# Praise for David Gemmell and his Druss the Legend adventures

"I am truly amazed at David Gemmell's ability to focus his writer's eye. His images are crisp and complete, a history lesson woven within the detailed tapestry of the highest adventure. Gemmell's characters are no less complete, real men and women with qualities good and bad, placed in trying times and rising to heroism or falling victim to their own weaknesses."
—R. A. SALVATORE
*New York Times* bestselling author
of *The Demon Awakens*

"Gemmell is very talented; his characters are vivid and very convincingly realistic."
—CHRISTOPHER STASHEFF
Author of the *Wizard in Rhyme* novels

"*Legend* is a rousing tale, all primary colors: think of Robert E. Howard meeting David Eddings. If you like headlong adventure, this one's for you."
—HARRY TURTLEDOVE

By David Gemmell
*Published by Ballantine Books:*

LION OF MACEDON
DARK PRINCE

KNIGHTS OF DARK RENOWN

MORNINGSTAR

*The Drenai Saga*
    LEGEND
    THE KING BEYOND THE GATE
    QUEST FOR LOST HEROES
    WAYLANDER
    IN THE REALM OF THE WOLF
    THE FIRST CHRONICLES OF DRUSS
      THE LEGEND
    THE LEGEND OF DEATHWALKER

*The Stones of Power Cycle*
    GHOST KING
    LAST SWORD OF POWER
    WOLF IN SHADOW
    THE LAST GUARDIAN
    BLOODSTONE

# The Legend of Deathwalker

## David Gemmell

A Del Rey® Book
THE BALLANTINE PUBLISHING GROUP • NEW YORK

A Del Rey® Book
Published by The Ballantine Publishing Group
Copyright © 1996 by David A. Gemmell

All rights reserved under International and Pan-American Copyright Conventions. Published in the United States by The Ballantine Publishing Group, a division of Random House, Inc., New York. Originally published in Great Britain by Bantam Press, a division of Transworld Publishers Ltd., in 1996.

Del Rey and colophon are registered trademarks of Random House, Inc.

www.randomhouse.com/delrey/

Library of Congress Catalog Card Number: 98-93423

ISBN 0-345-40800-4

Manufactured in the United States of America

First American Edition: May 1999

10  9  8  7  6  5  4  3  2  1

*The Legend of Deathwalker* is dedicated with love to the Hotz de Baars: to Big Oz, who walks the vales of dead computers and finds the novels lost in the void, a man who will give freely of his time, his energy, and his brilliance but never of his biscuits; to Young Oz, who taught me that *Civilization* was beyond me; to his sister Claire for the barbecue treats she didn't drop; and to Alison for the Upthorpe hospitality.

My thanks to my editor, Liza Reeves; test readers Val Gemmell, Edith Graham, and her daughter Stella; and to my copy editor, Jean Maund. Thanks also to the many readers who have written over the years demanding more stories of Druss. The volume of mail is so great these days that I can no longer answer all the letters. They are all read, and I do take note of the points raised.

# ◇ Prologue ◇

THE MOON HUNG like a sickle blade over Dros Delnoch, and Pellin stood quietly staring down at the Nadir camp in the lunar light below. Thousands of warriors were gathered there, and the next day they would come screaming across the narrow strip of bloodstained ground, hauling their ladders and carrying their grappling irons. They would be baying for battle and death, and just as on this day, the sound would terrify him, seeming to penetrate his skin like needles of ice. Pellin was more frightened than he had ever been in his young life, and he longed to run, to hide, to throw away his ill-fitting armor and race south to his home. The Nadir kept coming, wave after wave, their raucous battle cries sending their hatred ahead of them. The shallow wound in his upper left arm was both throbbing and itching. Gilad had assured him that this meant that it was healing well, but it had been a taste of pain, a bitter promise of worse pain to come. He had watched comrades writhing and screaming, their bellies opened by serrated swords . . . Pellin fought to push the memories away. A cold wind began to blow from the north, bunching dark rainclouds before it. He shivered and remembered his warm farmhouse with its thatched roof and large stone-built fireplace. On cold nights like this one he and Kara would lie in bed, her head resting on his shoulder, her left leg warm on his thighs. They would lie together in the soft red glow of the fading fire and listen to the wind howling mournfully outside.

Pellin sighed. "Please don't let me die here," he prayed aloud.

Of the twenty-three men who had volunteered from his village, only nine were left. He gazed back at the rows of sleeping defenders lying on the open ground between Walls Three and Four. Could these few men hold the greatest army ever assembled? Pellin knew they could not.

Returning his gaze to the Nadir camp, he scanned the area close to the mountains. The Drenai dead, stripped of armor and weapons, had been thrown there and burned. Oily black smoke had drifted over the Dros for hours afterward, bringing with it the sickly and nauseating smell of roasting flesh. It could have been me, thought Pellin, remembering the slaughter as Wall Two fell.

He shivered. Dros Delnoch, the mightiest fortress in all the world: six walls of rearing stone and a broad keep. Never had she been conquered by an enemy. But then, never had she faced an army of such numbers. It seemed to Pellin that there were more Nadir than there were stars in the sky. The defenders had fallen back from Wall One after bitter fighting, for it was the longest and therefore the hardest to hold. They had crept back in the night, conquering the wall without further losses. But Wall Two had been taken at great cost, with the enemy breaching the defenses and sweeping forward to encircle the defenders. Pellin had barely made it back to Wall Three and remembered the acid taste of fear in his throat and the terrible shaking of his limbs as he had hauled himself over the battlements and had sunk to the ramparts.

And what was it all for? he wondered. What difference would it make if the Drenai enjoyed self-rule or government by the warlord Ulric? Would the farm yield any less corn? Would his cattle sicken and die?

It had all seemed such an adventure twelve weeks earlier, when the Drenai recruiting officers had arrived at the village. A few weeks of patrolling the great walls and then a return home as heroes.

Heroes! Sovil was a hero until that arrow pierced his eye, ripping it from the socket. Jocan was a hero as he lay screaming, his blood-covered hands trying to hold his entrails in place.

Pellin added a little coal to the iron brazier and waved at the sentry thirty paces to the left. The man was stamping his feet against the cold. He and Pellin had swapped places an hour before, and soon it would be his turn to stand by the brazier. The knowledge of heat soon to be lost gave the fire an even greater significance, and Pellin stretched out his hands, enjoying the warmth.

A huge figure moved into sight, stepping carefully over the sleeping defenders and making his way toward the ramparts. Pellin's heart began to beat faster as Druss strode up the steps.

Druss the Legend, the Savior of Skeln Pass, the man who had battled his way across the world to rescue his wife. Druss the Axman, the Silver Slayer. The Nadir called him Deathwalker, and Pellin now knew why. He had watched him fighting on the battlements, his terrible ax cleaving and slaying. He was not mortal; he was a dark god of war. Pellin hoped the old man would stay away from him. What could a novice soldier find to say to a hero like Druss? To Pellin's great relief the Legend stopped by the other sentry, and the two men began to talk; he could see the sentry moving nervously from foot to foot as the old warrior spoke to him.

It struck him then that Druss was the human embodiment of this ancient fortress, unbeaten yet eroded by time, less than he was but magnificent for all that. Pellin smiled as he remembered the Nadir herald giving Druss the ultimatum to surrender or die. The old hero had laughed. "In the north," he had said, "the mountains may tremble when Ulric breaks wind. But this is Drenai land, and to me he is just another potbellied savage who couldn't wipe his ass without a Drenai map tattooed on his thigh."

Pellin's smile faded as he saw Druss clap the other sentry on the shoulder and move on toward him. The rain had eased, and the moon was bright once more. Pellin's hands began to sweat, and he wiped the palms on his cloak. The young sentry stood at attention as the Legend approached him, striding along the ramparts, his ax shining silver in the bright moonlight. Pellin's mouth was dry as he stood, fist clenched against his breastplate, to salute him.

"Relax, laddie," said Druss, laying the mighty ax on the ramparts. The old warrior stretched his huge hands to the brazier, warming them, then sat with his back to the wall, beckoning the youth to join him. Pellin had never been this close to Druss, and he saw the lines of age etched deep into his broad face, giving it the look of ancient granite. The eyes were bright and pale, though, beneath heavy brows, and Pellin found he could not stare into them. "They'll not come tonight," said Druss. "Just before first light they'll rush in. No war cries; it will be a silent assault."

"How do you know that, sir?"

Druss chuckled. "I'd like to tell you that my vast knowledge of war leads me to that conclusion, but the answer is more simple. The Thirty predict it, and they're a canny bunch. Normally I have little time for wizards and such, but these lads are great fighters." He lifted his black helm clear of his head and ran his fingers through his thick white hair. "Served me well, this helm," he told Pellin, twirling it so that moonlight shone on the silver ax motif on the brow. "And I don't doubt it will do its job tomorrow."

At the thought of the battle to come Pellin cast a nervous glance over the wall to where the Nadir waited. From there he could see many of them lying in their blankets, close to hundreds of campfires. Others were awake, sharpening weapons or talking in small groups. The young man turned and ran his gaze over the exhausted Drenai defenders lying on the ground behind the ramparts, wrapped in their blankets, trying to snatch a few hours of precious, refreshing sleep. "Sit down, laddie," said Druss. "You can't worry them away."

Resting his spear against the wall, the sentry sat. His scabbard clanged against the stone, and clumsily he swiveled it. "I cannot get used to wearing all this armor," said Pellin. "I trip over the sword all the time. I am not much of a soldier, I fear."

"You looked every inch the soldier three days ago on Wall Two," said Druss. "I saw you kill two Nadir, then fight your way back to the ropes on this wall. Even then you helped a comrade who had a wound in his leg; you climbed below him, supporting him."

"You saw that? But there was so much confusion, and you were in the midst of the battle yourself!"

"I see many things, boy. What is your name?"

"Pellin . . . Cul Pellin," he corrected himself. "Sir," he added swiftly.

"We can dispense with the formalities, Pellin," Druss told him amiably. "Here tonight we are just two veterans sitting quietly waiting for the dawn. Are you frightened?"

Pellin nodded, and Druss smiled. "And do you ask yourself, Why me? Why should I be standing here facing the might of the Nadir?"

"Yes. Kara didn't want me to go with the others. She told me I was a fool. I mean, what difference will it make if we win or lose?"

"In a hundred years? None at all," said Druss. "But all invading armies carry their own demons with them, Pellin. If they break through here, they will sweep across the Sentran Plain bringing fire and destruction, rape and slaughter. That's why we must stop them. And why you? Because you are the man for the role."

"I think I am going to die here," said Pellin. "I don't want to die. My Kara is pregnant and I want to see my son grow tall and strong. I want . . ." He stumbled to silence as the lump in his throat blocked further speech.

"You want what we all want, laddie," Druss said softly. "But you are a man, and men must face what they fear or be destroyed by it."

"I don't know if I can. I keep thinking of joining the other deserters. Creeping south in the night. Going home."

"Then why haven't you?"

Pellin thought for a moment. "I don't know," he said lamely.

"I'll tell you why, boy. Because you look around and see the others who must stay and fight all the harder because you are not standing by your post. You are not a man to leave others to do your work for you."

"I'd like to believe that. Truly I would."

"Believe it, laddie, for I am a good judge of men." Suddenly Druss grinned. "I knew another Pellin once. He was a spear thrower. A good one, too. Won the gold in the Fellowship Games when they were held in Gulgothir."

"I thought that was Nicotas," said Pellin. "I remember the parade when the team came home. Nicotas carried the Drenai flag."

The old man shook his head. "That feels like yesterday," Druss said, with a wide grin. "But I am talking about the Fifth Games. I would guess they took place around thirty years ago, long before you were a gleam in your mother's eye. Pellin was a good man."

"Were they the games you took part in, sir? At the court of the mad king?" asked the sentry.

Druss nodded. "It was no part of my plan. I was a farmer then, but Abalayn invited me to Gulgothir as part of the Drenai delegation. My wife, Rowena, urged me to accept the invitation; she thought I was growing bored with life in the mountains." He chuckled. "She was right! We came through Dros Delnoch, I remember. There were forty-five competitors and around another hundred hangers-on, whores, servants, trainers. I have forgotten most of their names now. Pellin I remember— but then, he made me laugh, and I enjoyed his company." The old man fell silent, lost in memories.

"So how did you become part of the team, sir?"

"Oh, that! The Drenai had a fistfighter named . . . damned if I can remember. Old age is eating away at my memory. Anyway, he was an ill-tempered man. All the fighters brought their own trainers with them and lesser fighters to spar with. This fellow—Grawal, that was it!—was a brute, and he disabled two of his sparring partners. One day he asked me to spar with him. We were still three days from Gulgothir, and I was *really* bored by then. That's one of the curses of my life, lad. Easily bored! So I agreed. It was a mistake. Lots of the camp women used to watch the fighters train, and I should have realized that Grawal was a crowd pleaser. Anyway, he and I began to spar. At first it went well; he was good, a lot of power in the shoulders but supple, too. Have you ever sparred, Pellin?"

"No, sir."

"Well, it looks the same as a genuine fight, but all the punches are pulled. The purpose of it is to increase the speed of the fighter's reflexes. But then a group of the camp women turned up and sat close by us. Grawal wanted to show the women how tough he was, and he let rip with a combination of blows at full power. It was like being kicked by a mule, and I have to admit that it irritated me. I stepped back and told him to ease up. The fool took no notice and then rushed me. So I hit him. Damned if his jaw didn't break in three places. As a result the Drenai had now lost their one heavy fighter, and I felt honor bound to take his place."

"What happened then?" Pellin asked as Druss eased himself to his feet and leaned over the ramparts. The faint light of predawn was showing in the east.

"That story had better wait until tonight, laddie," said Druss softly. "Here they come!"

Pellin scrambled to his feet. Thousands of Nadir warriors were streaming silently toward the wall. Druss bellowed a warning, and a bugler sounded the alert. Red-cloaked Drenai defenders came surging from their blankets.

Pellin drew his sword, his hand trembling as he gazed at the rushing tide of men. Hundreds were carrying ladders; others held coiled ropes and grappling hooks. Pellin's heart was hammering. "Sweet Missael," he whispered. "Nothing will stop them!" He took a backward step, but then Druss laid his huge hand on the boy's shoulder.

"Who am I, laddie?" he asked, his ice-blue eyes holding to Pellin's gaze.

"W-what?" stammered Pellin.

"Who am I?"

Pellin blinked back the sweat that trickled into his eyes. "You are Druss the Legend," he answered.

"You stand by me, Pellin," the old man said grimly, "and we'll stop them together." Suddenly the axman grinned. "I don't tell many stories, laddie, and I hate it when they're interrupted. So when we've seen off this little sortie, I'll stand you a goblet of Lentrian red and tell you the tale of the Gothir God-King and the Eyes of Alchazzar."

Pellin took a deep breath. "I'll stand with you, sir," he said.

## 1

A S THE HUGE crowd bayed for blood, Sieben the Poet found himself staring around the vast colosseum, its mighty columns and arches, its tiers and statues. Far below on the golden sand of the arena two men were fighting for the glory of their nations. Fifteen thousand people were shouting now, the noise cacophonous like the roaring of some inchoate beast. Sieben lifted a scented handkerchief to his face, seeking to blot out the smell of sweat that enveloped him from all sides.

The colosseum was a marvelous piece of architecture, its columns shaped into statues of ancient heroes and gods, its seats of finest marble covered by cushions of down-filled green velvet. The cushions irritated Sieben, for the color clashed with his bright blue silken tunic inset with shards of opal on the puffed sleeves. The poet was proud of the garment, which had cost a suitably enormous amount of money and had been bought from the best tailor in Drenan. To have it beggared by a poor choice of seat covering was almost more than he could stand. Still, with everyone seated, the effect was muted. Servants moved endlessly through the crowd, bearing trays of cool drinks or sweetmeats, pies, cakes, and savory delicacies. The tiers of the rich were shaded by silken coverings, also in that dreadful green, while the very rich sat in red-cushioned splendor with slaves fanning them. Sieben had tried to change his seat and sit among the nobility, but no amount of flattery or offers of bribes could purchase him a place.

To his right Sieben could just see the edge of the God-King's balcony and the straight backs of two of the Royal Guards in their silver breastplates and white cloaks. Their helms, thought the poet, were particularly magnificent, embossed with gold and crested with white horsehair plumes. That was the beauty of the simple colors, he thought; black, white, silver, and gold were rarely upstaged by upholstery, no matter what its color.

"Is he winning?" asked Majon, the Drenai ambassador, tugging at Sieben's sleeve. "He's taking a fearful battering. The Lentrian has never been beaten, you know. They say he killed two fighters last spring in a competition in Mashrapur. Damn, I bet ten gold Raq on Druss."

Sieben gently lifted the ambassador's fingers from his sleeve, brushing at the bruised silk, and forced his gaze away from the wonders of the architecture to focus briefly on the combat below. The Lentrian hit Druss with an uppercut, then a right cross. Druss backed away, blood seeping from a cut over his left eye. "What odds did you get?" asked Sieben.

The slender ambassador ran his hand over his close-cropped silver hair. "Six to one. I must have been mad."

"Not at all," said Sieben smoothly. "It was patriotism that drove you. Look, I know ambassadors are not well paid, so I will take your bet. Give me the token."

"I couldn't possibly ... I mean, he's being thrashed out there."

"Of course you must. After all, Druss is my friend, and I should have wagered on him out of loyalty." Sieben saw the glint of avarice in the ambassador's dark eyes.

"Well, if you are sure." The man's slim fingers darted into the pearl-beaded leather pouch at his side, producing a small square of papyrus bearing a wax seal and the amount wagered. Sieben took it, and Majon waited with hand outstretched.

"I didn't bring my purse with me," said Sieben, "but I will hand over the money tonight."

"Yes, of course," said Majon, his disappointment obvious.

"I think I'll take a walk around the colosseum," said Sieben. "There is so much to see. I understand there are art galleries and shops on the levels below."

"You don't show much concern for your friend," said Majon.

Sieben ignored the criticism. "My dear ambassador, Druss fights because he loves to fight. Generally one saves one's concern for the poor unfortunates he faces. I will see you later at the celebrations."

Easing himself from his seat, Sieben climbed the marble steps, making his way to the official gambling booth. A gap-toothed cleric was sitting inside the recess. Behind him stood a soldier, guarding the sacks of money already wagered.

"You wish to place a wager?" asked the cleric.

"No, I am waiting to collect."

"You have bet on the Lentrian?"

"No. I bet on the winner. It's an old habit," he answered, with a smile. "Be so good as to have sixty gold pieces available, plus my original ten."

The cleric chuckled. "You bet on the Drenai? It will be a cold day in hell before you see a return on that investment."

"My, I do think I sense a drop in the temperature," Sieben told him with a smile.

In the heat of the arena the Lentrian champion was tiring. Blood was seeping from his broken nose, and his right eye had swollen shut, but even so his strength was prodigious. Druss moved in, ducking beneath a right cross and thundering a blow to the man's midsection; the muscles of the Lentrian's stomach were like woven steel. A punch smashed down onto Druss' neck, and he felt his legs buckle. With a grunt of pain he sent an uppercut into the taller man's bearded chin, and the Lentrian's head snapped back. Druss hammered an overhand right that missed its mark, cracking against the man's temple. The Lentrian wiped blood from his face, then hit Druss with a thundering straight left followed by a right hook that all but spun Druss from his feet.

The crowd was baying, sensing that the end was close. Druss tried to move in and grapple, only to be stopped by a straight left that jarred him to his heels. Blocking a right, he fired home another uppercut. The Lentrian swayed but did not fall. He countered with a chopping blow that took Druss behind the right ear. Druss shrugged it off. The Lentrian's strength was fading; the punch lacked speed and weight.

This was the moment! Druss waded in, sending a combination of punches to the Lentrian's face: three straight lefts followed by a right hook that exploded against the man's chin. The Lentrian spun off balance, tried to right himself, then fell face first to the sand.

A sound like rolling thunder went up, booming around the packed arena. Druss took a deep breath and stepped back, acknowledging the cheers. The new Drenai flag, a white stallion on a field of blue, was hoisted high, fluttering in the afternoon breeze. Striding forward, Druss halted below the royal balcony and bowed to the God-King he could not see.

Behind him two Lentrians ran out and knelt beside their fallen champion. Stretcher bearers followed, and the unconscious man was carried from the arena. Druss waved to the crowd, then walked slowly to the dark mouth of the tunnel that led through to the bathhouses and rest areas for the athletes.

The spear thrower Pellin stood grinning at the tunnel entrance. "Thought he had you there, mountain man."

"It was close," said Druss, spitting blood from his mouth. His face was swollen, and several teeth had been loosened. "He was strong. I'll say that for him."

The two men walked down the tunnel, emerging into the first bathhouse. The sound from the arena was muted there, and around a dozen athletes were relaxing in the three heated pools of marble. Druss sat down beside the first. Rose petals floated on the steamy surface of the water, their fragrance filling the room.

The runner Pars swam across to him. "You look as if a herd of horses has run across your face," he said.

Leaning forward, Druss placed a hand on top of the man's balding head and propelled him down beneath the surface. Pars swam clear and surfaced several yards away; with a sweep of his hand he drenched Druss. Pellin, stripped now of his leggings and tunic, dived into the pool.

Druss peeled off his leggings and slid into the warm water. The relief to his aching muscles was instant, and for some minutes he swam around the pool; then he hauled himself clear. Pars joined him. "Stretch yourself out and I'll knead the aches away," he said. Druss moved to a massage table and lay face-down, where Pars rubbed oil into his palms and began to work expertly on the muscles of his upper back.

Pellin sat down close by, toweling his dark hair, then draping the white cloth over his shoulders. "Did you watch the other contest?" he asked Druss.

"No."

"The Gothir man, Klay, is awesome. Fast. Strong chin. That plus a right hand that comes down like a hammer. It was all over in less than twenty heartbeats. Never seen the like, Druss. The Vagrian didn't know what hit him."

"So I heard," Druss grunted as Pars' fingers dug deeply into the swollen muscles of his neck.

"You'll take him, Druss. What does it matter that he's bigger, stronger, faster, and better-looking?"

"And fitter," put in Pellin. "They say he runs five miles every day on the mountains outside the city."

"Yes, I forgot fitter. Younger, too. How old are you, Druss?" asked Pars.

"Thirty," grunted Druss.

"An old man," said Pellin with a wink at Pars. "Still, I'm sure you'll win. Well . . . fairly sure."

Druss sat up. "It is good of you youngsters to be so supportive."

"Well, we are a team," said Pellin. "And since you deprived us of Grawal's delightful company, we've sort of adopted you,

Druss." Pars began to work on Druss' swollen knuckles. "More seriously, Druss, my friend," said the runner, "your hands are badly bruised. Back home we'd use ice to bring the swelling down. I should soak them in cold water tonight."

"There's three days before the final. I'll be fine by then. How did you fare in your race?"

"I finished second and so will contest the final at least. But I'll not be in the first three. The Gothir man is far better than I, as are the Vagrian and the Chiatze. I cannot match their finish."

"You might surprise yourself," said Druss.

"We're not all like you, mountain man," observed Pellin. "I still find it hard to believe that you could come to these games unprepared and fight your way to the final. You really are a legend." Suddenly he grinned. "Ugly, old, and slow—but still a legend," he added.

Druss chuckled. "You almost fooled me there, laddie. I thought you might be showing some respect for me." He lay back and closed his eyes.

Pars and Pellin strolled away to where a servant stood holding a pitcher of cold water. Seeing them coming, the man filled two goblets. Pellin drained his and accepted a refill, while Pars sipped his slowly. "You didn't tell him about the prophecy," said Pars.

"Neither did you. He'll find out soon enough."

"What do you think he'll do?" asked the bald runner.

Pellin shrugged. "I have known him only for a month, but somehow I don't think he'll want to follow tradition."

"He'll have to!" insisted Pars.

Pellin shook his head. "He's not like other men, my friend. That Lentrian should have won, but he didn't. Druss is a force of nature, and I don't think politics will affect that one jot."

"I'll wager twenty gold Raq you are wrong."

"I'll not take that bet, Pars. You see, I hope for all our sakes that you are right."

* * *

From a private balcony high above the crowd the giant blond fighter Klay watched Druss deliver the knockout blow. The Lentrian carried too much weight on his arms and shoulders, and though it gave him incredible power, the punches were too slow and easy to read. But the Drenai made it worthwhile. Klay smiled.

"You find the man amusing, Lord Klay?" Startled, the fighter swung around. The newcomer's face showed no expression, no flicker of muscle. It is like a mask, thought Klay, a golden Chiatze mask, tight and unlined. Even the jet-black hair, dragged back into the tightest of ponytails, was so heavily waxed and dyed that it seemed false, painted onto the overlarge cranium. Klay took a deep breath, annoyed that he could have been surprised on his own balcony and angry that he had not heard the swish of the curtains or the rustle of the man's heavy ankle-length robe of black velvet.

"You move like an assassin, Garen-Tsen," said Klay.

"Sometimes, my lord, it is necessary to move with stealth," observed the Chiatze, his voice gentle and melodic. Klay looked into the man's odd eyes, as slanted as spear points. One was a curious brown, flecked with shards of gray; the other was as blue as a summer sky.

"Stealth is necessary only when among enemies, surely," ventured Klay.

"Indeed so. But the best of one's enemies masquerade as friends. What is it about the Drenai that amuses you?" Garen-Tsen moved past Klay to the balcony's edge, staring down into the arena below. "I see nothing amusing. He is a barbarian, and he fights like one." He turned back, his fleshless face framed by the high, arched collar of his robe.

Klay found his dislike of the man growing, but masking his feelings, he considered Garen-Tsen's question. "He does not *amuse* me, Minister. I admire him. With the right training he could be very good indeed. And he is a crowd pleaser. The mob always loves a plucky warrior. And by heaven, this Druss lacks nothing in courage. I wish I had the opportunity to train him. It would make for a better contest."

"It will be over swiftly, you think?"

Klay shook his head. "No. There is a great depth to the man's strength. It is born of his pride and his belief in his invincibility; you can see it in him as he fights. It will be a long and arduous battle."

"Yet you will prevail? As the God-King has prophesied?" For the first time Klay noticed a slight change in the minister's expression.

"I should beat him, Garen-Tsen. I am bigger, stronger, faster, and better trained. But there is always a rogue element in any fight. I could slip just as a punch connects. I could fall ill before the bout and be sluggish, lacking in energy. I could lose concentration and allow an opening." Klay gave a wide smile, for the minister's expression was openly worried.

"This will not happen," he said. "The prophecy will come true."

Klay thought carefully before answering. "The God-King's belief in me is a source of great pride. I shall fight all the better for it."

"Good. Let us hope it has the opposite effect on the Drenai. You will be at the banquet this evening, my lord? The God-King has requested your presence. He wishes you to sit alongside him."

"It is a great honor," Klay answered, with a bow.

"Indeed it is." Garen-Tsen moved to the curtained doorway, then swung back. "You know an athlete named Lepant?"

"The runner? Yes. He trains at my gymnasium. Why?"

"He died this morning during questioning. He looked so strong. Did you ever see signs of weakness in his heart? Dizziness, chest pain?"

"No," said Klay, remembering the bright-eyed garrulous boy and his fund of jokes and stories. "Why was he being questioned?"

"He was spreading slanders, and we had reason to believe he was a member of a secret group pledged to the assassination of the God-King."

"Nonsense. He was just a stupid boy who told bad-taste jokes."

"So it would appear," agreed Garen-Tsen. "Now he is a dead boy who will never again tell a bad-taste joke. Was he a very talented runner?"

"No."

"Good. Then we have lost nothing." The odd-colored eyes stared at Klay for several seconds. "It would be better, my lord, if you ceased to listen to jokes. In cases of treàson there is guilt by association."

"I shall remember your advice, Garen-Tsen."

After the minister had departed, Klay wandered down to the arena gallery. It was cooler there, and he enjoyed walking among the many antiquities. The gallery had been included on the arena plans at the insistence of the king—long before his diseased mind had finally eaten away his reason. There were some fifty stalls and shops there, where discerning buyers could purchase historical artifacts or beautifully made copies. There were ancient books, paintings, porcelain, even weapons.

People in the gallery stopped as he approached, bowing respectfully to the Gothir champion. Klay acknowledged each salutation with a smile and a nod of his head. Though huge, he moved with the easy grace of an athlete, always in balance and always aware. He paused before a bronze statue of the God-King. It was a fine piece, but Klay felt the addition of lapis lazuli for the pupils was too bizarre in a face of bronze. The merchant who owned the piece stepped forward. He was short and stout with a forked beard and a ready smile. "You are looking very fine, Lord Klay," he said. "I watched your fight—what little there was of it. You were magnificent."

"Thank you, sir."

"To think your opponent traveled so far only to be humiliated in such a fashion!"

"He was not humiliated, sir, merely beaten. He had earned his right to face me by competing against a number of very good fistfighters. And he had the misfortune to slip on the sand just as I struck him."

"Of course, of course! Your humility does you great credit, my lord," the man said smoothly. "I see you were admiring the bronze. It is a wonderful work by a new sculptor. He will go far." He lowered his voice. "For anyone else, my lord, the price would be one thousand in silver. But for the mighty Klay I could come down to eight hundred."

"I have two busts of the emperor; he gave them to me himself. But thank you for your offer."

Klay moved away from the man, and a young woman stepped before him. She was holding the hand of a fair-haired boy of around ten years of age. "Pardon me, lord, for this impertinence," she said, bowing deeply, "but my son would dearly like to meet you."

"Not at all," said Klay, dropping to one knee before the boy. "What is your name, lad?"

"Atka, sir," he replied. "I saw all your fights so far. You are . . . you are wonderful."

"Praise indeed. Will you watch the final?"

"Oh, yes, sir. I shall be here to see you thrash the Drenai. I watched him, too. He almost lost."

"I don't think so, Atka. He is a tough man, a man of rock and iron. I wagered on him myself."

"He can't beat you, though, sir. Can he?" asked the boy, his eyes widening as doubt touched him.

Klay smiled. "All men can be beaten, Atka. You will just have to wait a few days and see."

Klay stood and smiled at the blushing young woman. "He is a fine boy," said the champion. Taking her hand, he kissed it, then moved away, pausing to study the paintings on the far wall. Many were landscapes of the desert and the mountains; others depicted young women in various stages of undress. Some were of hunting scenes, while two, which caught Klay's eye, were of wildflowers. At the far end of the gallery was a long stall behind which stood an elderly Chiatze. Klay made his way to the man and studied the artifacts laid out so neatly. They were mostly small statuettes surrounded by brooches, amulets, bracelets, bangles, and rings. Klay lifted a small ivory figurine, no more than four inches tall. It was of a beautiful woman in a flowing dress. There were flowers in her hair, and in her hand she held a snake, its tail coiled around her wrist.

"This is very lovely," he said.

The small Chiatze nodded and smiled. "She is Shul-sen, the bride of Oshikai Demon-bane. The figurine is close to a thousand years old."

"How can you tell?"

"I am Chorin-Tsu, lord, the royal embalmer and a student of history. I found this piece during an archaeological survey near the site of the fabled Battle of Five Armies. I am certain that it is no less than nine centuries old." Klay lifted the figurine close to his eyes. The woman's face was oval, her eyes slanted; she seemed to be smiling.

"She was Chiatze, this Shul-sen?" he asked.

Chorin-Tsu spread his hands. "That depends, lord, on your perspective. She was, as I told you, the wife of Oshikai, and he is considered the father of the Nadir. It was he who led the rebel tribes from the lands of the Chiatze and fought his way to the lands now ruled by the Gothir. After his death the tribes roamed free, warring on one another, even as now. So if he was the first Nadir, then Shul-sen was . . . what? Nadir or Chiatze?"

"Both," said Klay. "And beautiful, too. What happened to her?"

The Chiatze shrugged, and Klay saw sorrow in the dark, slanted eyes. "That depends on which version of historical events you happen to believe. For myself I think she was murdered soon after Oshikai's death. All the records point to this, though some stories have her sailing to a mythic land beyond the sea. If you have romantic leanings, perhaps that is the story you should cling to."

"I tend to hold to the truth where I can," said Klay. "But in this case I would like to believe she lived happily somewhere. I would guess we will never know."

Chorin-Tsu spread his hands once more. "As a student I like to think that one day the mists will be opened. Perhaps I might find some documentary evidence."

"If you do so, let me know. Meanwhile I shall purchase this figurine. Have it delivered to my house."

"You wish to know the price, lord?"

"I am sure it will be a fair one."

"Indeed it will, sir."

Klay turned away, then swung back. "Tell me, Chorin-Tsu: How is it that the royal embalmer runs a stall of antiquities?"

"Embalming, lord, is my profession. History is my passion. And as with all passions, they must be shared to be enjoyed. Your delight in the piece brings me great pleasure."

Klay moved on through the gallery arch and to the Hall of Cuisine. Two guards opened the door to the beautifully furnished dining room of the nobility. Klay had long since lost any sense of nervousness on entering such establishments, for despite the lowliness of his birth, his legend was now so great among the people that he was considered higher than most nobles. There were few diners present, but Klay spotted the Drenai ambassador, Majon, engaged in a heated discussion with a fop in a bejeweled blue tunic. The fop was tall and slim and very handsome, his hair light brown and held in place by a silver headband adorned with an opal. Klay approached them. Majon did not at first notice the fighter and continued to rail at his companion.

"I do think this is unfair, Sieben. After all, you won—" At that moment he saw Klay, and instantly his face changed, a broad smile appearing. "My dear chap, so good to see you again. Please do join us. It would be such an honor. We were talking about you only moments ago. This is Sieben the Poet."

"I have heard your work performed," said Klay, "and I have read with interest the saga of Druss the Legend."

The poet gave a wolfish smile. "You've read the work, and soon you'll face the man. I have to tell you, sir, that I shall be wagering against you."

"Then you will forgive me for not wishing you luck," said Klay, sitting down.

"Did you watch today's bout?" asked Majon.

"I did indeed, Ambassador. Druss is an interesting fighter. It seems that pain spurs him to greater efforts. He is indomitable and very strong."

"He always wins," said Sieben happily. "It's a talent he has."

"Sieben is particularly pleased today," Majon put in icily. "He has won sixty gold pieces."

"I won also," said Klay.

"You bet on Druss?" asked Sieben.

"Yes. I had studied both men and did not feel the Lentrian had the heart to match your man. He also lacked speed in his left, which gave Druss the chance to roll with the punches. But you should advise him to change his attacking stance. He tends to duck his head and charge, which makes him an easy target for an uppercut."

"I'll be sure to tell him," promised Sieben.

"I have a training ground at my house. He is welcome to use it."

"That is a very kind offer," put in Majon.

"You seem very confident, sir," said Sieben. "Does it not concern you that Druss has never lost?"

"No more than it concerns me that I have never lost. Whatever else happens, one of us will surrender that perfect record. But the sun will still shine, and the earth will not topple. Now, my friends, shall we order some food?"

\* \* \*

The air was fresh and clean, and a slight wind whispered across the fountain pool, cooling the air as Sieben and Druss climbed the steep path to the summit of the highest hill in the Grand Park. Above them the sky was the glorious blue of late summer, dotted with thick white clouds drifting slowly from the east. Shafts of sunlight in the distance, breaking clear of the clouds, suddenly illuminated a section of the eastern mountains, turning them to deep shadowed red and gold, glowing like jewels in torchlight. And just as swiftly the wandering clouds blocked the sun, the golden rocks returning to gray. Druss gazed longingly at the mountains, remembering the smell of the pine and the song of the stream in his own high homeland. The clouds drifted on, and the sun shone down on the far mountains once more. The sight was beautiful, but Druss knew there would be no pine forests there. To the east of Gulgothir were the Nadir steppes, an enormous stretch of desert, dry, harsh, and inhospitable.

Sieben sat beside the fountain, trailing his hand in the water. "Now you can see why this is called the Hill of the Six Virgins," he said. At the center of the pool was a statue of six women exquisitely carved from a single block of marble. They stood in a circle, each leaning forward and extending her arms as if in entreaty. Behind and above them was the figure of an old man holding a huge urn from which came the fountain, spilling out over the white statues and flowing down to the pool. "Several hundred years ago," continued Sieben, "when a raiding army from the north surrounded Gulgothir, six virgins were sacrificed here to appease the gods of war. They were ritually drowned. After that the gods favored the defenders, and they beat off the attack."

Sieben smiled as he saw Druss' pale blue eyes narrow. The warrior's huge hand came up and idly tugged at his square-cut black beard, a sure sign of his growing irritation. "You don't believe in appeasing the gods?" Sieben asked innocently.

"Not with the blood of the innocent."

"They went on to win, Druss. Therefore, the sacrifice was worthwhile, surely."

The axman shook his head. "If they believed the sacrifice would appease the gods, then they would have been inspired to fight harder. But a good speech could have done that."

"Suppose the gods *did* demand that sacrifice and therefore *did* help win the battle."

"Then it would have been better lost."

"Aha!" Sieben exclaimed triumphantly. "But if it had been lost, a far greater number of innocents would have been slain: women raped and murdered, babes slain in their cribs. How do you answer that?"

"I don't feel the need to. Most people can smell the difference between perfume and cow dung; there's no need for a debate on it."

"Come on, old horse, you're not stretching yourself. The answer is a simple one: the principles of good and evil are not based on mathematics. They are founded on the desire of individuals to do—or not to do—what is right and just, both in conscience and in law."

"Words, words, words! They mean nothing!" snapped Druss. "The desire of individuals is what causes most evils. And as for conscience and law, what happens if a man has no conscience and the law promotes ritual sacrifice? Does that make it good? Now stop trying to draw me into another of your meaningless debates."

"We poets live for such 'meaningless' debates," said Sieben, battling to hold back his anger. "We tend to like to stretch our intelligence, to develop our minds. It helps make us more aware of the needs of our fellows. You are in a sour mood today, Druss. I would have thought you would have been delirious at the thought of another fight to come, another man to bash your fists against. The championship, no less. The cheers of the crowd, the adoration of your fellow countrymen. Ah, the blood and the bruises and the endless parades and banquets in your honor!"

Druss swore, and his face darkened. "You know I despise all that."

Sieben shook his head. "Part of you might, Druss. The best part loathes the public clamor, yet how is it that your every action always leads to more? You were invited here as a guest, an inspirational mascot, if you like. And what do you do? You break the jaw of the Drenai champion, then take his place."

"It was not my intention to cripple the man. Had I known his chin was made of porcelain, I would have struck him in the belly."

"I am sure you would like to believe that, old horse. Just as I am sure I do not. Answer me this: How do you feel as the crowd roars your name?"

"I have had enough of this, poet. What do you want from me?"

Sieben took a deep, calming breath. "Words are all we have to describe how we feel, what we need from one another. Without them, how would we teach the young or express our hopes for future generations to read? You view the world so simplistically, Druss, as if everything were either ice or fire. That in itself matters not a jot. But like all men with closed minds and small dreams you seek to mock what you can never comprehend. Civilizations are built with words, Druss. They are destroyed by axes. What does that tell you, *axman*?"

"Nothing I did not already know. Now, are we even yet?"

Sieben's anger fell away, and he smiled. "I like you, Druss, I always have. But you have the most uncanny power to irritate me."

Druss nodded, his face solemn. "I am not a thinker," he said, "nor am I stupid. I am a man like so many others. I could have been a farmer, or a carpenter, even a laborer. Never a teacher, though, or a cleric. Intellectual men make me nervous. Like that Majon." He shook his head. "I have met a great number of ambassadors, and they all seem identical: easy, insincere smiles and gimlet eyes that don't miss a thing. What do they believe in? Do they have a sense of honor? Of patriotism? Or do they laugh at us common men as they line their purses with our gold? I don't know much, poet, but I do know that men like Majon—aye, and you—can make all I believe in seem as insubstantial as summer snow. And make me look foolish into the bargain. Oh, I can understand how good and evil can come down to numbers. Like those women in the fountain. A besieging army could say, 'Kill six women and we'll spare the city.' Well, there's only one right answer to that. But I couldn't tell you why I know it is right."

"But I can," said Sieben. "And it is something, in part at least, that I learned from you. The greatest evil we can perpetrate is to make someone else do evil. The besieging army you speak of is actually saying: 'Unless you commit a small evil act, we will commit a great one.' The heroic response would naturally be to refuse. But diplomats and politicians are pragmatists, Druss. They live without any genuine understanding of honor. Am I right?"

Druss smiled and clapped Sieben's shoulder. "Aye, poet, you are. But I know that without turning a hair you could argue the opposite. So let us call an end to this."

"Agreed! We will call it even."

Druss switched his gaze to the south. Below them lay the center of Old Gulgothir, a tightly packed and apparently haphazard jumble of buildings, homes, shops, and workplaces intersected by scores of narrow alleyways and roads. The old Keep Palace sat at the center like a squat gray spider. Once the residence of kings, the palace was now used as a warehouse and granary. Druss looked to the west and the new Palace of the God-King, a colossal structure of white stone, its columns adorned with gold leaf, its statues—mostly of the king himself—crowned with silver and gold. Ornate gardens surrounded the palace, and even from there Druss could see the splendor of the royal blooms and the flowering trees. "Have you seen the God-King yet?" asked the warrior.

"I was close to the royal balcony while you were toying with the Lentrian. But all I saw was the backs of his guards. It is said he has his hair dyed with real gold."

"What do you mean 'toying'? The man was tough, and I can still feel the weight of his blows."

Sieben chuckled. "Then wait until you meet the Gothir champion, Druss. In combat the man is not human; it is said he has a punch like a thunderbolt. The odds are nine to one against you."

"Then maybe I'll lose," grunted Druss, "but don't wager on it!"

"Oh, I won't be wagering a copper coin this time. I've met Klay. He is unique, Druss. In all the time I have known you, I never met another man I thought could best you in combat. Until now."

"Pah!" snorted Druss. "I wish I had a gold Raq for every time someone has told me another man was stronger, or faster, or better, or more deadly. And where are they now?"

"Well, old horse," Sieben answered coolly, "they are mostly dead, slain by you in your endless quest to do what is good and pure and right."

Druss' eyes narrowed. "I thought you said we were even."

Sieben spread his hands. "Sorry. Couldn't resist it."

The Nadir warrior known as Talisman ducked into the alleyway and loped along it. The shouts of his pursuers were muted now, but he knew he had not lost them . . . not yet. Emerging into an open square, Talisman paused. There were many doors there; he counted six on each side of the square. "This way! This way!" he heard someone shout. The moonlight shone brightly on the north and west walls as he ran to the south of the square and pressed his back against a recessed doorway. There, in his long, black hooded cloak, he was all but invisible in the shadows. Talisman took a deep breath, fighting for calm. Absently his hand strayed toward his hip, where his long hunting knife should have been. Silently he cursed. No Nadir warrior was allowed to carry weapons inside any Gothir city. He hated this place of stone and cobbles with its seething masses and the resultant stench of humanity. Talisman longed for the open expanse of the Nadir steppes: awesome mountains beneath a naked burning sky, endless plains and valleys where a man could ride for a year and never see another soul. On the steppes a man was *alive*. Not so here in this rat's nest of a city, its foul, polluted air carrying the bowel stink of human excretion thrown from windows to lie rotting in the alleyways, alongside other garbage and waste.

A rat scuttled over his foot, but Talisman did not move. The enemy was close. *Enemy?* These scum from the poorest quarter of Gulgothir could hardly be considered worthy of the title. They were merely filling time in their worthless existence by hunting a Nadir tribesman through their vermin-infested streets, enjoying a transient moment of entertainment to brighten their poverty-stricken lives. He cursed again. Nosta Khan had warned him about the gangs, telling him which areas to avoid, though Talisman had barely listened. But then, he had never visited a city as large as Gulgothir and had no idea how easily a man could become lost within its warrens.

The sound of running feet came to him, and his hands clenched into fists. If they found him there, they would kill him.

"Did you see where he went?" came a guttural voice.

"Nah! What about down there?"

"You three take the alley; we'll cut through Tavern Walk and meet you in the square."

Drawing his hood around his face, leaving only his dark eyes showing, Talisman waited. The first of the three men ran past his hiding place, then the second. But the third glanced in his direction—and spotted him. Talisman leapt forward. The man lunged with a knife, but Talisman sidestepped and hammered his fist into the attacker's face. The man stumbled back as Talisman darted to the left and sprinted into another alleyway.

"He's here! He's here!" shouted the attacker.

Ahead was a wall around eight feet high. Talisman jumped, curling his fingers over the top and scrambling up. Beyond was a moonlit garden. Dropping to the grass, he ran to a second wall and scaled that also. On the other side was a narrow road; landing lightly, he loped along it, his anger mounting. It shamed him to run from these soft, round-eyed southerners.

He came to an intersection and cut to the north. There was no sound of pursuit, but he did not relax. He had no idea where he was; all these foul buildings looked the same. Nosta Khan had told him to seek out the home of Chorin-Tsu, the embalmer, which was on the Street of Weavers in the northwest quarter of the city. But where am I now? thought the tribesman.

A tall man moved from the shadows, a rust-pitted knife in his right hand. "Got you, you little Nadir bastard!" he said.

Talisman gazed into the man's cruel eyes, and his anger rose, cold and all-engulfing. "What you have found," said Talisman, "is death."

Knife hand raised, the man ran in and stabbed down toward Talisman's neck. But Talisman swayed to the right, his left forearm sweeping up to block the attacker's wrist. In the same flowing movement his right arm came up behind the man's shoulder; then, with a savage jerk, he brought his weight down on the knife arm, which snapped at the elbow. The man screamed and dropped the knife. Releasing him, Talisman swept up the blade, ramming it to the hilt between the man's ribs. As he dragged back on his victim's greasy hair, Talisman's dark eyes fixed on the terrified face. "May you rot in many hells," whispered the Nadir, twisting the knife blade. The mortally wounded man's mouth opened for one last scream of pain, but he died before he could draw breath.

Releasing the body, Talisman wiped the knife clean of blood on the man's filthy tunic and moved on into the darkness. All was silent there. Walls towered on both sides of him, decorated with lines of shuttered windows. Talisman emerged onto a wider alley, no more than sixty yards long, and saw glimmering lights from the windows of a tavern. Hiding the knife beneath his hooded cloak, he walked on. The tavern door opened, and a big man with a square-cut black beard stepped into sight. Talisman approached him.

"Your pardon, lord," said the Nadir, the words tasting like acid on the tongue, "but could you direct me to the Street of Weavers?"

"Laddie," said the man, slumping drunkenly to an oak bench, "I'd be surprised if I could find my own way home. I'm a stranger here myself and have been lost in this city maze more than once tonight. By heaven, I don't know why anyone would want to live in such a place. Do you?"

Talisman turned away. At that moment the men who had been pursuing him came into sight, five at one end of the alley and four at the other. "We're going to cut your heart out!" shouted the leader, a fat, balding ruffian. Talisman drew his knife as the first five attackers rushed in. Movement came unexpectedly from Talisman's left. His eyes flickered toward it. The drunken stranger had risen to his feet and appeared to be trying to move the oak bench. No, not move it, Talisman realized, but lift it! It was so incongruous and bizarre a moment that he had to jerk his eyes from the scene in order to face his attackers. They were close now, three armed with knives and two with cudgels of lead. Suddenly the heavy oak bench hurtled past Talisman like a spear. It struck the gang leader full in the face, smashing his teeth and punching him from his feet, then spun off into the others, sending two of them to the ground. The remaining two men leapt over the bodies and ran in close. Talisman met the first blade to blade, then hammered his elbow into the man's chin. The attacker fell face first to the cobbles. As he struggled to rise, Talisman kicked him twice in the face; at the second kick the man groaned and slumped unconscious to the ground.

Talisman swung, but the last assailant was vainly struggling in the iron grip of the stranger, who had lifted him by neck and groin and was holding him suspended above his head. Spinning on his heel, Talisman saw the four remaining attackers edging forward from the other end of the alley. The stranger ran toward them, gave a grunt of effort, and hurled his hapless victim straight into them. Three went down but struggled to their feet. The stranger stepped forward.

"I think that's enough now, lads," he said, his voice cold. "So far I haven't killed anyone in Gulgothir. So gather your friends and go on about your business."

One of the men moved carefully forward, peering at the stranger. "You're the Drenai fighter, aren't you? Druss?"

"True enough. Now be on your way, lads. The fun is over—unless you've an appetite for more."

"Klay will beat you to a bloody pulp in the final, you bastard!" Without another word the man sheathed his knife and turned to his comrades. Together they helped the injured from the alley, having to carry the leader, who was still unconscious.

The stranger turned to Talisman. "An ugly place," he said with a broad grin, "but it does have its delights. Join me in a jug?"

"You fight well," said Talisman. Glancing around, he could see the attackers milling at the mouth of the alley. "Yes, I'll drink with you, Drenai. But not here. My feeling is they will talk among themselves until their courage returns; then they will attack again."

"Well, walk with me, laddie. The Gothir gave us lodgings, which I believe are not far from here, and there's a jug of Lentrian red that has been calling my name all evening." Together they moved west, out onto the main avenue leading to the colosseum. The attackers did not follow.

Talisman had never been inside so luxurious a lodging, and his dark, slanted eyes soaked in the sights: the long oak-paneled staircase, the wall hangings of velvet, the ornate cushioned chairs, sculpted and gilded, the carpets of Chiatze silk. The huge warrior called Druss led him up the stairs and into a long corridor. Doors were set on both sides at every fifteen paces. The stranger paused at one of them, then pressed a bronze latch, and the door slid open to reveal a richly furnished apartment. When Talisman peered in, his first sight was of a six-foot-long rectangular mirror. He blinked, for he had seen his reflection before, but never full-length or quite so clearly. The stolen black cloak and tunic were travel-stained and dust-covered, and his jet-black eyes gazed back at him with undisguised weariness. The face he gazed upon—despite being beardless—looked far older than his eighteen years, the mouth set in a grim, determined line. Responsibility sat upon him like a vulture, eating away at his youth.

Stepping closer to the mirror, he touched the surface. It looked like glass. But glass was virtually transparent; how, then, did it reflect so wonderfully? Peering closer, he examined the mirror, and on the bottom right edge he saw what appeared to be a scratch. Dropping to his knee, he stared at it and found that he could look through the scratch at the carpet beyond the mirror. "They paint the glass with silver somehow," said Druss. "I don't know how it is done."

Turning from the mirror, Talisman walked into the room. There were six couches covered with polished leather, several chairs, and a long, low table on which was a jug of wine and four silver goblets. The room was as large as the home tent of his father, and that housed fourteen! Twin doors on the far side opened onto a wide balcony that overlooked the colosseum. Talisman padded across the lush carpets and out onto the balcony. The Great Arena was surrounded by tall brass poles on which stood burning lamps casting red light on the lower half of the colosseum. It was almost as if the enormous structure were on fire. Talisman wished that it was—and this entire city with it!

"Pretty, is it not?" asked Druss.

"You fight there?"

"Just once more. The Gothir champion, Klay. Then I'm going home to my farm and my wife."

Druss passed his guest a goblet of Lentrian red, and Talisman sipped it. "All the flags flying from so many nations. Why? Are you planning a war?"

"As I understand it," said Druss, "it is the opposite. The nations are here for the Fellowship Games. They are supposed to encourage friendship and trade between the nations."

"The Nadir were not invited to take part," said Talisman, turning from the window and reentering the main room.

"Ah, well, that's politics, laddie. I neither understand nor condone it. But even if they did wish to invite the Nadir, to whom would the invite be sent? There are hundreds of tribes, mostly at war with one another. They have no center—no leader."

"That will change," said Talisman. "A leader is prophesied, a great man. The Uniter!"

"I hear there have been many so-called Uniters."

"This one will be different. He will have eyes the color of violet and will bear a name no Nadir has ever chosen. He is coming. And then let your world beware!"

"Well, I wish you luck," said Druss, sitting back on a couch and raising his booted feet to the table. "Violet eyes, eh? That'll be something to see."

"They will be like the Eyes of Alchazzar," said Talisman. "He will be the embodiment of the Great Wolf in the Mountains of the Moon."

The door opened, and Talisman spun to see a tall, handsome young man enter. His fair hair was tied back in a tight ponytail, and he wore a cloak of crimson over a long blue tunic of opal-adorned silk.

"I hope you've left some of that wine, old horse," the newcomer said, addressing Druss. "I'm as dry as a lizard's armpit."

"I must be going," said Talisman, moving toward the door.

"Wait!" said Druss, rising. "Sieben, do you know the whereabouts of the Street of Weavers?"

"No, but there's a map in the back room. I'll fetch it." Sieben returned moments later and spread the map on the low table. "Which quarter?" he asked Talisman.

"Northwest."

Sieben's slender finger traced the map. "There it is! Beside the Hall of Antiquities." He glanced up at Talisman. "You leave here by the main entrance and continue along the avenue until you come to the statue of the war goddess—a tall woman carrying a long spear; there's a hawk on her shoulder. You bear left for another mile until you see the Park of Poets ahead of you. Turn right and keep going until you reach the Hall of Antiquities. There are four huge columns outside and a high lintel stone on which is carved an eagle. The Street of Weavers is the first on the right, past the hall. Would you like me to go over it again?"

"No," said Talisman. "I shall find it." And without another word the Nadir left the room.

As the door closed, Sieben grinned. "His gratitude overwhelms me. Where do you meet these people?"

"He was involved in a scuffle, and I gave him a hand."

"Many dead?" inquired Sieben.

"None, as far as I know."

"You're getting old, Druss. Nadir, was he not? He's got a nerve walking around Gulgothir."

"Aye, I liked him. He was telling me about the Uniter to come, a man with the Eyes of Alchazzar, whatever that means."

"That is fairly simple to explain," said Sieben, pouring himself a goblet of wine. "It's an old Nadir legend. Hundreds of years ago three Nadir shamans, men of great power reputedly, decided to create a statue to the gods of stone and water. They drew magic from the land and shaped the statue, which they called Alchazzar, from the stone of the Mountains of the Moon. It was, I understand, in the form of a giant wolf. Its eyes were huge amethysts, its teeth of ivory."

"Get to the point, poet!" snapped Druss.

"You have no patience, Druss. Now bear with me. According to the legends, the shamans drew all the magic from the land, placing it within the wolf. They did this so that they could control the destiny of the Nadir. But one of the shamans later stole the Eyes of Alchazzar, and suddenly the magic ceased. Robbed of their gods, the Nadir tribes—peaceful until then—turned on one another, fighting terrible wars, which continue to this day. There! A nice little fable to help you sleep."

"So what happened to the man who stole the eyes?" asked Druss.

"I have no idea."

"That's what I hate about your stories, poet. They lack detail. Why was the magic trapped? Why did he steal the eyes? Where are they now?"

"I shall ignore these insults, Druss, old horse," said Sieben with a smile. "You know why? Because when word got out that you were ill, your odds against Klay lengthened to twelve to one."

"Ill? I have never been ill in my life. How did such a rumor start?"

Sieben shrugged. "I would . . . guess it was when you failed to attend the banquet in the God-King's honor."

"Damn, I forgot about it! You told them I was sick?"

"I don't believe I said sick . . . more . . . injured. Yes, that was it. Suffering from your injuries. Your opponent was there, and he asked after you. Such a nice fellow. Said he hoped the prophecy did not affect your style."

"What prophecy?"

"Something about you losing the final," said Sieben airily. "Absolutely nothing to worry about. Anyway, you can ask him yourself. He has invited you to his home tomorrow evening, and I should be grateful if you would accept."

"You would be grateful? Do I take it there is a woman involved in this?"

"Now that you mention it, I did meet a delightful serving maid at the palace. She seems to think I'm some kind of foreign prince."

"I wonder how she formed that opinion," muttered Druss.

"No idea, old lad. However, I did invite her to dine with me here tomorrow. Anyway, I think you'll like Klay. He's witty and urbane, and his arrogance is carefully masked."

"Oh, yes," grunted Druss. "I like him already."

## 2

**T**HE HOUSE ON the Street of Weavers was an old gray stone Gothir building, two stories under a roof of red terra-cotta tiles. However, the rooms inside had been redesigned after the fashion of the Chiatze. No square or rectangular rooms remained; the walls now flowed in perfect curves: ovals or circles or circles upon ovals. Doors and door frames followed those lines; even the heavy, square-framed Gothir windows, so bleak and functional from the outside, had been decorated on the interior frames with exquisitely sculpted circular covers.

In the small central study Chorin-Tsu sat cross-legged on an embroidered rug of Chiatze silk, his deep brown eyes staring unblinking at the man kneeling before him. The newcomer's eyes were dark and wary, and though he was kneeling, as was customary in the presence of one's host, his body was tense and ready. He reminded Chorin-Tsu of a coiled snake, very still but ready to strike. Talisman flicked his gaze to the rounded walls, the reliefs of sculpted lacquered wood, and the delicate paintings in their lacquered frames. His gaze flowed over the works of art, never pausing to examine them. Swiftly he returned his attention to the little Chiatze. Do I like you? Chorin-Tsu wondered, as the silence lengthened. Are you a man to be trusted? Why did destiny choose you to save your people? Without blinking, Chorin-Tsu studied the young man's face. He had a high brow, which often denoted intelligence, and his skin was closer to the gold of the Chiatze than to the jaundiced yellow of the Nadir. How old was he? Nineteen? Twenty? So young! And yet he radiated power, strength of purpose. You have gained experience beyond your years, thought the old man. And what do you see before you, young warrior? A wrinkled ancient, a lantern whose oil is almost gone, the flame beginning to stutter? An old man in a room of pretty pictures! Well, once I was strong like you, and I had great dreams also. At the thought of those dreams his mind wandered briefly, and he came to with a start and found himself staring into Talisman's jet-black eyes. Fear touched him fleetingly, for now the eyes were cold and impatient.

"Be so kind as to show me the token," said Chorin-Tsu, speaking in the southern tongue, his voice barely above a whisper. Talisman reached into his tunic and produced a small coin stamped with the head of a wolf. He offered it to the old man, who took it with trembling fingers, leaning forward to examine it. Talisman found himself staring at the small white braid of hair on the crown of Chorin-Tsu's otherwise shaven head. "It is an interesting coin, young man. Sadly, however, anyone can possess such a piece," said the embalmer, his breath wheezing from him. "It could have been taken from the true messenger."

Talisman gave a cold smile. "Nosta Khan told me you were a mystic, Chorin-Tsu. You should therefore have little difficulty judging my integrity."

There were two shallow clay cups of water set on a silk rug. The young Nadir reached for one, but the old man waved a hand and shook his head. "Not yet, Talisman. Forgive me, but I shall tell you when to drink. As to your point, Nosta Khan was not speaking of psychic powers. I was never a true mystic. What I have been all my life, Talisman, is a student. I have studied my craft, I have examined the great sites of history, but most of all I have studied men. The more I studied the race, the better I understood its foibles. But the curious thing about study, when conducted with an open mind, is that it makes one smaller. But forgive me; philosophy is not a Nadir preoccupation."

"Being savages, you mean?" answered the Nadir without rancor. "Perhaps I should therefore leave the answer to the priest-philosopher Dardalion, who said, 'Every question answered leads to seven other questions. Therefore, to a student the gathering of knowledge merely increases the awareness of how much more there is still to know.' Will that suffice, Master Embalmer?"

Chorin-Tsu masked his surprise and bowed deeply. "Indeed it will, young man. And I pray you will forgive this old one for such rudeness. These are heady days, and I fear my excitement is affecting my manners."

"I take no offense," said Talisman. "Life is harsh on the steppes. There is little opportunity for a contemplative existence."

The old man bowed again. "I do not wish to compound my rudeness, young sir, but I find myself intrigued as to where a Nadir warrior would come upon the words of Dardalion of the Thirty."

"It is said that a little mystery adds spice to a relationship," Talisman told him. "However, you were talking about your studies."

Chorin-Tsu found himself warming further to the young man. "My studies also involve astrology, numerology, the casting of runes, the reading of palms, the fashioning of spells. And yet there remain so many things to baffle the mind. I shall give you an example." From his belt he pulled an ivory-handled throwing knife, which he pointed toward a round target set on the wall some twenty paces away. "When I was younger, I could hurl this blade into the golden center of that target. But now, as you see, my fingers are gnarled and bent. Do it for me, Talisman." The young Nadir caught the tossed blade. For a moment he weighed it in his hand, feeling the balance. Then he drew back his arm and let fly. The silver steel shimmered in the lantern light and flashed across the room to lance home into the target. It missed the gold by a finger's breadth. "The target is covered with small symbols. Go and tell me the symbol that the blade pierced," ordered Chorin-Tsu.

Talisman rose and walked across the room. The target had been decorated with curious Chiatze hieroglyphs traced in gold paint. He did not recognize most of them. But the knife blade had pierced an oval at the center of which was a delicately drawn talon, and this image he understood. "Where did it strike?" called Chorin-Tsu. Talisman told him.

"Good, good. Come and rejoin me, my boy."

"I have passed your test?"

"One of them. Here is the second. Drink from one of the cups."

"Which one contains the poison?" asked Talisman.

Chorin-Tsu said nothing, and Talisman stared at the cups. "Suddenly I am not thirsty."

"Yet you must drink," Chorin-Tsu insisted.

"Tell me the purpose of the game, old one. Then I shall decide."

"I know you can throw a knife, Talisman; this I have seen. But can you *think*? Are you worthy to serve the Uniter, to bring him to our people? As you rightly surmise, one of the cups contains a deadly poison. Death will follow if it even touches your lips. The other contains nothing but water. How will you choose?"

"There is insufficient information," said Talisman.

"You are wrong."

Talisman sat quietly, his mind working at the problem. He closed his eyes, recalling every word spoken by the old man. Leaning forward, he lifted the left-hand cup, twirling it in his fingers, and then the right. Both were identical. Transferring his gaze to the rug, he gave a rare smile. It was embroidered with the same set of symbols as the target. And below the left-hand cup was the oval and the talon. Lifting the cup, he tasted the water. It was sweet and cool.

"Good, you are observant," said Chorin-Tsu. "But is it not

amazing that you should have thrown the knife to the exact symbol, when there were twelve others to strike?"

"How did you know I would strike it?"

"It was written thus in the stars. Nosta Khan knew it also. He knew it through his talent, whereas I knew it through study. Now, answer me this: What is the third test?"

Talisman took a deep breath. "The talon was the mark of Oshikai Demon-bane, the oval the symbol of his wife, Shul-sen. When Oshikai wished to wed Shul-sen, her father set him three tasks. The first was one of marksmanship, the second concerned intelligence, the third . . . required a sacrifice. Oshikai had to slay a demon who had been his friend. I know no demons, Chorin-Tsu."

"As with all myths, my boy, they serve a purpose beyond the richness of the tales. Oshikai was a reckless man, given to great rages. The demon was merely a part of himself, the wild and dangerous side of his personality. Shul-sen's father knew this and wanted Oshikai to pledge himself to love her till the end of his days, never to harm her, never to put her aside for another."

"What has this to do with me?"

"Everything." Chorin-Tsu clapped his hands together. The door opened, and a young Chiatze woman entered. She bowed to both men, then knelt and touched her head to the floor at Chorin-Tsu's feet. Talisman gazed at her in the candlelight. She was exquisitely beautiful, with raven-dark hair and wide almond-shaped eyes. Her mouth was full, and her figure was trim within a white silk blouse and long satin skirt.

"This is Zhusai, my granddaughter. It is my wish that you take her with you on your quest. It is also the wish of Nosta Khan and your father."

"And if I refuse?"

"No more will be said. You will leave my home and journey back to the tents of your people."

"And my quest?"

"Will continue without my aid."

"I am not ready for a wife. I have dedicated my life to the pursuit of revenge and the Day of the Uniter. But even were I to consider marriage, then as the son of a chieftain, it would be my right to choose my own woman. It would certainly be my wish that she be Nadir. I have great respect for the Chiatze, but they are not my people."

Chorin-Tsu leaned forward. "Leaders have no rights; that is one of the great secrets of leadership. However, you miss the point, young man. Zhusai is not to be your wife. She is pledged to the Uniter; she will be the Shul-sen to his Oshikai."

"Then I do not understand," admitted Talisman, relieved. "What sacrifice is required of me?"

"Do you accept Zhusai into your custody? Will you protect her with your life?"

"If that is required, so be it," promised Talisman. "Now, what is the sacrifice?"

"Perhaps there will be none. Zhusai, show our guest to his room." The young woman bowed once more, then rose silently and led Talisman from the chamber.

At the end of a short corridor Zhusai opened a door and stepped inside. Rugs were set around the room, and blankets had been spread on the floor. There were no chairs or ornaments. "This is your room," she said.

"Thank you, Zhusai. Tell me, have you ever been in the desert?"

"No, lord."

"Does the prospect of our journey cause you concern? We will be traveling through hostile lands, and there will be many dangers."

"There is only one danger I fear, lord," she said.

"And that is?" As he asked the question he saw a gleam appear in her eyes and a tightening of the muscles of her face. In that moment the quiescent, agreeable Chiatze girl-child disappeared, replaced by a hard-eyed woman. Then, just as suddenly, the girl mask fell back into place.

"It is best not to speak of fears, lord. For fear is akin to magic. Good night. Sleep well."

The door closed behind her.

Sieben's laughter was rich, the sound filling the room, and the Drenai ambassador reddened. "I think you'll find that this is no subject for humor," he said coldly. "We are talking here about international diplomacy, and the whims of individuals have no place in it." The poet sat back and studied the ambassador's thin face. His steel-colored hair was carefully combed and delicately perfumed, his clothes immaculate and very costly. Majon wore a white woolen cloak and a blue silk tunic edged with gold. The ambassador's fingers toyed with his crimson neck scarf and the ceremonial brooch—a silver horse rearing— that denoted his rank. The man was angry and was allowing it to show. This, Sieben decided, was a calculated insult. Diplomats were masters of oily charm, their expressions endlessly amiable when they dealt with superiors. "Do you disagree?" asked Majon.

"I rarely disagree with politicians," Sieben told him. "It seems to me that the worst of you could convince me that a horse turd tastes like a honey cake. And the best would leave me believing that I alone in all the world had failed to enjoy its flavor."

"That is a highly insulting remark," snapped Majon.

"I do apologize, Ambassador. It was meant as a compliment."

"Will you seek to convince him or not? This matter is of the highest importance. I swear, by the memory of Missael, that we could be talking of war!"

"Oh, I don't doubt that, Ambassador. I saw the God-King, remember?" Majon's eyes widened, and he swiftly raised his hand to his mouth, holding a finger to his lips in warning. Sieben merely grinned. "An inspired leader," he said with a wink. "Any ruler who would sack a politician and raise his pet cat to ministerial rank has my support."

Majon rose from his chair and walked to the door, opening it and peering out into the corridor. Swinging back into the room, he stood before the poet. "It is not wise to mock any ruler, most especially when in the capital city of such a man. The peoples of the Drenai and the Gothir are at peace. Long may it remain so."

"Yet in order to ensure that peace," said Sieben, his smile fading, "Druss must lose against Klay?"

"Put simply, that is indeed the situation. It would not be . . . appropriate . . . for Druss to win."

"I see. You have little faith, then, in the God-King's prophecy?"

Majon poured himself a goblet of wine and sipped it before answering. "It is not a question of faith, Sieben; it is simply politics. The God-King makes a prophecy at this time every year. They come true. There are those who believe that since his prophecies generally concern the actions of men, the men themselves ensure their accuracy. Others simply accept that their ruler is divine. However, in this instance the point is academic. He has predicted that Klay will take the gold. If Druss were to win, it would be seen as an insult to the God-King and interpreted as a Drenai plot to destabilize the administration. The consequences of such an action could be disastrous."

"I suppose he could put his cat in charge of the army and attack Dros Delnoch. A terrifying prospect!"

"Is there a brain inside that handsome head? The army you speak of numbers more than fifty thousand men, many of them battle-hardened by war against Nadir tribes and Sathuli raiders. But that is not the point. Here in Gothir there are three main factions. One faction believes in the divine right of the Gothir to conquer the world. The other seeks to conquer the world without concerning themselves with the question of divine rights. You understand? For reasons best known to themselves, each faction hates the other. This nation stands constantly on the brink of civil war. While they are thus fighting among themselves, the Drenai are free from the appalling cost of resisting an invasion."

"Cost? Are we talking coin here?"

"Of course we are talking coin," said Majon, his irritation flaring. "Mobilization of men, training, new armor, swords, breastplates. Food for the recruits. And where do we find the recruits? The land. Peasants and farmers. When they are soldiers, who gathers the crops? The answer is that many fields are left unharvested. What happens to the price of grain? It soars. And at the end, what has been achieved? The fortress will hold, and the men will go home to find that their taxes have risen to pay for the war. Fifty thousand trained soldiers angry at the government."

"You didn't mention the dead," said Sieben softly.

"A good point. The threat of disease from corpses, the costs of burial. Then there are the cripples, who become an endless drag on the benevolence of the state."

"I think you have made your point, Ambassador," put in Sieben. "Your humanity does you credit. But you mentioned three factions, and you have described only two."

"Lastly there is the Royal Guard, ten thousand men, the elite of the Gothir army. They placed the God-King on the throne after the last insurrection, and they keep him there. Neither of the other two factions is yet powerful enough to be guaranteed victory *without* the support of the guards. Therefore, everyone stands frozen, unable to move. Ideally, that situation should be encouraged to continue."

Sieben laughed. "And meanwhile a madman sits on the throne, his reign punctuated by murder, torture, and enforced suicides?"

"That is a problem for the Gothir, Sieben. Our concern is the Drenai, of whom there are also close to three thousand living in Gothir lands whose lives would be forfeit if any general hostilities were announced. Merchants, laborers, physicians—aye, and diplomats. Are their lives without meaning, Sieben?"

"Smoothly done, Majon," said Sieben, clapping his hands. "And now we come to the horse-turd–honey cake. Of course their lives have meaning. But Druss is not responsible for them or for the actions of a madman. Don't you understand, Ambassador? Nothing you or the God-King can do will change that. Druss is not a stupid man, yet he sees life very clearly. He will go out and face Klay and give everything he has to win. There is nothing anyone could say that would induce him to do less. Nothing at all. All your arguments here would be meaningless. Druss would say that whatever the God-King chooses to do—or not to do—is up to his own conscience. But even more than that, Druss would refuse for one very simple reason."

"And that is?"

"It wouldn't be right."

"I thought you said he was intelligent!" snapped Majon. "Right, indeed! What has right to do with this? We are dealing with a . . . sensitive and . . . unique ruler."

"We are dealing with a lunatic who, if he wasn't king, would be locked away for his own safety," responded Sieben.

Majon rubbed his tired eyes. "You mock politics," he said softly. "You sneer at diplomacy. But how do you think we hold the world at peace? I'll tell you, Sieben. Men like me travel to places like this, and we're fed those horse-turd cakes of yours. And we smile, and we say how nourishing they are. We move in the space between other men's egos, massaging them as we walk. We do this not for gain but for peace and prosperity. We do it so that Drenai farmers, merchants, clerics, and laborers can raise their families in peace. Druss is a hero; he can enjoy the luxury of living his own life and speaking his own truths. Diplomats cannot. Now, will you help me convince him?"

Sieben rose. "No, Ambassador, I will not. You are wrong in this, though I give you the benefit of the doubt as to your motives." He walked to the door and turned. "Perhaps you've been eating those cakes too long. Perhaps you have acquired a taste for them."

Behind the paneled walls a servant slipped away to report the conversation.

Garen-Tsen lifted the hem of his long purple robe and stepped carefully down the worn stone steps to the dungeon level. The stench there was great, but the tall Chiatze closed his mind to it. Dungeons were supposed to stink. Prisoners dragged into such places were assailed by the gloom, the damp, and the awful smell of fear. It made interrogation that much more simple.

In the dungeon corridor he paused and listened. Somewhere to his left a man was crying, the noise muffled by the heavy stone of his cell. Two guards stood by. Garen-Tsen summoned the first. "Who weeps?" he asked.

The guard, a fat, bearded man with stained teeth, sniffed loudly. "Maurin, sir. He was brought in yesterday."

"I will see him after speaking to the senator," said Garen-Tsen.

"Yes, sir." The man backed away, and Garen-Tsen walked slowly to the interrogation room. An elderly man was seated there, his face blotched and swollen, his right eye almost shut. Blood had stained his white undertunic.

"Good morning, Senator," said Garen-Tsen, moving to a high-backed chair that a guard slid into position for him. He sat opposite the injured man, who glared at him balefully. "I understand that you have decided to remain uncooperative."

The prisoner took a deep, shuddering breath. "I am of the royal line, Garen-Tsen. The law expressly forbids torture."

"Ah, yes, the law. It also expressly forbids plotting to kill the king, I understand. And it frowns on conspiracies to overthrow the rightful government."

"Of course it does!" snapped the prisoner. "Which is why I would never be guilty of such dealings. The man is my nephew; you think I would plan to murder my own blood kin?"

"And now you add heresy to the charges," said Garen-Tsen mildly. "The God-King is never to be referred to as 'a man.' "

"A slip of the tongue," muttered the senator.

"Such slips are costly. Now, to matters at hand. You have four sons, three daughters, seven grandchildren, fourteen cousins, a wife, and two mistresses. Let me be frank with you, Senator. You are going to die. The only question that remains is whether you die alone or with your entire family."

All color drained from the prisoner's face, but his courage remained. "You are a vile devil, Garen-Tsen. There is an excuse for my nephew, the king—poor boy—for he is insane. But you—you are an intelligent, cultured man. May the gods curse you!"

"Yes, yes, I am sure they will. Shall I order the arrest of your family members? I do not believe your wife would relish the atmosphere of these dungeons."

"What do you desire from me?"

"A document is being prepared for your signature. When it is completed and signed by you, you will be allowed to take poison. Your family will be spared." Garen-Tsen rose. "And now you must excuse me. There are other traitors awaiting interrogation."

The old man looked up at the Chiatze. "There is only one traitor here, you Chiatze dog. And one day you will be dragged screaming to this very room."

"That may indeed prove true, Senator. You, however, will not be here to see it."

An hour later Garen-Tsen rose from his scented bath. A young manservant applied a hot towel to his wet body, gently rubbing away the drops of water clinging to the golden skin. A second servant brought a phial of scented oil, which he massaged into Garen-Tsen's back and shoulders. When he had finished, a third boy stepped forward carrying a fresh purple robe. The Chiatze raised his arms, and the robe was expertly settled in place. Two ornate slippers were laid on the rug at his feet. Garen-Tsen slipped his feet into them and walked to his study. The ornate desk of carved oak had been freshly polished with beeswax and scented with lavender. Three inkwells had been placed there, along with four fresh white quill pens. Seating himself in a padded leather chair, Garen-Tsen took up a quill and a virgin sheet of thick paper and began his report.

As the noon bell was struck in the courtyard beyond, there came a tap at his door. "Enter!" he called. A slim, dark-haired man moved to the desk and bowed.

"Yes, Oreth, make your report."

"The sons of Senator Gyall have been arrested. His wife committed suicide. Other family members have fled, but we are hunting them now. The wife of the noble Maurin has transferred funds to a banker in Drenan: eighty thousand gold pieces. His two brothers are already in the Drenai capital."

"You will send a message to our people in Drenan. They must deal with the traitors."

"Yes, sir."

"Anything else, Oreth?"

"Only one small matter, sir. The Drenai fighter, Druss. It seems he will probably attempt to win. His ambassador will try to persuade him, but the fighter's friend, Sieben, maintains he will not be convinced."

"Who do we have following the fighter?"

"Jarid and Copass."

"I have spoken to Klay, and he says the Drenai will prove a tough opponent. Very well, arrange to have him waylaid and cut. Any deep wound will suffice."

"It might not be so simple, lord. The man was engaged in a fracas recently and thrashed several robbers. It may be necessary to kill him."

"Then kill him. There are far more important matters needing my attention, Oreth. I have little time for consideration of such tiny problems." Lifting his quill, Garen-Tsen dipped it into an inkwell and began once more to write.

Oreth bowed and backed away.

Garen-Tsen continued to work for almost a full hour. The

words of the senator, however, continued to echo through his mind. *"And one day you will be dragged screaming to this very room."* Such an event was at present extremely likely. As of this moment Garen-Tsen was perched on the very top of the mountain. The hold, however, was precarious, for his position of eminence depended entirely on a madman. Laying aside his quill, he contemplated the future. So far, mainly through his own efforts, both rival factions remained in balance. Such harmony could not be maintained for much longer, not with the king's illness proceeding at such a terrifying rate. Soon his insanity would become too difficult to control, and a bloodbath would surely follow. Garen-Tsen sighed.

"On top of the mountain," he said aloud. "It is not a mountain at all but a volcano waiting to erupt."

At that moment, the door opened and a middle-aged soldier stepped inside. He was powerfully built and wore the long, black cloak of the Royal Guards. Garen-Tsen's odd-colored eyes focused on the man. "Welcome, Lord Gargan. How may I be of service?"

The newcomer moved to a chair and sat down heavily. Removing his ornate helm of bronze and silver, he laid it on the desktop. "The madman has killed his wife," he said.

Two Royal Guards led Chorin-Tsu into the grounds of the palace. Two more came behind, carrying the trunk in which lay the objects and materials necessary to the trade of the embalmer. The old man's breath was wheezing from him as he hurried to keep up. He asked no questions.

The guardsmen led him through the servants' halls and up a richly carpeted stairway into the warren of royal apartments. Skirting the fabled Hall of Concubines, the guards entered the royal chapel, bowing before the golden image of the God-King. Once through the rear of the chapel, they slowed, as if to make less noise, and Chorin-Tsu took the opportunity to regain his breath. At last they came to a double-doored private chamber.

Two men were waiting outside. One was a soldier with a forked beard the color of iron; the second was the purple-garbed first minister, Garen-Tsen. He was tall and wand-thin, and his face bore no expression.

Chorin-Tsu bowed to his countryman. "May the lords of high heaven grant you blessings," said Chorin-Tsu, speaking in Chiatze.

"It is unseemly and discourteous to use a foreign language in the royal chambers," admonished Garen-Tsen in the southern tongue. Chorin-Tsu bowed once more. Garen-Tsen's long fingers tapped at the second knuckle of his right hand. Then he folded his arms, his index finger touching his bicep. Chorin-Tsu read the sign language: *Do what is required and you will live!*

"My apologies, lord," said Chorin-Tsu. "Forgive your humble servant." Bringing his hands together, he bowed even lower than before, touching his thumbs to his chin.

"Your skills are needed here, Master Embalmer. No one else will enter this room until you have completed your . . . craft. You understand?"

"Of course, lord." The guardsmen placed Chorin-Tsu's trunk by the door. Garen-Tsen opened the door just wide enough for the elderly Chiatze to enter, dragging the trunk behind him.

Chorin-Tsu heard the door close behind him, then gazed around the apartments. The rugs were of the finest Chiatze silk, as were the hangings around the royal bed. The bed itself had been exquisitely carved and then gilded. Every item in the room spoke of riches and the extremes of wealth only monarchs could afford.

Even the corpse . . .

She was hanging by her arms from golden chains attached to rings in the ceiling above the bed, and blood had drenched the sheets below her. Chorin-Tsu had seen the queen only twice before: once during the parade at her wedding and then, two weeks ago, when the Fellowship Games began. In her new role as Bokat, goddess of wisdom, she had blessed the opening ceremony. Chorin-Tsu had seen her closely then. Her eyes had seemed vacant, and she had slurred the words of the blessing. Now he moved to a chair and sat, staring at the still body.

The old man sighed. Just as at the games ceremony, the queen was wearing the Helm of Bokat, a golden headpiece with flaring wings and long cheek guards. Chorin-Tsu was not well versed in Gothir myths, but he knew enough. Bokat was the wife of Missael, the god of war. Their son, Caales, future lord of battle, sprang fully grown from his mother's belly.

But that was not the myth that inspired this insanity. No. Bokat had been captured by the enemy. The gods of the Gothir had gone to war, the world burning from the flame arrows of Missael. Bokat had been taken by one of the other gods and hung from chains outside the Magical City. Her husband, Missael, was warned that if he attacked, she would be the first slain. He had taken his bow and shot her through the heart; then he and his companions had rushed forward, scaling the walls and slaying all within. When the battle was over, he drew the arrow from his wife's breast and kissed the wound. It healed instantly, and she awoke and took him in her arms.

Here in this room someone had tried to duplicate the myth. The blood-covered arrow was lying on the floor. Wearily Chorin-Tsu climbed to the bed, loosening the bolts that held the golden chains to the slender wrists of the dead queen. The body fell to the bed, the helm rolling clear and striking the floor with a dull clang. The queen's blond hair fell free, and Chorin-Tsu noticed that the roots were a dull, mousy brown.

Garen-Tsen entered, and the two men spoke in sign.

*"The God-King tried to save her. When the bleeding would not stop, he panicked and sent for the royal physician."*

*"There is blood everywhere,"* said Chorin-Tsu. *"I cannot perform my arts on her in these conditions."*

*"You must! No one will be allowed to know of this"*— Garen-Tsen's fingers hesitated. *"—this stupidity."*

*"The physician is dead, then?"*

"Yes."

"As I will be when my work is done."

"No. I have arranged for you to be smuggled from the palace. You will flee to the south and Dros Delnoch."

"I thank you, Garen-Tsen."

"I will have a chest left outside these apartments. Place all the . . . soiled linen within it." "How long will you need to prepare her?" he concluded aloud.

"Three hours, perhaps more."

"I shall return then."

The minister left the room, and Chorin-Tsu sighed. The man had lied to him; there would be no escape to the south. Putting the thought from his mind, Chorin-Tsu moved to the trunk by the door and began to remove the jars of embalming fluid, the cutters and the scrapers, setting them out neatly on a table by the bed.

A gilded panel at the rear of the apartment slid open. Chorin-Tsu dropped to his knees, averting his gaze, but not before he had seen the gold paint on the royal face and the dried blood on his lips from when he had kissed the wound on his wife's breast.

"I shall awaken her now," said the God-King. Moving to the body, he knelt and pressed his lips to hers. "Come to me, sister-wife. Open your eyes, Goddess of the Dead. Come to me, I command you!"

Chorin-Tsu remained on his knees, eyes closed. "I command you!" shouted the God-King. Then he began to weep, and for long moments the sobbing continued. "Ah," he said suddenly. "She is teasing me; she is pretending to be dead. Who are you?"

Chorin-Tsu jerked as he realized that the king was addressing him. Opening his eyes, he looked up into the face of madness. The blue eyes shone brightly within the mask of gold; they were friendly and gentle. Chorin-Tsu took a long slow breath. "I am the royal embalmer, sire," he said.

"Your eyes are slanted, but you are not Nadir. Your skin is gold, like my friend Garen. Are you Chiatze?"

"I am, sire."

"Do they worship me there? In your homeland?"

"I have lived here for forty-two years, sire. Sadly, I do not receive news from my homeland."

"Come, talk to me. Sit here on the bed."

Chorin-Tsu rose, his dark eyes focusing on the young God-King. He was of medium build and slender, much like his sister. His hair was dyed gold, and his skin was painted the same color. His eyes were a remarkable blue. "Why is she not waking? I have commanded it."

"I fear, sire, that the queen has . . . moved to her second realm."

"Second? Oh, I see, goddess of wisdom, queen of the dead. Do you think so? When will she come back?"

"How could any mortal man predict such a happening, sire? The gods are far above mere mortals like myself."

"I suppose that we are. I think you are correct in your assumption, embalmer. She is ruling the dead now. I expect she will be happy. A lot of our friends are there to serve her. Many, many. Do you think that's why I sent them all there? Of course it was. I knew Bokat would return to the dead, and I sent lots of her friends ahead to welcome her. I only pretended to be angry with them." He smiled happily and clapped his hands. "What is this for?" he asked, lifting a long brass instrument with a forked end.

"It is an . . . aid to me, sire, in my work. It helps to . . . make the object of my attentions remain beautiful always."

"I see. It is very sharp and wickedly hooked. And why all the knives and scrapers?"

"The dead have little use for their internal organs, sire. They putrefy. For a body to remain beautiful, they must be removed."

The God-King stood and wandered to where Chorin-Tsu's chest stood open by the door. He peered inside, then lifted out a glass jar in which were stored many sets of crystal eyes. "I think I shall leave you to your craft, Master Embalmer," he said brightly. "I have many matters to attend to. There are so many of Bokat's friends who will want to follow her. I must prepare their names."

Chorin-Tsu bowed deeply and said nothing.


Sieben had been wrong. When Majon broached the subject of the prophecy with Druss, there was no immediate refusal. The Drenai warrior listened, his face impassive, his cold, pale eyes expressionless. As the ambassador concluded, Druss rose from his chair. "I'll think on it," he said.

"But Druss, there are so many considerations that—"

"I said I'll think on it. Now leave." The coldness of the warrior's tone cut through Majon like a winter wind.

During the late afternoon Druss, dressed casually in a wide-sleeved shirt of soft brown leather, woolen leggings, and knee-length boots, walked through the city center, oblivious to the crowds surging around him: servants buying supplies and wares for their households, men gathered around inns and taverns, women moving through the marketplaces and shops, lovers walking hand in hand in the parks. Druss weaved his way among them, his mind focused on the ambassador's plea.

When slavers had attacked Druss' village and captured the young women—Rowena among them—Druss had instinctively followed the raiders, hunting them down. That had been right! There had been no moral or political questions to be addressed.

But here and now it was all blurred. *"There would be honor in such a decision,"* Majon had assured him. And why? Because thousands of Drenai lives would be saved. Giving in to the wishes of a madman, suffering humiliation and defeat? This was honor?

Yet to win could mean, at worst, a terrible war. Was winning a fight worth such a risk? Majon had asked. For the satisfaction of pounding a man to the ground?

Druss crossed the Park of Giants and cut to the left, through the Arch of Marble and on toward the low Valley of the Swans in which Klay's house was situated. Here were the homes of the rich, the roads lined with trees, the houses elegantly designed, the grounds boasting small lakes and fountains or beautifully sculpted statues set around widening paths that ran through immaculately tended gardens.

Everything spoke of money, enormous amounts of gold. Druss had been raised in mountain communities where homes were built of rough-cut timber sealed with clay, places where coin was as rare as a whore's honor. Now he stood gazing at palace after palace of white marble, with gilded pillars, painted frescoes, and carved reliefs, each topped with red terra-cotta tile or black Lentrian slate.

Walking on, he sought out the home of the Gothir champion. Two sentries stood before the high wrought-iron gates; both men wore silver breastplates and were armed with short swords. The house was imposing, though not as ostentatious as the other homes nearby. It was square-built with a sloping red tile roof and boasted no ornate columns, no frescoes, no paint work. The home of the champion was of simple white stone. The main door was set beneath a stone lintel, and the many windows were functional, displaying no colored glass, no leaded figures, no ornamentation at all. Much to his own annoyance, Druss found himself liking the man who owned the house, which was set amid gardens boasting willow and beech.

There was one gesture toward the dramatic. A statue of the fighter, almost twice life size, was set on a pedestal at the center of a well-tended lawn. Like the house, it was of white stone, unpainted and unadorned, and showed Klay with his fists raised defiantly.

For a while Druss stood on the broad avenue outside the gates. A movement in the shadows caught his eye, and he saw a small boy crouched by the bole of an elm tree. Druss grinned at him. "Waiting for a glimpse of the great man, are you?" he asked amiably. The boy nodded but said nothing. He was painfully thin and scrawny, his eyes deep-set, his face pinched and tight. Druss fished in the small pouch at his belt, producing a silver coin, which he tossed to the urchin. "Go on with you. Buy yourself some food."

Catching the coin, the child stowed it in his ragged tunic but remained where he was.

"You really want to see him, don't you? Even hunger can't draw you away? Come with me then, boy. I'll take you in." The child's face brightened instantly, and he scrambled forward. Standing, he was even thinner than he had appeared, his elbows and knees seeming swollen larger than his biceps and thighs. Beside the huge form of the Drenai fighter he appeared no more than a frail shadow.

Together they walked to the gates, where the sentries stepped forward, blocking the way.

"I am Druss. I have been invited here."

"The beggar boy hasn't been invited," said one of the guards.

Druss stepped in close, his cold gaze locking to the man's eyes, their faces only inches apart. The guard stepped back, trying to create space between himself and Druss, but the Drenai followed him, and the man's breastplate clanged against the gate. "I invited him, laddie. You have a problem with that?"

"No. No problem."

The sentries stepped aside, pushing open the wrought-iron gates. Druss and the boy moved slowly on. The axman paused to gaze at the statue, then once more scanned the house and the grounds. The statue was out of place here, at odds with the natural contours of the garden. As he approached the house, an elderly servant opened the main door and bowed.

"Welcome, Lord Druss," he said.

"I am no lord nor would ever wish to be. This child was waiting in the shadows for a glimpse of Klay. I promised him a closer look."

"Mmm," said the old man. "I think he could do with a meal first. I'll take him to the kitchen. My master is waiting for you, sir, in the training grounds at the rear of the house. Just follow the hallway; you cannot miss it." Taking the boy by the hand, the old man moved away.

Druss strode on. In the grounds behind the house there were some twenty athletes engaged in training or sparring. The area was well designed, with three sand circles, punching bags, weights, massage tables, and two fountains supplying running water. At the far end was a deep pool where Druss could see several men swimming. The setting was simple, and he warmed to it, feeling the tension drain from him. Two men were sparring in one of the sand circles, while a third, the colossal Klay, stood close by, watching intently. In the fading sunlight Klay's short-cropped blond hair shone like gold. His arms were folded, and Druss noted the powerful muscles of his shoulders and back and the way his body tapered at the waist and hips. Built for speed and power, thought Druss.

"Break away!" ordered Klay. As the fighters moved apart, the Gothir champion stepped into the circle. "You are too stiff, Calas," he said, "and that left hand moves like a sick turtle. I think your training is out of harmony. You are building weight in your shoulders and arms, which is good for power, but you are ignoring the lower body. The most deadly punches are powered by the legs, the force flowing up through the hips and *then* to the shoulders and arms. When it reaches the fist, the impact is like a lightning bolt. Tomorrow you will work with Shonan." Swinging to the other man, he laid a hand on his shoulder. "You have great skill, boy, but you lack instinct. You have courage and style but not the heart of a fighter. You see with your eyes only. Shonan tells me your spear work is excellent. I think we will concentrate on that for the time being." Both men bowed and moved away.

Klay swung and saw Druss. He gave a broad smile and walked across the training area, his hand extended. A head taller than Druss, he was broader across the shoulders. His face was flat, with no sharpness to the bones on the brow and cheek.

It was unlikely that a blow would split the skin above or below his eyes, and his chin was square and strong. He had the face of a natural fighter.

Druss shook his hand. "This is what a training area should be," said Druss. "It is very fine. Well considered."

The Gothir fighter nodded. "It pleases me, though I wish it were bigger. No room for spear throwing or hurling the discus. My trainer, Shonan, uses a field close by. Come, I will show you our facilities." There were four masseurs at work, skillfully kneading and stretching the muscles of tired athletes, and a bathhouse with two heated pools set back from the training area. For some time the two men wandered the grounds, then at last Klay led Druss back into the house.

The walls of Klay's study were covered with drawings and paintings of the human form, showing muscle structures and attachments. Druss had never seen the like. "Several of my friends are physicians," said the Gothir fighter. "Part of their training involves the dissection of corpses and the study of the workings of the human body. Fascinating, is it not? Most of our muscles appear to work in an antagonistic fashion. For the biceps to swell, the triceps must relax and stretch."

"How does this help you?" asked Druss.

"It enables me to find balance," said Klay. "Harmony, if you will. Both muscles are vital, one to the other. Therefore, it would be foolish to develop one at the expense of the other. You see?"

Druss nodded. "I had a friend back in Mashrapur, a fighter named Borcha. He would have been as impressed as I am."

"I have heard of him. He trained you and helped you become a champion. After you left Mashrapur, he was the first fighter in circle history to regain his championship. He retired six years ago after losing to Proseccis in a bout that lasted almost two hours."

A servant brought a jug and filled two goblets. "Refreshing," Druss observed, as he drank.

"The juices of four fruits," said Klay. "I find them invigorating."

"I prefer wine."

"They say red wine feeds the blood," agreed Klay, "but I have always found it inhibits full training." For several heartbeats the men sat in silence, then Klay leaned back on his couch. "You are wondering why I invited you here, are you not?"

"I had thought it was an attempt at intimidation," said Druss. "Now I do not believe that."

"That is gracious of you. I wanted you to know that I was dismayed to hear of the prophecy. It must be galling for you. I know that I always find it hateful when politics intrudes on what should be honest competition. Therefore, I wanted to set your mind at rest."

"How do you plan to do that?"

"By convincing you to fight to win. To give it your very best."

Druss leaned back and looked hard at the Gothir champion. "Why is it," he asked, "that my own ambassador urges me to an opposite course of action? Do you wish to see your king humbled?"

Klay laughed. "You misunderstand me, Druss. I have watched you fight. You are very good, and you have heart and instinct. When I asked Shonan how he saw us both, he said, 'If I had to put all my money on a fighter, it would be you, Klay. But if I had to have someone fight for my life, it would be Druss.' I am an arrogant man, my friend, but it is not an arrogance born of false pride. I know what I am, and I know what I am capable of. In some ways, as my physician friends tell me, I am a freak of nature. My strength is prodigious, but my speed is extraordinary. Stand up for a moment."

Druss did so, and Klay positioned himself an arm's length away. "I shall pluck a hair from your beard, Druss. I want you to block me if you can." Druss readied himself.

Klay's hand snapped forward and back, and Druss felt the sting as several hairs were torn clear. His own arm had barely moved in response. Klay returned to his couch. "You cannot beat me, Druss. No man can. *That* is why you must not concern yourself with prophecies."

Druss smiled. "I like you, Klay," he said, "and if there was gold to be won for plucking hairs, I think you'd win. But we can talk about that after the final bout."

"You will fight to win?"

"I always do, laddie."

"By heavens, Druss, you are a man after my own heart. No give in you, is there? Is this why they call you the Legend?"

Druss shook his head. "I made the mistake of befriending a saga poet. Now everywhere I go he makes new stories, each more outlandish than those which came before. What astonishes me is that they are believed. The more I deny them, the more widespread is the belief they are true."

Klay led Druss back outside into the garden training area. The other athletes had gone, but servants had lit torches. "I know the feeling, Druss. Denial is seen as modesty. And people like to believe in heroes. I once lost my temper during training and struck a stone statue with the blade of my hand. Broke three bones. There are now a hundred men who claim the power of my blow shattered the statue into a thousand pieces. And there are at least twenty more who swear they saw it done. Will you stay and dine with me?"

Druss shook his head. "There's a tavern I passed coming here. I smelled a spiced meat dish being prepared and have had a taste for it ever since."

"Were the windows of the place stained blue?"

"Yes. You know it?"

"It's called the Broken Sword and has the finest chef in Gulgothir. I wish I could join you, but I have business to discuss with my trainer, Shonan."

"I would have been glad of the company. My friend Sieben is

entertaining a lady at our quarters and would not relish the sight of me arriving home early. Perhaps after tomorrow's final?"

"That would be pleasant."

"By the way, you have a guest. An urchin I found waiting outside. I would be grateful if you treated him kindly and offered him a word or two."

"Of course. Enjoy your meal."

## ◇ 3 ◇

**K**ELLS LICKED HIS fingers, then tore another chunk of dark bread with which to scour the bowl for the last of the stew. The old servant chuckled. "It's all right, boy; there is more where that came from." Lifting the pot from the stove, he ladled the bowl full. Kells' pleasure was undisguised. Taking up his spoon, he attacked the stew with renewed gusto, and within moments it had vanished. He belched loudly.

"I am Carmol," said the old servant, holding out his hand.

Kells looked at it, then reached out with his own grimy palm. Carmol shook hands. "I think this is the point where you tell me your name," he said.

Kells looked up into the old man's face. It was heavily lined, especially around the eyes, which were blue and merry. "Why?" There was no insolence in Kells' tone, merely innocent inquiry.

"Why? Well, it is considered polite when two people share a meal. It is also the way friendships begin." The old man was friendly, and his smile was not sly.

"I am called Fastfinger," said Kells.

"Fastfinger," echoed Carmol. "Is that what your mother calls you?"

"No, she calls me Kells. But everyone else calls me Fastfinger. The stew is very good. And the bread is soft. Fresh. I've had fresh bread, and I know the taste." Kells climbed down from the bench and belched again. The kitchen was warm and cozy, and it would have been nice to curl up on the floor beside the stove and sleep. Yet he could not, for his mission was not yet complete. "When can I see . . . Lord Klay?"

"What is your business with him?" inquired Carmol.

"I have no business with him," said Kells. "I have no business. I am . . . a beggar," he announced, thinking it sounded better than thief or cutpurse.

"So you have come to beg?"

"Yes, to beg. When can I see him?"

"He is a very busy man. But I can give you a coin or two and another bowl of stew."

"I don't want coins . . ." He stumbled to silence, his brow furrowing. "Well, I *do* want coins from you, but not from him. Not from Lord Klay."

"Then what do you want?" asked Carmol, sitting down at the bench.

Kells leaned in close. It could surely do no harm to tell Lord Klay's servant about his mission. The old man might even prove an ally. "I want him to lay his hands on my mother."

The old man laughed suddenly, which embarrassed Kells; this was no subject for laughter, and his eyes narrowed. Carmol saw his expression, and his smile faded. "I am sorry, boy. You took me by surprise. Tell me why you require such . . . such an act from my master."

"Because I *know* the truth," said Kells, dropping his voice. "I haven't told anyone; the secret is safe. But I thought that he could spare a little magic for my mam. He could make the lump go away. Then she could walk again and laugh. And she could work and buy food."

There was no smile on Carmol's face now. Tenderly he laid his hand on Kells' shoulder. "You . . . believe Lord Klay has magic?"

"He is a god," whispered Kells. The old man was silent for a moment, but Kells watched him closely. His face softened, and he looked worried. "I swear I won't tell anyone," said the boy.

"And how did you come by this intelligence, young Kells?"

"I saw him perform the miracle—last year it was. My mam had one of her . . . friends with her, so I was sitting in the alley mouth under cover. There was a storm raging, and the lightning was fierce. I saw the flash of it in the alley, and I heard the loud crack as it struck nearby. A body came hurtling by me and cracked into the wall. I ran out. It was Tall Tess; she's my mam's partner, and she works the Long Avenue. She must have been coming home. The lightning hit her, it did. Killed her dead. I felt her neck, and there was no thumping in the veins. I pushed my ear to her breast, and the heart was stopped. Then a carriage came by. I run swiftly back into the darkness for fear they'd think I killed her. Then Lord Klay jumps down from the carriage and goes to her. He feels for the thumping and listens for her heart. And then he did it." Kells felt his breathing quicken at the memory, his heart beating fast.

"What did he do?" asked Carmol.

"He bent over her and kissed her! I couldn't believe my eyes. He kissed a dead woman. Full on the lips, like a lover. You know what happened then?"

"Tell me."

"She groaned and come back from the dead. That's when I knew. I said nothing, not even to Tess. She had burns on her feet, and one earring had melted to her skin. But even she don't know as how she was dead."

The old man sighed. " 'Tis a powerful tale, boy. And I think you should speak with Lord Klay. Sit here, and I will see if he can spare you a moment or two. There is some fruit there. Help yourself to whatever you can eat."

Kells needed no second invitation. Even before Carmol had left the room, the boy had grabbed two ripe oranges and several bananas. These he devoured at speed, washing them down with fruit juice he discovered in a stone jug.

This was bliss. Fine food and a miracle for his mam!

It was a good day's work. Sitting down by the warm stove, Kells thought about what he would say to the god, how he would explain that his mother was sick and could not work. She was not lazy-sick. When the first lump had appeared on her breast, she had continued to work the Short Avenue even though dizziness often caused her to faint during the labor. As the lump had grown harder and more unsightly, some of her clients had turned away from her, and she had been forced to work longer hours, many of them in the alleys, where business was brisk and was conducted in darkness. But then came the second lump on the side of her neck, as big as one of the oranges he had just eaten. Nobody wanted to pay for her favors then. Her color had changed, too, ghost-gray her face was now with dark rings under the eyes. And thin! Terribly thin despite all the food Kells stole for her.

All this he would tell the god, and he would make it right.

Not like that surgeon Tall Tess had paid for. Five silver coins he took, and he did nothing! Oh, he felt the lumps and moved his hands over the rest of her body. Dirty skike! Then he whispered to Tess and shook his head a lot. Tess cried after that and spoke to his mam. Mam cried, too.

Kells lay down by the fire and dozed.

He awoke suddenly and found the god leaning over him. "You are tired, boy," said the god. "You may sleep if you wish."

"No, lord," said Kells, rising to his knees. "You must come with me! Me mam is sick."

Klay nodded, then sighed. "Carmol has told me what you saw; it was not a miracle, Kells. One of my physician friends taught me the trick. The shock of the lightning stopped her heart. I blew air into her lungs, then massaged the heart. There was no magic, I swear it."

"She was dead! You brung her to life!"

"But without magic."

"You won't help me, then?"

Klay nodded. "I'll do what I can, Kells. Carmol has gone to fetch the physician I spoke of. When he returns, we'll go to your mother and see what can be done."

\* \* \*

Kells sat quietly in the corner as the gray-haired physician examined Loira. The old man's fingers pressed gently at the lumps, then probed her belly and back and loins. All the time the dying woman was groaning, semidelirious, only the pain keeping her conscious. Her red hair was lank and greasy, her face pale and glistening with sweat. But even now she looked beautiful to Kells. He listened as the physician spoke to Klay, but he did not understand the conversation. Nor did he need to. The sepulchral tones conveyed it all. She was dying, and there was no god to lay his hands upon her. Anger rose as bile in Kells' throat. He swallowed it down as hot tears flowed to his cheeks, streaking the dirt. Blinking rapidly, he fought for control. Tall Tess stood by the opposite corner, her skinny arms crossed. She was still wearing the tattered red dress that denoted her calling.

"We need to get her to the hospice," he heard the physician say.

"What is that?" asked Kells, pushing himself up from the floor.

The old surgeon knelt before him. "It is a place Lord Klay paid for, where people in great pain can spend . . . can be when their sickness is too great to heal. We have medicines there to take away the pain. You may come, too, young man. You can sit with her."

"She's going to die, isn't she?"

Klay placed his hand on Kells' shoulder. "Aye, boy. There is nothing we can do. Eduse is the finest physician in Gulgothir. No one knows more than he."

"We can't pay for it," said Kells bitterly.

"It is already paid for by Lord Klay," said Eduse. "It was built for those who have nothing. You understand? Lord Klay—"

"He needs no lecture about me, my friend. I am far less than he believed, and no amount of words will take away his disappointment." Leaning over the bed, he lifted the woman, cradling her head against his chest.

The sick woman groaned again, and Tess moved to her, stroking her head. "It's all right, my little dove. We'll look after you. Tess'll be there, Loira. And Kells."

Klay carried Loira to the black carriage and opened the door. Kells and Tess scrambled in. Klay laid the unconscious woman on a padded seat and sat beside her. The physician, Eduse, climbed up alongside the driver. Kells heard the slap of reins on the backs of the four horses, then the carriage lurched forward. His mother awoke and cried out in pain, and Kells felt that his heart would burst.

The journey did not take long, for the hospice was built close to the poor quarter, and Kells followed as Klay carried her inside the white-walled building. Orderlies in long white tunics rushed forward to help, laying Loira on a stretcher and covering her with a thick blanket of white wool. Eduse led them down a long corridor to a room as large as any Kells had ever seen. The north and south walls were lined with pallet beds in which lay the sick and the dying. Many people were moving around the room: orderlies dressed in white, visitors arriving to see relatives or friends, physicians preparing medicines. The stretcher bearers carried his mother the length of the room and out into another corridor, coming at last to a small room some twelve feet long. They transferred Loira to one of the two narrow beds, both covered in fresh white linen, then covered her with a blanket. After the orderlies had gone, Eduse produced a phial of dark liquid. Lifting Loira's head, he poured the liquid into her mouth. She gagged, then swallowed. Some of the medicine dribbled to her chin. Eduse dabbed at it with a cloth, then eased her head back to the pillow.

"You may sleep here with her, Kells," said Eduse. "You, too," he told Tess.

"I can't stay," she said. "Have to work."

"I'll pay your . . . wages," said Klay.

Tess gave him a gap-toothed grin. "That's not it, lovely man. If I'm away from my patch, some other whore will take my trade. I need to be there. But I'll come here when I can." Stepping in close, she took Klay by the hand, raising it to her lips and kissing it. Then she swung away, embarrassed, and left the room.

Kells walked to the bedside and took his mother's hand. She was sleeping now, but the skin was hot and scaly to the touch. The boy sighed and sat down on the bed.

Klay and Eduse walked from the room. "How long?" he heard Klay ask, his voice little more than a whisper.

"Difficult to say. The cancers are very advanced. She could die in the night or last another month. You should get home; you've a fight tomorrow. I saw the Drenai fight. You'll need to be at your best."

"I shall be, my friend. But I'll not go home yet. I think I'll take a stroll. Get some air. You know, I have never wanted to be a god. Not until tonight."

Kells heard him move away.

Jarid was a careful man, a thinker. Few understood this, for what they saw was a large, round-shouldered, shambling bear of a man, slow of speech and therefore dim-witted. This was a misconception Jarid did not seek to change. Far from it. Born in the slums of Gulgothir, he had learned fast that the only way for a man to prosper was to outwit his fellow men. The first lesson to be learned was that morality was merely a weapon used by the rich. There was not—and never would be—an ultimate right or wrong. All life was theft in one form or another. The rich called their theft taxes, and a king could steal a nation by invasion and conquest and men would proclaim it a glorious victory. Yet a beggar could steal a loaf of bread and the same men would label it larceny and hang the man. Jarid would have none of it. He had killed his first man just after his twelfth birthday, a fat merchant whose name he could no longer remember. He had stabbed him in the groin, then slashed his purse clear of its retaining belt. The man had screamed loud and long, the sound following Jarid as he had sped through the alleyways. The money had bought medicines for his mother and sister and food for their shrunken bellies.

Now, at forty-four, Jarid was an accomplished killer, so accomplished that his skills had come to the attention of the state, and his work was now paid for out of public funds. He had even been allotted a tax number, the ultimate symbol of citizenship, giving him the right to vote in local elections. He had a small house in the southeastern quarter and a housekeeper who also warmed his bed. Far from rich, Jarid was still a long way from the urchin thief he once had been.

From his position in the alleyway he had watched Druss enter the Broken Sword tavern and had followed him inside, listening as he ordered his meal and noting the tavern maid telling him that the house was almost full and that the food would take a little time to prepare.

Jarid had left the tavern and run to where Copass waited; he gave the man his orders and stood back in the shadows, waiting. Copass soon returned with a dozen men, tough capable fighters mostly armed with knives and clubs. The last man carried a short crossbow.

Jarid took the thin-faced bowman by the arm and led him away from the others, then spoke to him in a low voice. "You don't shoot unless all else fails. You will be paid whether you loose a bolt or not. Your target is a black-bearded Drenai in a dark leather shirt; you will have no trouble picking him out."

"Why don't I just kill him as he appears in the doorway?"

"Because I am telling you not to, half-wit. He is the Drenai champion. It will suit our purposes if he is merely injured—you understand?"

"Whose purposes are we talking about?"

Jarid smiled. "Large sums have been wagered on tomorrow's fight. If you wish, I shall speak the name of my master.

Know, however, that once I have done so, I will take your neck in my hands and snap the bones beneath. Your choice. You wish to know?"

"No. I understand. But *you* have to understand that if your men fail, then I'll be sending a bolt into the darkness at a moving target. I can't guarantee I won't kill him! What happens then?"

"You'll still get paid. Now take up your position." Swinging to the others, Jarid gathered them in a tight group and spoke, his voice scarcely above a whisper. "The Drenai is a fearsome fighter, very powerful. Once any of you have planted a knife in his upper body, shoulders, chest, or arm, the rest of you must break away and run. You understand? This is not a fight to the death; a deep wound is all we require."

"Begging your pardon, sir," said a lean man with missing front teeth, "but I've bet on Klay. Won't that bet be voided if the Drenai can't fight?"

Jarid shook his head. "The bet would be on Klay taking gold. If the Drenai doesn't fight, then the gold is automatically given to Klay."

"What if a knife goes too deep and he dies?" asked another man.

Jarid shrugged. "All life is a game of chance."

Moving away from the men, he ducked into an alley, then cut left across a section of waste ground, ducking into a shadowed doorway. Tall Tess was standing by a broken mirror, her red dress unfastened at the breast and pushed down to her hips. She was sponging cool water on her naked upper body.

"It's hot tonight," she said, grinning at Jarid. He did not return the smile but, in close, grabbed her arm, twisting it painfully. Tess cried out.

"Shut up!" he ordered. "I told you no other clients tonight, my girl. I like my women fresh."

"There haven't been any, lovely man," she said. "I had to run from the hospice, all the way. That's why I'm sweating!"

"Hospice? What you talking about, girl?" Releasing her arm, he took a step back. Tess rubbed at her scrawny bicep.

"Loira. They took her in today. Klay come for her. Took her in his carriage, he did. It was wonderful, Jarid. All dark wood, lacquered black, and padded leather seats and cushions of satin. And she's in a bed now, with linen so white, it could have been spun from clouds."

"I didn't know Klay was one of her marks."

"He wasn't. Her snipe, Fastfinger, went and begged him to help. And he did. So Loira's being looked after now, with medicines and food."

"You'd better be telling me the truth, girl," said Jarid huskily, moving in close and cupping his hand to Tess' sagging breast.

"I'd never lie to you, lovely man," she whispered. "You're my darling. My only darling." Tess slid her hand downward and allowed her mind to drift. Everything now was performance, and so mind-numbingly familiar was every move that she no longer needed to think. Instead, as she moaned and touched, teased and caressed, Tess was thinking about Loira. It seemed so wrong that a woman should be laid on such clean sheets merely to die. Many was the time that she and Loira had been huddled together under a thin blanket on cold winter nights, when the freezing winds had kept marks from the street. Then they had spoken of such luxuries as all-day fires, down-filled pillows and quilts, and blankets of softest wool. And they had giggled and laughed and cuddled in close for warmth. Now poor Loira had the kind of sheets she had dreamed of and would never know it. One day soon she would die, and her bowels would open and gush out their contents on those clean white sheets.

The pounding of the man's hips increased in power and speed. Instantly Tess began to moan rhythmically, arching her thin body up against his. His breathing was hoarse in her ear, then he groaned and sank his weight down upon her. Curling her arm around him, she stroked the nape of his neck. "Ah, you are a wonder, lovely man. You are my darling. My only darling."

Jarid heaved himself from her, pulled his leggings up from around his ankles, and rolled to his feet. Tess smoothed down her red dress and sat up. Jarid tossed her a full silver piece. "You want to stay for a little, Jarid? I have some wine."

"No, I have work to do." He smiled at her. "It was good tonight."

"The best," she assured him.

**D**RUSS FINISHED HIS meal and pushed away the wooden platter. The meat had been good, lean and tender, covered with savory spices and a rich, dark gravy. Yet despite the quality of the meal he had barely tasted it. His thoughts remained confused and melancholy. Meeting Klay had not helped. Damn it, he liked the man.

Druss lifted his tankard and swallowed half the contents. The ale was thin but refreshing and brought back memories of his youth and the beer brewed in the mountains. He had grown to manhood among common folk, men and women of simple pleasures who worked from first light to dusk and lived for their families, battling to put enough bread on the table. Often on summer evenings they would gather in the communal hall and drink ale, sing songs, and swap stories. Not for them the great questions of politics, the compromises, the betrayals of ideals. Life was hard yet uncomplicated.

He had been torn from that life when the renegade Collan had led an attack on the village, slaughtering the men and the older women and taking the young girls captive to be sold as slaves.

Among them had been Druss' wife, Rowena, his love and his life. He had been felling trees high in the timberline when the attack had taken place. He had returned to the ruins of the village and set off after the killers, and he had found them.

Druss had slain many of the raiders and freed the girls, but

Rowena had not been with them; Collan had taken her to Mashrapur and sold her to a Ventrian merchant. In order to earn money for his passage to Ventria, Druss had become a fighter in the sand circles of Mashrapur. And moment by bone-crunching moment the young farmer had changed, his natural strength and ferocity honed until he became the most feared fighter in the city.

At last he had journeyed on, in the company of Sieben and the Ventrian officer Bodasen, joining in the Ventrian Wars and quickly earning a deadly reputation. The Silver Slayer, they called him for his deeds with the shining double-headed ax Snaga.

Druss had fought in a score of battles and hundreds of skirmishes. Many times he had been wounded, yet always he had emerged triumphant.

When, after many years, he had found Rowena and brought her home, he had truly believed that his wanderings and his battles were blood dreams of the past. Rowena knew differently. Day by day Druss grew more morose. He was no longer a farmer and could find no pleasure in tilling the earth or tending his cattle. A little more than a year had passed when he journeyed to Dros Delnoch to join a militia force formed to counter raids by Sathuli tribesmen. Six months later, with the Sathuli forced back into the mountains, he had returned home with fresh scars and fond memories.

Closing his eyes, he recalled Rowena's words on the night he had returned from the Sathuli campaign. Sitting on the goatskin rug before a log fire, she had reached out and taken his hand. "My poor Druss. How can a man live for war? It is so futile."

He had seen the sorrow in her hazel eyes and had struggled to find an answer. "It is not the fighting alone, Rowena. It is the comradeship, the fire in the blood, the facing of fear. When danger threatens, I become . . . a man."

Rowena had sighed. "You are what you are, my love. But it saddens me. There is great beauty here—bringing food from the earth, watching the sun rise over the mountains and the moon's reflection dancing on the lakes. There is contentment and joy. Yet it is not for you. Tell me, Druss: Why did you cross the world for me?"

"Because I love you. You are everything to me."

She had shaken her head. "If that were true, you would have no desire to leave me and go wandering in search of war. Look around you at the other farmers. Do they rush off to battle?"

Druss had risen and walked to the window, pushing the shutters wide and staring out at the distant stars. "I am not like them anymore. I do not know if ever I was. I am a man fitted for war, Rowena."

"I know," she had said sadly. "Oh, Druss, I know."

Draining his tankard now, Druss caught the eye of a blond serving maid. "Another!" he called out, waving the tankard in the air.

"Just a moment, sir," she answered him.

The tavern was almost full, the atmosphere bright and noisy. Druss had found a booth in the corner of the room, where he could sit with his back to the wall and watch the crowd. Usually he enjoyed the gently chaotic rhythms of a tavern, the mix of laughter and conversation, the clattering of plates, the clinking of tankards, the shuffling of feet, and the scraping of chairs. But not tonight.

The maid brought him a second tankard of ale; she was a buxom girl, full-breasted and wide-hipped. "Did you enjoy your meal, sir?" she asked, leaning forward with her hand on his shoulder. Her fingers stroked up into his short-cropped dark hair. Rowena often did the same thing when he was tense or angry. Always it soothed him. He smiled at the girl.

"It was a meal fit for a king, lass, but I didn't enjoy it as I should. Too many weighty problems that I haven't the brain to solve."

"You need to relax in the company of a woman," she said, her fingers stroking his dark beard.

Taking her hand, he gently moved it away from his face. "My woman is a long way from here, girl. But always she is close to my heart. And pretty as you are, I'll wait to enjoy her company." Dipping into the pouch at his belt, Druss drew out two silver pieces. "The one is for the meal, the second for you."

"You are very kind. If you change your mind . . ."

"I won't."

As she moved away, Druss felt a cold draft on his cheek.

In that instant all sound died away. Druss blinked. The serving maid was standing statue-still, her wide skirt, which swished as she walked, motionless. All around him the diners and revelers were frozen in their places. When Druss flicked his gaze to the fire, the tongues of flame were no longer dancing between the logs but were standing steady, the smoke above them hanging solid in the chimney. And the normal smells of a tavern—roasted meats, wood smoke, and stale sweat—had disappeared, to be replaced by the sickly-sweet odor of cinnamon and burning sandalwood.

A small Nadir dressed in a tunic of goat's hair stepped into sight, weaving his way through the silent revelers. He was old but not ancient, his thinning black hair greasy and lank. Swiftly he crossed the room and seated himself opposite Druss. "Well met, axman," he said, his voice soft, almost sibilant.

Druss looked deep into the man's dark, slanted eyes and read the hatred there. "Your magic will need to be very strong to stop me from reaching across and snapping your scrawny neck," he said.

The old man grinned, showing stained and broken teeth. "I am not here to bring you harm, axman. I am Nosta Khan, shaman to the Wolfshead tribe. You aided a young friend of mine, Talisman; you fought alongside him."

"What of it?"

"He is important to me. And we Nadir like to repay our debts."

"I have no need of repayment. There is nothing you can offer me."

Nosta Khan shook his head. "Never be too sure, axman.
Firstly, would it surprise you to know that even now there are a
dozen men waiting outside, armed with clubs and knives? Their
purpose is to prevent you from fighting the Gothir champion.
They have been told to cripple you if they can and kill you if
they must."

"It seems everyone wants me to lose," said Druss. "Why do
you warn me? And don't insult me with talk of repayment. I can
see the hatred in your eyes."

The shaman was silent for a moment, and when he spoke, his
voice was rich with both malice and a sense of regret. "My
people need you, axman."

Druss gave a cold smile. "It cost you to say that, did it not?"

"Indeed it did," admitted the little man. "But I would swallow burning coals for my people, and telling a small truth to a
roundeye is a pain I can live with." He grinned again. "An an-
cestor of yours aided us in the past. He hated the Nadir, yet he
helped my grandfather in a great battle against the Gothir. His
heroism brought us closer to the days of the Uniter. He was
known as Angel, but his Nadir name was Hard-to-Kill."

"I've never heard of him."

"You roundeyes disgust me! You call us barbarians, yet you
know not the deeds of your own ancestors. Pah! Let us move
on. My powers are not limitless, and soon this stinking tavern
will return with all its foul noise and stench. Angel was linked
to the Nadir, Druss. Linked by blood, held by destiny. So are
you. I have risked my life in many fever dreams, and always
your face floats before me. I do not know as yet what role you
have to play in the coming drama. It may be small, though I
doubt it. But whatever it is, I know where you must be in the
coming days. It is necessary that you travel to the Valley of
Shul-sen's Tears. It is a five-day ride to the east. There is a

shrine there, dedicated to the memory of Oshikai Demon-bane, the greatest of Nadir warriors."

"Why would I wish to go there?" asked Druss. "*You* say it is necessary, but I do not think so."

The shaman shook his head. "Let me tell you of the healing stones, axman. There is said to be no wound they cannot mend. Some even claim they can raise the dead. They are hidden at the shrine."

"As you can see," said Druss, "I have no wound."

The little man averted his eyes from Druss' gaze, and a secretive smile touched his weather-beaten features. "No, you have not. But much can happen in Gulgothir. Have you forgotten the men who wait? Remember, Druss, a five-day ride due east, in the Valley of Shul-sen's Tears."

Druss' vision swam, and the noise of the tavern covered him once more. He blinked. The tavern maid's skirt swished as she walked. Of the shaman there was no sign.

Draining the last of his ale, Druss pushed himself to his feet. According to the shaman, a dozen men waited outside, rogues hired to prevent him from fighting Klay. He gave a deep sigh and moved to the long trestle bar. The tavern keeper, fat of belly and red of face, approached him. "Another ale, sir?"

"No," said Druss, placing a silver coin on the bar. "Loan me your club."

"My club? I don't know what you mean."

Druss smiled and leaned forward conspiratorially. "I've never met a tavern keeper yet, friend, who did not keep a weighted club at hand. Now, I am the Drenai fighter Druss, and I am told there is a gang outside waiting for me. They seek to stop my fight with Klay."

"I've got money on that," muttered the innkeeper. "Now look, lad, why don't you just come with me and I'll take you downstairs to the ale cellar? There's a secret door that will allow you to sneak past them all."

"I don't need a secret door," said Druss patiently. "I need to borrow your club."

"One day, lad, you might realize that it is more sensible to avoid trouble. No one is invincible." Reaching down, he produced an eighteen-inch truncheon of black metal, which he laid on the bar. "The outer casing is iron," he said, "but the inner is lead. Return it when you are done."

Druss hefted the weapon; it was twice as heavy as most short swords. Sliding it up the right sleeve of his shirt, he eased himself through the crowd. As he opened the door, he saw several big men standing outside. Dressed in shabby tunics and leggings, they looked like beggars. Switching his gaze to the right, he saw a second group gathered close by. They stiffened as he appeared, and for a moment no one moved. "Well, lads," said Druss with a broad grin. "Who wants to be first?"

"That would be me," answered a tall man with a shaggy beard. He had wide, powerful shoulders and despite his grimy clothing was no beggar, Druss knew. The skin of his neck was white and clean, as were his hands. And the knife he carried was of Ventrian steel; weapons like that did not come cheap. "I can tell by your eyes that you're frightened," said the knifeman as he moved in. "And I can smell your fear."

Druss stood very still, and the man suddenly leapt forward, his knife flashing toward Druss' shoulder. With his left forearm Druss blocked the thrust, and in the same movement he sent a left hook exploding against the man's chin; he hit the cobbles face first and did not move. Opening his fingers, Druss allowed the truncheon to slide from his sleeve. Figures darted from the shadows, and he charged into them, turning his shoulder into the first and cannoning him from his feet. The truncheon hammered left and right, hurling men from their feet. A knife blade grazed the top of his shoulder. Grabbing the wielder by his tunic, he head-butted the man, smashing his nose and cheekbone, then spun him into the path of two more attackers. The first fell clumsily, landing on his own knife; as the blade tore into his side, his screams rent the air. The second backed away. But more men gathered: eight fighters, all with weapons of sharp steel. Druss knew they were no longer thinking of crippling him; he could sense their hatred and the blood lust surging within them.

"You're dead meat, Drenai!" he heard one of them shout as the group edged forward.

Suddenly a voice boomed out. "Hold on, Druss, I'm coming."

Druss glanced to his left to see Klay charging from the mouth of a nearby alley. As the giant Gothir hurtled into them the men, recognizing him, scattered and ran. Klay walked over to Druss. "Such an exciting life you lead, my friend," he said with a broad grin.

Something bright flashed toward Druss' face, and in that one terrifying moment he saw so many things: the moonlight shining on the dagger blade, the thrower with a look of triumph on his dirty face, and Klay's hand snaking out with impossible speed, catching the hurled knife by the hilt to stop the blade mere inches from Druss' eye.

"I told you, Druss, speed is everything," said Klay.

Druss let out a long, deep breath. "I don't know about that, laddie, but you saved my life, and I'll not forget it."

Klay chuckled. "Come on, my friend, I need to eat." Throwing his arm around Druss' shoulder, he turned toward the tavern. In that moment a black-feathered crossbow bolt slashed across the open ground to plunge into the back of the Gothir champion. Klay cried out and collapsed against Druss. The axman staggered under the weight, then saw the bolt low in the fighter's back. Gently he lowered him to the ground. Scanning the shadows for signs of the attacker, he saw two men running away. One carried a crossbow, and Druss longed to give chase, but he could not leave the wounded Klay.

"Lie still. I'll fetch a surgeon."

"What's happened to me, Druss? Why am I lying down?"

"You've been struck by a crossbow bolt. Lie still!"

"I cannot move my legs, Druss . . ."

The interrogation room was cold and damp, fetid water leaving a trail of slime on the greasy walls. Two bronze lanterns on one wall put out a flickering light but no heat. Seated at a crudely fashioned table on which he could see bloodstains both old and new, Chorin-Tsu waited patiently, gathering his thoughts. The little Chiatze said nothing to the guard, a burly soldier in a grubby leather tunic and torn breeches who stood with arms folded by the door. The man had a brutal face and cruel eyes. Chorin-Tsu did not stare at him but gazed about the room with clinical detachment. Yet his thoughts remained with the guard. *I have known many good, ugly men,* he thought, *and even a few handsome, evil men. Yet one had only to look at this guard to recognize his brutality,* as if his coarse and vile nature had somehow reached up from within and molded his features, swathing his eyes in pockets of fat set close together above a thick pockmarked nose and thick, slack lips.

A black rat scurried across the room, and the guard jumped, then kicked at it, missing wildly. The creature vanished into a hole by the far corner of the wall. "Bastard rats!" hissed the guard, embarrassed that he had allowed himself to be startled in front of the prisoner. "You obviously like 'em. Good! You'll be living with them soon enough. Have 'em running all over you then, biting your skin, leaving their little fleas to suck your blood in the dark."

Chorin-Tsu ignored him.

Garen-Tsen's arrival was sudden, the door whispering open. In the lantern light the minister's face glowed with a sickly yellow sheen, and his eyes seemed unnaturally bright. Chorin-Tsu offered no greeting. Nor, as should have been Chiatze custom in the presence of a minister, did he rise and bow. Instead he sat, his expression calm and impassive.

Dismissing the guard, the minister sat down opposite the

little Chiatze embalmer. "My apologies for the inhospitable surroundings," said Garen-Tsen, speaking in Chiatze. "It was necessary for your safety. You did wonderfully well with the queen. Her beauty has never been so radiant."

"I thank you, Garen-Tsen," Chorin-Tsu answered coolly. "But why am I here? You promised I would be freed."

"As indeed you will be, countryman. But first let us talk. Tell me of your interest in Nadir legends."

Chorin-Tsu stared at the slender minister, holding his gaze. It was all a game now, with only one ending. I am to die, he thought. Here, in this cold, miserable place. He wanted to scream his hatred at the monster before him, to rage and show defiance. The strength of feeling surprised him, going against all Chiatze teaching, but not a trace of his inner turmoil showed on his face as he sat very still, his expression serene. "All legends have a basis in fact, Garen-Tsen. I am a student of history, and it pleases me to study."

"Of course. But your studies have been focused in recent years, have they not? You have spent hundreds of hours in the Great Library, studying scrolls concerning Oshikai Demonbane and the legend of the stone wolf. Why is that?"

"I am indeed gratified by your interest, though puzzled as to why a man of your status and responsibilities should concern himself with what is, after all, no more than a hobby," countered Chorin-Tsu.

"The movements and interests of all foreign nationals are scrutinized. But my interest goes beyond such mundane matters. You are a scholar, and your work deserves a wider audience. I would be honored to hear your views on the stone wolf. But since time is pressing, perhaps it would be best if you merely outlined your findings concerning the Eyes of Alchazzar."

Chorin-Tsu gave an almost imperceptible bow of his head. "Perhaps it would be better to postpone this conversation until we are both sitting in more comfortable apartments."

The minister leaned back in his chair and steepled his fingers under his long chin. When he spoke, his voice was cold. "Spiriting you away will be both costly and dangerous, countryman. How much is your life worth?"

Chorin-Tsu was surprised. The question was vulgar and considerably beneath any high-born Chiatze. "Far less than you would think but far more than I can afford," he replied.

"I think you will find that the price is well within your reach, Master Embalmer. Two jewels, to be precise," said Garen-Tsen. "The Eyes of Alchazzar. It is my belief that you have located their hiding place. Am I wrong?"

Chorin-Tsu remained silent. He had known for many years that death would be his only reward and had believed himself prepared for it. But now, in this cold, damp place, his heart began to beat in panic. He wanted to live! Looking up, he met the reptilian gaze of his countryman. Keeping his voice steady, he said, "Let us, for the sake of argument, assume that you are correct. In what way would sharing this information prove of benefit to this humble embalmer?"

"Benefit? You will be free. You have the sacred word of a Chiatze nobleman. Is that not enough?"

Chorin-Tsu took a deep breath and summoned the last of his courage. "The word of a Chiatze nobleman is indeed sacred. And in the presence of such a man I would not hesitate to surrender my knowledge. Perhaps you should send for him so that we may conclude our conversation."

Garen-Tsen's color deepened. "You have made the most unfortunate error, for now you will have to make the acquaintance of the royal torturer. Is this what you truly desire, Chorin-Tsu? He will make you speak; you will scream and babble, weep and beg. Why put yourself through such agony?"

Chorin-Tsu considered the question carefully. All his long life he had cherished Chiatze teaching, most especially the laws governing the subjugation of the self to the rigors of an iron etiquette. That alone was the foundation of Chiatze culture. Yet here he sat seeking an answer to a question no *true* Chiatze would dream of asking. It was obnoxious and invasive, indeed, the kind of question only a barbarian would utter. He looked deeply into Garen-Tsen's eyes. The man was waiting for an answer. Chorin-Tsu sighed and for the first time in his life spoke like a barbarian.

"To thwart you, you lying dog," he said.

The ride had been long and dry, the sun beating down on the open steppes, the strength-sapping heat leaving both riders and ponies near exhaustion. The rock pool was high in the hills, beneath an overhang of shale and slate. Few knew of its existence, and once Talisman had found the dried bones of a traveler who had died of thirst less than fifty feet from it. The pool was no more than twenty feet long and only twelve feet wide. But it was very deep, and the water was winter-cold. After tending to the ponies and hobbling them, Talisman threw off his jerkin and tugged his shirt over his head. Dust and sand scraped against the skin of his arms and shoulders. Kicking off his boots, he loosened his belt, stepped out of his leggings, and walked naked to the pool's edge. The sun beat down on his skin, and he could feel the heat of the rock beneath his feet. Taking a deep breath, he launched himself out over the sparkling water in an ungainly dive that sent up a glittering spray. He surfaced and swept his sleek black hair back from his face.

Zhusai sat, fully clothed, by the poolside. Her long, black hair was soaked with sweat, her face was streaked with dust, and her pale green silk tunic—a garment of bright, expensive beauty back in Gulgothir—was now travel-stained and dirt-streaked.

"Do you swim, Zhusai?" he asked her. She shook her head. "Would you like me to teach you?"

"That is most kind of you, Talisman. Perhaps on another occasion."

Talisman swam to the poolside and levered himself to the

rock beside her. Kneeling, she leaned over the edge, cupping her hands to the water and dabbing her fingers to her brow and cheeks. In the two days they had been together Zhusai had not initiated a conversation. If Talisman spoke, she would respond with typical Chiatze politeness and courtesy. Replacing her wide straw hat on her head, she sat in the stifling heat without complaint, her eyes averted from him.

"It is not difficult to swim," he said. "There is no danger, Zhusai, for I shall be in the pool with you, supporting you. Also, it is wondrously cool."

Bowing her head, she closed her eyes. "I thank you, Lord Talisman. You are indeed a considerate companion. The sun is very hot. Perhaps you should dress now or your skin will burn."

"No, I think I will swim again," he told her, jumping into the pool. His understanding of the Chiatze people was limited to their methods of warfare, which were apparently ritualistic. According to Gothir reports, many campaigns were conducted and won without bloodshed, armies maneuvering across battlefields until one side or the other conceded the advantage. It helped not at all with his understanding of Zhusai. Rolling to his back, Talisman floated on the cool surface. Her good manners, he realized, were becoming hard to tolerate. He smiled and swam to the pool's edge, hooking his arm to the warm stone.

"Do you trust me?" he asked her.

"Of course. You are the guardian of my honor."

Talisman was surprised. "I can guard your life, Zhusai, to the best of my ability. But no one but you can guard your honor. It is something no man—or woman—can *take*. Honor can only be surrendered."

"As you say, so must it be, lord," she said meekly.

"No, no! Do not agree for the sake of courtesy, Zhusai." Her eyes met his, and for a long moment she did not speak. When she did, her voice was strangely different, still lilting and soft yet with an underlying confidence that touched a chord in Talisman.

"I fear my translation of your title was not sufficiently exact. The *honor* you speak of is essentially a male concept, born in blood and battle. A man's *word*, a man's *patriotism*, a man's *courage*. Indeed, this form of honor can only be surrendered. Perhaps 'guardian of my virtue' would suffice. And though we could enter a fine philosophical debate on the meaning of the word 'virtue,' I use it in the sense that a male would apply to a woman, most especially a Nadir male. I understand that among your people a raped woman is put to death, while the rapist is merely banished." She fell silent and averted her eyes once more. It was the longest speech he had heard from her.

"You are angry," he said.

She bowed and shook her head. "I am merely hot, my lord. I fear it has made me indiscreet."

Levering himself from the pool, he walked to the hobbled ponies and pulled a clean shirt and leggings from his saddle pack. Once dressed, he returned to the seated woman. "We will be resting here today and tonight." Pointing to the southern section of the pool, he told her, "There is a shelf there, and the water is no more than four feet deep. You may bathe there. So that you may have privacy, I shall walk back down the trail and gather wood for tonight's fire."

"Thank you, lord," she said, bowing her head.

Pulling on his boots, Talisman looped an empty canvas bag over his shoulder. Slowly he walked back up the trail, stopping short of the crest and scanning the steppes below. There was no sign of other riders. Above the crest the heat was searing and intense. Talisman walked slowly down the hillside, pausing to gather sticks, which he dropped into the bag. Desert trees and bushes grew there, their roots deep in the dry earth, their arid existence maintained by the few days of heavy rain in what passed for winter there. Fuel was plentiful, and soon his bag was crammed full. He was just starting back up the slope when he heard Zhusai cry out. Throwing the bag to one side, Talisman sprinted up the trail and over the crest. Zhusai, her arms thrashing wildly, had slipped from the shelf, and her head sank below the surface.

Talisman ran to the pool's edge and dived after her. Below the surface he opened his eyes to see that Zhusai, still struggling, was sinking some twenty feet below him. Bubbles of air were streaming from her mouth. Talisman dived toward her, his fingers hooked into her hair, and twisting in the water, he kicked out for the surface. At first he did not rise, and panic touched him. She was too heavy. If he hung on to her, they would both drown. Looking around, he saw the shelf from which she had slipped; it was no more than ten feet to his left. The surface must be close, he thought. Zhusai was a dead weight now, and Talisman's breath was failing. But he hung on—and kicked out with renewed force. His head splashed clear of the water. Taking a great lungful of air, he dragged Zhusai to the shelf and heaved her body onto it. She rolled in the shallow water, facedown. Talisman scrambled alongside her and with his feet on solid rock lifted her to his shoulder and climbed from the pool. Laying her down on her stomach, he straddled her and pushed down against her back. Water bubbled from her mouth as again and again he applied pressure. Suddenly she coughed, then vomited. Talisman stood, then ran to her pony and unfastened her blanket. Zhusai was sitting up as he returned. Swiftly he wrapped the blanket around her.

"I was dying," she said.

"Yes. But now you are alive once more."

For a moment she was silent, then she looked up at him. "I would like to learn to swim," she told him.

Talisman smiled. "Then I shall teach you, but not today."

The sun was setting, and already it was cooler. Talisman rose and fetched the bag of wood. When he returned, Zhusai had dressed in a blue tunic and leggings and was washing the dust from their travel-stained clothes. In a wide niche in the rock wall Talisman lit a fire above the ashes of a previous blaze. Zhusai joined him, and together they sat for some time in comfortable silence.

"Are you a student of history, like your grandfather?" he asked her.

"I have assisted him since I was eight years old, and many times since I have traveled with him to the sacred sites."

"You have been to Oshikai's shrine?"

"Yes, twice. It was once a temple. My grandfather believes it is by far the oldest building in all the Gothir lands. Oshikai is said to have been carried there after the Battle of the Vale. His wife was with him when he died; thereafter they named it the Valley of Shul-sen's Tears. Some visitors claim you can still hear her weeping if you sit close to the shrine on cold winter nights. Did you hear her weeping, Lord Talisman?"

"I have never been there," admitted the warrior.

"Forgive me, lord," she said swiftly, bowing and closing her eyes. "I fear my words, which were intended lightly, have caused offense."

"Not at all, Zhusai. Now tell me of the shrine. Describe it for me."

She glanced up. "It is three years since last I was there. I was fourteen, and my grandfather gave me my woman name, Zhusai."

"What was your child name?"

"Voni. It means 'Chittering Rat' in the Chiatze tongue."

Talisman chuckled. "It has a . . . similar . . . meaning in Nadir."

"In Nadir it means 'Windy Goat,'" she said, tilting her head and giving a smile so dazzling that it struck him between the eyes with the power of a fist. He blinked and took a deep breath. Before that smile her beauty had seemed cold and distant, leaving Talisman untroubled by their journeying together. But now? He felt curiously short of breath. When he had saved her from drowning, he had not been unduly affected by her nakedness. Now, however, the memory of her golden skin shone in his

mind, the curve of her hips and belly, the large dark nipples on
her small breasts. He realized that Zhusai was speaking to him.
"Are you well, lord?"

"Yes," he replied more tersely than he had intended. Rising, he walked away from the bemused girl, moving up the
trail to sit on a rock close to the crest. Her smile shone in his
mind, and his body ached for her. It was as if a spell had been
cast. Nervously he glanced back down to the fire, where Zhusai was sitting quietly. She is not a witch, he thought; no, far
from it. She was simply the most beautiful woman Talisman
had ever known.

And he was honor bound to take her to another man.

Chorin-Tsu had spoken of sacrifice.

Talisman knew now what it meant . . .

Zhusai sat quietly by the small fire, a multicolored blanket
wrapped around her shoulders. Talisman slept nearby, his
breathing deep and steady. When one of the ponies moved in its
sleep, its hoof scraping on stone, Talisman stirred but did not
wake. She gazed down on his face in the moonlight. He was not
a handsome man or an ugly one. Yet you are attractive, thought
Zhusai, remembering the gentle touch as he had laid the blanket
around her shoulders and the concern in his eyes as she had recovered from the terrifying experience in the water. During her
seven years in the company of her grandfather, Zhusai had met
many Nadir tribesmen. Some she had liked; others she had
loathed. But all were frightening, for there was a ferocity lurking close to the surface of the Nadir personality, a terrible
hunger for blood and violence. Talisman was different. He had
strength and a power not often found in one so young. But she
sensed that he had no love of cruelty, no lust for bloodletting.

Zhusai added the last of the fuel to the fire. The night was not
cold, but the little blaze was comforting. Who are you, Talisman? she wondered. Talisman was Nadir—of that there was no
doubt. And he was past the age of manhood. Why then did he

carry no Nadir name? Why *Talisman*? Then there was his speech. The Nadir tongue was guttural, with many sounds created from the back of the throat, which usually made for clumsiness when they spoke the softer language of the round-eyed southerners. Not so with Talisman, whose speech was fluent and well modulated. Zhusai had spent many months among the Nadir as her grandfather traveled widely, examining sites of historical interest. They were a brutal people, as harsh and unyielding as the steppes on which they lived. Women were treated with casual cruelty. Zhusai sat back and considered the events of the day.

When Talisman had stripped himself and dived into the water, Zhusai had been both outraged and wonderfully stirred. Never had she seen a man naked. His skin was pale gold, his body wolf-lean. His back, buttocks, and thighs were crisscrossed with white scars: the marks of a whip. While the Nadir were cruel to women, they rarely whipped their children, certainly not with enough force to leave the marks that Talisman bore.

There was no question about it: Talisman was an enigma.

"He will be one of the Uniter's generals," her grandfather had told her. "He is a thinker yet also a man of action. Such men are rare. The Nadir will have their day of glory with men such as he."

His zeal had confused Zhusai. "They are not our people, Grandfather. Why should we care?"

"Their origins are the same, little one. But that is not the whole reason. The Chiatze are a rich, proud nation. We pride ourselves on our individuality and our culture. These round-eyes are the true savages, and their evil soars far beyond our comprehension. How long before they turn their eyes to the Chiatze, bringing their wars, their diseases, their foulness to our homeland? A united Nadir nation would be a wall against their invasion."

"They have never been united. They hate one another," she said.

"The one who is coming, the man with violet eyes—has the power to draw them together, to bind up the wounds of centuries."

"Forgive my slow-wittedness, Grandfather, but I do not understand," she said. "If he is already coming—if it is written in the stars—why do you have to spend so much time studying, traveling, and meeting with shamans? Will he not rise to power regardless of your efforts?"

He smiled and took her small hands into his own. "Perhaps he will, Voni. Perhaps. A palm reader can tell you much about your life, past and present. But when he looks into the future, he will say, 'This hand shows what *should* be, and this hand shows what *could* be.' He will never say, 'This hand shows what *will* be.' I have some small talent as an astrologer. I know the man with violet eyes is out there somewhere. But I also know what dangers await him. It is not enough that he has the courage, the power, the charisma. Great will be the forces ranged against him. He exists, Zhusai, one special man among the multitude. He *should* rise to rule. He *could* change the world. But *will* he? Or will the enemy find him first, or a disease strike him down? I cannot sit and wait. My studies tell me that somehow I will prove to be the catalyst in the coming drama, the breath of wind that births the storm."

And so they had continued their travels and their studies, seeking always the man with the violet eyes.

Then had come the day when the vile little shaman Nosta Khan had arrived at their home in Gulgothir. Zhusai had disliked him from the first; there was about him an almost palpable sense of evil and malice. He and her grandfather had been closeted together for several hours, and only when he had gone did Chorin-Tsu reveal the full horror of what was to be. So great was the shock that all Chiatze training fled from her, and she spoke bluntly.

"You wish me to marry a savage, Grandfather? To live in

filth and squalor among a people who value women less than they value their goats? How could you do this?"

Chorin-Tsu had ignored the breach of manners, though Zhusai could see that he was stung and disappointed by her outburst. "The savage, as you call him, is a special man. Nosta Khan has walked the mist. I have studied the charts and cast the runes. There is no doubt; you are vital to this quest. Without you the days of the Uniter will pass us by."

"This is your dream, not mine! How could you do this to me?"

"Please control yourself, Granddaughter. This unseemly display is extremely disheartening. The situation is not of my making. Let me also say this, Zhusai: I have cast your charts many times, and always they have shown you are destined to marry a great man. You know this to be true. Well, that man is the Uniter. I know this without any shade of doubt."

Under the moon and stars Zhusai gazed down at Talisman. "Why could it not have been you?" she whispered.

His dark eyes opened. "Did you speak?"

She shivered. "No. I am sorry to have disturbed you."

He rolled to his elbow and saw that the fire was still burning. Then he lay down and slept once more.

When she awoke, she found that Talisman's blanket, as well as her own, was laid across her. Sitting up, she saw the Nadir sitting cross-legged on the rocks some distance away, his back to her. Pushing the blankets aside, she rose. The sun was clearing the peaks, and already the temperature was rising. Zhusai stretched, then made her way to where Talisman sat. His eyes were closed, his arms folded to his chest, palms flat and thumbs interlinked. Zhusai's grandfather often adopted that position when meditating, usually when he was trying to solve a problem. Silently Zhusai sat opposite the warrior.

Where are you now, Talisman? she wondered. Where does your restless spirit fly?

*  *  *

He was a small boy who had never seen a city. His young life had been spent on the steppes, running and playing among the tents of his father's people. At the age of five he had learned to tend the goats, to make cheese from their milk, to stretch and scrape the skins of the slaughtered animals. At seven he could ride a small pony and shoot a bow. But at twelve he was taken from his father by men in bright armor who journeyed far beyond the steppes, all the way to a stone city by the sea.

It had been the first real shock of Talisman's life. His father, the strongest and bravest of Nadir chieftains, had sat by in silence as the round-eyed men in armor came. This man who had fought in a hundred battles had said not a word, had not even looked his son in the eye. Only Nosta Khan had approached him, laying his scrawny hand on Talisman's shoulder. "You must go with them, Okai. The safety of the tribe depends on it."

"Why? We are Wolfshead, stronger than all."

"Because your father orders it."

They had lifted Okai to the back of a tall horse, and the long journey had begun. Not all Nadir children were fully taught the tongue of the roundeye, but Talisman had a good ear for language and Nosta Khan had spent many months teaching him the subtleties. Thus it was that he could understand the shining soldiers. They made jokes about the children they were gathering, referring to them as dung puppies. Other than that, they were not unkind to their prisoners. Twenty-four days they traveled, until at last they came to a place of nightmare that the Nadir children gazed upon with awe and terror. Everything was stone, covering the earth, rearing up to challenge the sky, huge walls and high houses, narrow lanes, and a mass of humanity continually writhing like a giant snake through its marketplaces, streets, alleys, and avenues.

Seventeen Nadir youngsters, all the sons of chieftains, were brought to the city of Bodacas in that late summer. Talisman-Okai remembered the ride through the city streets, children pointing at the Nadir, then baying and screeching and making gestures with their fingers. Adults, too, stood and watched, their faces grim. The cavalcade came to a stop at a walled structure on the outskirts of the city, where the double gates of bronze and iron were dragged open. For Okai it was like riding into the mouth of a great dark beast, and fear rose like bile in his throat.

Beyond the gates was a flat, paved training area, and Okai watched as young men and older boys practiced with sword and shield, spear and bow. They were dressed identically in crimson tunics, dark breeches, and knee-length boots of shining brown leather. All exercise ceased as the Nadir youngsters rode in with their escort.

A young man with blond hair stepped forward, his training sword still in his hand. "I see we are to be given proper targets for our arrows," he said to his comrades, who laughed loudly.

The Nadir were ordered to dismount, then led into a six-story building and up a seemingly interminable winding stair to the fifth level. There was a long, claustrophobic corridor leading to a large room in which, behind a desk of polished oak, sat a thickset warrior with a forked beard. His eyes were bright blue, his mouth wide and full-lipped. A scar ran from the right side of his nose, curving down to his jawbone. His forearms, too, showed the scars of close combat. He stood as they entered.

"Get in two lines," he ordered them, his voice deep and cold. The youngsters shuffled into place. Okai, being one of the smallest, was in the front line. "You are here as janizaries. You do not understand what that means, but I will tell you. The king—may he live forever—has conceived a brilliant plan to halt Nadir raids both now and in the future. You are here as hostages so that your fathers will behave. More than that, however, you will learn during your years with us how to be civilized, what constitutes good manners and correct behavior. You will learn to read, to debate, to think. You will study poetry and literature, mathematics and cartography. You will also be taught the arts of war, the nature of strategy, logistics, and command. In short you are to become cadets and then officers in the great Gothir army." Glancing up, he addressed the two officers who had led the boys into the room. "You may go now and bathe the dust of travel from your bodies. I have a few more words to say to these . . . cadets."

As the officers departed and the door clicked shut, the warrior moved to stand directly before the boys, towering over Okai. "What you have just heard, you dung-eating monkeys, is the *official* welcome to Bodacas Academy. My name is Gargan, the Lord of Larness, and most of the scars I carry come from battles with your miserable race. I have been killing Nadir scum for most of my life. You cannot be taught, for you are not human; it would be like trying to teach dogs to play the flute. This foolishness springs from the addled mind of a senile old man, but when he dies, this stupidity will die with him. Until that blessed day work hard, for the lash awaits the tardy and the stupid. Now get downstairs, where a cadet awaits you. He will take you to the quartermaster, who will supply you with tunics and boots."

Talisman was jerked back to the present as he heard Zhusai move behind him. He opened his eyes and smiled. "We must move with care today. This area is, your grandfather tells me, controlled by a Notas group called Chop-backs. I wish to avoid them if I can."

"Do you know why they are called Chop-backs?" she asked him.

"I doubt that it is connected with the study of philanthropy," he said, moving past her to the ponies.

"The study of philanthropy?" echoed Zhusai. "What kind of a Nadir are you?"

"I am the dog who played the flute," he told her as he tightened the cinch of his saddle and vaulted to the pony's back.

They rode through most of the morning, halting at noon in a gully to rest the horses and eat a meal of cold meat and cheese. No riders had been seen, but Talisman had spotted fresh tracks, and once they had come across horse droppings that were still moist. "Three warriors," said Talisman. "They are ahead of us."

"That is most disconcerting. Is it not possible that they are merely travelers?"

"Possible but not likely. They are not carrying supplies, and they are making no effort to disguise their tracks. We will avoid them if we can."

"I have two throwing knives, one in each boot, lord," she said, bowing her head. "I am skilled with them. Though, of course," she added hurriedly, "I have no doubt that a warrior such as yourself can easily kill three Notas."

Talisman absorbed the information. "I shall think on what you have said, but I hope there will be no need for bloodshed. I will try to talk my way through them. I have no wish to kill any Nadir."

Zhusai bowed again. "I am sure, lord, you will devise a suitable plan."

Talisman pulled the cork from the water canteen and took a sip, swishing the warm liquid around his mouth. According to Chorin-Tsu's map, the closest water was half a day to the east; that was where he intended to camp, though it occurred to him that the Notas were probably thinking along similar lines. He passed the canteen to Zhusai and waited while she drank. Then he took the canteen to the hobbled ponies and, wetting a cloth, cleaned the dust and sand from their nostrils. Returning to Zhusai, he squatted down before her. "I accept your offer," he said. "But let us be clear: you will use your knife only upon my explicit command. You are right-handed?" She nodded. "Then your target will be the farthest man to your left. If we meet the Notas, you must draw your knife surreptitiously. Listen for the command. It will be when I say your name."

"I understand, lord."

"There is one other matter we must settle. Chiatze politeness is legendary and well suited to a world of silk-covered seats, vast libraries, and a ten-thousand-year-old civilization. Not so here. Put from your mind thoughts of guardian and ward. We have just established our battle plan and are now two warriors traveling together in a hostile land. From now on it would please me to have you speak less formally."

"You do not wish me to call you 'lord'?"

Talisman looked into her eyes and felt his mouth go dry. "Save that honorific for your husband, Zhusai. You may call me Talisman."

"As you command, so be it . . . Talisman."

The afternoon sun beat down on the steppes, and the ponies plodded on, heads down, toward the distant mountains. Although the land looked flat and empty, Talisman knew that there were many hidden gullies and depressions and that the three Notas could be in any one of a hundred different hiding places. Narrowing his eyes, Talisman scanned the shimmering heat-scorched landscape. There was nothing to be seen. Loosening his saber, he rode on.

Gorkai was a killer and a thief, usually—but not exclusively—in that order. The sun beat down on him, but not a bead of sweat shone on his flat, ugly face. The two men with him both wore wide-brimmed straw hats, protecting their heads and necks from the merciless heat, but Gorkai gave no thought to the heat as he waited for yet another victim. Once he had aspired to be more than a thief. He had longed to possess his own goat herd and a string of fine ponies sired from the hardy stallions of the north passes. Gorkai had dreamed of the day when he could afford a second wife, even though he had not yet won his first. And further, on those evenings when his imagination took flight, he saw himself invited to sit among the Elders. All his dreams were like remembered smoke now, merely an acrid aftertaste on the memory.

Now he was Notas—no tribe.

As he sat in the blazing sunshine, staring out over the

steppes, he had no dreams. Back at the camp the nose-slit whore who waited for him would expect some pretty bauble before bestowing her favors on him.

"You think they turned off the trail?" asked Baski, crouching alongside him. The horses were hobbled in the gully below, and the two men were partly hidden behind the overlapping branches of several *sihjis* bushes. Gorkai glanced at the stocky warrior beside him.

"No. They are riding slowly, conserving the strength of their ponies."

"We attack when he comes into view?"

"You think he will be easy to take?" countered Gorkai.

Baski cleared his throat and spit, then he shrugged. "He is one man. We are three."

"Three? You would be wise not to consider Djung in your estimate."

"Djung has killed before," said Baski. "I have seen it."

Gorkai shook his head. "He is a *killer*, yes. But we are facing a *fighter*."

"We have not seen him yet. How do you know this, Gorkai?"

The older man sat back on his haunches. "A man does not have to know birds to see that the hawk is a hunter, the pigeon his prey. You understand? The sharpness of the talons, the wicked curve of the beak, the power and speed of the wings. So it is with men. This one is careful and wary, avoiding areas of ambush, which shows he is skilled in the ways of the raid. Also, he knows he is in hostile territory, yet he rides anyway. This tells us he has courage and confidence. There is no hurry, Baski. First we observe, then we kill."

"I bow to your wisdom, Gorkai."

A sound came from behind, and Gorkai twisted around to see Djung scrambling up the slope. "Slowly," hissed Gorkai. "You are making dust!"

Djung's fat face adopted a sulky expression. "It cannot be seen from any distance," he said. "You worry like an old woman."

Gorkai turned away from the younger man. There was no need for further conversation. Djung had a gift for stupidity, an almost mystic ability to withstand any form of logic.

There was still no sign of the riders, and Gorkai allowed his mind to relax. Once he had been considered a coming man, a voice for the future. Those days were far behind now, trodden into the dust of his past. When he was first banished, he had believed himself unlucky, but now, with the nearly useless gift of hindsight, he knew this was not so. He had been impatient and had sought to rise too far, too fast. The arrogance of youth. Too clever to recognize its own stupidity.

He had been just seventeen when he had taken part in the raid on the Wolfshead tribe, and it was Gorkai who had captured thirty of their ponies. Suddenly rich, he had learned to swagger. At the time it had seemed that the gods of stone and water had smiled upon him. Looking back, he saw that it was a gift laced with poison. Capturing two ponies would have helped him find a wife; ten would have gained him a place among the elite. But thirty was too many for a young man, and the more he had swaggered, the more he had become disliked. This was hard for a young man to understand. At the midsummer gathering he had made an offer for Li-shi, the daughter of Lon-tsen. Five ponies! No one had ever offered five ponies for a virgin.

And he had been rejected! The flush of remembered shame stained his cheeks even now. Before all he had been humiliated, for Lon-tsen had given his daughter to a warrior who had offered only one pony and seven blankets.

Angry beyond reason, Gorkai had nursed his humiliation, fanning it into a hatred so strong that when the plan came to him, he saw it as a blindingly brilliant scheme to restore his shattered pride. He had abducted Li-shi, raped her, then returned her to her father. "Now see who desires Gorkai's leavings," he had told the old man. Nadir custom was such that no other man would marry her. Nadir law decreed that her father would have to give her to Gorkai or kill her for bringing shame to her family.

They had come for him in the night and dragged him before the council. Once there, he had witnessed the execution of the girl, strangled by her own father, and had heard the words of banishment spoken by the Elders.

Despite all the killing since, he still remembered the girl's death with genuine regret. Li-shi had not struggled at all but had turned her eyes upon Gorkai and watched him until the light fled from her and her jaw fell slack. Guilt remained with him, a stone in the heart.

"There they are," whispered Baski.

Gorkai forced the memories away and narrowed his eyes. Still some distance away, the man was riding just ahead of the woman. This was the closest they had been. Gorkai narrowed his eyes and studied the man. A bow and a quiver were looped over his saddle horn, and a cavalry saber was scabbarded at his waist. The man drew rein some sixty paces from Gorkai. He was young, and that surprised Gorkai; judging by the skill he had shown so far, the Notas leader had expected him to be a seasoned warrior in his thirties.

The woman rode alongside the man, and Gorkai's jaw dropped. She was exquisitely beautiful, raven-haired and slender. But what shook him was the resemblance to the girl he had once loved. Surely the gods were giving him a chance to find happiness at last. The sound of rasping steel broke the silence, and Gorkai swung an angry glance at Djung, who had drawn his sword.

Out on the steppes the rider swung his mount, cutting to the left. Together he and the woman galloped away.

"Idiot!" said Gorkai.

"There are three of us. Let's ride them down," urged Baski.

"No need. The only water within forty miles is at Kall's Pool. We will find them."

\* \* \*

Talisman was sitting back from the fire when the three riders rode into the camp he had prepared some two hundred yards from Kall's Pool. It was yet another rock tank, fed in part by deep wells below the strata. Slender trees grew by the poolside, and brightly colored flowers clung to life on the soft mud of the water's edge. Zhusai had wanted to camp by the water, but Talisman had refused, and they had built their fire against a rock wall in sight of the water. The girl was asleep by the dying fire as the riders made their entrance, but Talisman was wide awake with his saber drawn and resting on the ground before him. By his side was his hunting bow, three arrows drawn from the quiver and plunged into the earth.

The riders paused, observing him as he observed them. In the center was a thickset warrior, his hair closely cropped, a widow's peak extending like an arrowhead over his brow. To his right was a shorter, slimmer rider with burning eyes, and to his left was a fat-faced man wearing a fur-rimmed iron helm.

The riders waited, but Talisman made no move and did not speak. At last the lead rider dismounted. "A lonely place," he said softly. Zhusai woke and sat up.

"All places are desolate to a lonely man," said Talisman.

"What does that mean?" asked the warrior, beckoning his comrades to join him.

"Where in all the land of stone and water can a Notas feel welcome?"

"You are not very friendly," said the man, taking a step forward. The other two moved sideways, hands on their sword hilts.

Talisman rose, leaving the saber by his feet, his hands hanging loosely by his sides. The moon was bright above the group. Zhusai made to rise, but Talisman spoke to her. "Remain where you are . . . Zhusai," he said. "All will be well in a little while."

"You seem very sure of that," said the widow-peaked leader. "And yet you are in a strange land and not among friends."

"The land is not strange to me," Talisman told him. "It is Nadir land, ruled by the gods of stone and water. I am a Nadir, and this land is mine by right and by blood. You are the strangers here. Can you not feel your deaths in the air, in the breeze? Can you not feel the contempt that this land has for you? Notas! The name stinks like a three-day-dead pig."

The leader reddened. "You think we chose the title, you arrogant bastard? You think we wanted to live this way?"

"Why are you talking to him?" snarled the fat-faced warrior. "Let's be done with him!" The man's sword snaked from its leather scabbard, and he ran forward.

Talisman's right hand came up and back, the knife blade slashing through the air to hammer home into the man's right eye, sinking in to the ivory hilt. The warrior ran on for two more paces, then pitched to his left, striking the ground face first. As the second warrior leapt forward, Zhusai's knife thudded into the side of his neck. Blood bubbled into his windpipe. Choking, he let go of his sword and tore the knife clear, staring down at the slender blade in shock and disbelief. Sinking to his knees, he tried to speak, but blood burst from his mouth in a crimson spray. Talisman's foot flipped the saber into the air, and he caught it expertly.

"Your dead friend asked you a question," he told the stunned leader. "But I would like to hear the answer. Why *are* you talking to me?"

The man blinked and then suddenly sat down by the fire. "You are right," he said. "I can feel the contempt. And I am alone. It was not always thus. I made a mistake born of pride and foolishness, and I have paid for it these last twenty years. There is no end in sight."

"What tribe were you?" asked Talisman.

"Northern Gray."

Talisman walked to the fire and sat opposite the man. "My name is Talisman, and I live to serve the Uniter. His day is almost upon us. If you wish to be Nadir again, then follow me."

The man smiled and shook his head. "The Uniter? The hero

with violet eyes? You believe he exists? And if he did, why would he take me?"

"He will take you—if you are with me."

"You know where he is?"

"I know what will bring us to him. Will you follow me?"

"What tribe are you?"

"Wolfshead. As you will be."

The man stared gloomily into the fire. "All my troubles began with the Wolfshead. Perhaps they will end there." Glancing up, he met Talisman's dark gaze. "I will follow you. What blood oath do you require?"

"None," said Talisman. "As you have said it, so shall it be. What is your name?"

"Gorkai."

"Then keep watch, Gorkai, for I am tired."

So saying, Talisman laid down his saber, covered himself with a blanket, and slept.

Zhusai sat quietly as Talisman stretched himself out, his head resting on his forearm; his breathing deepened. Zhusai could scarcely believe he would do such a thing. Nervously she glanced at Gorkai, reading the confusion in the man's expression. Moments before, this man and two others had ridden into the camp to kill them. Now two were dead, and the third was sitting quietly by the fire. Gorkai rose, and Zhusai flinched. But the Nadir warrior merely walked to the first of the corpses, dragging it away from the camp; he repeated the action with the second body. Returning, he squatted before Zhusai and extended his hand. She glanced down to see that he was holding her ivory-handled throwing knife. Silently she took it. Gorkai stood and gathered firewood before settling down beside the fire. Zhusai felt no need of sleep, convinced that the moment she shut her eyes, this killer would cut Talisman's throat, then abuse and murder her.

The night wore on, but Gorkai made no movement toward

her or the sleeping Talisman. Instead he sat cross-legged, deep in thought. Talisman groaned in his sleep and spoke suddenly in the tongue of the Gothir. "Never!" he said.

Gorkai glanced at the woman, and their eyes met. Zhusai did not look away. Rising, Gorkai gestured to her to walk with him. He did not look back but strode to the ponies and sat on a rock. For a while Zhusai made no move to follow, then, knife in hand, she followed him.

"Tell me of him," said Gorkai.

"I know very little."

"I have watched you both. You do not touch; there is no intimacy."

"He is not my husband," she said coldly.

"Where is he from? Who is he?"

"He is Talisman of the Wolfshead."

"Talisman is not a Nadir name. I have given him my life, for he touched upon my dreams and my needs. But I need to know."

"Believe me, Gorkai, you know almost as much as I. But he is strong, and he dreams great dreams."

"Where do we travel?"

"To the Valley of Shul-sen's Tears and the tomb of Oshikai."

"Ah," said Gorkai, "a pilgrimage, then. So be it." He rose and took a deep breath. "I, too, have dreams, though I had all but forgotten them." He hesitated, then spoke again. "Do not fear me, Zhusai. I will never harm you." Gorkai walked back to the fire and sat.

Zhusai returned to her blanket.

The dawn sun was hidden by a thick bank of cloud. Zhusai awoke with a start. She had been determined not to sleep but at some point in the night had drifted into dreams. Talisman was up and talking to Gorkai. Zhusai opened their pack and re-kindled the fire, preparing a breakfast of salted oats and dried meat. The two men ate in silence, then Gorkai gathered the wooden platters and cleaned them in the pool. It was the work of a woman or a servant, and Zhusai knew it was Gorkai's way of establishing his place with them. Zhusai placed the platters within the canvas pack and tied it behind her saddle. Gorkai helped her mount, then handed her the reins of the other two ponies.

Talisman led the way out onto the steppes, Gorkai riding beside him. "How many Notas raid in this area?" Talisman asked.

"Thirty," answered Gorkai. "We . . . they call themselves Chop-backs."

"So I have heard. Have you been to Oshikai's tomb?"

"Three times."

"Tell me of it."

"It is a simply carved sarcophagus set in a building of white stone. Once it was a Gothir fort; now it is a holy place."

"Who will be guarding it now?"

Gorkai shrugged. "Hard to say. There are always warriors from at least four tribes camped close by. A blind priest sends messages to each, telling them when they may take up their duties. He also tells them when to return to their own lands, and at such times other tribes send warriors. It is a great honor to be chosen to guard the resting place of Oshikai. The last time I was there the Green Monkey tribe patrolled the tomb. Waiting were the Northern Grays, the Stone Tigers, and the Fleet Ponies."

"How many in each group?"

"No more than forty."

The clouds began to break, and the burning sun shone clear. Zhusai lifted a wide-brimmed straw hat from the pommel of her saddle and tied it into place. The shifting dust dried her throat, but she resisted the urge to drink.

And the trio rode on through the long day.

## ◇ 5 ◇

THE RIOTS LASTED three days, beginning in the poorest section and spreading fast. Troops were called in from surrounding areas, cavalry charging into the rioters. The death toll rose, and by the end of the third day some four hundred people were reported killed and hundreds more injured.

The games were suspended during the troubles, the athletes advised to remain in their quarters, the surrounding area patrolled by soldiers. As darkness fell, Druss stared gloomily from the upstairs window, watching the flames leap from the burning buildings of the western quarter.

"Madness," he said as Sieben moved alongside him.

"Majon was telling me they caught the crossbowman and hacked him to pieces."

"And yet the killing still goes on. Why, Sieben?"

"You said it yourself: madness. Madness and greed. Almost everyone had money on Klay, and they feel betrayed. Three of the gambling houses have been burned to the ground." Outside a troop of cavalry cantered along the wide avenue, heading for the riot area.

"What is the news of Klay?" asked Druss.

"There is no word, but Majon told me he has many friends among the physicians. And Klay is a rich man, Druss; he can afford the best."

"I would have died," Druss said softly. "A knife was flashing toward my eye. In that moment I could do nothing. His hand moved like lightning, poet. I have never seen anything like it. He plucked the blade from the air." Druss shook his head. "I still do not believe it. Yet moments later a coward's bolt had smashed him to the ground. He'll not walk again, Sieben."

"You can't say that, old horse. You are no surgeon."

"I know his spine was smashed. I have seen that injury a score of times. There's no coming back from it. Not without . . ." He fell silent.

"Without what?"

Druss moved away from the window. "A Nadir shaman came to me just before the fight. He told me of magical gems to heal any wound."

"Did he also try to sell you a map to a legendary diamond mine?" Sieben asked with a smile.

"I'm going out," said Druss. "I need to see Klay."

"Out? Into that chaos? Come on, Druss; wait till morning."

Druss shook his head.

"Then take a weapon," Sieben urged. "The rioters are still looking for blood."

"Then they had better stay away from me," snarled Druss, "or I'll spill enough of it to drown them all!"


The grounds were deserted, and the gates were open. Druss paused and stared at the broken statue lying on the lawn. It looked as if the legs had been shattered by hammers. The neck was sheared away, the head lying on the grass, its stone eyes staring unseeing at the black-bearded warrior standing in the gateway.

Druss gazed around. The flower beds had been uprooted, the lawn churned into mud around the statue. He strode to the front door, which was open. No servants greeted him as he moved through to the training area. There was no sound. The sand circles were empty of fighters, the fountains silent. An old man came in sight, carrying a bucket of water; he was the servant who had looked after the beggar boy. "Where is everyone?" asked Druss.

"Gone. All gone."

"What of Klay?"

"They moved him to a hospice in the southern quarter. The scum-sucking bastards!"

Druss wandered back into the main building. Couches and chairs had been smashed, the curtains ripped down from the windows. A portrait of Klay had been slashed through, and the place smelled of stale urine. Druss shook his head in puzzlement. "Why would the rioters do this? I thought they loved the man."

The old man set down the bucket, righted a chair, and slumped down. "Oh, aye, they loved him, until his back broke. Then they hated him. People had wagered their life savings on him. They heard that he was involved in a drunken brawl and that all bets were dead. Their money gone, they turned on him. Turned on him like animals! After all he'd won for them, done for them. You know," he said, glancing up, his ancient face flushed with anger, "the hospice they carried him to was built from money donated by Klay. Many of the people who came here and screamed abuse had been helped by him in the past. No gratitude. But the worst of them was Shonan."

"Klay's trainer?"

"Pah!" spit the old man. "Trainer, handler, owner? Call him what you will, but I call him a blood-sucking parasite. Klay's gone now, and so is his wealth. Shonan even says that this house belongs to him. Klay, it seems, had nothing. Can you believe that? The bastard didn't even pay for the carriage that took Klay to the hospice. He will die there penniless." The old man laughed bitterly. "One moment he was the hero of the Gothir, loved by all, flattered by all. Now he is poor, alone, and friendless. By the gods, it makes you think, doesn't it?"

"He has you," said Druss. "And he has me."

"You? You're the Drenai fighter; you hardly knew him."

"I *know* him, and that is enough. Can you take me to him?"

"Aye, and gladly. I'm finished here now. I'll gather my gear and meet you at the front of the house."

Druss strolled through to the front lawn. A group of about a dozen athletes was coming through the gate, and the sound of laughter pricked Druss' anger. At the center of the group was a bald-headed man wearing a gold torque studded with gems. They stopped by the statue, and Druss heard a young man say, "By Shemak, that monstrosity cost over three thousand Raq. Now it is just rubble."

"What's past is past," said the man with the gold torque.

"So what will you do now, Shonan?" asked another.

The man shrugged. "Find another fighter. It will be hard, mind, for Klay was gifted. No doubt about that."

The old man moved alongside Druss. "Doesn't their grief move you to tears? Klay supported them all. See the young blond one? Klay paid off his gambling debts no more than a week ago. Just over a thousand Raq. And this is the way they thank him!"

"Aye, they're a shoddy bunch," said Druss. Striding across the lawn, he approached Shonan.

The man grinned at Druss. "How fall the mighty," he said, pointing to the statue.

"And the not so mighty," said Druss, his fist thundering into the man's face and catapulting him from his feet. Several of the athletes surged forward, but Druss glared at them, and they stopped in their tracks. Slowly they backed away, and Druss moved to the fallen Shonan. Both of the man's front teeth had been smashed through his lips, and his jaw was hanging slack. Druss ripped the gold torque from his neck and tossed it to the old man. "This might pay a bill or two at the hospice," he said.

"It will that," agreed the old man. The athletes were still standing close by. Druss pointed to the young man with long blond hair.

"You, come here." The man blinked nervously but then stepped forward.

"When this piece of offal wakes, you tell him that Druss is going to find him again. You tell him that I expect Klay to be looked after. I expect him to be back in his own house, with his own servants, and with money enough to pay them. If this is not done, I will come back and kill him. And after that I will find you, and I will rip your pretty face from your skull. You understand me?" The young man nodded, and Druss swung to the others. "I have marked all you maggots in my mind. If I find that Klay wants for anything, I shall come looking for each of you. Make no mistake: if Klay suffers one more ounce of indignity, you will all die. I am Druss, and that is my promise."

Druss walked away from them, the old man alongside him. "My name is Carmol," the servant said with a broad grin. "And it is a pleasure to meet you again!"

Together they walked across the riot-torn city. Here and there bodies could be seen lying by the wayside, and the smell of burning buildings wafted to them on the wind.

The hospice was sited in the center of the poorest quarter, its white walls out of place among the squalid buildings that surrounded it. The riots had begun near there but had moved on since. An elderly priest showed them to Klay's room, which was small and clean with a single cot placed beneath the window. Klay was asleep when they entered, and the priest brought two chairs for the visitors. The fighter awoke as Druss sat beside the bed.

"How are you feeling?" asked the Drenai.

"I've known better days," answered Klay, forcing a smile. His face was gray beneath his tan, his eyes sunken and blue-ringed.

Druss took hold of the fighter's hand. "A Nadir shaman told me of a place to the east where there are magical jewels to heal any wound. I leave tomorrow. If they exist, I shall find them and bring them to you. You understand?"

"Yes," said Klay, despair in his voice. "Magical jewels to heal me!"

"Do not give up hope," said Druss.

"Hope is not on offer here, my friend. This is a hospice, and we come here to die. Throughout this building there are people waiting for death, some with cancers, others with lung rot, still more with wasting diseases for which there are no names. There are wives, husbands, children. If such jewels exist, there are other, more deserving cases than mine. But I thank you for your words."

"They are not just words, Klay. I am leaving tomorrow. Promise me you will fight for life until my return."

"I always fight, Druss. That's my talent. The east, you say? That is Nadir heartland, filled with robbers and thieves and deadly killers. You wouldn't want to meet them."

Druss chuckled. "Trust me, laddie. They wouldn't want to meet me!"

Garen-Tsen stared down at the body of the embalmer, his face twisted in death, frozen in midscream, eyes wide and staring. Blood had ceased to flow from the many wounds, and the broken fingers twitched no longer.

"He was a tough one," said the torturer.

Garen-Tsen ignored the man. The information gleaned from the embalmer had been far from complete; he had held something back to the end. Garen-Tsen stared at the dead face. You knew exactly where they were, he thought. Through his years of study Chorin-Tsu had finally pieced together the route taken by the renegade shaman who originally had stolen the Eyes of Alchazzar. The man ultimately had been found hiding in the Mountains of the Moon, and he had been slain there. Of the eyes there was no sign. He could have hidden them anywhere, but a number of incidents suggested that they were concealed in or near the tomb of Oshikai Demon-bane. Miraculous healings were said to have taken place there: several blind men regained their sight, a cripple walked. In themselves those miracles meant nothing. Tombs of heroes or prophets always attracted such claims, and being Chiatze, Garen-Tsen well understood the nature of hysterical paralysis or blindness. Even so, it was the only indication of the whereabouts of the jewels. The problem remained, however, that the tomb had been surreptitiously searched on at least three occasions. No hidden jewels had been found.

"Dispose of it," Garen-Tsen ordered the torturer, and the man nodded. The university paid five gold coins for every fresh corpse, though this one was in such a wretched state that he probably would receive only three.

The Chiatze minister lifted the hem of his long velvet robe and walked from the chamber. Am I clutching at leaves in the wind? he wondered. Can I send troops to Shul-sen's valley with any surety of success?

Back in his own rooms he emptied his mind of the problem and pored over the reports of the day. A secret meeting at the home of Senator Borvan, an overheard criticism of the God-King in a tavern on Eel Street, a scuffle at the home of the fighter Klay. The name Druss caught his eye, and he remembered the awesome Drenai fighter. He read on, skimming through the reports and making notes. Druss' name figured once more; he had visited Klay in the hospice that morning. Garen-Tsen blinked as he read the small script. "The subject made reference to healing jewels, which he would fetch for the fighter . . ." Picking up a small silver bell, Garen-Tsen rang it twice. A servant entered and bowed.

An hour later the informant was standing nervously before Garen-Tsen's desk. "Tell me all that you heard. Every word. Leave nothing out," ordered Garen-Tsen. The man did so. Dismissing him, the Chiatze walked to the window, staring out over the towers and rooftops. A Nadir shaman had told Druss about the jewels, and he was heading east. The Valley of Shul-sen's Tears was in the east. Chorin-Tsu's daughter was riding east with the Nadir warrior Talisman.

He rang the bell once more.

"Go to Lord Larness," he told the servant, "and say that I must meet with him today. Also have a warrant drawn up for the arrest of the Drenai fighter Druss."

"Yes, lord. What accusation should be logged against him?"

"Assault on a Gothir citizen, leading to the man's death."

The servant looked puzzled. "But lord, Shonan is not dead; he merely lost some teeth." Garen-Tsen's hooded eyes fastened to the man's face, and the servant reddened. "I will see to it, lord. Forgive me."

The haggle had reached the crucial point, and Sieben the Poet steeled himself for the kill. The horse dealer had moved from politeness, to polite disinterest, to irritation, and now he was displaying an impressively feigned anger. "This probably just looks like a horse to you," said the dealer, patting the beast's steel-dust flanks, "but to me Ganael is a member of my family. We love this horse. His sire was a champion, and his dam had the speed of the east wind. He is brave and loyal. And you insult me by offering the price normally paid for a swaybacked nag?"

Sieben adopted a serious expression and held to the man's gray-eyed gaze. "I do not disagree with your description of this . . . gelding. And were it five years younger, I might be tempted to part with a little more silver. But the horse is worth no more than I have offered."

"Then our business is concluded," snapped the dealer. "There are many noblemen in Gulgothir who would pay twice what I am asking of you. And I offer you this special price only because I like you and feel that Ganael likes you, too."

Sieben glanced up at the steel dust and looked into the gelding's eye. "He has a mean look," he said.

"Spirited," the dealer said swiftly. "Like me, he doesn't suffer fools gladly. But he is fearless and strong. You are riding into the steppes. By heaven, man, you will need a horse with the power to outrun those Nadir hill ponies."

"Thirty pieces is too much. Ganael may be strong, but he is also verging on the old."

"Nonsense. He is no more than nine—" As the dealer spoke, Sieben raised a quizzical eyebrow. "Well, perhaps nearer ten or eleven. Even so, he has years of service left in him. His legs are strong, and there is no weakness in the hoof. And I'll reshoe him for the steppes. How does that sound?"

"It would sound very fine at twenty-two pieces of silver."

"Gods, man, have you come here merely to insult me? Did you wake this morning and think, I'll spend the day bringing an honest Gothir businessman to the threshold of heart failure? Twenty-seven."

"Twenty-five, and you can throw in the old mare in the farthest stall and two saddles."

The dealer swung around. "The mare? Throw in? Are you trying to bankrupt me? That mare is of the finest pedigree. She—"

"Is a member of the family," Sieben put in with a wry smile. "I can see she is strong, but more importantly, she is old and steady. My friend is no rider, and I think she will suit him. You will have no buyers for her, save for prison meat or glue. The price for those mounts is one half-silver."

The dealer's thin face relaxed, and he pulled at his pointed beard. "I do happen to have two old saddles—beautiful workmanship, equipped with bags and canteens. But I couldn't let them go for less than a full silver each. Twenty-seven and we will grip hands upon it. It is too hot to haggle further."

"Done," agreed Sieben. "But I want both horses reshod and brought to me in three hours." From his pouch he took two silver pieces and passed them to the man. "Full payment will be upon receipt," he said.

After giving the dealer the address, Sieben strolled out into the marketplace beyond. It was nearly deserted, mute testimony to the riots that had taken place there the previous night. A young whore approached him, stepping from the doorway of a smoke-blackened building. "Do you seek delight, lord?" she asked him. Sieben gazed down; her face was young and pretty, but her eyes were world-weary and empty.

"How much?"

"For a nobleman like you, lord, a mere quarter-silver. Unless you need a bed, and that will be a half."

"And for this you will delight me?"

"I will give you hours of pleasure," she promised.

Sieben took her hand and saw that her fingers were clean, as was the cheap dress she wore. "Show me," he said.

Two hours later he wandered back into the house of lodging. Majon was sitting by the far window, composing a speech he was to make at the royal funeral the next day. He glanced up as Sieben entered and laid aside his quill. "We must talk," he said, beckoning Sieben to join him.

The poet was tired and already regretting his decision to join Druss on his journey. He sat on a padded couch and poured himself a goblet of watered wine. "Let us make this swift, Ambassador, for I need an hour's sleep before I ride."

"Yes, the ride. This is not seemly, poet. The queen's funeral is tomorrow, and Druss is an honored guest. To ride out now is an insult of the worst kind. Especially following the riots, which began over Druss, after all. Could you not wait for a few days at least?"

Sieben shook his head. "I am afraid we are dealing here with something you don't understand, Ambassador. Druss sees this as a debt of honor."

"Do not seek to insult me, poet. I well understand the notion. But Druss did not ask for this man's help and therefore is in no way responsible for his injury. He owes him nothing."

"Amazing," said Sieben. "You prove my point exactly. I talk of honor and you speak of transactions. Listen to me. A man was crippled trying to help Druss. Now he is dying, and we cannot wait any longer. The surgeon told Druss that Klay has perhaps a month to live. Therefore, we are leaving now, as soon as the horses are delivered."

"But it is all nonsense!" roared Majon. "Magical jewels hidden in a Nadir valley! What sane man would even consider such . . . such a fanciful tale? I have been researching the area you plan to visit. There are many tribes raiding in those parts. No convoys pass through there unless heavily guarded. There is one particular group of raiders known as Chop-backs. How do you like the sound of that? You know how they got their name? They smash the lower spines of their prisoners and leave them out on the steppes for the wolves to devour."

Sieben drained his wine and hoped his face had not shown the terror he felt. "You have made your point, Ambassador."

"Why is he *really* doing this?"

"I have already told you. Druss owes the man a debt, and he would walk through fire to repay it."

As Sieben rose, Majon also stood. "Why are you going with him? He is not the brightest of men, and I can . . . just . . . understand his simplistic view of the world. But you? You have wit and rare intelligence. Can you not see the futility of this venture?"

"Yes," admitted Sieben. "And it saddens me that I can, for it merely highlights the terrible flaws of what you call intelligence."

Back in his room Sieben bathed and then stretched himself out on his bed. The delights the whore had promised had proved to be ephemeral and illusory. Just like all the delights of life Sieben had ever sampled. Lust followed by a gentle sorrow for all that had been missed. The ultimate experience, like the myth of the ultimate woman, was always ahead.

*Why are you going with him?*

Sieben loathed danger and trembled at the thought of approaching fear. But Druss, for all his faults, lived life to the full, relishing every breath. Sieben had never been more alive than when he had accompanied Druss on his search for the kidnapped Rowena, in the storm when the *Thunderchild* had been hurled and tossed like a piece of driftwood, and in the battles and wars when death had seemed but a heartbeat distant.

They had returned in triumph to Drenan, and there Sieben had composed his epic poem *Druss the Legend*. It was now the most widely performed saga in all the Drenai lands and had been translated into a dozen languages. The fame had brought riches, the riches had bought women, and Sieben had fallen back with astonishing speed into a life of idle luxury. He sighed and rose from the bed. Servants had laid out his clothes: leggings of pale blue wool and soft thigh-length riding boots of creamy beige. His puff-sleeved shirt was of blue silk, the wrists slashed to reveal gray silk inserts decorated with mother-of-pearl. A royal blue cape completed the ensemble, fastened at the neck with a delicate braided chain of gold. Once dressed, he stood before the full-length mirror and looped his baldric over his shoulder. From it hung four black sheaths, each housing an ivory-hilted throwing knife.

*Why are you going with him?* It would be fine if he could say, "Because he is my friend." Sieben hoped there was at least a semblance of truth in that. The reality, however, was altogether different. "I need to feel alive," he said aloud.

"I have purchased two mounts," said Sieben, "a fine thoroughbred for myself and a cart horse for you. Since you ride with all the grace of a sack of carrots, I thought it would be fitting."

Druss ignored the jibe. "Where did you get the pretty knives?" he asked, pointing at the ornate leather baldric slung carelessly over Sieben's shoulder.

"Pretty? These are splendidly balanced weapons of death." Sieben slid one from its sheath. The blade was diamond-shaped and razor-sharp. "I practiced with them before I bought them. I hit a moth at ten paces."

"That could come in handy," grunted Druss. "Nadir moths can be ferocious, I'm told."

"Ah, yes," muttered Sieben, "the old jokes are the best. But I should have seen that one staggering over the horizon."

Druss carefully packed his saddlebags with supplies of dried meat, fruit, salt, and sugar. Fastening the straps, he dragged a blanket from the bed and rolled it tightly before tying it to the saddlebags.

"Majon is not best pleased that we are leaving," said Sieben. "The queen's interment is tomorrow, and he fears the king will take our departure at this juncture as an insult to his dearly departed."

"Have you packed yet?" asked Druss, swinging the saddlebag to his shoulder.

"I have a servant doing it," said Sieben, "even as we speak. I hate these bags; they crumple the silk. No shirt or tunic ever looks right when produced from one of these grotesqueries."

Druss shook his head in exasperation. "You're bringing silk shirts into the steppes? You think there will be many admirers of fashion among the Nadir?"

Sieben chuckled. "When they see me, they'll think I'm a god!"

Striding to the far wall, Druss gathered up his ax, Snaga. Sieben stared at the awesome weapon with its glittering butterfly blades of shining silver steel and its black haft fashioned with silver runes. "I detest that thing," he said with feeling.

Leaving the bedroom, Druss walked out into the main lounge and through to the entrance hall. The ambassador Majon was talking to three soldiers of the Royal Guard, tall men in silver breastplates and black cloaks. "Ah, Druss," he said smoothly. "These gentlemen would like you to accompany them to the Palace of Inquisition. There's obviously been a mistake, but there are questions they would like to ask you."

"About what?"

Majon cleared his throat and nervously swept a hand over his neatly groomed silver hair. "Apparently there was an altercation at the house of the fighter Klay, and someone named Shonan died as a result."

Druss laid Snaga on the floor and dropped the saddlebags from his shoulder. "Died? From a punch to the mouth? Pah! I don't believe it. He was alive when I left him."

"You will come with us," said a guard, stepping forward.

"Best that you agree, Druss," said Majon soothingly. "I am sure we can—"

"Enough talk, Drenai," said the guard. "This man is wanted for murder, and we're taking him." From his belt the guard produced a set of manacles, and Druss' eyes narrowed.

"I think you might be making a mistake, officer," said Sieben. But his words came too late, as the guard stepped forward straight into Druss' right fist, which cannoned into his jaw. The officer pitched to his right, his head striking the wall, dislodging his white-plumed helm. The other two guards sprang forward. Druss felled the first with a left hook, the second with a right uppercut.

One man groaned, then all was still. Majon spoke, his voice trembling. "What have you done? You can't attack Royal Guards!"

"I just did. Now, are you ready, poet?"

"Indeed I am. I shall fetch my bags, and then I think it best we quit this city with all due speed."

Majon slumped to a padded chair. "What will I tell them when they . . . wake?"

"I suggest you give them your discourse on the merits of diplomacy over violence," said Sieben. Gently he patted Majon's shoulder, then ran to his apartments and gathered his gear.

The horses were stabled at the rear. Druss tied his saddlebags into place, then clumsily hauled himself into the saddle. The mare was sixteen hands and, though swaybacked, was a powerful beast. Sieben's mount was of similar size, but as he had told Druss, the horse was a thoroughbred, steel-gray and sleek.

Sieben vaulted into the saddle and led the way out into the main street. "You must have hit that Shonan awfully hard, old horse."

"Not hard enough to kill him," said Druss, swaying in the saddle and grabbing the pommel.

"Grip with your thighs, not your calves," advised Sieben.

"I never liked riding. I feel foolish perched up here."

There were a number of riders making for the eastern gate, and Druss and Sieben found themselves in a long convoy threading through the narrow streets. At the gates soldiers were questioning each rider, and Sieben's nervousness grew. "They can't be looking for you already, surely." Druss shrugged.

Slowly they approached the gates. A sentry walked forward. "Papers," he said.

"We are Drenai," Sieben told him. "Just out for a ride."

"You need papers signed by the exit officer of the watch," said the sentry, and Sieben saw Druss tense. Swiftly he reached into his pouch and produced a small silver coin; leaning over the saddle, he passed it to the soldier.

"One feels so cooped up in a city," said Sieben with a bright smile. "An hour's ride in open country frees the mind."

The sentry pocketed the coin. "I like to ride myself," he said. "Enjoy yourselves." He waved them through, and the two riders kicked their mounts into a canter and set off for the eastern hills.

After two hours in the saddle, Sieben drank the last of his water and stared about him. With the exception of the distant mountains, the landscape was featureless and dry.

"No rivers or streams," said the poet. "Where will we find water?" Druss pointed to a range of rocky hills some miles farther on. "How can you be sure?" asked the poet. "I don't want to die of thirst out here."

"You won't." He grinned at Sieben. "I have fought campaigns in deserts, and I know how to find water. But there's one trick I learned that's better than all the others."

"And that is?"

"I bought a map of the water holes! Now let's walk these horses for a while."

Druss slid from the saddle and strode on. Sieben dismounted and joined him. For a time they walked on in silence.

"Why so morose, old horse?" asked Sieben as they neared the outcrop of rocks.

"I've been thinking of Klay. How can people just turn on him like that? After all he did for them."

"People are sometimes vile creatures, Druss, selfish and self-regarding. But the real fault is not in them but in us for expecting better. When Klay dies, they'll all remember what a fine man he was, and they'll probably shed tears for him."

"He deserves better," grunted Druss.

"Maybe he does," agreed Sieben, wiping sweat from his brow with a perfumed handkerchief. "But when did that ever matter? Do we get what we deserve? I do not believe so. We get what we can win—what we can take, whether it be employment, or money, or women, or land. Look at you! Raiders stole your wife; they had the power to take, and they took her. Sadly for them you had the power to hunt them down and the sheer determination to pursue your love across the ocean. But you didn't win her back by luck or by the whim of a capricious deity. You did it by force of arms. You might have failed for a hundred reasons: illness, war—the flight of an arrow, the flash of a sword blade—a sudden storm at sea. You didn't get what you deserved, Druss; you got what you fought for. Klay was unlucky. He took a bolt that was meant for you. That was your good luck."

"I don't argue with that," said Druss. "Yes, he was unlucky. But they tore down his statue, and his friends robbed and then deserted him—men he had supported, aided, protected. That's what I find hard to swallow."

Sieben nodded. "My father told me that a man is lucky if in his life he can count on at least two good friends. He always maintained that a man with many friends had to be either rich or stupid, and I think that is largely true. In all my life I have had only one friend, Druss, and that is you."

"Do you not count your women?"

Sieben shook his head. "Everything with them has always been transactional. They require something of me; I require something of them. We each supply the other. They give me the warmth of their bodies and their yielding flesh; I give them the incredible expertise of the perfect lover."

"How can you call yourself a lover when love is never present in your encounters?"

"Don't be a pedant, Druss. I am worth the title. Even accomplished whores have told me I'm the best lover they ever had."

"How surprising," Druss said, with a grin. "I'll wager they don't say that to many men."

"Mockery does not suit you, axman. We all have our skills. Yours is with that appalling weapon; mine is in lovemaking."

"Aye," agreed Druss. "But it seems to me my weapon ends problems. Yours causes them."

"Oh, very droll. Just what I need as I walk through this barren wilderness, a lecture on morals!" Sieben stroked the neck of the steel-dust gelding, then stepped into the saddle. Lifting his hand, he shaded his eyes. "It is all so green. I've never seen a land that promised so much and gave so little. How do these plants survive?"

Druss did not answer. He was trying to hook his foot into the stirrup, but the mare began walking in circles. Sieben chuckled and rode alongside, taking the mare's reins and holding her steady while the axman mounted. "They are deep-rooted," said Druss. "It rains here for a full month every winter. The plants and bushes soak it in, then battle to survive for another year. It is a hard land. Harsh and savage."

"Like the people who dwell here," said Sieben.

"Aye. The Nadir are a fierce people."

"Majon was telling me about a group called Chop-backs."

"Renegades," said Druss. "They call them Notas, no tribe. They are outcasts, robbers and killers. We'll try to avoid them."

"And if we can't?"

Druss laughed. "Then you can show me your skills with the pretty knives!"

Nosta Khan sat in the shade of an overhanging rock, his scrawny left hand dipped in the cool water of the rock pool. The sun was high overhead, the heat beyond the shade pitiless, relentless in its power. It caused Nosta Khan no distress. Neither heat nor cold, pain nor sorrow could touch him now. For he was a master of the way, a shaman.

He had not desired this mystic path. No, as a young man he had dreamed the dreams of all Nadir warriors: many ponies, many women, many children. A short life filled with the savage joy of battle and the grunting, slippery warmth of sex.

It was not to be. His talent had denied him his dreams. No wives for Nosta Khan, no children at play at his feet. Instead he had been taken as a boy to the cave of Asta Khan, and there had learned the way.

Lifting his hand from the water, he touched it to his brow, closing his eyes as several drops of cold water fell to the wrinkled skin of his face.

He had been seven years old when Asta had taken him and six other boys to the crest of Stone Hawk Peak to sit in the blazing sunshine, dressed only in breechclouts and moccasins. The old shaman had covered their heads and faces with wet clay and told them to sit until the clay baked hard and fell clear. Each child had two reed straws through which to breathe. There was no sense of time within the clay, no sound and no light. The skin of his shoulders had burned and blistered, but Nosta had not moved. For three blazing days and three frozen nights he had sat thus within that tomb of drying clay.

It did not fall clear, and he had longed to lift his hands and rip it away. Yet he did not even when the terror gripped him. What if the wolves came? What if an enemy was close? What if Asta had left him there to die because he, Nosta, was not worthy? Still he sat unmoving, the ground beneath him soiled with his urine and excrement, ants and flies crawling over him. He felt their tiny legs on his skin and shivered. What if they were not flies but scorpions?

Still the child did not move. On the morning of the fourth day, as the sun brought warmth and pain to his chilled yet raw flesh, a section of the clay broke clear, allowing him to move the muscles of his jaw. Tilting his head, he forced open his mouth. The two reed straws dropped away, then a large chunk of baked clay split above his nose. A hand touched his head, and he flinched. Asta Khan peeled away the last of the clay.

The sunlight was brutally bright, and tears fell from the boy's eyes. The old shaman nodded. "You have done well," he said. They were the only words of praise he ever heard from Asta Khan.

When at last he could see, Nosta looked around. He and the old man were alone on Stone Hawk Peak. "Where are the other boys?"

"Gone. They will return to their villages. You have won the great prize."

"Then why do I feel only sadness?" he asked, his voice a dry croak.

Asta Khan did not answer at first. He passed a water skin to the boy and sat silently as he drank his fill. "Each man," he said at last, "gives something of himself to the future. At the very least the gift is in the form of a child to carry his seed onward. But a shaman is denied that pleasure." Taking the boy by the hand, he led him to the edge of the precipice. From there they gazed down over the plains and the distant steppes. "See there," said Asta Khan, "the goats of our tribe. They worry about little save to eat, sleep, and rut. But look at the goat herder. He must watch for wolves and lions, for the flesh-eating worms of the blowfly, and he must find pastures that are safe and rich with grass. Your sadness is born of the knowledge that you cannot be a goat. Your destiny calls for more than that."

Nosta Khan sighed and once more splashed his face with water. Asta was long dead now, and he remembered him with little affection.

A golden lioness and three cubs came into sight on the trail. Nosta took a deep breath and focused his concentration.

*The rearing rocks are part of the body of the gods of stone and water, and I am one with the rocks.*

The lioness moved warily forward, her great head sniffing the air. Satisfied that her family was safe, she edged to the pool, the cubs gamboling behind her. The last of the cubs leapt on the back of one of the others and commenced a play fight. The lioness ignored them and drank deeply. She was thin, her pelt patchy. When she had drunk her fill, she moved into the shade and lay beside Nosta Khan. The cubs followed her, nuzzling her teats. One scrambled over Nosta Khan's bare legs, then settled down in the old man's lap with its head resting on his thigh.

Reaching out, he laid his hand on the lioness's broad head. She did not flinch. Nosta Khan allowed his mind to float free. High above the hills he floated, scanning the folds and gullies. Less than a mile to the east he found a small family group of *ochpi*, wild mountain goats with short curved horns. There were a male, three females, and several young. Returning to his body, Nosta touched the lioness with his spirit. Her head came up, nostrils flaring. There was no way she could pick up the scent from this distance, with the wind against her, but Nosta Khan filled her mind with the vision of the *ochpi*. The lioness rose, scattering the cubs, then loped away. At first the cubs remained where they were, but she gave a low growl, and they ran after her.

With luck she would feed.

Nosta sat back and waited. The riders would be there within the hour. He pictured the axman, his broad, flat face and deep, cold eyes. Would that all these southerners could be so easily manipulated, he thought, remembering his spirit meeting in the tavern. Once outside, it had been so easy to mesmerize the crossbowman and command him to shoot down the Gothir fighter. Nosta recalled with pleasure the flight of the bolt, the sickening impact, and the intense shock of the crossbowman when he realized what he had done.

The threads were drawing together well now, but there was so much still to weave. Nosta rested his body and his mind, floating in half sleep in the warmth.

Two riders came into view. The shaman took a deep breath and focused, as he had when the lioness had come to the pool. He was a rock, eternal, unchanging, except to the slow eroding winds of time. The lead rider, a tall, slim young man with fair hair, dressed in garish silks, dismounted smoothly, holding firm to the reins, preventing the steel-dust gelding from reaching the cool water. "Not yet, my lovely," he said softly. "First we must cool you down." The second rider, the black-bearded axman, lifted his leg over the saddle pommel and jumped down. His mount was old and more than tired. Laying his ax to the ground, Druss unbuckled the saddle, hauling it clear of the mare's back. She was lathered in sweat and breathing heavily; he wiped her down with a cloth and tethered her next to the tall gelding in the partial shade of the east side of the pool. The fair one moved to the pool and stripped off his clothing, shaking off the dust and folding it neatly. His body was as pale as ivory, smooth and soft. No warrior this, thought Nosta Khan as the young man dived into the water. Druss gathered his ax and moved to the shade, where Nosta Khan sat. Squatting down, he cupped his hands and drank, then splashed water to his thick dark hair and beard.

Nosta Khan closed his eyes and reached out to touch Druss' arm and read his thoughts. An iron grip closed around his wrist, and his eyes flared open. Druss was looking directly at him.

"I have been waiting for you," said Nosta, fighting for calm.

"I do not like men creeping up on me," said the axman, his voice cold. Nosta glanced down at the pool, and the tension eased from him. The spell of concealment had not failed him; Druss had merely seen the reflection of his hand on the water. Druss released his grip and drank once more.

"You are seeking the healing jewels, eh? That is good. A man should stand by his friends in their darkest moments."

"Exactly where are they?" asked Druss. "I do not have much time. Klay is dying."

"I cannot tell you *exactly*. They were stolen several hundred years ago by a renegade shaman. He was hunted and stopped to rest at the Shrine of Oshikai; after that he was found and killed. Despite the most severe torture he refused to reveal the hiding place. I now believe they are hidden at the shrine."

"Then why have you not searched for them?"

"I think he placed them within the tomb of Oshikai Demon-bane. No Nadir may defile that sacred object. Only a . . . foreigner . . . would desecrate it."

"How much more are you concealing from me, little man?"

"A great deal," admitted Nosta. "But then, there is much that you do not need to know. The only truth that is of value to you is this: the jewels will save the life of your friend and return him to full health."

Sieben emerged from the water and padded across the hot stones to the shade. "Ah, made a friend, I see," he said as he sat beside the shaman. "I take it this is the old man who spoke to you in the tavern." Druss nodded, and Sieben extended his hand. "My name is Sieben. I am the poet. You may have heard of me."

"I have not heard of you," said Nosta, ignoring the outstretched hand.

"What a blow to one's vanity," said Sieben with an easy smile. "Do you have poets among the Nadir?"

"For what purpose?" asked the old man.

"Art, joy, entertainment . . ." Sieben hesitated as he saw the blank look of incomprehension on the old man's face.

"History!" he said suddenly. "How is your history retained among the tribe?"

"Each man is taught the history of his tribe by his mother and the history of his family by his father. And the tribe's shaman knows all their histories and the deeds of every Nadir hero."

"You have no art, no sculptors, actors, painters?"

Nosta Khan's coal-dark eyes glittered. "Three in five Nadir babies die in infancy. The average age of death among Nadir men is twenty-six. We live in a state of constant war, one with another, and in the meanwhile being hunted for sport by Gothir noblemen. Plague, pestilence, the constant threat of drought or famine—these are matters that concern the Nadir. We have no time for *art*." Nosta Khan spit out the last word as if the taste on his tongue were offensive.

"How excruciatingly dull," said Sieben. "I never felt sorry for your people until now. Excuse me while I water the horses."

Sieben rose and dressed. Nosta Khan swallowed his irritation and returned his gaze to Druss. "Are there many like him in the southlands?"

Druss smiled. "There are not many like him anywhere." Reaching into his pack, he produced a round of cheese wrapped in muslin and some dried beef. He offered a portion to Nosta Khan, who refused. Druss ate in silence. Sieben returned and joined him. When they had completed the meal, Druss yawned and stretched out in the shade; within moments he was asleep.

"Why do you travel with him?" Nosta Khan asked Sieben.

"For the adventure, old horse. Wherever Druss goes, one is sure to find adventure. And I like the idea of magical jewels. I'm sure there'll be a song or a story in it."

"On that we will agree," said Nosta Khan. "Even now two thousand Gothir warriors are being marshaled. Led by Gargan, Lord of Larness, they will march to the Shrine of Oshikai Demon-bane and lay siege to it with the intention of killing everyone there and taking the jewels as a gift to the madman who sits on the throne. You are riding into the eye of the hurricane, poet. Yes, I am sure there will be a song in it for you."

Nosta relished the fear that showed in the young man's soft eyes. Stretching his scrawny frame, he struggled to his feet and walked away from the pool. All was moving as he had planned, yet Nosta felt uneasy. Could Talisman marshal the Nadir troops to withstand Larness? Could he find the Eyes of Alchazzar? Closing his eyes, Nosta let his spirit fly to the east, soaring over the mountains and dry valleys. Far below he saw the shrine, its curved white walls shining like a ring of ivory. Beyond it were the tents of the Nadir guardians. Where are you, Talisman? he wondered.

Concentrating on the face of the young man, he allowed his spirit to drift down, drawn by the pull of Talisman's personality. Opening the eyes of his spirit, Nosta Khan saw the young Nadir warrior breasting the last rise before the valley. Behind him came the Chiatze woman Zhusai. Then a third rider came in sight, leading two ponies. Nosta was surprised. Floating above this stranger, he reached down, his spirit fingers touching the man's neck. The rider shivered and drew his heavy coat more closely about his powerful frame.

Satisfied, Nosta drew back. In the one instant of contact he had witnessed the attempted attack on Talisman and the girl and Gorkai's conversion to the cause of the Uniter. It was good; the boy had performed well. The gods of stone and water would be pleased.

Nosta flew on, hovering over the shrine. Once it had been a small supply fort, its walls boasting wooden parapets but no towers. Less than twenty feet high, they had been constructed to keep out marauding tribesmen, not two thousand trained soldiers. The west-facing gates were rotting on their hinges of bronze, while the west wall had crumbled at the center, leaving a pile of rubble below a V-shaped crack.

Fear touched Nosta Khan with fingers of dread.

Could they hold against Gothir guards?

And what of Druss? What role would the axman play? It was galling to see so much yet know so little. Was his purpose to stand, ax in hand, upon the walls? In that moment a fleeting vision flickered in his mind: a white-haired warrior standing on a colossal wall, his ax raised in defiance. As suddenly as it had come, it faded away.

Returning to his body, Nosta took a deep, shuddering breath.

By the pool the poet was sleeping alongside the giant axman. Nosta sighed and walked away into the east.

Talisman sat on the highest wall, staring out over the Valley of Shul-sen's Tears. The sun was bright, yet a light breeze was blowing, robbing the heat of its withering power. In the distance the mountains looked like banks of dark storm clouds hugging the horizon, and overhead two eagles were circling on the thermals. Talisman's dark eyes scanned the valley. From this southern wall of Oshikai's resting place he could see two camps. At the first a long horsehair standard bearing the skull and horns of a wild ox was planted before the largest tent. The thirty warriors of the Curved Horn tribe were sitting in the fading sunshine cooking their evening meals. Three hundred paces to the west was a second series of goathide tents; the standard of the Fleet Ponies was pitched there.

Out of sight on the northern side of the shrine were two more camps, of the Lone Wolves and the Sky Riders, each guarding a compass point near the resting place of the greatest Nadir warrior. The breeze died away, and Talisman strolled down the rickety wooden steps to the courtyard, making his way to a table near the well. From there he could see where the west wall had crumbled away at the center. Through the jagged hole he could just make out the distant tree line of the western hills.

This place is rotting away, he thought, just like the dreams of the man whose bones lie here. Talisman was fighting to control a cold, gnawing anger deep in his belly. They had arrived the previous night just in time to witness a sword duel between two Nadir warriors, that had ended in the sudden and bloody disemboweling of a young man from the Fleet Ponies tribe. The victor, a lean warrior wearing the white fur wrist ring of the Sky Riders, leapt upon the dying man, plunging his sword into his victim's neck, seesawing the blade through the vertebrae, tearing the head from the shoulders. Blood-drenched, he had surged to his feet, screaming his triumph.

Talisman had heeled his pony on through the gates. Leaving Gorkai to tend the mounts, he had walked across the courtyard to stand before the shrine entrance.

But he did not enter; he could not enter. Talisman's mouth was dry, his stomach knotted with fear. Out there in the bright moonlight his dreams were solid, his confidence unshakable. Once through that door, however, they could disappear like wood smoke.

Calm yourself! The shrine has been plundered before. The eyes will be hidden. Step inside and pay homage to the spirit of the hero.

Taking a deep breath, he moved forward and pushed open the ancient wooden door. The dust-covered room was no more than thirty feet long and twenty feet wide. Wooden pegs were hammered into the walls, but nothing hung from them now. Once Oshikai's armor had been displayed there, his breastplate and helm, and Kolmisai, the single-bladed hand ax that had felled a hundred foes. There had been tapestries and mosaics detailing his life and his victories. Now there were only bare and empty walls. The shrine had been ransacked hundreds of years ago. They had, so Nosta Khan had informed him, even opened the coffin and torn off the fingers of the corpse to get the golden rings worn by Oshikai. The chamber was bleak, the stone coffin resting on a raised platform at the center. The coffin itself was unadorned except for a square of black iron set into the stone. Upon it, in raised letters, were the words

Talisman laid his hand on the cold stone of the coffin lid. "I live," he said aloud, "to see your dreams return. We will be united again. We will be Nadir, and the world will tremble."

"Why do the dreams of men always lead to war?" asked a voice. Talisman spun to see that sitting in the shadows was an old blind man wearing a gray robe and cowl. He was stick-thin and hairless. Taking hold of his staff, he levered himself to his feet and approached Talisman. "You know," he said, "I have studied the life of Oshikai, sifting through the legends and the myths. He never wanted war. Always it was thrust upon him. That was when he became a terrible enemy. The dreams you speak of were mostly of finding a land of promise and plenty where his people could grow in peace. He was a great man."

"Who are you?" asked Talisman.

"I am a priest of the Source." As the man stepped into the beam of moonlight coming through the open western window, Talisman saw that he was Nadir. "I live here now, writing my histories."

"How does a blind man write?"

"Only the eyes of my body are blind, Talisman. When I write, I use the eyes of my spirit."

Talisman shivered as the man spoke his name. "You are a shaman?"

The priest shook his head. "I understand the way, though my own path is different. I cast no spells, Talisman, though I can heal warts and read the hearts of men. Sadly, I cannot alter them. I can walk the paths of the many futures but do not know which will come to pass. If I could, I would open this coffin and raise the man within. But I cannot."

"How is it that you know my name?"

"Why should I not? You are the flaming arrow, the messenger."

"You know why I am here," said Talisman, his voice dropping to a whisper.

"Of course. You are seeking the Eyes of Alchazzar, hidden here so many years ago."

Talisman fingered the dagger at his belt and silently drew it. "You have found them?"

"I know they are here. But they were not left for me to find. I write history, Talisman; it is not for me to create it. May the Source give you wisdom."

The old man turned away and walked to the sunlit doorway, where he stood for a moment, as if waiting. Then his voice sounded once more. "In at least three of the futures I have seen, you struck me down as I stood here, your dagger deep in my back. Why did you not do so in this one?"

"I considered it, old man."

"Had you committed the deed, you would have been dragged from this chamber, your arms and legs tied with ropes attached to the saddles of four ponies. You would have been ripped apart, Talisman. That also happened."

"Obviously it did not, for you still live."

"It happened somewhere," said the old man. Then he was gone.

Talisman followed him into the light, but he had vanished into one of the buildings. Seeing Gorkai drawing water from the well, he strolled across to him. "Where is Zhusai?"

"The woman sleeps," said Gorkai. "It looks as if there will be another fight today. The head of the boy who was killed now sits atop a pole at the Sky Rider camp. His comrades are determined to punish this insult."

"Stupidity," said Talisman.

"It seems to be in our blood. Maybe the gods cursed us."

Talisman nodded. "The curse came when the Eyes of Alchazzar were stolen. When they are returned to the stone wolf, we shall see a new day."

"You believe this?"

"A man must believe in something, Gorkai. Otherwise we are merely shifting grains of sand, blown by the wind. The

Nadir number in the hundreds of thousands, perhaps in the millions, yet we live in squalor. All around us there is wealth, controlled by nations whose armies do not exceed twenty thousand men. Even here the four tribes guarding the shrine cannot live in peace. Their purpose is identical—the shrine they protect is of a man who is a hero to all Nadir—yet they stare at each other with undisguised hatred. I believe that will change. We will change it."

"Just you and I?" Gorkai asked softly.

"Why not?"

"I have still seen no man with violet eyes," said Gorkai.

"You will. I swear it."

When Druss awoke, Nosta Khan had gone. It was approaching dusk, and Sieben was sitting by the poolside, his naked feet resting in the cool water. Druss yawned and stretched. Rising, he stripped off his jerkin, boots, and leggings and leapt into the pool, where the water was welcomingly cool. Refreshed, he climbed out and sat beside the poet. "When did the little man leave?" he asked.

"Soon after you fell asleep," Sieben told him, his voice flat.

Druss looked into his friend's face and saw the lines of tension there. "You are concerned about the two thousand warriors heading for the shrine?"

Sieben bit back an angry retort. " 'Concerned' does not quite cover it, old horse. I see it doesn't surprise you, though."

Druss shook his head. "He told me he was repaying a debt because I helped his young friend. That is not the Nadir way. No, he wanted me at the shrine because he knew there would be a battle."

"Oh, I see, and the mighty Druss the Legend will turn the tide, I suppose."

Druss chuckled. "Perhaps he will, poet. Perhaps he will not. Whatever the answer, the only way I'll find the jewels is if I go there."

"And what if there are no magical jewels? Suppose he lied about that also?"

"Then Klay will die, and I will have done my best."

"It is all so simple for you, isn't it?" stormed Sieben. "Black and white, light and dark, pure and evil? Two thousand warriors are going to ransack that shrine. You won't stop them. And why should you even try? What is it about Klay that has touched you so? Other men have suffered grievous wounds before now. You have seen comrades cut down beside you for years."

Druss stood and dressed, then wandered to the horses and unhooked a sack of grain from the saddle pommel. From his pack he took two feed bags and looped them over the ears of the mounts. Sieben joined him. "They say a grain-fed horse will outrun anything fed on grass," said Druss. "You are a horseman. Is that true?"

"Come on, Druss, answer my question, damn you! Why Klay?"

"He reminds me of a man I never knew," answered Druss.

"Never knew! What does that mean?"

"It means that I must try to find the jewels, and I don't give a damn about two thousand Gothir whoresons or the entire Nadir nation. Leave it there, poet!"

The clatter of hooves sounded on the trail, and both men swung toward the source of the noise. Six Nadir warriors riding in single file approached the pool. They were dressed in goatskin tunics and wore fur-rimmed helms. Each carried a bow and two short swords. "What do we do?" whispered Sieben.

"Nothing. Water holes are sacred places, and no Nadir will fight a battle at one. They'll merely water their horses, then leave."

"Then what?"

"Then they'll try to kill us. But that is a problem for another time. Relax, poet. You wanted adventure. Now you'll have it."

Druss strolled back to the shade and sat down beside the

fearsome ax. The Nadir affected to ignore him, but Sieben could see them cast furtive glances in his direction. Finally the leader—a middle-aged stocky warrior with a thin, wispy beard—came and sat opposite him.

"You are far from home," he said, speaking haltingly in the southern tongue.

"Yet I am at ease," replied Druss.

"The dove is rarely at ease in the home of the hawk."

"I am not a dove, laddie. And you are no hawk."

The man rose. "I think we will meet again, roundeye." He strolled back to his companions, vaulted to the saddle, and led the riders on toward the east.

Sieben sat down beside Druss. "Oh, well done, old horse. Always best to appease an enemy who outnumbers you three to one."

"There was no point. He knows what he must do. As do I. You wait here with the horses; get them saddled and ready."

"Where are you going?"

"East a little way. I want to see what sort of trap they will set."

"Is this wise, Druss? There are six of them."

Druss grinned. "You think it would make it fairer if I left my ax behind?" With that he gathered up Snaga and set off up and over the rocks. Sieben watched him go, then settled down to wait. Darkness came swiftly in the mountains, and he wished he had thought to gather deadwood back along the trail. A fire would be a welcome friend in this desolate place. The moon was bright, however, and Sieben wrapped himself in his blanket and sat deep in the shadows of the rock wall. Never again, he thought. From now on I'll welcome boredom with open arms and a mighty hug!

What was it Druss had said about Klay? *He reminds me of a man I never knew?* Suddenly it came clear to Sieben. Druss was speaking of Michanek, the man who had loved and wed Rowena back in Ventria. Like Druss, Michanek had been a mighty warrior and a champion among the rebels opposed to

Prince Gorben. And Rowena, robbed of her memory, had grown to love him, had even attempted suicide when she had learned of his death. Druss had been there as Michanek faced the elite of Gorben's Immortals. Alone he had killed many, until at last even Michanek's prodigious strength had failed him, sapped from his body in the gushing of blood from a score of wounds. As he died, he asked Druss to look after Rowena.

Once, when visiting Druss and his lady at their farm in the mountains, Sieben had walked with Rowena across the high meadow. He had asked her then about Michanek, and she had smiled fondly. "He was like Druss in many ways but he was also gentle and kind. I did love him, Sieben, and I know Druss finds that hard to bear. But they took my memory from me. I did not know who I was and remembered nothing of Druss. All I knew was that this huge man loved me and cared for me. And it still saddens me to know that Druss had a part in his death."

"He didn't know Michanek," Sieben had said. "All he had dreamed of through those long years was finding you and bringing you home."

"I know."

"Given the choice between the two men, who would you have chosen?" Sieben had asked suddenly.

"That is a question I never ask myself," she had told him. "I merely know that I was fortunate to be loved by, and to love, both of them."

Sieben had wanted to ask more, but she had touched a finger to his lips. "Enough, poet! Let us go back to the house."

A cold wind blew around the rock pool now, and Sieben wrapped his cloak more tightly about him. There was no sound except for the wind whistling through the rocks, and Sieben felt terribly alone. Time passed with a mind-numbing lack of speed, and the poet dozed several times, always waking with a start, terrified that hidden Nadir assassins were creeping up on him.

Just before the dawn, with the sky brightening, he heard the sound of hooves on stone. Scrambling to his feet, he drew one of his knives, dropped it, gathered it, and stood waiting. Druss came into sight leading four Nadir ponies, and Sieben walked out to meet him. There was blood on Druss' jerkin and leggings. "Are you hurt?" asked Sieben.

"No, poet. The way is now clear, and we have four ponies to trade."

"Two of the Nadir got away?"

Druss shook his head. "Not the Nadir, but two of the ponies broke loose and ran off."

"You killed all six?"

"Five. One fell from the cliff as I was chasing him. Now, let us be moving on."

⋄ **6** ⋄

**J**UST BEFORE MIDNIGHT Talisman entered the tomb of Oshikai Demon-bane. While Gorkai stood guard outside the door, the Nadir warrior crept inside and placed four small pouches on the ground before the coffin. From the first he poured a small amount of red powder; then, with his index finger, he formed it into a circle no bigger than his palm. Faint moonlight shin- ing through the open window made his task more easy. From the second pouch he took three long dried leaves, which he rolled into a ball and placed in his mouth, under his tongue. The taste was bitter, and he almost gagged. Taking a tinder- box from the pocket of his goatskin tunic, he struck a flame and held it to the red powder, which flared instantly with a crimson light. Smoke billowed up. Talisman breathed it in, then swal- lowed the ball of leaves.

He felt faint and dizzy, and as if from a great distance he heard the sound of soft music, then a sigh. His vision blurred, then cleared. Upon the walls of the shrine there were flickering lights that made his eyes water. He rubbed them with finger and thumb and looked again. Shimmering in place beneath the pegs on the wall was the armor of Oshikai Demon-bane: the breast- plate with its 110 leaves of hammered gold, the winged helm of black iron set with silver runes, and the dread ax Kolmisai. Tal- isman slowly scanned the chamber. Beautiful tapestries deco- rated the walls, each showing an incident from the life of Oshikai: the hunt for the black lion, the razing of Chien-Po, the flight over the mountains, the wedding to Shul-sen. The last tapestry was a spectacular piece, showing a host of ravens carrying the bride to the altar while Oshikai stood waiting with two demons beside him.

Talisman blinked and battled to hold his concentration against the waves of narcotics coursing through his blood. From the third pouch he took a ring of gold, and from the fourth a small finger bone. As Nosta Khan had commanded, he slid the ring over the bone and placed it before him. With his dagger he made a narrow cut in his left forearm, allowing the blood to drip onto the bone and the ring. "I call to thee, Lord of War," he said. "I humbly ask for your presence."

At first there was nothing, then a cool breeze seemed to blow across the chamber, though not a mote of dust was disturbed. A figure began to materialize over the coffin. The armor of gold flowed over him, the ax floating down to rest in his right hand. Talisman almost ceased to breathe as the spirit descended to sit cross-legged opposite him. Though broad of shoulder, Oshikai was not huge, as Talisman had expected. His face was flat and hard, the nose broad, the nostrils flared. He wore his hair tied back in a tight ponytail, and he sported no beard or mustache. His violet eyes glowed with power, and he radiated strength of purpose.

"Who calls Oshikai?" asked the translucent figure.

"I, Talisman of the Nadir."

"Do you bring news of Shul-sen?"

The question was unexpected, and Talisman faltered. "I . . . I know nothing of her, lord, save legends and stories. Some say she died soon after you, others that she crossed the oceans to a world without darkness."

"I have searched the Vales of Spirit, the Valleys of the Damned, the Fields of Heroes, the Halls of the Mighty. I have crossed the Void for time without reckoning. I cannot find her."

"I am here, lord, to see your dreams return to life," said Talisman, as Nosta Khan had ordered. Oshikai seemed not to hear him. "The Nadir need to be united," continued Talisman. "To do this we must find the violet-eyed leader, but we do not know where to look."

The spirit of Oshikai gazed at Talisman, then sighed. "He will be found when the Eyes of Alchazzar are set in their rightful sockets. The magic will flow back into the land, and then he will be revealed."

"I seek the eyes, lord," said Talisman. "They are said to be hidden here. Is this true?"

"Aye, it is true. They are close by, Talisman of the Nadir. But you are not destined to find them."

"Then who, lord?"

"A foreigner will take them. More than this I will not tell you."

"And the Uniter, lord. Can you not tell me his name?"

"His name will be Ulric. Now I must go. I must keep searching."

"Why do you search, lord? Is there no paradise for you?"

The spirit stared at him. "What paradise could there be without Shul-sen? Death I could bear, but not this parting of souls. I will find her though it take a dozen eternities. Fare you well, Talisman of the Nadir."

Before Talisman could speak the figure was gone. The young Nadir warrior rose unsteadily and backed to the door.

Gorkai was waiting in the moonlight. "What happened in there? I heard you speak, but there was no answer."

"He came, but he could not help me. He was a soul in torment, seeking his wife."

"The witch Shul-sen. They say she was burned alive, her ashes scattered to the four winds and her spirit destroyed by sorcery."

"I have never heard that story," said Talisman. "Among others we were taught that she crossed the sea to a land where there was no nightfall, and there she lives forever in the hope that Oshikai will find her."

"It is a prettier tale," admitted Gorkai, "and both would

explain why the lord of war cannot find her. What will we do now?"

"We will see what tomorrow brings," said Talisman, striding off to the rooms Gorkai had found for them. There were thirty small chambers set within the main building, all constructed for the use of pilgrims. Zhusai had spread her blankets on the floor beneath the window and pretended to be asleep as Talisman entered. He did not go to her but pulled up a chair and sat staring out at the stars.

Unable to bear the silence any longer, she spoke. "Did the spirit not come to you?" she asked.

"Aye, he came." Slowly he told her the full story of Oshikai's search for Shul-sen and the two legends that told of her passing.

Zhusai sat up, holding the blanket around her. "There are other stories of Shul-sen—that she was thrown from a cliff high on the Mountains of the Moon, that she committed suicide, that she was turned into a tree. Every tribe has a different tale. But it is sad that he cannot find her."

"More than sad," said Talisman. "He said that without her there could be no paradise."

"How beautiful," she said. "But then, he was Chiatze, and we are a people who understand sensitivity."

"I have found in my life that people who boast of their sensitivity are sensitive only to their own needs and utterly indifferent to the needs of others. However, I am in no mood to argue the point." Taking up his blanket, he lay down beside her and slept. His dreams, as always, were filled with pain.

The lash cut deeply into his back, but he did not cry out. He was Nadir, and no matter how great the pain, he would never show his suffering to these *gajin*, these round-eyed foreigners. The whip he had been forced to make himself, the leather wound tightly around a wooden handle and then sliced into thin strips, each tipped with a small pellet of lead. Okai counted each stroke to the prescribed fifteen. As the last slashing swipe lanced across his bleeding back, he allowed himself to slump forward against the stake. "Give him five more," came the voice of Gargan.

"That would exceed the regulations, my lord," answered Premian. "He has received the maximum allowed for a cadet of fifteen." Okai could scarcely believe that Premian had spoken up for him. The house prefect had always made clear his loathing of the Nadir boys.

Gargan spoke again. "That regulation is for human beings, Premian, not Nadir filth. As you can see, he has not suffered at all. Not a sound has he made. Where there is no sense, there is no feeling. Five more!"

"I cannot obey you, my lord."

"You are stripped of your rank, Premian. I had thought better of you."

"And I of you, Lord Gargan." Okai heard the lash fall to the floor. "If one more blow is laid upon this young man's back, I shall report the incident to my father at the palace. Fifteen strokes was bad enough for a misdemeanor. Twenty would be savage beyond belief."

"Be silent!" thundered Gargan. "One more word and you will suffer a similar punishment and face expulsion from this academy. I'll not tolerate disobedience or insubordination. You!" he said, pointing at a boy Okai could not see. "Five more lashes if you please."

Okai heard the whisper of the lash being swept up from the floor and tried to brace himself. Only when the first blow fell did he realize that Premian had been holding back. Whoever now held the lash was laying it on with a vengeance. At the third stroke a groan was torn from him that shamed him even more than the punishment, but he bit down hard on the leather belt between his teeth and made no further sound. Blood was running freely down his back now, pooling above the belt of his leggings. At the fifth stroke a great silence fell upon the hall. Gargan broke it. "Now, Premian, you may go and write to your father. Cut this piece of offal down."

Three Nadir boys ran forward, untying the ropes that bound Okai. Even as he fell into their arms, he swung to see who had wielded the whip, and his heart sank. It was Dalsh-chin of the Fleet Ponies tribe.

His friends half carried him to the infirmary, where an orderly applied salve to his back and inserted three stitches into a deeper cut on his shoulder.

Dalsh-chin entered and stood before him. "You did well, Okai," he said, speaking in the Nadir tongue. "My heart swelled with pride for you."

"Why, then, did you make me cry out before the *gajin*?"

"Because he would have ordered five more had you not, and five more still. It was a test of will and one that might have killed you."

"You stop talking in that filthy language," said the orderly. "You know it is against the rules, and I won't have it!"

Dalsh-chin nodded, then reached out and laid his hand on Okai's head. "You have a brave heart, young one," he said in the southern tongue. Then he turned and strode from the room.

"Twenty lashes for defending yourself," said his closest friend, Zhen-shi. "That was not just."

"You cannot expect justice from *gajin*," Okai told him. "Only pain."

"They have stopped hurting me," said Zhen-shi. "Perhaps it will be better for all of us from now on."

Okai said nothing, knowing that they had stopped hurting his friend because Zhen-shi ran errands for them, cleaned their boots, bowed and scraped, acted like a slave. As they mocked him, he would smile and bob his head. It saddened Okai, but there was little he could do. Every man had to make his own choices. His own was to resist them in every way yet learn all they could teach. Zhen-shi did not have the strength for that course; he was soft and remarkably gentle for a Nadir boy.

After a short rest in the infirmary, Okai walked unaided to the room he shared with Lin-tse. From the Sky Rider tribe, Lin-tse was taller than most Nadir youths, his face square and his eyes barely slanted. It was rumored that he had *gajin* blood, but no one said that to his face. Lin-tse was short of temper and long on remembered wrongs.

He stood as Okai entered. "I have brought you food and drink, Okai," he said. "And some mountain honey for the wounds upon your back."

"I thank you, Brother," Okai replied formally.

"Our tribes are at war," said Lin-tse, "and therefore we cannot be brothers. But I respect your courage." He bowed, then returned to his studies.

Okai lay facedown on the narrow pallet bed and tried to block the hot pain that flowed from his lacerated back. "Our tribes are at war *now*," he said, "but one day we will be brothers, and the Nadir will sweep down on these *gajin* and wipe them from the face of the earth."

"May it be so," responded Lin-tse. "You have an examination tomorrow, do you not?"

"Yes. The role of cavalry in punitive expeditions."

"Then I shall question you on the subject. It will help shield your mind from the pain you are suffering."

Talisman awoke just before dawn. Zhusai still slept as he silently rose and left the room. In the courtyard below, the blind Nadir priest was drawing water from the well. In the half light of the predawn the man looked younger, his face pale and serene. "I trust you slept well, Talisman?" he inquired as the Nadir approached.

"Well enough."

"And were the dreams the same?"

"My dreams are my concern, old man, and should you wish to live to complete your history, you would be advised to remember my words."

The priest laid down the bucket and sat on the lip of the well, his pale opal eyes glinting in the last of the moonlight. "Dreams are never secret, Talisman, no matter how hard we try to protect them. They are like regrets, always seeking the light, always shared. And they have meaning far beyond our understanding. You will see. Here in this place the circle will be complete."

The priest carried the bucket to a nearby table and with a copper ladle slowly began to fill clay water pots that hung on slender ropes from the beams of the porch.

Talisman walked to the table and sat. "What are these histories you write?" he asked.

"They mostly involve the Chiatze and the Nadir. But I have become fascinated by the life of Oshikai. Do you know the origin of the name *'Nadir'*?"

Talisman shrugged. "In the southern tongue it means 'the point of greatest hopelessness.' "

"In Chiatze it means 'the crossroads of death,' " said the priest. "When Oshikai first led his people out of Chiatze lands, a great army followed them, seeking to exterminate what they perceived as his rebel force. He met them on the plain of Chu-chien and destroyed them. But two more armies were closing in on him, and he was forced to lead his people across the Ice Mountains. Hundreds died, and many more lost fingers and toes, arms and legs, to the terrible cold. As they cleared the frozen passes, they emerged onto the terrible desert of salt beyond. The despair was almost total. Oshikai called a meeting of his council. He told them that they were a people born in hardship and danger and that they had now reached their nadir. From that moment he changed their name. Then he addressed the multitude and told them that Shul-sen would lead them to water and that a land full of promise would await them beyond the salt desert. He spoke of a dream where the Nadir grew and prospered from shimmering sea to snow-topped peaks. That is when he gave them the verse all Nadir children learn as they suck their mothers' milk:

*Nadir we,*
*youth born,*
*ax wielders,*
*bloodletters,*
*victors still.*

"What happened to Shul-sen?" asked Talisman.

The priest smiled as, laying down his bucket once more, he sat at the table. "There are so many tales, most embroidered upon, some mere fancy, others crafted with such mystical symbolism that they become meaningless. The truth, I fear, is more mundane. It is my belief that she was captured by Oshikai's enemies and slain."

"If that were so, he would have found her."

"Who would have found her?"

"Oshikai. His spirit has searched for her for hundreds of years, but he has never found her. How could that be?"

"I do not know," admitted the priest, "but I will think on it. How is it you know these things?"

"Accept merely that I know," answered Talisman.

"We Nadir are a secretive people and yet also curious," said the priest with a smile. "I will return to my studies and consider the question you pose me."

"You claim to walk the many paths of the future," said Talisman. "Why can you not walk the single path of the past and see for yourself?"

"A good question, young man. The answer is simple. A true historian must remain objective. Anyone who witnesses a great event immediately forms a subjective view of it, for it has affected him. Yes, I could go back and observe, yet I will not."

"Your logic is flawed, priest. If the historian cannot observe events, he must then rely on the witness of others who, by your own words, can offer only a subjective view."

The priest laughed aloud and clapped his hands together. "Ah, my boy! If only we had more time to talk. We could debate the hidden circle of deceit in the search for altruism or the lack of evidence for the nonexistence of a supreme being." His smile faded. "But we do not have the time."

The priest returned the bucket to the well and walked away. Talisman leaned back and watched the majesty of the dawn sun rising above the eastern peaks.

Quing-chin emerged from his tent and into the sunlight. A tall man with deep-set eyes and a solemn face, he stood enjoying the warmth of the sun on his face. He had slept without dreams and had woken feeling refreshed and ready for the sweet taste of revenge, his anger of the previous day replaced by a cold, resolute sense of purpose. His men were seated in a circle nearby. Quing-chin lifted his powerful arms above his head and slowly stretched the muscles of his upper back. His friend Shi-da rose from the circle and brought him his sword. "It is sharp now, comrade," said the smaller man, "and ready to slice the flesh of the enemy." The other six men in the circle rose. None were as tall as Quing-chin.

The sword brother of Shanqui, the warrior slain by the Sky Rider champion, moved before Quing-chin. "The soul of Shanqui waits for vengeance," he said formally.

"I shall send him a servant to tend his needs," quoted Quing-chin.

A young warrior approached the men, leading a dappled pony. Quing-chin took the reins from him and swung into the saddle. Shi-da handed him his long lance decorated with the dark double twist of horsehair that denoted a blooded warrior of the Fleet Ponies and a black helm of lacquered wood rimmed with fur. Pushing back his shoulder-length dark hair, Quing-chin donned the helm. Then, touching heels to the pony's flanks, he rode from the camp and out past the white walls of Oshikai's resting place.

Men were already moving around the camp of the Sky Riders, setting their cook fires, as Quing-chin rode in. He ignored them all and headed his pony toward the farthest of the eighteen tents. Outside the entrance a lance had been plunged into the ground, and set atop the weapon was the head of Shanqui. Blood had dripped to the ground below it, and the flesh on the dead face was ashen gray.

"Come forth," called Quing-chin. The tent flap was pulled open, and a squat warrior stepped into view. Ignoring Quing-chin, he opened his breeches and emptied his bladder on the ground. Then he looked up at the severed head.

"Here to admire my tree?" he asked. "See, it is blooming already." Most of the Sky Riders had gathered around the two men now, and they began to laugh. Quing-chin waited until the sound had died down. When he spoke, his voice was cold and harsh.

"It is perfect," said Quing-chin. "Only a Sky Rider tree would have rotting fruit on it."

"Ha! This tree will have fresh fruit today. So sad you will not be able to admire it."

"Ah, but I shall. I will tend it myself. And now the time for talk is past. I shall await you in the open, where the air is not filled with the stench of your camp."

Tugging on the reins, Quing-chin galloped his pony some two hundred paces to the north. The twenty-eight warriors of the Fleet Ponies had already gathered there, sitting their mounts in silence. Within moments the thirty Sky Riders rode out, forming a line opposite Quing-chin and his men.

The squat Sky Rider, long lance in hand, heeled his pony forward, then swung to the right and galloped some fifty yards before savagely hauling on the reins. Quing-chin rode his pony between the lines of the two tribes, then turned and raised his lance. The squat warrior leveled his lance and kicked his mount into a run, charging at Quing-chin. The Fleet Ponies' leader remained motionless as his opponent closed the gap between them. Closer and closer came the Sky Rider, until at the last possible moment Quing-chin jerked the reins and barked out a command. His pony bunched its muscles and sprang to the right. In the same heartbeat Quing-chin lifted his lance over his pony's head and rammed it to the left. The move was intended to spear the opposing rider through the side and belly, but the Sky Rider had dragged back on his reins more swiftly than Quing-chin had anticipated, and the lance slammed into the neck of his opponent's pony, which stumbled and fell, dragging Quing-chin's lance from his hand. The Sky Rider was thrown clear and spun in the air to land heavily on his back. Quing-chin leapt from his mount and ran forward, drawing his sword. The Sky Rider rolled to his feet, still groggy from the fall, but even so he drew his blade and blocked the first cut. Quing-chin closed in, his left foot lashing out into the Sky Rider's unprotected knee. The Sky Rider jumped back and half fell. Quing-chin followed him, sending his sword in a vicious cut that ripped open the other man's jerkin and sliced up across his left cheek, tearing the flesh and sending a spray of blood into the air. The Sky Rider screamed in pain and attacked. Quing-chin blocked a belly thrust, spun on his heel, and hammered his left elbow into the Sky Rider's blood-covered face. The man was hurled from his feet, but he scrambled up as Quing-chin closed in; he was fast and sent a lightning thrust at Quing-chin's face. The taller man swayed aside, the blade slicing his earlobe. His sword flashed out in a neck cut that was too low, the blade slicing into the Sky Rider's left shoulder. The squat warrior stumbled forward but swung just in time to block a second blow aimed at his neck. The two warriors circled each other more warily, respect growing between them. Quing-chin had been surprised by the man's speed, and the Sky Rider, blood pouring from the wounds to his shoulder and face, knew he was in desperate trouble.

Quing-chin darted forward to feint a cut to the throat. The Sky Rider's sword swept across to block, but his speed betrayed him. The block was too fast. Quing-chin's blade plunged into the man's upper chest, but at the moment of impact the Sky

Rider hurled himself backward so that Quing-chin's sword penetrated no more than two inches before the blade was ripped clear. The Sky Rider fell, rolled, and staggered to his feet.

"You are very skilled," he said. "I shall be proud to add your head to my tree." His left arm was hanging uselessly, blood streaming over his hand and dripping to the ground. In that instant Quing-chin experienced a moment of regret. Shanqui had been an arrogant, boastful young man who had challenged this warrior and had died for it. And now, according to Nadir custom, Quing-chin would send this man's soul to serve him for eternity. He sighed.

"I, too, feel pride," he said. "You are a man among men. I salute you, Sky Rider."

The Sky Rider nodded and then ran forward into the attack. Quing-chin swayed aside from the desperate thrust, slamming his blade into the man's belly and up through the heart. The Sky Rider fell against him, his head falling to Quing-chin's shoulder as his knees gave way. Quing-chin caught him as he fell and lowered him to the ground. With a shuddering sigh the Sky Rider died.

This was the moment. Kneeling beside the body, Quing-chin drew his knife. The two lines of riders waited, but Quing-chin rose. "I will not take this man's eyes," he said. "Let his friends bear him away for burial."

Shi-da leapt from his pony and ran to him. "You must, Brother! Shanqui must have the eyes in his hand or he will have no servant in the netherworld!"

A Sky Rider nudged his pony forward, then dismounted alongside Quing-chin. "You fought well, Dalsh-chin," he said.

The Fleet Ponies warrior turned at the sound of his childhood name and looked into the sorrowful eyes of the Sky Rider. Lintse had changed little in the two years since they had left the Bodacas Academy; he was broader in the shoulder, and his head had been shaved clean except for a short braid of dark hair at the crown. "It is good to see you again, Lin-tse," he said. "It saddens me that it should be on such an occasion."

"You talk like a Gothir," said Lin-tse. "Tomorrow I will come to your camp. And when I have killed you, I will take your eyes and give them to my brother. You will serve him until the stars are ground to dust."

Back at his own tent Quing-chin stripped off his bloodstained jerkin and knelt on the ground. In the two years since he had left the Bodacas Academy he had fought to reestablish his Nadir roots, aware that his own people felt he was somehow tainted by his years among the Gothir. He had denied it even to himself, but today he knew that it was true.

Outside he heard the riders returning with the head of Shanqui, but he remained in the tent, his thoughts somber. The rituals of the revenge duel differed from tribe to tribe, but the principles remained the same. If he had cut out the eyes of the Sky Rider and placed them in the dead hand of Shanqui, the spirit of the Sky Rider would have been bonded to Shanqui for eternity. The belief was that the Sky Rider would be blind in the Void unless Shanqui lent him the use of his eyes. This would ensure obedience. Now Quing-chin had broken the ritual. And to what purpose? Tomorrow he must fight again. If he won, another warrior would challenge him.

His friend Shi-da entered the tent and squatted down before him. "You fought bravely," said Shi-da. "It was a good fight. But tomorrow you must take the eyes."

"The eyes of Lin-tse," whispered Quing-chin. "The eyes of one who was my friend? I cannot do this."

"What is wrong with you, my brother? These are our enemies!"

Quing-chin rose. "I shall go to the shrine. I need to think."

Leaving Shi-da, he ducked under the tent flap and stepped out into the sunshine. The body of Shanqui, wrapped in hide, had been left within yards of his tent. The right hand of the corpse had been left exposed, the fingers clawed and open. Striding to his dappled pony, Quing-chin mounted and rode to the white-walled shrine.

In what way did they poison my Nadir spirit? he wondered. Was it the books, the manuscripts, the paintings? Or perhaps the teachings concerning morality or the endless discussions of philosophy? How can I know?

The gates were open, and Quing-chin rode inside and dismounted. Leaving his pony in the shade, he strode toward the shrine.

"We shall make them suffer as Zhen-shi suffered," said a voice. Quing-chin froze. Slowly he turned toward the speaker.

Talisman stepped from the shadows and approached the taller man. "It is good to see you again, my friend," he said.

Quing-chin said nothing for a moment, then he gripped Talisman's outstretched hand. "You gladden my heart, Okai. All is well with you?"

"Well enough. Come, share water and bread with me."

The two men strolled back to the shade, where they sat beneath a wooden awning. Filling two clay cups with cool water from a stone jug, Talisman passed one to Quing-chin. "What happened in the fight this morning?" he asked. "There was so much dust, I could see nothing from the walls."

"A Sky Rider died," said Quing-chin.

"When will such madness end?" Talisman asked sadly. "When will our eyes be opened to the real enemy?"

"Not soon enough, Okai. Tomorrow I fight again." He looked into Talisman's eyes. "Against Lin-tse."

Lin-tse sat on a rock sharpening his sword, his face impassive and his anger masked. Of all the men in the world, the last he wished to kill was Dalsh-chin. Yet such was his fate, and a true man never whined when the gods of stone and water twisted the knife. The whetstone slid along the saber's edge, and Lin-tse imagined the silver steel blade slicing through

Dalsh-chin's neck. He swore softly, then stood and stretched his back.

At the last there had been only four Nadir janizaries at the academy: himself, Dalsh-chin, the miserable Green Monkey boy Zhen-shi, and the strange one from the Wolfshead, Okai. Some of the others had fled; most had simply failed their examinations miserably, much to the delight of Gargan, Lord Larness. One had been hanged after killing an officer; another had committed suicide. The experiment—as Lord Larness had intended—had been a failure. Yet much to the Gothir general's chagrin four Nadir youngsters had consistently passed the examinations. And one—Okai—excelled above all other students, including the general's own son, Argo.

Lin-tse scabbarded his sword and walked out onto the steppes. His thoughts turned to Zhen-shi, with his frightened eyes and his nervous smile. Tormented and abused, he had fawned around the Gothir cadets, especially Argo, serving him like a slave. "Grinning Monkey," Argo had called him, and Lin-tse had despised the youth for his cowardice. Zhen-shi carried few scars, but then, he was everything the Gothir boys had been taught to expect of a barbarian: subservient and inferior to the civilized races.

Yet he had made a mistake, and it had cost him his life. In the end-of-year examinations he had outscored all but Okai. Lin-tse still remembered the look on Zhen-shi's face when the results were announced. At first his delight was obvious, but then, as he gazed at Argo and the others, the full horror of his plight dawned on him. Grinning Monkey had beaten them all. No longer did they see him as an object of scorn or derision. Now he had become a figure of hate. Little Zhen-shi had withered under their malevolent gazes.

That night Zhen-shi had plunged from the roof, his body crushed to pulp on the snow-covered cobbles below.

It was winter, the night harsh and cold, ice forming on the insides of the glass windows. Yet Zhen-shi had been dressed only in a loincloth. Hearing the scream as he fell, Lin-tse had looked out of the window and saw his scrawny body leaking blood onto the snow. He and Okai had run out with scores of other boys and had stood over the corpse. The body bore the red weals of a lash on the back, buttocks, and thighs. The wrists were also bleeding.

"He was tied," said Lin-tse. Okai did not answer; he was staring up at the gable from which Zhen-shi had fallen. The rooms on that top level were reserved for the senior cadets from noble families. But the nearest window was that of Argo. Lin-tse followed Okai's gaze. The blond-haired son of Gargan was leaning on his windowsill and gazing down with mild interest on the scene below.

"Did you see what happened, Argo?" someone shouted.

"The little monkey tried to climb the roof. I think he was drunk." Then he leaned back and slammed shut his window.

Okai turned to Lin-tse, and the two boys walked back to their room. Dalsh-chin was waiting for them. Once inside, they squatted on the floor and spoke Nadir in low voices.

"Argo sent for Zhen-shi," whispered Dalsh-chin, "three hours ago."

"He was tied and beaten," said Okai. "He could not stand pain and therefore must have also been gagged. Otherwise we would have heard the screams. There will be an inquiry."

"It will find," said Lin-tse, "that Grinning Monkey, having consumed too much alcohol in celebration of his success, fell from the roof. A salutary lesson that barbarians have no tolerance for strong drink."

"That is true, my friend," said Okai. "But we will make them suffer as Zhen-shi suffered."

"A pleasing thought," said Lin-tse. "And how will this miracle be accomplished?"

Okai sat silently for a moment. Lin-tse would never forget what followed. Okai's voice dropped even lower: "The rebuilding work on the north tower is not yet complete. The laborers will not return for three days. It is deserted. Tomorrow night we will wait until everyone is asleep, then we will go there and prepare the way for vengeance."

Gargan, Lord of Larness, removed his helm and drew in a deep breath of hot desert air. The sun was beating down, shimmering heat haze forming over the steppes. Twisting in the saddle, he glanced back along the column. A thousand lancers, eight hundred infantry guardsmen, and two hundred archers were moving slowly in line, dust rising in a cloud around them. Gargan tugged on the reins and cantered back along the column, past the water wagons and supply carts. Two of his officers joined him, and together they rode to the crest of a low hill, where Gargan drew rein and scanned the surrounding landscape.

"We will make camp by that ridge," said Gargan, pointing to a rocky outcrop some miles to the east. "There is a series of rock pools there."

"Yes, sir," answered Marlham, a grizzled, white-bearded career officer coming close to the age for mandatory retirement.

"Put out a screen of scouts," Gargan ordered. "Any Nadir seen should be killed."

"Yes, sir."

Gargan swung to the second officer, a handsome young man with clear blue eyes. "You, Premian, will take four companies and scout the marshes. No prisoners. All Nadir are to be treated as hostiles. Understand?"

"Yes, Lord Gargan." The boy had not yet learned how to keep his feelings from showing in his expression.

"I had you transferred to this force," said Gargan. "Do you know why?"

"No, Lord Gargan."

"Because you are soft, boy," snapped the general. "I saw it at the academy. The steel in you—if steel there is—has not been tempered. Well, it will be during this campaign. I mean to soak the steppes in Nadir blood." Spurring his stallion, Gargan galloped down the hillside.

"Watch yourself, my boy," said Marlham. "The man hates you."

"He is an animal," said Premian. "Vicious and malevolent."

"All of that," Marlham agreed. "He always was a hard man, but when his son disappeared . . . well, it did something to him. He's never been the same since. You were there at the time, weren't you?"

"Aye. It was a bad business," said Premian. "There was to be an inquiry into the death of a cadet who fell from Argo's window. On the night before the inquiry Argo vanished. We searched everywhere; his clothes were gone, as was a canvas shoulder pack. We thought at first that he had feared being implicated in the boy's death. But that was ridiculous, for Gargan would have protected him."

"What do you think happened?"

"Something dark," said Premian. With a flick of the reins he moved away, returning to the rear of the column and signaling his junior officers to join him. Swiftly he told them their new orders. The news was greeted with relief by the two hundred men under his command, for it would mean no more swallowing the dust of the column.

While the men were being issued with supplies, Premian found himself thinking back to his last days at the academy that summer two years earlier. Only Okai remained of the original Nadir contingent, his two comrades having been sent home after failing the toughest of the prefinal examinations. Their failure had concerned Premian, for he had worked with them and knew that their mastery of the subjects was no less proficient than his own. And he had passed with a credit. Only Okai remained, a student so brilliant that there was no way he could fail. Even he, however, had barely scraped by with a pass.

Premian had voiced his concerns to the oldest and best of the tutors, a former officer named Fanlon. Late at night, in the old man's study, he told Fanlon he believed the youths had been unfairly dismissed.

"We speak much of honor," said Fanlon sorrowfully, "but in reality it is in short supply. It always was. I was not allowed to take part in the judging of their papers; Lord Larness and two of his cronies marked them. But I fear you are correct, Premian. Both Dalsh-chin and Lin-tse were more than capable students."

"Okai was allowed to pass. Why?" asked Premian.

"He is exceptional, that one. But he will not be allowed to graduate; they will find a way to mark him down."

"Is there no way we can help him?"

"Tell me first, Premian, why you would wish to. You are not friends."

"My father taught me to loathe injustice," answered Premian. "Is that not enough?"

"Indeed it is. Very well, then. I shall help you."

On the day of the finals, upon entering the examination room, each cadet was handed a small numbered disk taken from a black velvet sack held by the chief prefect, a tall, spindly youth named Jashin. Each disk was wrapped in paper to keep the number from being seen by the prefect. It was a ritual intended to ensure that no preferential treatment could be given to any student during the examinations; each cadet would merely write the number of the disk at the top of his paper. At the close of the examination the gathered papers would be taken to the judges, who would mark them immediately.

Premian stood in line behind Okai and noticed that Jashin's fist was already clenched as he delved into the bag before handing the Nadir boy his disk. Premian followed Okai into the examination room, where desks had been set out in rows.

The examination lasted three hours and involved first establishing a logistical formula and a strategy for supplying an invading army of twenty thousand men conducting a campaign across the Ventrian Sea and second constructing a letter of ad-

vice to the commanding officer of the expedition, outlining the
hazards he must expect to face during his invasion of Ventria.

Premian felt exhausted by the close but was fairly certain
he had performed well. The questions were based on a real
campaign of two centuries earlier led by the legendary Gothir
general Bodacas, after whom the academy had been named.
Happily, Premian had studied the campaign fairly recently.

As the cadets trooped out, Premian saw General Gargan
enter the room along with the other judges. Premian avoided
eye contact and sought out Fanlon. The elderly tutor poured the
cadet a goblet of watered wine, and the two of them sat for a
while in silence by the upper window overlooking the bay.

The afternoon wore on, and finally the keep bell sounded.
Premian joined the other students streaming toward the main
hall to hear the results.

Gargan and the senior tutors stood on the raised stage at the
south end of the hall as the two hundred senior cadets filed in.
This time Premian looked squarely at the general, who was now
wearing the full armor of his rank, a gilded breastplate and
the white cloak of a senior guards officer. Behind him, set on
wooden stands, were scores of shining sabers. When the cadets
had taken up their positions, Gargan moved to the front of the
stage.

His voice thundered out. "One hundred forty-six cadets have
passed the final examination and will receive their sabers this
day," he said. "A further seventeen passed with credit. One
cadet gained an honor pass. Thirty-six failed and leave this
honored place bearing the shame earned by their slothful behavior. In the time-honored tradition, we will begin with the
passes and progress to the honor cadet. As your disk number is
called, move forward."

One by one the cadets moved forward and handed in their
disks, receiving their sabers and bowing to their tutors before
marching to the back of the hall and standing in a rank.

The credit students followed. Premian was not among them,

nor was Okai. Premian's mouth was dry; he was standing close to the stage and staring up at Gargan.

"Now," said Gargan, "we come to the honor student, the cream of the academy and a man whose martial skills will help maintain the glory of Gothir." Turning, he took the last saber from the stand. Its blade was shining silver steel, its hilt embellished with gold. "Step forward, number seventeen."

Okai marched from the ranks and up the short wooden steps as whispers began all around the hall. Premian focused on Gargan's broad face; the man's eyes widened, and Premian saw his jaw twitch. He stood silently, staring with undisguised hatred at the young Nadir.

"There has been a mistake," he said at last. "This cannot be! Fetch his paper!"

There was silence in the hall as the chief prefect ran from the stage. Minutes passed, and no one moved or spoke. The chief prefect returned and handed the sheaf of papers to Gargan, who stood and studied them.

Fanlon stepped forward. "There is no question as to the handwriting, Lord Gargan," he said softly. "These are Okai's papers. And I see that you marked them yourself. There can be no mistake."

Gargan blinked. Okai stepped forward, hand outstretched. Gargan stared at him, then looked down at the saber in his own trembling hands. Suddenly he thrust the saber at Fanlon. "You give it to him!" he hissed. And he strode from the stage.

The elderly tutor smiled at Okai. "This was well merited, young man," he said, his voice carrying to all in the hall. "For five years you have endured much, both in physical hardship and in emotional cruelty. For what it is worth—and I hope it is something—you have my respect and my admiration. I hope that when you go from here, you will carry with you some fond memories. Would you like to say a few words to your fellow cadets?"

Okai nodded. Stepping forward, he stood and ran his gaze

over the assembled cadets. "I have learned much here," he said. "One day I will put that knowledge to good use." Without another word he walked from the stage and out of the hall.

Fanlon followed him from the stage and approached Premian. "I shall appeal on your behalf and have your papers reexamined."

"Thank you, sir. For everything. You were right about the disks. I saw that Jashin's fingers were closed as he dipped his hand into the bag; he already had a disk ready for Okai."

"Jashin will be in serious trouble," said Fanlon. "Lord Gargan is not a forgiving man."

Later that day Premian was summoned to Gargan's study. The general was still in his armor, and his face was gray. "Sit down, boy," he said. Premian obeyed. "I am going to ask you a question, and I put you on your honor to answer it with truth."

"Yes, sir," Premian answered, with a sinking heart.

"Is Okai a friend of yours?"

"No, sir. We rarely speak; we have little in common. Why do you ask, sir?"

For a long moment Gargan stared at him, then he sighed. "It does not matter. It broke my heart to see him take the saber. However, that is of no interest to you. I called you here to tell you there has been an error in the marking. You have gained a credit pass."

"Thank you, sir. How . . . did it happen?"

"It was an honest mistake, and I hope you will accept my apologies for it."

"Of course, sir. Thank you, sir."

Premian left the study and returned to his room, where at midnight he was awakened by a tapping at the door. Rising, he lifted the latch. Okai stood there; the Nadir was fully dressed for travel. "You are leaving? But the prize giving is not until tomorrow."

"I have my saber," said Okai. "I came to thank you. I had thought Gothir honor was all sham. I was wrong."

"You have suffered here, Okai, but you emerged triumphant, and I admire you for it. Where will you go now?"

"Back to my tribe."

Premian held out his hand, and Okai shook it. As the Nadir turned away, Premian spoke. "Do you mind if I ask a question?"

"Not at all."

"When we were at the burial of your friend Zhen-shi, you opened the coffin and pressed a small package into his hand. There was blood on it. I have often wondered what it was. Is it part of some Nadir ritual?"

"Yes," said Okai. "It gave him a servant in the next life."

With that Okai walked away.

Three days later, after continuing complaints of a bad smell coming from behind a wall in the new section of the north tower, laborers dug out several blocks of stone. Behind them they found a rotting body from which the eyes had been cut out.

◇ **7** ◇

N UANG XUAN WAS a wily old fox, and he would never have brought his people into Chop-back territory if fortune had not ceased to smile upon him. Shading his eyes, he scanned the surrounding land, pausing at the pinnacles of rock to the west. His nephew Meng rode alongside him. "Are they the Towers of the Damned?" he asked, keeping his voice low to avoid invoking the spirits who dwelled there.

"They are indeed," Nuang told the boy, "but we will not be going close enough for the demons to strike us." The boy reined his pony around, galloping back to the little convoy. Nuang's gaze followed him. Fourteen warriors, fifty-two women, and thirty-one children; it was not a great force with which to enter such lands. But then, who could have supposed that a Gothir cavalry force would be so close to the Mountains of the Moon? When Nuang had led the raid on the Gothir farmers of the marches, seeking to seize horses and goats, he had done so in the knowledge that no soldiers had been stationed there for five years. He had been lucky to escape with fourteen men when the lancers had charged. More than twenty of his warriors had been hacked down in that first charge, among them two of his sons and three nephews. With the cursed *gajin* following his trail, he had had no choice but to lead the remnants of his people into this cursed place.

Nuang kicked his pony into a run and rode to the high ground, squinting against the morning sun and studying the

163

back trail. There was no sign of the lancers. Perhaps they, too, feared the Chop-backs. Yet why had they been so close to the marches? No Gothir force ever entered the eastern flatlands except in time of war. Were they at war with someone? The Wolfshead, perhaps, or the Green Monkeys? No, surely he would have heard from passing merchants and traders.

It was a mystery, and Nuang disliked mysteries. Once more he glanced at his small company—too small now to build his clan into a full tribe. I will have to lead them back to the north, he thought. He hawked and spit. How they would laugh when Nuang begged for readmittance to the tribal grounds. Nuang No-luck, they would call him.

Meng and two of the other young men galloped their ponies up the rise. Meng arrived first. "Riders," he said, pointing to the west. "*Gajin,* two of them. Can we kill them, Uncle?" The boy was excited, his dark eyes gleaming.

Nuang swung his gaze to where Meng had pointed. At that distance, through the heat haze, he could barely make out the riders, and just for a moment he envied the eyes of the young. "No, we will not attack yet. They may be scouts from a larger force. Let them approach."

Heeling his pony, he rode down to the flatlands, his fourteen warriors alongside him, fanning out in a skirmish line. Summoning Meng, he said, "What do you see, boy?"

"Still only two, Uncle. *Gajin.* One has a beard and wears a round black helm and a black jerkin with silver armor on the shoulders; the other is yellow-haired and carries no sword. He has knife sheaths on his chest. Ah!"

"What?"

"The black-bearded one carries a great ax with two shining blades. They ride Gothir horses but are leading four saddled ponies."

"I can see that myself now," Nuang said testily. "Go to the rear."

"I want my part in the kill, Uncle!"

"You are not yet twelve, and you will obey me or feel my whip across your buttocks!"

"I'm almost thirteen," contradicted Meng, but reluctantly he dragged on his reins and backed his pony to the rear of the group.

Nuang Xuan waited, his gnarled hand resting on his ivory-hilted saber. Slowly the two riders closed the distance until Nuang could see their features clearly. The fair-haired *gajin* was very pale, his manner betraying his nervousness and fear, with his hands gripping the reins tightly and his body stiff in the saddle. Nuang flicked his gaze to the axman. No fear could be seen in that one. Still, one man and a coward against fourteen? Surely Nuang's luck had changed. The riders drew rein just ahead of the group, and Nuang took a deep breath, ready to order his men to the attack. As he did so, he looked at the axman and found himself staring into the coldest eyes he had ever seen, the color of winter storm clouds, gray and unyielding. A nagging doubt struck him, and he thought of his remaining sons and nephews, many of whom already carried wounds, as their bloody bandages bore witness. The tension grew. Nuang licked his lips and prepared once more to give the signal. The axman gave an almost imperceptible shake of his head; then he spoke, his voice deep and, if anything, colder than his stare.

"Think carefully about your decision, old one. It seems that luck has not favored you recently," he said. "Your women outnumber your men by—what?—three to one. And the riders with you look bloodied and weary."

"Perhaps our fortune has changed," Nuang heard himself say.

"Perhaps it has," agreed the rider. "I am in a mood for trade. I have four Nadir ponies and a few swords and bows."

"You have a fine ax. Is that also for trade?"

The man smiled; it was not a comforting sight. "No, this is Snaga, which in the old tongue means 'the Sender,' the blade of no return. Any man who wishes to test her name need only ask."

Nuang felt the men around him stirring. They were young and, despite their recent losses, eager for battle. Suddenly he felt the full weight of his sixty-one years. Swinging his horse, he ordered his men to prepare a night camp close to the towers of rock and sent out riders to watch for signs of any enemy force. He was obeyed instantly. Turning back to the axman, he forced a smile. "You are welcome in our camp. Tonight we will talk of trade."

Later, as dusk fell, he sat at a small fire with the axman and his companion. "Would it not be safer within the rocks?" asked the black-bearded warrior.

"Safer from *men*," Nuang told him. "They are the Towers of the Damned, and demons are said to stalk the passes. An ancient sorcerer is entombed there, his devils with him. At least that is how the stories tell it. Now, what do you desire in exchange for those scrawny ponies?"

"Food for the journey and a guide to take us to the next water and then on to the Shrine of Oshikai Demon-bane."

Nuang was surprised, but his expression remained neutral. What would *gajin* seek at the shrine? "That is a difficult journey and perilous. These are the lands of the Chop-backs. Two men and a guide would be . . . tempting . . . prey."

"They have already been tempted," the axman told him. "That is why we have ponies and weapons to trade."

Bored by the continued bartering, Sieben stood and wandered away from the fire. The Nadir clan had pitched its tents in a rough circle and had erected wind screens between them. The women were cooking over small fires, the men sitting in three small groups sharing jugs of *lyrrd*, a liquor fermented from rancid goat's milk. Despite the fires and the screens, the night was cold. Sieben moved to the horses and unstrapped his blanket, tossing it carelessly over his shoulder. When he had first seen the Nadir riders, he had assumed that death would be swift despite the awesome power of Druss. Now, however, reaction had set in and he felt an almost overwhelming sense of fatigue. A young Nadir woman rose from a cooking fire and brought him a wooden bowl of braised meat. She was tall and slim, her lips full and tempting. Sieben forgot his weariness instantly as he thanked her and smiled. She moved away without a word, and Sieben's eyes lingered on her swaying hips. The meat was hot and heavily spiced, the flavor new to him, and he ate with relish, returning the bowl to where the woman sat with four others. He squatted down among them. "A meal fit for a prince," he told her. "I thank you, my lady."

"I am not your lady," she said, her voice flat and disinterested.

Sieben flashed his best smile. "Indeed no, which is my loss, I am sure. It is merely an expression we . . . *gajin* use. What I am trying to say is: Thank you for your kindness and for the quality of your cooking."

"You have thanked me three times, and dog is not difficult to prepare," she told him, "as long as it has been hung until the worms appear in the eye sockets."

"Delightful," he said. "A tip I shall long remember."

"And it mustn't be too old," she continued. "Young dogs are better."

"Of course," he said, half rising.

Suddenly she cocked her head, and her eyes met his. "My man was killed," she said, "by Gothir lancers. Now my blankets are cold, and there is no one to stir my blood on a bitter night."

Sieben sat down again more swiftly than he had intended. "That is a tragedy," he said softly, looking deep into her almond-shaped eyes. "A beautiful woman should never suffer the solitude of a cold blanket."

"My man was a great fighter; he killed three lancers. But he rutted like a dog in heat. Fast. Then he would sleep. You are not a fighter. What are you?"

"I am a scholar," he said, leaning in to her. "I study many things: history, poetry, art. But most of all I study women. They fascinate me." Lifting his hand, he stroked his fingers through her long dark hair, pushing it back from her forehead. "I love the smell of a woman's hair, the touch of skin on skin, the softness of lips on lips. And I am not fast."

The woman smiled and said something in Nadir to her friends. All the women laughed. "I am Niobe," she told him. "Let us see if you rut as well as you talk."

Sieben smiled. "I've always appreciated directness. But is this allowed? I mean, what of the . . ." He gestured toward the men at the campfires.

"You come with me," she said, rising smoothly. "I wish to see if what they say about *gajin* is true." Reaching out, she took his hand and led him to a night-dark tent.

Back at the leader's fire, Nuang chuckled. "Your friend has chosen to mount the tiger. Niobe has fire enough to melt any man's iron."

"I think he will survive," said Druss.

"You want a woman to warm your blankets?"

"No. I have a woman back home. What happened to your people? It looks as if you've been mauled."

Nuang spit into the fire. "Gothir lancers attacked us; they came from nowhere on their huge horses. Twenty men I lost. You spoke with great truth when you said fortune has not favored me. I must have done something to displease the gods of stone and water. But it does no good to whine about it. Who are you? You are no Gothir. Where are you from?"

"The lands of the Drenai, the far blue mountains to the south."

"You are far from home, Drenai. Why do you seek the shrine?"

"A Nadir shaman told me I might find something there to help a dying friend."

"You take a great risk to help this friend; these are not hospitable lands. I considered killing you myself, and I am among the more peaceable of my people."

"I am not an easy man to kill."

"I knew that when I looked into your eyes, Drenai. You have seen many battles, eh? Behind you there are many graves. Once, a long time ago, another Drenai came among my people. He, too, was a fighter; they called him Old-Hard-to-Kill, and he fought a battle against the Gothir. Years later he came to live among us. I was told these stories when I was a child; they are the only stories I have heard of Drenai. His name was Angel."

"I have heard the name," said Druss. "What more do you know of him?"

"Only that he was wed to the daughter of Ox-skull and they had two sons. One was tall and handsome and did not look like Angel, but the other was a powerful warrior. He married a Nadir maiden, and they left the tribe to journey south. That is all I know."

Two women came and knelt beside them, offering bowls of meat to the men. A short series of keening cries came from the tent of Niobe, and the women laughed. Druss reddened and ate his meal in silence. The women moved away. "Your friend will be a tired man come the dawn," said Nuang.

Druss lay quietly looking up at the stars. He rarely found sleep difficult, but this night he was restless. Sitting up, he threw back his blanket. The camp was silent, the fires having faded to glowing ash. Nuang had offered him the shelter of his own tent, but Druss had refused, preferring to sleep in the open.

Gathering his ax and helm and silver-skinned gauntlets, he stood and stretched. The night was cold, and a chilly breeze whispered under the windbreaks stretching between the tents. Druss was uneasy. Pushing his helm into place and pulling on his gauntlets, he silently strode through the camp, easing himself past a stretched canvas windbreak and out onto the open steppes. A sentry was sitting by a creosote bush, a goatskin cloak drawn about him. As Druss approached him, he saw it was the slender boy Meng, whom Nuang had introduced as his youngest nephew. The youth looked up but said nothing.

"All quiet?" asked Druss. The boy nodded, obviously ill at ease.

Druss strolled on toward the towers of black rock and sat down on a boulder some fifty feet from the boy. By day the steppes were hot and inhospitable, but the cold magic of the night gave the land a sense of brooding malevolence that spoke of nameless horrors stalking the shadow-haunted rocks. The eyes played tricks on the brain. Gnarled boulders became crouching demons that seemed to shimmer and move, and the wind hissing over the steppes became a sibilant voice promising pain and death. Druss was not oblivious to this lunar sorcery. Pushing such thoughts from his mind, he gazed up at the moon and thought of Rowena, back on the farm. He had tried so hard during the years since the rescue to make her feel loved, needed. But deep down there was a gnawing pain in him that he could not ignore. She had loved the warrior Michanek, and he had loved her. It was not jealousy that hurt Druss; it was a deep sense of shame. When the raiders had stolen her so many years before, Druss had set out to find her with a single-minded determination that would brook no opposition. He had journeyed to Mashrapur and there, to gain enough money for passage to Ventria, had become a fistfighter. After that he had crossed the ocean, engaged in battles with corsairs and pirates, and joined the demoralized army of Prince Gorben, becoming his champion. All that so that he could find Rowena and rescue her from what he perceived as a life of abject slavery.

At the last, though, he had learned the truth. Her memory lost to her, she had fallen in love with Michanek and was a respected and loved wife, living in luxury, happy and content. Yet knowing this, Druss had still fought alongside the soldiers who destroyed the city in which she lived and butchered the man she loved.

Druss had watched Michanek stand against the best of the Immortals and had seen them fall back in awe as he stood bleeding from a score of wounds, a dozen assailants dead around him.

"You were a man, Michanek," whispered Druss with a sigh. Rowena had never once shown bitterness for his part in Michanek's death. Indeed, they had never spoken of the man. Out here in this lonely wilderness Druss realized that this was wrong. Michanek deserved better. As did Rowena—sweet, gentle Rowena. All she had wanted was to marry the farmer Druss would have become, build a house, and raise children. Druss had been a farmer once but never could be again. He had tasted the joys of battle, the exhilarating narcotic of violence, and not even his love for Rowena could keep him chained to the mountains of home. And as for children? They had not been blessed. Druss would have liked a son. Regret touched him, but he swiftly blocked it from his mind. His thoughts drifted to Sieben, and he smiled. We are not so different, he thought. We are both skilled in a dark sterile art. I live for battle without need of a cause; you live for sex without thought of love. What do we offer this tormented world? he wondered. The breeze picked up, and Druss' restlessness increased. Narrowing his eyes, he scanned the steppes. All was silent. Standing, he walked back to the boy. "What do the riders report?" he asked.

"Nothing," replied Meng. "No sign of *gajin* or Chop-backs."

"When is the next change of watch?"

"When the moon touches the tallest peak."

Druss glanced up. That would be soon. Leaving the boy, he strolled out once more, his unease growing. They should have camped within the rocks, and to hell with fears of demons! A rider came into sight; he waved at Meng and then cantered into the camp. Minutes later his replacement rode out. Another rider came in, then another. Druss waited for some time, then returned to the boy. "Were not four sent out?"

"Yes. I expect Jodai is sleeping somewhere. My uncle will not be pleased."

The breeze shifted. Druss' head came up, and he sniffed the

air. Grabbing the boy by his shoulder, he hauled him to his feet. "Wake your uncle *now*! Tell him to get everyone back into the rocks."

"Take your hand off me!" Feebly the boy lashed out, but Druss dragged him in close. "Listen to me, boy. Death is coming! You understand? There may be no time left. So run as if your life depended on it, for it probably does."

Meng turned and sprinted back toward the camp. Druss, ax in hand, stared out at the seemingly empty steppes. Then he, too, turned and loped back to the camp. Nuang was already moving as Druss ducked under the windbreak. Women were hastily gathering blankets and food and shushing the children into silence.

Nuang ran to Druss. "What have you seen?" he asked.

"Not seen, *smelled*. Thickened goose grease. The lancers use it to protect the leather on their mounts and also to prevent rust on their chain mail. They have hidden their horses, and they are close."

Nuang swore and moved away. As Sieben emerged from a tent, looping his knife baldric over his shoulder, Druss waved to him, pointing to the rocks some hundred paces away. Leaving their tents, the Nadir opened a gap in the windbreaks and ran across the open ground. Druss saw the remaining warriors leading the ponies into a deep cleft in the rocks. Taking up the rear, he moved behind the column. A running woman fell, and Druss helped her to her feet. She was carrying a baby and also holding the hand of a toddler. Druss swept the boy into his arms and ran on. There were only a handful of Nadir women still short of the rocks when fifty lancers emerged from a nearby gully. On foot they charged, blades bright in the moonlight.

Passing the toddler to his terrified mother, Druss hefted Snaga and turned to face the advancing soldiers. Several of the Nadir warriors had scrambled high into the rocks, and they sent black-shafted arrows into the enemy. But the Gothir lancers were well armored with breastplates, chain mail, and full-faced helms. Each carried a round buckler strapped to his left forearm. Most of the arrows bounced harmlessly clear, except for one that took a man deep in the thigh. He stumbled and fell, his white horsehair-plumed helmet falling clear. "Shoot low!" yelled Druss.

The entrance to the rocks was narrow, and Druss backed into it. The first three lancers ran into the cleft, and with a roar he leapt to meet them, smashing Snaga through the helm of the first and killing the second with a reverse cut that smashed his hip and tore open his belly. The third tried to bring his saber to bear, but the blade bounced from Druss' black helm. Snaga sang out, thundering against the man's chain-mail neck guard. The mail was well made and prevented the blades from reaching the skin, but the sheer weight of the blow drove the links against the man's neck, smashing his spine to shards. More soldiers ran in. The first tried to block the sweep of the ax with his iron-reinforced wooden buckler, but the silver blades sliced it cleanly, half severing the arm beneath. With a scream of pain the man fell, tripping two men behind him. The narrow opening would allow only three to attack at any one time, and the rest of the lancers milled behind the entrance. From above, the Nadir hurled rocks down on them and sent shafts into unprotected legs.

Druss hacked and cut, the mighty ax drenched in blood.

And the lancers fell back. A man groaned at Druss' feet; it was the soldier with the half-severed arm. Kneeling, Druss dragged the soldier's helm clear and seized the wounded man's hair. "How many in your force?" asked the axman. "Speak and you live, for I'll let you go back to your friends."

"Two companies. I swear it!"

"Get up and run, for I cannot swear for the archers above."

The man stumbled out into the open and began to run. Two arrows bounced from his breastplate, a third stabbing into the back of his thigh. Gamely he limped on and managed to reach his comrades.

Two companies ... fifty men. Druss glanced down at the bodies he could see. Seven were dead by his ax, and several more had been struck by shafts and would not fight again. That still left around forty, not enough to storm the rocks but enough to pin them down until a second force could be sent for.

Three young Nadir climbed down to where he stood and began to strip the dead of armor and weapons. Nuang clambered down also. "You think they will pull back?"

Druss shook his head. "They will look for another way in. We must get farther back into the rocks; otherwise they'll find a way to get behind us. How many in the group that attacked you on the marches?"

"No more than a hundred."

"Then the question remains: Where are the other two companies?"

Suddenly the lancers charged again. The Nadir youngsters ran back, and Druss stepped forward. "Come in and die, you whoresons!" he bellowed, his voice booming and echoing in the rocks. The first of the lancers sent his saber in a hissing arc toward Druss' throat, but Snaga flashed up to shatter the blade. The soldier hurled himself back, cannoning into two of his comrades. As Druss leapt at them, they turned and fled.

Nuang, sword in hand, appeared alongside Druss. Flames leapt up from the Nadir camp, and Nuang cursed, but Druss chuckled. "Tents can be replaced, old man. It seems to me that your luck has changed for the better."

"Oh, yes," said Nuang bitterly. "I leap with joy at this change of fortune!"

Niobe lay on her stomach, staring down into the narrow cleft of black basaltic rock. "Your friend is a very great fighter," she said, pushing her raven hair back from her face.

Sieben hunkered down beside her. "That is his talent," he admitted, annoyed at her admiring tone and the way her dark, almond-shaped eyes were focused on the axman below.

"Why did you not fight alongside him, po-et?"

"My dear, when Druss starts swinging that dreadful ax, the last place you want to be is beside him. Anyway, Druss always likes the odds to be against him. Brings out the best in him, you know."

Niobe rolled to her elbow and gazed into his eyes. "Why is it you are no longer frightened, po-et? When we ran in here, you were trembling."

"I don't like violence," he admitted, "especially when it is directed toward me. But they won't follow us in here. They are lancers, heavily armored; they are trained for cavalry charges on open ground. Their boots are metal-reinforced and high-heeled to keep their feet in the stirrups. They are entirely unsuited to scrambling over volcanic rock. No, they will pull back now and try to catch us in the open. Therefore, for the moment we are safe."

She shook her head. "No one is safe here," she told him. "Look around you, po-et. These black rocks are part of the Towers of the Damned. Evil dwells here. Even now there may be demons creeping toward us!"

Sieben shivered, but even in the fading moonlight he could see the amused gleam in her eyes. "You don't believe that for a moment," he said.

"Perhaps I do."

"No, you are just trying to frighten me. Would you like to know why the Nadir believe there are demons here?" She nodded. "Because this area is—or once was—volcanic. It would have spewed fire, poisoned ash, and red-hot lava. Travelers close by would have heard great rumblings below the earth." He swung around and pointed to the twin towers rearing toward the brightening sky. "Those are just cones of hollow, cooled lava."

"You don't believe in demons?" she asked him.

"Aye," he said somberly, "I do. There are beasts that can be summoned from the pit, but they are like puppy dogs compared with the demons every man carries in his heart."

"Your heart has demons in it?" she whispered, eyes widening.

"Such a literal people," he said, shaking his head and rising. Swiftly he climbed down to where Druss was waiting with Nuang and several Nadir. He noted wryly how the Nadir stood close to the axman, hanging on his words and grinning as he spoke. Only hours before they had been lusting to kill him. Now he was a hero to them, a friend.

"What ho, old horse!" Sieben called, and Druss swung toward him.

"What do you think, poet? Have we seen the last of them?"

"I believe so. But we had better find another way out of these hills. I wouldn't want to be caught by them on open ground."

Druss nodded. Blood was staining his jerkin and beard, but he had cleaned his ax blades.

The dawn sun glinted above the distant mountains, and Druss strode to the mouth of the cleft. The lancers had pulled back in the darkness and were nowhere in sight.

For another hour the Nadir waited nervously in the rocks, then several of them crept down to the smoking ruins of their camp, gathering the possessions that had not been lost to the fires.

Nuang approached Druss and Sieben. "Niobe tells me you believe the rocks are safe," he said, and Sieben explained once more about volcanic activity. Nuang did not look impressed, his dark flat face expressionless and his eyes wary.

Druss laughed. "Given a choice between demons we haven't seen and lancers we have, I know what I'd choose."

Nuang grunted, then cleared his throat and spit. "Does your ax kill demons?"

Druss gave a cold smile and hefted Snaga, holding the blades close to Nuang's face. "What it can cut, it can kill."

Nuang gave a broad smile. "I think we will walk the Hills of the Damned," he said.

"Never a dull moment with you, Druss," muttered Sieben. As Druss clapped him on the shoulder, he glanced down at the blood-smeared hand. "Oh, thank you. Just what a blue silk shirt needs, a spot of drying blood!"

"I'm hungry," Druss announced, swinging away with a grin. Taking a handkerchief from the pocket of his leggings, Sieben dabbed at the offending mark, then followed the axman back into the rocks. Niobe brought him cold meat and goat's cheese and sat beside him as he ate.

"Is there any water?" he asked.

"Not yet. The *gajin* destroyed all but one of our barrels. Today will be dry and hot. That is a pretty shirt," she added, reaching out and stroking the silk, her fingers lingering over the mother-of-pearl buttons at the neck.

"I had it made in Drenan," he told her.

"Everything is so soft," she murmured, stroking her hand down over his woolen leggings and resting her palm on his thigh. "So soft."

"Raise your hand any higher and it won't stay soft," he warned her.

Glancing up at him, she raised one eyebrow, then slid her hand along the inside of his thigh. "Ah," she said, "how true."

"Time to be moving, poet!" called Druss.

"Your timing is impeccable," replied Sieben.

For two hours the convoy moved into the black hills. There was no vegetation there, and walls of dark volcanic rock reared above them. Silently the group pushed on, the Nadir casting fearful glances around them. Even the children remained quiet. No one rode, for the footing was treacherous. Toward midday the ground gave way under a pony, which fell, its left front leg snapping. It thrashed around until a young Nadir warrior leapt upon it, slicing open its throat; blood gushed to the rocks. The women moved forward, dragging the pony clear of the hole and butchering it. "Fresh meat tonight," Niobe told Sieben.

The heat was intense now, so strong that Sieben had ceased

to sweat and felt that his brain was shriveling to the size of a walnut. By dusk the exhausted party had reached the center of the hills, and they made camp beneath one of the twin towers. For more than an hour Sieben had been lusting after a drink of water from the one remaining barrel, and he lined up with the warriors for a single cup. The taste was beyond nectar.

Later, just before sunset, he wandered away from the camp and climbed the jagged rocks toward the west-facing summit. The climb was not difficult, but it was tiring. Even so Sieben had a need to get away from the others, to find solitude. At the peak he sat down and stared out over the land. White clouds dotted the sky, peaceful and serene, and the setting sun was falling behind them, bathing the distant mountains in golden light. The breeze was deliciously cool, the view extraordinary. The far mountains lost their color as the sun sank lower, becoming black silhouettes like storm clouds gathering at the horizon, the sky above them turning mauve, then gray-silver, and finally pale gold. The clouds also changed color, moving from pristine white to coral red in a sea of royal blue. Sieben leaned back against a rock and soaked in the sight. At last the sky darkened and the moon appeared, bright and pure. Sieben sighed.

Niobe clambered up to sit alongside him.

"I wanted to be alone," he said.

"We are alone," she pointed out.

"How stupid of me. Of course we are." Turning from her, he gazed down into the cone of the tower. A shaft of moonlight broke through the clouds and illuminated the core.

Niobe's hand touched his shoulder. "Look at the ledge down there," she said.

"I am in no mood for sex, my pretty. Not at this moment."

"No, look! At the far end of the ledge." His gaze followed her pointing finger. Some twenty feet below and to the right there was—or appeared to be—an entrance carved into the rock.

"It is a trick of the light," he said, peering down into the cone.

"And there," she said, "steps!" It was true. At the far end of the ledge a series of steps had been cut into the wall of the cone.

"Go and fetch Druss," he commanded.

"That is where the demons live," she whispered as she walked away.

"Tell him to bring a rope, torches, and a tinderbox."

Niobe stopped and looked back. "You are going down there? For why?"

"Because I am a naturally curious man, my darling. I want to know why anyone would carve an opening on the inside of a volcano."

The moonlight was brighter as the clouds dispersed, and Sieben edged around the crater, moving closer to the ancient steps. Immediately above the first of them there were rope grooves in the soft rock. The steps themselves had been hacked with great speed or had weathered badly, perhaps both, he thought. Leaning over the rim, he pushed his fingers against the first step. The rock crumbled away at his touch. Under no circumstances would those steps any longer support the weight of a man.

Druss, Nuang, and several Nadir warriors climbed up toward him. Niobe was not with them. The old Nadir chieftain leaned over the rim and stared at the rectangular entrance below. He said nothing.

Druss squatted down beside Sieben. "The girl says you want to go down there. Is that wise, poet?"

"Perhaps not, old horse. But I don't want to spend the rest of my life wondering about it."

Druss peered down into the cone. "That's a long way to fall."

Sieben gazed down into the black depths. The moonlight, though bright, did not reach the bottom of the cone. "Lower me down to the ledge," he said, hanging on to the last of his courage. There was no way now that he could withdraw. "But don't release your hold when I reach the ledge. The rock crumbles like salt crystals, and the ledge may not support me."

Tying a rope around his waist and waiting until Druss looped it over his huge shoulders, he swung out over the rim. Slowly Druss let out the rope until Sieben's feet touched the ledge, which was solid and strong.

He stood before the entrance. There was no doubt it had been carved by men. Strange symbols had been etched into the rock, swirls and stars surrounding what appeared to be the outline of a broken sword. Just inside the entrance a series of iron bars had been cemented into the black rock; they were now red with rust. Sieben gripped one of them and pulled hard, but it did not budge.

"What is happening?" called Druss.

"Come down and see. I'll untie the rope."

Moments later Druss, holding a lighted torch, joined him. "Stand back," said the axman, handing the torch to Sieben and removing his rope. Taking a firm grip with both hands, Druss wrenched at the first of the bars. With a grinding groan it bent in the middle, then ripped away from the surrounding rock. Druss hurled it over his shoulder, and Sieben heard it clanging and bouncing down the walls of the cone. Two more bars were prized loose in the same fashion. "After you, poet," said Druss.

Sieben eased himself through the gap in the bars and held up the torch. He found himself standing in a small round chamber. Turning, he saw two chains hanging from the ceiling. Druss appeared alongside him and approached the chains, from one of which something dangled. "Bring the torch closer," ordered the axman, and Sieben did so.

The chain held a dried and withered arm that had torn loose from the shoulder as the corpse had decayed. Lowering the torch, Sieben gazed down at the long-dead, almost mummified body. The flickering torchlight shone on a long dress of decaying white silk, still strangely beautiful in that dark and gloomy setting.

"It was a woman," said Druss. "Someone entombed her here alive."

Sieben knelt by the corpse. Glints of light came from the sunken eye sockets, and he almost dropped the torch. Druss peered closer. "The whoresons put out her eyes with nails of gold," he said. Touching the corpse's head, he turned it. Gold also glinted in the ear canals on both sides.

Sieben wished Niobe had never seen the ledge. His heart sank with sorrow for this long-dead woman and her terrible suffering. "Let's get out of here," he said softly.

At the rim they told Nuang what they had seen. The old leader sat silently until they had finished. "She must have been a great sorceress," he said. "The swirls and the stars on the entrance show that spells were cast there to chain her spirit to this place. And the nails would stop her from hearing or seeing in the world of spirit. It is likely that they also pierced her tongue."

Sieben rose and retied his rope. "What are you doing?" asked Druss.

"I'm going back, old horse."

"For why?" queried Nuang. Sieben gave no answer but swung himself once more over the rim.

Druss grinned at him as he took up the rope. "Ever the romantic, eh, poet?"

"Just hand me the torch."

Once more in the chamber, Sieben knelt by the corpse and forced himself to push his fingers deep into the dry eye sockets, drawing out the nails of gold. They came away cleanly, as did the longer nail in the right ear. The left nail was wedged deep, and Sieben had to loosen it with a knife blade. As he opened the mouth of the corpse, the jaw fell clear. Steeling himself, he lifted clear the last golden nail. "I do not know," he said softly, "if your spirit is now free, lady. I hope that it is." As he was about to rise, he saw a glint of bright metal within the rotted folds of the woman's dress. Reaching down, he lifted it; it was a round medallion ringed with dark gold. Holding it up to the light, he saw that the center was tarnished silver and raised with a relief he could not make out. Pocketing it, he walked back out to the ledge and called out to Druss to haul him up.

Once back in the camp, Sieben sat in the moonlight, polishing the medallion, bringing back its brightness. Druss joined him. "I see you found a treasure," said the axman, and Sieben passed it to him. On one surface was the profile of a man; on the obverse was a woman. Around the woman's head were words in a language Sieben did not recognize.

Druss peered at it. "Perhaps it was a coin—a king and queen," he said. "You think the woman was her?"

Sieben shrugged. "I do not know, Druss. But whoever she was, her murder was administered with the foulest cruelty. Can you imagine what it must have been like? To be dragged to that soulless place and to have your eyes put out? To be left hanging and bleeding while death crept up with agonizing lack of speed?"

Druss handed the medallion back to him. "Perhaps she was a terrible witch who ate babies. Perhaps her punishment was just."

"Just? There is no crime, Druss, for which that punishment was just. If someone is evil, then you kill them. But look what they did to her. Whoever was responsible took delight in it. It was so carefully planned, so meticulously executed."

"Well, you did what you could, poet."

"Little enough, wasn't it? You think I freed her spirit to see, to talk, to hear?"

"It would be good to think so."

Niobe moved alongside them and sat next to Sieben. "You have great tension, po-et. You need lovemaking."

Sieben grinned. "I think you are entirely correct," he said, rising and taking her by the hand.

Later, with Niobe sleeping beside him, Sieben sat in the moonlight, thinking about the woman in the tomb. Who was she, and for what crime had she been executed? he wondered. She was a sorceress—of that there was no doubt. Her killers had gone to great lengths—and greater cost—to destroy her.

Niobe stirred beside him. "Can you not sleep, po-et?"

"I was thinking about the dead woman."

"For why?"

"I don't know. It was a cruel way to die, blinded, chained, and left alone in a volcanic cave. Brutal and vicious. And why did they bring her here, to this desolate place? Why hide the body?"

Niobe sat up. "Where does the sun go to sleep?" she asked. "Where are the bellows of the winds? Why do you ask yourself questions you cannot answer?"

Sieben smiled and kissed her. "That is how knowledge is gained," he said. "People asking questions for which there are no immediate answers. The sun does not sleep, Niobe. It is a great ball of fire in the heavens, and this planet is a smaller ball spinning around it." She looked at him quizzically but said nothing. "What I am trying to say is that there are always answers even if we cannot *see* them right away. The woman in that cave was rich, probably highborn, a princess or a queen. The medallion I found has two heads engraved on it, a man and a woman. Both have Nadir or Chiatze features."

"Show me."

Sieben took the medallion from his pouch and dropped it into her hand. The moonlight was bright, and Niobe studied the heads. "She was very lovely. But she was not Nadir."

"Why do you say that?"

"The writings on the *lon-tsia*. They are Chiatze; I have seen the symbols before."

"Can you read what it says?"

"No." She passed it back to him.

"What did you call it? A *lon-tsia*?"

"Yes. It is a love gift. Very expensive. Two would have been made for the wedding. The man is her husband, and her *lon-tsia* would have been worn with the man's head facing inward, over her heart. He would wear his in the reverse way, her head upon his heart. Old Chiatze custom—but only for the rich."

"Then I wonder what happened to her husband."

Niobe leaned in close. "No more questions, po-et," she whispered. "I shall sleep now." Sieben lay down beside her. Her fingers stroked his face, then slid over his chest and belly.

"I thought you said you wanted sleep."

"Sleep is always better after lovemaking."

By the afternoon of the following day the group came to the last outcrop of rocks before the steppes. Nuang sent out scouts, and the last of the water was doled out to the women and children. Druss, Nuang, and the boy Meng climbed the rocks and scanned the bleak, apparently empty steppes. There was no sign of any enemy.

After an hour the scouts returned to report that the lancers had moved on. The riders had followed their tracks to a water hole in a deep gully, which had been drunk dry and was now deserted.

Nuang led his weary people to the hole and there made camp. "They have no patience, these *gajin*," he told Druss as they stood beside the mud-churned water hole. "It is a seep, yet they allowed their horses to ride into it. Had they waited and taken only a little water at a time, it would have fully nourished both men and mounts. Now? Ha! Their horses will have barely wet their tongues and will be useless to them by sunset."

Several of the Nadir women began digging in the mud and the gravel below, slowly clearing the hole. Then they sat back and waited. After an hour the small seep began to fill.

Later Nuang sent out scouts once more. They returned an hour before dusk. Nuang spoke to them, then moved to where Druss and Sieben were saddling their horses. "The *gajin* have cut to the northwest. My men saw a great cloud of dust there. They rode as close as they dared and saw an army on the march. For why is an army here? What is here for them to fight?"

Druss laid his huge hand on the old man's shoulder. "They are riding for the Valley of Shul-sen's Tears. They seek to pillage the shrine."

"They want Oshikai's bones?" asked the old man incredulously.

"How far is it to the shrine?" Druss asked.

"If you take two spare mounts and ride through the night to the northeast, you will see its walls in two days," said Nuang. "But the *gajin* will not be far behind you."

"May your luck be good," said Druss, holding out his hand. The Nadir leader nodded and shook hands.

Sieben moved away to where Niobe stood. "I hope we meet again, my lady," he said.

"We will or we won't," she said, and turned away from him. The poet walked to his horse and vaulted to the saddle. Druss mounted the mare, and, leading two spare ponies, the two men left the camp.

Even before Nosta Khan's arrival at the shrine, news of the Gothir invasion had reached the four camps. A rider from the Curved Horn tribe came in, his pony lathered in sweat. Galloping to the tents of his own people, he leapt from the saddle. A cavalry group had attacked two Curved Horn villages, slaughtering men, women, and children. Thousands more soldiers were heading toward the valley, he said.

The leader of the Curved Horn contingent, a middle-aged warrior named Bartsai, sent for the other leaders, and they gathered at noon in his tent: Lin-tse of the Sky Riders, Quingchin of the Fleet Ponies, and Kzun, the shaven-headed war chief of the Lone Wolves. They sat in silence as the rider told them what he had seen: a Gothir army on the march, killing all Nadir in its path.

"It makes no sense," said Kzun. "Why have they made war on the Curved Horn?"

"And why is their army heading for this valley?" put in Lin-tse.

"Perhaps more importantly," said Quing-chin, "we should be asking ourselves what we intend to do. They are less than two days from us."

"Do?" queried Bartsai. "What can we do? Do you see an army around you? We have fewer than 120 men."

"We are the guards of the sacred shrine," said Lin-tse. "Numbers mean nothing. Were we but four, we should fight."

"You speak for yourself!" snapped Bartsai. "I see no point in throwing away our lives. If there are no warriors here, then the *gajin* will pass by the shrine. There is nothing here for them save the bones of Oshikai. No treasures, no plunder. Therefore, we keep the shrine safe by fleeing."

"Pah!" sneered Lin-tse. "What more could be expected from a Curved Horn coward?"

Bartsai surged to his feet, snatching a curved dagger from his belt as Lin-tse reared up, reaching for his saber. Quing-chin jumped between them. "No!" he shouted. "This is madness!"

"I will not be insulted in my own tent," shouted Bartsai, glowering at the taller Lin-tse.

"Then do not talk of flight," said Lin-tse, slamming his saber back into its scabbard.

"What else is there to talk of?" asked Kzun. "I do not wish to run from *gajin*. Neither do I wish to throw away the lives of my men needlessly. I have no love for the Curved Horn, but Bartsai is a warrior who has ridden in many battles. He is no coward. Neither am I. What he says is true. Whatever their purpose, the *gajin* are looking to kill Nadir. If there are none of us here, they must move on. We should draw them farther into the steppes, away from water. Their horses will die there."

The tent flap opened, and a small man stepped inside. He was old and wizened and wore a necklace of human finger bones.

"Who are you?" asked Bartsai warily, aware from the bones that the man was a shaman.

"I am Nosta Khan." Moving forward, he sat between Kzun and Bartsai. Both men moved sideways, making more room for him. "You now know the threat facing you," said the shaman. "Two thousand Gothir warriors, led by Gargan Nadir-bane, are marching on this holy place. What you do not know is why, but I shall tell you. They come to destroy the shrine, to raze the walls, to take the bones of Oshikai and grind them to dust."

"For what purpose?" asked Kzun.

"Who can read the minds of the *gajin*?" said Nosta Khan. "They treat us like vermin, to be destroyed at their whim. I care nothing for their reasons. It is enough that they are coming."

"What do you advise, shaman?" asked Lin-tse.

"You must appoint a war leader and resist them with all your might. The shrine must not fall to the *gajin*."

"Stinking round-eyed vermin!" hissed Kzun. "It is not enough that they hound us and kill us. Now they wish to desecrate our holy places. I will not suffer this. The question is, Which of us should lead? I do not wish to sound arrogant, but I have fought in thirty-seven battles. I offer myself."

"Hear me," Quing-chin said softly. "I respect every leader here, and my words are not intended to cause insult. Of the men here in this tent only two could lead—myself and Lin-tse—for we were both trained by the *gajin* and well know the ways of the siege. But one among us here is a man who understands the strategies of *gajin* warfare better than any other."

"Who is this . . . hero?" asked Bartsai.

Quing-chin turned toward Lin-tse. "Once he was named Okai. Now he is called Talisman."

"And you believe this man can lead us to victory?" put in Kzun. "Against a force twenty times our number?"

"The Sky Riders will follow him," said Lin-tse suddenly.

"As will the Fleet Ponies," added Quing-chin.

"What tribe is this man from?" Bartsai asked.

"Wolfshead," Lin-tse told him.

"Then let us go to him. I wish to see him myself before I

commit my men to him," said Bartsai. "In the meantime I will send out riders, for there are many Curved Horn villages close by. We will need more fighters."

Zhusai had endured a troubled night with strange dreams filling her mind. Men were dragging her through a twisted landscape, chaining her in a dark, gloomy chamber. Names were screamed at her: "Witch! Whore!" Blows struck her face and body.

She had opened her eyes, her heart hammering in panic. Jumping from her bed, she had run to the window, throwing it open and breathing deeply of the cool night air. Too frightened to return to sleep, she had walked òut into the open yard before the shrine. Talisman and Gorkai were sitting there as she approached, and Talisman rose.

"Are you well, Zhusai?" he asked, taking her arm. "You are very pale."

"I had a terrible dream, but it is fading now." She smiled. "May I sit with you?"

"Of course."

The three of them had discussed the search for the Eyes of Alchazzar. Talisman had checked the shrine room thoroughly, scanning the walls and floor for hidden compartments, but there were none. Together with Gorkai he had even lifted the stone coffin lid and examined the dried bones within. There was nothing to be found except a *lon-tsia* of heavy silver bearing the heads of Oshikai and Shul-sen. He had left it with the bones and had carefully replaced the lid.

"Oshikai's spirit told me the eyes were hidden here, but I cannot think where else to look," said Talisman.

Zhusai stretched herself out beside the men, and drifted to sleep.

*A slim man with burning eyes pushed his face into her own, biting her lip until it bled. "Now you die, witch, and not before your time." She spit in his face.*

*"Then I shall be with my love,"* she said, *"and will never have to look upon your worthless face again!"* He struck her then, savagely, repeatedly. Then he grabbed her hair.

*"You'll never see him this side of eternity."* Holding up his hand, he showed her five small golden spikes. *"With these I shall put out your eyes and pierce your eardrums. The last I will drive through your tongue. Your spirit will be mine throughout time. Chained to me, as you should have been in life. Do you want to beg? If I cut you loose, will you fall down on your knees and swear loyalty to me?"*

Zhusai wanted to say yes, but the voice that came from her mouth was not hers. *"Swear loyalty to a worm? You are nothing, Chakata. I warned my lord of you, but he would not listen. Now I curse you, and my curse will follow you until the stars die!"*

Her head was dragged back. His hand came up, and she felt the glittering spike push into her eyeball.

With a cry of pain Zhusai woke to find Talisman sitting beside her bed. "How did I get here?" she asked.

"I carried you. You began speaking in Chiatze. It is not a tongue with which I am familiar; it changed your voice incredibly."

"I had the dream again, Talisman. It was so real. A man . . . many men . . . took me to a dark chamber, and there they put out my eyes. It was horrible. They called me a witch and a whore. They had . . . I think . . . murdered my husband."

"Rest," said Talisman. "You are distraught."

"I am distraught," she agreed, "but . . . I have never experienced a dream like this one. The colors were so sharp, and . . ." Gently he stroked her head, and exhausted, she slept again. This time there were no dreams.

When she awoke, she was alone, and bright sunlight filled the room. There was a jug of water and a basin on a table by the window. Rising from the narrow bed, she took off her clothes, filled the basin, added three drops of perfume from a tiny bottle, and washed her face and upper body. From her pack she took a long tunic of white silk; it was crumpled but clean. Once dressed, she washed the clothes she had been wearing the previous day and laid them over the windowsill to dry. Barefoot, she left the room, walked down the narrow wooden stairs, and emerged into the courtyard below.

Talisman was sitting alone, eating a breakfast of bread and cheese. Gorkai was grooming the ponies on the other side of the courtyard. Zhusai sat beside Talisman, and he poured her a goblet of water. "Did you dream again?" he asked her.

"No." He is bone-tired, she thought, his eyes dull. "What will you do now?" she asked him.

"I know . . . believe . . . the eyes are here, but I cannot think where else to look."

Five men came walking through the open gates. Zhusai's heart sank as she recognized Nosta Khan, and she stood and moved back into the shadows. Talisman's face was impassive as the men approached. The first of the men, a shaven-headed warrior with a gold earring, halted before him. "I am Kzun of the Lone Wolves," he said, his voice deep and cold. His body was lean and hard, and Zhusai felt a flicker of fear as she gazed at him. His posture was challenging as he stood looming over Talisman. "Quing-chin of the Fleet Ponies claims you are a war leader to follow. You do not look like a war leader."

Talisman rose and stepped past Kzun, ignoring him. He walked to a tall, solemn-faced warrior. "It is good to see you, Lin-tse," he said.

"And you, Okai. The gods of stone and water have brought you here at this time."

A burly middle-aged man stepped forward. "I am Bartsai of the Curved Horn." Dropping into a crouch, he extended his right arm with the palm upward. "Quing-chin of the Fleet Ponies speaks highly of you, and we are here to ask of you a service."

"Not yet we don't," snapped Kzun. "First let him prove himself."

"Why do you need a war leader?" asked Talisman, directing his question at Lin-tse.

"Gargan is coming with an army. The Gothir seek to destroy the shrine."

"They have already attacked several Nadir camps," added Quing-chin.

Talisman walked away from the group and sat cross-legged on the ground. Three of the others followed and sat around him. Kzun hesitated, then joined them. Gorkai moved across the courtyard and stood, arms folded across his chest, behind Talisman.

"How many men in the Gothir army?" Talisman asked.

"Two thousand," said Nosta Khan. "Lancers and foot soldiers."

"How long before they arrive?"

"Two days. Perhaps three," Bartsai answered.

"And you intend to fight?"

"Why else would we need a war leader?" asked Kzun.

For the first time Talisman looked the man in the eye. "Let us be clear, Kzun of the Lone Wolves," he said, no anger in his voice. "The shrine is ultimately indefensible. A sustained assault by two thousand men will take it eventually. There is no hope here of victory. At best we could hold for a few days, perhaps a week. Look around you. One wall has already crumbled, and the gates are useless. All the defenders would die."

"Exactly what I said," put in Bartsai.

"Then you advocate flight?" Kzun asked.

"At this moment I am not advocating anything," said Talisman. "I am stating the obvious. Do you intend to fight?"

"Yes," said Kzun. "This is the one place sacred to all Nadir. It cannot be surrendered without a fight."

Lin-tse spoke up. "You know the ways of the Gothir, Okai. You know how they will fight. Will you lead us?"

Talisman rose. "Go back to your warriors. Tell them to

assemble here in one hour; I will speak with them." Leaving them sitting there, Talisman walked across the courtyard and climbed to the east-facing parapet. Bewildered, the leaders rose and left the shrine. Nosta Khan followed Talisman.

Zhusai stood quietly by the wall as Gorkai approached her. "I don't think we will live to see the day of the Uniter," he said grimly.

"And yet you will stay," she said.

"I am Wolfshead," he told her proudly. "I will stay."

On the wall Nosta Khan came alongside Talisman. "I did not foresee this," said the shaman.

"It does not matter," Talisman told him. "Win or lose, it will speed the day of reckoning."

"How so?"

"Four tribes will fight together. It will show the way we must follow. If we succeed, then the Nadir will know the Gothir can be beaten. If we fail, then the sacrilege they commit upon this shrine will bind the tribes with chains of fire."

"Succeed? You said we would all die."

"We must be prepared for death. But there is a chance, Nosta. They have no water, so we must guard the wells, denying them access. Two thousand men will require 250 gallons of water a day, the horses three times that. If we deny them water for more than a few days, the horses will start to die, then the men."

"Surely they will have thought of that," argued Nosta Khan.

"I doubt it. They will expect to take the shrine within a day. And here there are three deep wells."

"Can you hold them with a hundred men and guard the wells and water holes outside?"

"No, we need more warriors. But they will come."

"From where?" asked the shaman.

"The Gothir will send them," Talisman told him.

◇ **8** ◇

TALISMAN SAT ALONE on the parapet, cross-legged, arms outstretched, eyes closed, and face upward to the blazing sun. There were so many ambitions he had longed to achieve, the foremost of them being to ride into the city of Gulgothir beside the Uniter, to see the Gothir humbled, their high walls brought down and their army in ruins. Anger flooded him, and for a while he allowed the richness of the emotion to rage in his veins; then, slowly, he calmed himself. What he had told Nosta Khan was true. The battle for the shrine would unite the tribes as never before. Even if he were to die here, which was probable, the effect would be to speed the day of the Uniter.

He had told the tribal leaders that victory was impossible. That also was true. Yet a general who fought with defeat in mind would surely lose. Slowing his breathing and calming his heart, Talisman floated above the sense of rage and frustration. Two armies were about to meet. He had to put aside thoughts of numbers and examine the essentials. He saw again Fanlon's paneled study back at the Bodacas Academy and heard the old soldier's voice whisper across the years. *"The responsibility for a martial host lies in one man. He is its spirit. If an army is deprived of its morale, its general also will lose heart. Order and confusion, bravery and cowardice, are qualities dominated by the heart. Therefore, the expert at controlling his enemy frustrates him and then moves against him. Aggravation and harassment will rob the enemy of his heart, making him fearful, affecting his ability to plan."*

Talisman pictured Gargan, and once again anger flickered. He waited for it to pass. The Lord of Larness had failed against him once, when all the odds were in his favor. Can I make him do so again? wondered Talisman.

The man was full of hate yet still a mighty general and a warrior of courage, and when calm he was not stupid. The secret was to steal his calm, allowing his hatred to swamp his intellect.

Opening his eyes, Talisman rose and stared out to the west. From there he could see where the enemy would camp, at the foot of the dry hills, where there would be shade for their horses in the afternoon. Would they surround the shrine? No. They would have lancers patrol the area.

Sitting on the wall, he gazed in at the buildings and walls of the shrine. There was the resting place of Oshikai with its flat roof, a two-story dwelling beside it with ten rooms, built for pilgrims. Beyond that there was the fallen ruin of an old tower. Three of the twenty-foot walls surrounding the buildings were still strong, but this west-facing barrier with its long *v*-shaped crack was the weak spot; this was where the main attack would come. Gargan would send archers to pin down the defenders and foot soldiers armed with trench tools to tear at the crack, opening it out. Then the sheer force of numbers would carry the Gothir inside.

Talisman walked down the stone steps and along the base of the wall, halting below the damaged section. Given enough men and enough time, he could repair it or at worst reinforce it with rocks from the fallen tower.

Men and time. The gods of stone and water had robbed him of both.

Through the gates rode Kzun and his Lone Wolves. Talisman stripped off his shirt, dropping it to the dust, then once more climbed the steps to the parapet. Quing-chin followed with the Fleet Ponies contingent, then came Lin-tse and his Sky Riders.

The last to arrive was Bartsai of the Curved Horn. The Nadir warriors sat on their ponies in silence, their eyes on Talisman on the wall above them.

"I am Talisman," he said. "My tribe is Wolfshead, my blood Nadir. These lands are ruled by the Curved Horn. Let the leader Bartsai join me upon this wall." Bartsai lifted his leg over the pommel of his saddle and jumped to the ground; he walked up the steps to stand beside Talisman. Drawing his knife, Talisman drew the blade across the palm of his left hand. Blood welled from the wound. Holding out his arm, he watched as the red drops fell to the ground below. "This is my blood, which I give to the Curved Horn," he said. "My blood and my promise to fight unto death for the bones of Oshikai Demon-bane." For a moment longer he stood in silence; then he called the other leaders forward. When they had joined him, he gazed down on the waiting riders. "At this place far back on the river of time Oshikai fought the Battle of the Five Armies. He won, and he died. In the days to come the Nadir will speak of our struggle as the Battle of the Five Tribes. They will speak of it with pride in their hearts. For we are warriors and the sons of men. We are Nadir. We fear nothing." His voice rose. "And who are these men who ride against us? Who do they think they are? They slaughter our women and our children. They pillage our holy places." Suddenly he pointed at a rider of the Curved Horn. "You!" he shouted. "Have you ever killed a Gothir warrior?" The man shook his head. "You will. You will slash your sword into his throat, and his blood will pour out onto the land. You will hear his death scream and see the light fade from his eyes. So will you. And you! And you! Every man here will get the chance to pay them back for their insults and their atrocities. My blood—Nadir blood—stains the earth here. I shall not leave this place until the Gothir are crushed or withdraw. Any man who cannot make the same oath should leave now." Not one of the riders moved.

Lin-tse stepped up alongside Talisman. With a curved dagger

he cut his left hand, then raised it high. One by one the other leaders joined them. Kzun turned to Talisman, stretching out his bloody hand, and Talisman gripped it. "Brothers in blood!" declared Kzun. "Brothers unto death!"

Talisman strode to the edge of the parapet. Drawing his saber, he looked down on the riders. "Brothers unto death!" he shouted. Swords hissed into the air.

"Brothers unto death!" they roared.

The blind priest sat in his quarters, listening as the roar went up. The dreams of men, he thought, revolve always around war. Battle and death, glory and pain. Young men lust for it, old men talk of it fondly. A great sadness settled on him, and he slowly moved around the room, gathering his papers.

Once he, too, had been a warrior, riding the steppes on raids, and he remembered well the heady excitement of battle. A small part of him wished he could remain with these young men and smite the enemy. But it was a very small part.

There was only one real enemy in all the world, he knew: hatred. All evil was born of that vile emotion. Immortal, eternal, it swept through the hearts of men of every generation. When Oshikai and his armies had reached these lands hundreds of years before, they had found a peaceful people living in the lush southlands. After Oshikai's death they had subjugated them, raiding their villages and taking their women, sowing the seeds of hatred. The seeds had grown, and the southerners had fought back, becoming more organized. At the same time the Nadir had splintered into many tribes. The southerners became the Gothir, and their remembrances of past iniquities made them hate the Nadir, visiting upon them the terror of the killing raids.

When will it end? he wondered.

Slowly he packed his manuscripts, quills, and ink into a canvas shoulder bag. There was not room for all of them, and the others he hid in a box below the floorboards. Hoisting the pack to his back, he walked from the room and out into a sunlit morning he could not see.

The riders had returned to their camps, and he heard footsteps approaching. "You are leaving?" asked Talisman.

"I am leaving. There is a cave a few miles to the south. I often go there when I wish to meditate."

"You have seen the future, old man. Can we beat them?"

"Some enemies can never be overcome," said the priest, and without another word he walked away.

Talisman watched him go. Zhusai came to him and wrapped a linen bandage around his wounded hand. "You spoke well," she said admiringly. Reaching out, he stroked his hand through her dark hair.

"You must leave this place."

"No, I shall stay."

Talisman gazed on her beauty then, the simple white tunic of silk shining in the sunlight, the sheen of her long black hair. "I wish," he said, "that you could have been mine."

"I am yours," she told him. "Now and always."

"It cannot be. You are pledged to the Uniter. To the man with violet eyes."

She shrugged. "So says Nosta Khan. But today you united five tribes, and that is enough for me. I stay." Stepping in to him, she took his hand and kissed the palm.

Quing-chin approached them. "You wished to see me, Talisman?"

Zhusai drew away, but Talisman caught her hand and lifted it to his lips. Then he turned and beckoned Quing-chin to follow him. "We must slow their advance," he said, leading the warrior to the breakfast table.

"How so?"

"If they are still two days from us, they will make one more night camp. Take ten men and scout the area. Then, when they are camped, scatter as many Gothir horses as you can."

"With ten men?"

"More would be a hindrance," said Talisman. "You must follow the example of Adrius. You remember your studies with Fanlon?"

"I remember," Quing-chin said with a wry smile. "But I didn't believe it then."

"Make it true now, my friend, for we need the time."

Quing-chin rose. "I live to obey, my general," he said, speaking in Gothir and giving the lancers' salute. Talisman grinned.

"Go now. And do not die on me. I need you."

"That is advice I shall keep close to my heart," the warrior promised.

Next Talisman summoned Bartsai. The Curved Horn leader sat down and poured himself a cup of water. "Tell me of all the water holes within a day's ride of here," he said.

"There are three. Two are small seeps. Only one would supply an army."

"That is good. Describe it to me."

"It is twelve miles to the east and high in the mountains. It is very deep and cold and is full even in the driest seasons."

"How easy is it to approach?"

Bartsai shrugged. "As I said, it is high. There is only one path to it, snaking up through the passes."

"Could wagons reach it?"

"Yes, though the trail would have to be cleared of large rocks."

"How would you defend it?"

"Why would I defend it?" countered Bartsai. "The enemy is coming here!"

"They will need water, Bartsai. It must be denied them."

Bartsai grinned, showing broken teeth. "That is so, Talisman. With fifty men I could hold the trail against any army."

"Fifty cannot be spared. Pick twenty—the finest you have."

"I will lead them myself," said Bartsai.

"No, you are needed here. As the Gothir approach, other

Curved Horn riders will come to the shrine, and they will look to you for leadership."

Bartsai nodded. "This is true. Seven came in last night, and I have men scouting for others." The older man sighed. "I have lived for almost fifty years, Talisman. And I have dreamed of fighting the Gothir. But not like this—a handful of men in a rotting shrine."

"This is only the beginning, Bartsai. I promise you that."

Kzun heaved another rock into place and stepped back, wiping sweat from his face with a grimy hand. For three hours he and his men had been moving stone blocks from the ruined tower and packing them against the west wall, just below the crack, creating a platform that Talisman had ordered to be twenty feet long, ten feet wide, and five feet tall. It was backbreaking work, and some of his men had complained. But Kzun had silenced them; he would suffer no whining before the other tribesmen.

He glanced to where Talisman was deep in conversation with the long-faced Sky Rider Lin-tse. Sweat dripped into his eyes. He hated the work, for it reminded him of the two years he had spent in the Gothir gold mines to the north. He shivered at the memory, remembering the day when he had been dragged in ankle chains to the mouth of the shaft and ordered to climb down. They had not removed the chains, and twice Kzun's feet had slipped and he had hung in darkness. Eventually he had arrived at the foot of the shaft, where two guards carrying torches had been waiting. One had smashed a fist into Kzun's face, propelling him into the wall. "That's to remind you, dung monkey, to obey every order you hear. Instantly!" The fifteen-year-old Kzun had struggled to his feet and looked up into the man's bearded, ugly face. He saw the second blow coming but could not avoid it. It split his lips and broke his nose. "And that is to tell you that you never look a guard in the eye. Now get up and follow."

Two years in the dark followed, with weeping sores on his

ankles where the chains bit, boils on his back and neck, and the kiss of the whip when his weary body failed to move at the speed the guards demanded. Men died around him, their spirits broken long before their bodies surrendered to the dark. But Kzun would not be broken. Every day he chipped at the tunnel walls with his pick of iron or a short-handled shovel, gathering up baskets of rock and hauling them back to the carts drawn by blind ponies. And every sleep time—for who could tell what was day and what was night?—he would fall to the ground on the order and rest his exhausted body on the rock of the ever-lengthening tunnel. Twice the tunnel at the face collapsed, killing miners. Kzun was half buried in the second fall but dug himself clear before the rescuers came.

Most of the slave workers around him were Gothir criminals, petty thieves and housebreakers. The Nadir contingent were known as "picked men." In Kzun's case that meant that a troop of Gothir soldiers had ridden into his village and arrested all the young men they could find. Seventeen had been taken. There were mines all over the mountains here, and Kzun had never seen his friends again.

Then, during a shift, a workman preparing support timbers broke the tip of his file. With a curse he strode back down the tunnel, seeking a replacement. Kzun picked up the tip; it was no longer than his thumb. Every sleep time for days and days he slowly filed away at the clasps of his ankle chain. There was always noise in the tunnels: the roaring of underground rivers, the snoring of sleepers whose lungs were caked with dirt and dust. Even so Kzun was careful. Finally, having worked evenly on both clasps, he got the first to give way. Feverishly Kzun filed the second. It, too, fell clear. Rising, he made his way back down the tunnel to where the tools were stored. It was quieter there, and a man wearing chains would have been heard by the guards in the small chamber by the shaft. But Kzun was wearing no chains. Selecting a short-handled pick, he hefted it clear of the other tools and padded silently to the guards' chamber.

There were two men inside; they were playing some kind of game involving bone dice. Taking a deep breath, Kzun leapt inside, swinging his pick into the back of the first man, the iron point driving through the rib cage and bursting from his chest. Releasing the weapon, Kzun drew the dying man's knife and hurled himself across the table at the second guard. The man surged to his feet, scrabbling for his own knife, but he was too late.

Kzun's weapon punched into his neck, down past the collar-bone, and into his heart.

Swiftly Kzun stripped the man, then climbed into his clothes. The boots were too big, and he hurled them aside.

Moving to the shaft, he began to climb the iron rungs set into the stone. The sky was dark above him, and he saw the stars shining clear. A lump came to his throat then. Climbing more slowly, he reached the lip of the shaft and warily looked out. There was a cluster of buildings beyond, where they milled the ore, and a barracks for the guards. Scrambling clear, Kzun walked slowly across the open ground. The smell of horse came to him on the night breeze, and he followed it to a stable.

Stealing a fine horse, he rode from the settlement and out into the clean, sweet air of the mountains.

Returning to his village, he found that no one recognized him as the young man taken only two years before. He had lost his hair, and his skin and face had the pallor of the recently dead. The teeth on the right side of his mouth had rotted away, and his once-powerful body was now wolf-lean.

The Gothir had not come for him. They took no names of the Nadir "picked men" or had any record of which village they had raided to capture him.

Now Kzun heaved another slab of old stone into place and stepped back from the new wall. It was just under four feet high. A beautiful woman appeared alongside him, carrying a bucket of water in which was a copper ladle. She bowed deeply and offered him a short scarf of white linen. "It is for the head, lord," she said formally.

"I thank you," he replied, not smiling for fear of showing his ruined teeth. "Who are you?" he asked as he tied the scarf over his bald head.

"I am Zhusai, Talisman's woman."

"You are very beautiful, and he is most fortunate."

She bowed again and offered him a ladle of water. He drank deeply, then passed the bucket to his waiting men. "Tell me, how is it that Talisman knows so much of the ways of the Gothir?"

"He was taken by them as a child," answered Zhusai. "He was a hostage. He was trained at the Bodacas Academy, as were Quing-chin and Lin-tse."

"A janizary. I see. I have heard of them."

"He is a great man, lord."

"Only a great man would deserve someone like you," he said. "I thank you for the scarf."

With a bow she moved away, and Kzun sighed. One of his men made a crude comment, and Kzun rounded on him. "Not one word more, Chisk, or I will rip your tongue from your mouth!"

"How do you read the other leaders?" asked Talisman.

Lin-tse let the question hang for a moment, marshaling his thoughts. "The weakest of them is Bartsai. He is old. He doesn't want to die. Quing-chin is as I remember him, brave and thoughtful. I am grateful to Gargan. Had he not been marching here with his army, I would have been forced to kill Quing-chin. It would have scarred my soul. Kzun? The man has a demon within him. He is unhinged, Talisman, but I think he will stand tall."

"And what of Lin-tse?"

"He is as you knew him. My people call me the man with two souls. I do not think it is true, but the years at Bodacas changed me. I now have to *try* to be Nadir. It is worse for Quing-chin. He killed my best fighter and refused to take his eyes. I would not have done that, Talisman, but I would have wished to. You understand?"

"I understand," said Talisman. "They took from us. But we also took from them. We will put it to good use here."

"We will die here, my friend," Lin-tse said softly. "But we will die well."

"Brothers unto death," said Talisman. "And perhaps beyond. Who knows?"

"Now, what orders do you have for me, General?"

Talisman looked into Lin-tse's dark, brooding eyes. "It is important that we begin this venture with a victory, no matter how small. Gargan will come with the main van of the army. Ahead will be several companies of lancers. They will reach us first, and I want you and your Sky Riders to bloody them. Bartsai tells me there is a narrow pass twelve miles west. When the lancers reach it, attack them—not head on but with arrows. Then run back through the pass. You will have most of today and early tomorrow to prepare your surprises. Bring back spoils if you can."

Lin-tse nodded. "You are thinking of Fecrem and the Long Retreat."

"I am indeed. As I said, a victory is important. What is vital, however, is that you take no unnecessary risks. If there are more than three companies, do not engage them. Your thirty men are irreplaceable."

Lin-tse rose. "I will do my utmost, General."

"Of that I have no doubt. You have the coolest head, Lin-tse. That is why I chose you for this mission."

Lin-tse's expression did not change. Without a word he strode away. Gorkai stepped forward. "He is a hard man, that one," he observed.

"A man of stone," agreed Talisman. "Where is Zhusai?"

"She went into the shrine to pray."

Talisman followed and found her standing by the stone sarcophagus. It was cool in the shadowed chamber, and he stood for a moment, watching her. She turned toward him and smiled. "It is so quiet here," she said.

"I saw you give the scarf to Kzun. Why did you do it?"

"He is a dangerous man and one who might . . . question your orders."

"A man gold could not buy, and you won him with a piece of linen. You are a surprising woman, Zhusai."

"There is nothing I would not do for you, Talisman. You will forgive me for being forward, but time is precious, is it not?"

"It is," he admitted, moving to her side. She took his hand and held it to her breast.

"Have you been with a woman?" she asked him.

"No."

"Then there is much for us both to discover." Drawing her to him, he touched his lips to hers. The scent of her hair filled his nostrils, and the taste of her mouth swamped his senses. He felt dizzy and weak and drew back from her. "I love you, my Talisman," she whispered.

For just those fleeting seconds he had forgotten the perils that awaited them both. Now realization struck him like a fist. "Why now?" he asked, pulling away.

"Because that is all there is," she said. Swinging to the sarcophagus, she ran her hand over the iron plate. "Oshikai Demon-bane, Lord of War," she read. "He was beset by enemies when he wed Shul-sen. And they had so little time, Talisman. They were together only four years. But great was their love. Ours will be as great. I know it. I feel it, here in this place. And if we die, we shall walk hand in hand through the Void. I know this, too."

"I do not want you to die," he said. "I wish I had never brought you here. I wish it with all my heart."

"And I am glad you did. You will win, Talisman. Your cause is just. The evil comes from the Gothir."

"It is a touching sentiment, Zhusai, and one that I wish were true. Sadly, the good do not always conquer. I must go, for there is much to do."

"When you have done all that you can and the night grows long, come to me, Talisman. Will you do that?"

"I will come to you," he promised.

The sky was black with crows and vultures as Druss and Sieben came over a ridge and down into a shadow valley. Below them were some forty goathide tents. Bodies were strewn everywhere under a writhing mass of carrion birds. Elsewhere small desert dogs tugged at rotting flesh.

"Sweet heaven," whispered Sieben, pulling back on the reins.

Druss touched his heels to the mare and rode down the hillside. Leading their extra ponies, Sieben followed him. Vultures too fat to fly spread their wings and waddled away from the horses. The stench of death caused the horses to shy away from the scene, but the riders forced them on. At first Sieben just stared ahead, trying not to look at the bodies. There were children there and women, some huddled together, others who had been slain as they ran. A brown dog edged into a flapping tent, then yelped and ran away. Druss dragged on the reins.

"Why are we stopping?" asked Sieben.

Druss dismounted, passing the mare's reins to the poet. Ax in hand, he strode to the tent and, ducking down, moved inside. Sieben sat on his horse and forced himself to view the scene. It was not hard to see what had happened there. The killers had attacked late in the evening as the cook fires were under way. The Nadir had fled in all directions but had been cut down with ruthless efficiency. Several of the bodies had been mutilated: beheaded or dismembered.

Druss emerged from the tent and moved to the horses, lifting clear a water canteen. "There's a woman inside," he said. "She's alive, but only just. She has a babe."

Sieben dismounted and tethered the horses to a tent pole. The Gothir mounts were skittish and nervous of the dogs and vultures, but the Nadir ponies stood by calmly. Swiftly he hobbled the horses with lengths of rawhide, then joined Druss. Inside the tent lay a naked young woman, a terrible wound in her belly and side. Blood had drenched the brightly colored blankets on which she lay. Her eyes were open, but her mouth was hanging slack. Druss raised her head, holding the canteen to her lips; water dribbled over her chin, but she managed to swallow a little. Sieben gazed at the wound; it was deep, the blade having completely pierced her body. The babe, partly hidden beneath a pile of furs, was whimpering softly. Druss picked it up and held it to the woman's swollen breast. It began to suck, weakly at first. The woman groaned and moved her arm around the child, drawing it in to her.

"What can we do?" asked Sieben. Druss' cold eyes met his. The axman said nothing. When Sieben reached up to stroke the woman's face, her dead eyes stared at him. The babe continued to feed.

"This one they kept for rape," said Druss. "What a pack of mongrels!"

"May they rot in seven hells," said Sieben. The babe ceased to suck, and Druss lifted it to his broad shoulder, supporting its head and gently rubbing its back. Sieben's eyes were drawn to the woman's swollen nipple. Milk and blood were seeping from it.

"Why, Druss?" he asked.

"Why what?"

"Why did they do it? What was the purpose?"

"I am not the man to ask, poet. I have seen the sack of cities and watched good men become evil as they were fired by rage and lust and fear. I don't know why they do it. The soldiers who did this will go home to their wives and families and be good husbands and fathers. It is a mystery to me."

Wrapping the naked babe in a blanket, he carried him out

into the sunlight. Sieben followed him. "Will they write it as a victory, do you think?" asked Sieben. "Will they sing songs about this raid?"

"Let's hope there are some women with milk in their breasts at the shrine," said Druss. Sieben freed the horses and held the babe until Druss had mounted. Passing the child to the axman, he stepped into the saddle of the gelding.

"He fed on milk and blood," said Sieben. "He drank from the dead."

"But he lives," said Druss. "He breathes."

The two rode on. Druss lifted the blanket over the top of the infant's head, shielding him from the bright sun. The child was asleep. Druss could smell the newness of life upon him, the creamy scent of milk-fed breath. He thought of Rowena and her longing for such a child to hold at her breast.

"I will be a farmer," he said suddenly. "When I get home, I shall stay there. No more wars. No more vultures."

"You believe that, my friend?" asked Sieben.

Druss felt the sinking of his heart. "No," he said.

They rode on across the burning steppes for another hour, then transferred the saddles to the two Nadir ponies. The baby awoke and cried for a while. Druss tried to calm him, then Sieben took him. "How old is he, do you think?" the poet asked.

"Perhaps a month. Two—I don't know."

Sieben swore, and Druss laughed. "Anointed you, too, has he?"

"During my short, eventful life I have learned many things, Druss, old horse," he said, holding the babe at arm's length. "But I never thought I would have to worry about urine stains on silk. Will it rot the fabric, do you think?"

"We can only hope not."

"How does one stop them from crying?"

"Tell him one of your stories, poet. They always put me to sleep."

Sieben cradled the babe close and began to sing a gentle song about Princess Ulastay and her desire to wear stars in her hair. He had a good voice, strong and melodic. The Nadir child rested its head against his chest and was soon asleep. Toward dusk they saw a dust cloud ahead, and Druss led them off the trail and into a small gully. Two companies of lancers rode by above them, heading west, their armor bright, the helms gleaming red in the fading sunshine. Sieben's heart was hammering fast. The babe murmured in his arms, but the sound did not carry above the drumming of hoofbeats.

Once they had passed, Druss headed northeast.

With the dying of the sun the air grew cooler, and Sieben felt the warmth of the child in his arms. "I think he has a fever," he told Druss.

"All babies are hot," said Druss.

"Really? I wonder why."

"They just are. By heavens, poet, do you have to question everything?"

"I have a curious mind."

"Then set it to work on how we are going to feed the child when he wakes. He looks a lusty infant to me, and his cries are likely to travel far. And we are unlikely to meet friends out here."

"That's it, Druss. Always try to finish on a comforting note."


Gargan, Lord of Larness, waited patiently as his manservant Bren unbuckled the heavy breastplate and removed it. The flesh around his middle had spread since last he had worn it, and the freedom of release caused him to sigh with pleasure. He had ordered new armor the previous month, but it had not been ready when Garen-Tsen had told him of the jewels and the need for speed.

Bren unfastened the thigh plates and greaves, and Gargan sat down on a canvas chair and stretched out his legs. The nation was sliding into the pit, he thought bitterly. The emperor's madness was growing daily, and the two factions were hovering in the shadows. Civil war loomed. Madness!

And we are all caught up in it, he realized. Magical jewels, indeed! The only magic that counted was contained in the swords of the Royal Guards, the shining points of the royal lances.

What was needed now was an outside threat to pull the Gothir nation together. A war with the tribes would focus the minds of the people wonderfully. It would buy time. The emperor had to go. The question was when, and how, and who would replace him? Until that day Gargan would have to give the factions something else to think about.

Bren left the tent, returning with a tray of wine, butter, cheese, and bread. "The captains wish to know when you will see them, my lord," he said. Gargan looked up at him. The man was getting old, worn out.

"How many campaigns have you served with me?" asked Gargan.

"Twelve, my lord," answered Bren, cutting the bread and buttering three slices.

"Which do you remember most fondly?"

The old man paused in his preparations. "Gassima," he said.

Pouring the wine into a silver goblet, Bren added water and passed it to his general. Gargan sipped it. Gassima! The last civil war, almost twenty-five years in the past now. Outnumbered, Gargan had led a retreat across the marshes, then had swung his force and launched an attack that ought to have been suicidal. On his giant white stallion Skall he had thundered into the heart of the enemy camp and killed Barin in hand-to-hand combat. The war had been won on that day, the civil war ended. Gargan drained his wine and handed the goblet to Bren, who refilled it.

"That was a horse, by Missael! Feared nothing. It would have charged into the fires of hell."

"A mighty steed," agreed Bren.

"Never known another like him. You know the stallion I ride

now? He is of the blood of Skall, his great-grandson. But he does not have the same qualities. Skall was a prince of horses." Gargan chuckled. "Mounted three mares on the day he died, at the ripe age of thirty-two. I have wept only twice in my life, Bren. The first was on the death of Skall."

"Yes, my lord. What shall I tell the captains?"

"One hour from now. I have letters to read."

"Yes, my lord." Leaving the meal on the table, Bren stepped back through the tent flap. Gargan stood and poured a third goblet of wine; this time he added no water. The mail riders had caught up with the vanguard of the army at dusk, and there were three letters for him. He opened the first, which bore the seal of Garen-Tsen. Gargan tried to focus on the spidery script. Lifting a lantern from its pole, he lowered it to the desk. His eyes were not what they once had been. Nothing is what it was, he thought.

The letter told of the funeral of the queen, and how Garen-Tsen had smuggled the king from the city, having him taken to the winter palace at Siccus. The factions were beginning to speak openly in the Senate about "a need for change." Garen-Tsen urged a speedy end to the campaign and a swift return to the capital.

The second letter was from his wife. He scanned it: four pages containing little of interest, detailing small incidents from the household and the farms. A maidservant had broken an arm falling from a chair as she cleaned windows, a prize foal had been sold for a thousand Raq, and three slaves had fled the north farm but had been recaptured in a local brothel.

The last letter was from his daughter, Mirkel. She had given birth to a baby boy, and she was calling him Argo. She hoped Gargan could see him soon.

The old soldier's eyes misted.

Argo. Finding his mutilated body had been like a blow to the heart, and Gargan could still feel the pain of it. He had known all along that allowing Nadir filth to attend the academy would lead to disaster. But never had he remotely considered the possibility that it would lead to the death of his own son. And what a death to suffer!

Anger and sorrow vied in him.

The old emperor had been a wise man, ruling well in the main. But his later years had seen a rise in confusion, a softening of his attitudes. It was for this man that Gargan had fought at Gassima. I gave you that crown, he thought. I placed it on your head. And because of you my son is dead.

Nadir janizaries! A foul and pernicious idea. Why was it that the old man could not see the stupidity of it? The Nadir were numberless and dreamed only of the day when a Uniter would draw them together into one unstoppable army. And yet the emperor had wished the sons of their chiefs to be trained in the ways of Gothir warfare. Gargan could still scarcely believe it.

The day when Okai had been the prize student was a grim one to recall. What was worse was to know that the man who had walked up to the dais was the murderer of his son. He had had him close then; he could have reached out and torn away his throat.

Gargan reached for the jug but hesitated. The captains would be there soon, and strong drink was no aid to planning.

Rising from the table, he rubbed at his weary eyes and stepped outside the tent. Two guards came to attention. Gargan stared out over the campsite, pleased with the orderly placing of tents and the neatness of the five picket lines. The ground had been well cleared around the campfires, dug over and wetted down, so that no spark could land on the tinder-dry grass of the steppes.

Gargan walked on, scanning the camp for signs of disorderliness or complacency. He found none except that one of the latrine trenches had been dug in an area where the prevailing wind would carry the stench back into the camp. He noted it in his mind. Two Nadir heads had been tied to a pole outside one tent. A group of lancers were sitting around a campfire close by.

When Gargan strode up, the men leapt to their feet, saluting smartly.

"Bury them," said Gargan. "They are attracting flies and mosquitoes."

"Yes, sir!" they chorused.

Gargan returned to his tent. Sitting down at the table, he took quill and ink and wrote a short letter to Mirkel, congratulating her and stating his hope and his intention to be with her soon. "Take good care of little Argo," he wrote. "Do not rely on wet nurses. A child draws much from his mother's milk, taking in not only nourishment but also spirit and courage. One should never allow a babe of noble birth to suckle at a common breast. It dissipates character."

Traveling carefully, using dry gullies and low terrain, Quing-chin and his nine riders avoided the Gothir patrols. As darkness fell, they were hidden to the south of the Gothir encampment. His friend Shi-da crept alongside him as he knelt behind a screen of dry bushes, scanning the camp.

The night breeze was picking up, blowing from the south-east. Shi-da tapped Quing-chin's shoulder. "It is done, my brother."

Quing-chin settled back on his haunches. The breeze was picking up. "Good."

"When?" asked Shi-da, eagerness showing on his young face.

"Not yet. We wait until they settle for the night."

"Tell me of Talisman," said Shi-da, settling down alongside him. "Why is he the chosen one? He is not as strong as you."

"Strength of body counts for nothing in a general," said Quing-chin. "He has a mighty heart and a mind sharper than a dagger."

"You also have a great heart, my brother."

Quing-chin smiled. The boy's hero worship was a source of both irritation and delight. "I am the hawk; he is the eagle. I am the wolf; he is the tiger. One day Talisman will be a war leader among the Nadir. He will lead armies, little brother. He has a mind for . . ." He hesitated. There was no Nadir word for "logistics." "A mind for planning," he said at last. "When an army marches, it must be supplied. It needs food and water, and just as important, it needs information. It takes a rare man to be able to plan for all eventualities. Talisman is such a man."

"He was at the academy with you?"

"Yes. And at the last he was the honor student, beating all others."

"He fought them all?"

"In a way." Behind them a pony whinnied, and Quing-chin glanced back to where the others were hidden. "Get back to them," he said, "and tell Ling that if he does not control his pony better than that, I shall send him back in disgrace."

As the boy eased himself back from the gully's crest, Quing-chin settled down to wait. Fanlon had often said that a captain's greatest gift was patience: knowing when to strike and having the nerve to wait for the right moment.

As the air cooled, the wind would increase. So would the moisture as a result of the change in temperature. All these factors combined to make good timing essential. Quing-chin looked out at the enemy camp and felt his anger rise. They were not in a defensive formation, as was required when in enemy territory. There was no outer perimeter of fortifications. They had constructed the encampment according to the regulations for a peacetime maneuver: five picket lines, each with two hundred horses, the tents set out in squares by regiment. How arrogant they were, these *gajin*. How well they understood Nadir mentality.

Three Gothir scouts came riding from the east. Quing-chin ducked down below the crest until they had passed. They were talking and laughing as they rode. Tomorrow there would be no laughter; they would be biting on a leather strap as the whip lashed their backs.

Quing-chin carefully made his way down the slope to where

his men were waiting. Tinder and brush had been packed into a net of twine and tied to a long rope. "Now is the time," he said.

Shi-da stepped forward. "May I ride the fire?" he asked.

"No." The boy's disappointment was intense, but Quing-chin walked past him, stopping before a short, bowlegged warrior. "You have the glory, Nien," he said. "Remember, ride south for at least a quarter of a mile before releasing the rope. Not too fast, then double back along the line."

"It will be done," said the man. Swiftly they mounted and rode to the top of the gully. Quing-chin and two others leapt from their saddles and, using tinderboxes, lit the tinder bundle tied behind Nien's pony. Flames licked up, then roared into life.

Nien kicked his horse and set off at a slow trot across the dry grass of the steppes. Fire flickered behind him, and dark oily smoke spiraled up. The wind fanned the blaze, and soon a roaring wall of flames swept toward the Gothir camp.

"Might I inquire, sir, the purpose of this mission?" asked Premian as he and the other ten senior officers gathered in Gargan's tent.

"You may," said the general. "Our intelligence reports show that a Nadir uprising is planned, and it is our duty to see that it does not happen. Reports have been gathered and compiled showing that the Curved Horn tribe has been mustering for a major raid on the lands around Gulgothir. We shall crush this tribe; it will send a message to other Nadir chieftains. First, however, we shall march to the Shrine of Oshikai and dismantle it stone by stone. The bones of their hero will be crushed to powder and scattered on the steppes."

The veteran Marlham spoke up. "But surely, sir, the shrine is a holy place to all the tribes. Will this not be seen by all the leaders as a provocation?"

"Indeed it will," snarled Gargan. "Let them know once and for all that they are a slave race. Would that I could bring an army of forty thousand into the steppes. By Shemak, I would slay them all!"

Premian was tempted to speak again, but Gargan had been drinking and his face was flushed, his temper short. He was leaning on the desk, the muscles of his arms sharp and powerful in the lantern light, his eyes gleaming. "Does any man here have a problem with this mission?"

The other officers shook their heads. Gargan straightened and moved around the desk, looming over the shorter Premian. "How about you? As I recall, you have a soft spot for these scum."

"I am a soldier, sir. It is my duty to carry out all orders given to me by a superior officer."

"But you don't agree with them, do you?" sneered Gargan, pushing his bearded face so close to Premian's that the officer could smell the sour taste of wine on the other man's breath.

"It is not my place to disagree with policy, sir."

"Not my place," mimicked Gargan. "No, sir, it is not your place. Do you know how many tribesmen there are?"

"No, sir."

"No, sir. Neither do I, boy. Nor does any man. But they are numberless. Can you imagine what would happen if they joined together under one leader? They would sweep over us like a tide." He blinked and returned to his table, sitting heavily on the canvas chair, which groaned under the sudden weight. "Like a tide," he mumbled. Sucking in a great breath, he fought to overcome the wine in his system. "They must be humbled. Crushed. Demoralized."

A commotion began outside, and Premian heard men shouting. With the other officers he left the tent. A wall of flame was lighting the night sky, and smoke was swirling around the camp. Horses began whinnying in fear. Premian swung his gaze around the camp. The fire would sweep right over it. "The water wagons!" he yelled. "Harness the wagons!" Premian began to run across the camp to where the twenty wagons had been drawn up in a square. Each carried sixteen barrels. A man ran by him in panic, and Premian grabbed his shoulder.

"Fetch horses for the wagons," he said, his voice ringing with authority.

"Yes, sir," replied the soldier, saluting. He moved away.

Premian saw a group of soldiers trying to gather their belongings from a communal tent. "Leave them," he shouted. "If the wagons go up, we'll all die. You three get to the picket line. Fetch horses. The rest of you start dragging these wagons into line for harness."

The flames were licking at the edge of the camp now. Hundreds of men were trying to beat out the fires with blankets and cloaks, but Premian saw that it was pointless. Soldiers came running back, leading frightened horses. A tent caught fire. The first of the wagons was harnessed, and a soldier climbed to the driving board and lashed out with the reins. The four horses leaned into the harnesses, and the wagon lurched forward.

A second wagon followed, then a third. More men came to help. Premian ran to the nearest picket line. "Cut the rest of the horses loose," he told a soldier standing by. "We'll round them up tomorrow!"

"Yes, sir," responded the man, slashing his knife through the picket rope. Premian grabbed the reins of the nearest horse and vaulted to its bare back. The beast was panicked and reared, but Premian was an expert horseman. Leaning forward, he patted the horse's long neck.

"Courage, my beauty," he said. Riding back to the wagons, he saw that another six had been harnessed and were moving east, away from the line of fire. More tents were ablaze now, and smoke and cinders filled the air. To the left a man screamed as his clothes caught fire. Several soldiers threw him to the ground, covering him with blankets to smother the flames. The heat was intense now, and it was hard to breathe. Flames were licking at the last of the wagons, but two more were harnessed.

"That's it!" Premian yelled at the struggling soldiers. "Save yourselves!"

The men mounted the last of the horses and galloped from

the burning camp. Premian turned to see other soldiers running for their lives. Several stumbled and fell and were engulfed in flames. He swung his horse and saw Gargan walking through the smoke. The general looked bewildered and lost. "Bren!" he was shouting. "Bren!"

Premian tried to steer his horse to the general, but the beast would not move toward the flames. Dragging off his shirt, Premian leaned forward, looping it over the horse's eyes and tying it loosely in place. Heeling the now-blind stallion forward, he rode to Gargan.

"Sir! Mount behind me!"

"I can't leave Bren. Where is he?"

"He may already be clear, sir. If we stay any longer, we'll be cut off!"

Gargan swore, then reached up to take Premian's outstretched hand. With the practiced ease of a skilled horseman, he swung up behind. The young officer kicked the stallion into a gallop across the burning steppes, swerving around the walls of flame that swept toward the northwest. The heat was searing, and Premian could hardly see through the smoke as the horse thundered on, its flanks scorched.

At last they outran the fire, and Premian dragged the exhausted stallion to a stop. Leaping from its back, he turned and watched the camp burn.

Gargan slid down beside him. "You did well, boy," he said, placing his huge hand on Premian's shoulder.

"Thank you, sir. I think we saved most of the water wagons."

The stallion's flanks were charred and blistered, and the great beast stood shivering. Premian led him to the east, where the main body of soldiers had gathered.

Slowly, as the fire died away in the distance, men began making their way back to the camp, searching through the wreckage. By dawn all the bodies had been recovered. Twenty-six men and twelve horses had died in the flames. All the tents had been destroyed, but most of the supplies had survived; the fire had passed too quickly to burn through all the sacks of flour, salt, oats, and dried meat. Of the nine water wagons left behind, six had caught fire and were now useless, though most of the barrels containing the precious water had been saved. Only three had split their caulks.

As the early-morning sun rose above the blackened earth of the campsite, Gargan surveyed the wreckage. "The fire was set in the south," he told Premian. "Find the names of the night sentries in that section. Thirty lashes per man."

"Yes, sir."

"Less destruction than we might have expected," said the general.

"Yes, sir. Though more than a thousand arrows were lost and around eighty lances. I'm sorry about your manservant. We found his body behind the tent."

"Bren was a good man. Served me well. I took him out of the line when the rheumatism ruined his sword arm. Good man! They'll pay for his death with a hundred of their own."

"We've also lost six water wagons, sir. With your permission, I will adjust the daily ration to allow for the loss and suspend the order that every lancer must be clean-shaven daily."

Gargan nodded. "We'll not get all the horses back," he said. "Some of the younger ones will run clear back to Gulgothir."

"I fear you are correct, sir," said Premian.

"Ah, well. Some of our lancers will have to be transferred to the infantry; it'll make them value their mounts more in the future." Gargan hawked and spit. "Send four companies through the pass. I want reports on any Nadir movements. And prisoners. Last night's attack was well executed; it reminds me of Adrius and the winter campaign, when he slowed the enemy army with fire."

Premian was silent for a moment, but he saw that Gargan was staring at him, awaiting a response. "Okai was Wolfshead, sir. Not Curved Horn. In fact, I don't believe we had any Curved Horn janizaries."

"You don't know your Nadir customs, Premian. Four tribes guard the shrine. Perhaps he is with them. I hope so. I would give my left arm to have him in my power."

The moon was high above the Valley of Shul-sen's Tears, and Talisman, weary to the bone, took a last walk to the battlements, stepping carefully over sleeping Nadir warriors. His eyes were gritty and tired, his body aching with unaccustomed fatigue as he slowly climbed the rampart steps. The new wooden platform creaked under his feet. In the absence of nails the planks had been tied into place, but it was solid enough, and the next day it would be more stable yet as Bartsai and his men continued to work on it. The fighting platform constructed by Kzun and his Lone Wolves was nearing completion. Kzun had worked well, tirelessly, but the man worried Talisman. Often during the day he would walk from the shrine compound and stand out on the steppes. And now he was sleeping not with his men but outside, back at the former Lone Wolves camp.

Gorkai strode up to join him. On Talisman's instructions, the former Notas had worked alongside Kzun's men throughout the day. "What did you find out?" asked Talisman, keeping his voice low.

"He is a strange one," said Gorkai. "He never sleeps inside his tent; he takes his blankets out and spreads them under the stars. He has never taken a wife. And back in Curved Horn lands he lives alone, away from the tribe; he has no sword brothers."

"Why, then, was he placed in command of the tomb guards?" asked Talisman.

"He is a ferocious fighter. Eleven duels he has fought—he has not been cut once. All his enemies are dead. His men hate him, but they respect him."

"What is your evaluation?"

Gorkai shrugged and scratched at the widow's peak on his brow. "I don't like him, Talisman, but if I was faced with many enemies, I would want him by my side." Talisman sat down on the rampart wall, and Gorkai looked at him closely. "You should sleep."

"Not yet. I have much to think on. Where is Nosta Khan?"

"In the shrine. He casts spells there," said Gorkai, "but he finds nothing. I heard him curse a while back."

Gorkai gazed along the wall. When first he had seen the shrine, he had thought it small, but now the walls—at sixty paces each—looked ridiculously long. "Can we hold this place?" he asked suddenly.

"For a time," said Talisman. "Much depends on how many ladders the enemy has. If they are well equipped, they will sweep over us."

"A thousand curses on all of them," hissed Gorkai.

Talisman grinned. "They will not have enough ladders. They would not have expected a siege. And there are no trees to hack down here to make them. We have close to two hundred men now, fifty per wall if they try to attack on all sides. We will hold them, Gorkai—at least for some days."

"And then what?"

"We live or die," Talisman answered with a weary shrug.

Far away to the southwest the sky began to glow a dull, flickering red. "What is that?" asked Gorkai.

"With luck it is the enemy camp burning," said Talisman grimly. "It will not slow them overmuch, but it will rob them of their complacency."

"I hope many die."

"Why do you stay?" asked Talisman.

Gorkai looked puzzled. "What do you mean? Where else would I be? I am Wolfshead now, Talisman. You are my leader."

"I may have led you to a path of no returning, Gorkai."

"All paths lead to death, Talisman. But here I am at one with the gods of stone and water. I am Nadir again, and that has meaning."

"Indeed it does. And I tell you this, my friend: it will have more meaning in the years to come. When the Uniter leads his armies, the world will tremble at the sound of the name 'Nadir.' "

"That is a pleasant thought to take to my bed," said Gorkai with a smile.

Just then both men saw the figure of Zhusai emerge from the sleeping quarters. She was dressed only in a shift of white linen, and she walked slowly, dreamily, toward the gates. Talisman ran down the steps, closely followed by Gorkai, and they caught up with her on the open steppes. Gently Talisman took her by the arm. Her eyes were wide open and unblinking. "Where is my lord?" she asked.

"Zhusai? What is wrong?" whispered Talisman.

"I am lost," she said. "Why is my spirit chained in the dark place?" A tear formed and fell to her cheek. Talisman took her in his arms and kissed her brow.

"Who speaks?" said Gorkai, taking Zhusai's hand.

"Do you know my lord?" she asked him.

"Who are you?" asked Gorkai. Talisman released his hold and turned toward the warrior. Gorkai gestured him to silence and stepped before the woman. "Tell me your name," he said.

"I am Shul-sen, the wife of Oshikai. Can you help me?"

Gorkai took her hand and kissed it. "What help do you require, my lady?"

"Where is my lord?"

"He is . . ." Gorkai fell silent and looked to Talisman.

"He is not here," said Talisman. "Do you recall how you came here?"

"I was blind," she said, "but now I can see and hear and speak." Slowly she looked around. "I think I know this valley," she said, "but I do not remember the buildings here. I tried to leave the dark place, but there are demons there. My spells have no effect. The power is gone, and I cannot leave."

"And yet you have," said Gorkai. "You are here."

"I do not understand," she said. "Am I dreaming? Someone called me, and I awoke here. These clothes are not mine. And where is my *lon-tsia*? Where are my rings?"

Suddenly she jerked as if struck. "No!" she cried. "It is drawing me back. Help me! I cannot abide the dark place!" Wildly she reached out, grabbing Talisman's arm, then she went limp and fell against him. Her eyelids fluttered, and she looked up at Talisman. "What is happening, Talisman?" she asked.

"What do you remember?"

"I was dreaming. You remember? The woman in the cave? She was walking hand in hand with a man. Then the sun died away, and walls of black rock formed around us . . . her. All light faded until the darkness was absolute. The man was gone. I . . . she . . . tried to find a door in the rock, but there was none. And there were moans and snarls coming from close by. That is all I can remember. Am I going mad, Talisman?"

"I do not think so, my lady," Gorkai said softly. "Tell me, have you ever seen visions?"

"No."

"Have you ever heard voices though there was no one near?"

"No. What are you saying?"

"I believe the spirit of Shul-sen is somehow drawn to you. I don't know why. But I do know you are not insane. I have seen spirits and spoken with them. It was the same with my father. What we have just experienced here was no dream walking. Your voice was different, as was your manner. You agree, Talisman?"

"This is beyond my understanding," admitted the Nadir leader. "What must we do?"

"I do not know what we can do," said Gorkai. "You told me that Oshikai is searching for his wife, and now we know that Shul-sen is also seeking him. But their world is not ours, Talisman. We cannot bring them together."

The moon vanished behind a bank of clouds, plunging the steppes into darkness. A man cried out in the distance. Talisman saw a light hastily struck, and a lantern flickered to life outside the tent of Kzun.

# ◇ 9 ◇

**T**HE BLIND NADIR priest Enshima sat silently on the edge of the rocks overlooking the steppes below. Behind him, at the hidden spring, some two dozen refugees—mostly older women and young children—sat forlornly in the shade. He had seen the distant fire in the night and felt the passing of souls into the Void. The priest's pale blue robes were dust-stained, and his feet were sore and bleeding from walking on the sharp volcanic rock that blighted this area of the mountains.

Silently Enshima offered up a prayer of thanks for the ragged band of Curved Horns who had reached the spring two days before. They had been part of a larger group attacked by Gothir lancers but had managed to flee to higher ground where the heavily armed horsemen could not follow. Now they were safe for the moment. Hungry, bereaved, desolated but safe. Enshima thanked the Source for their lives.

Releasing the chains of his spirit, Enshima soared high above the mountains, gazing down on the vast emptiness of the steppes. Twelve miles to the northwest he could see the tiny battlements of the shrine, but he did not fly there. Instead he scanned the land for the two riders he knew would soon be approaching the spring.

He saw them riding out of a gully some two miles from the rocks in which his body sat. The axman was leading two horses while the poet, Sieben, rode at the rear, carrying the babe wrapped in its red blanket. Floating closer to the lead rider, he looked closely at the man. Riding a swaybacked mare, he was dressed in a jerkin of black leather with shining silver shoulder guards and was carrying a huge double-headed ax.

The route they were taking would lead them past the hidden spring. Enshima floated closer to the poet. Reaching out with his spirit hand, he touched the rider's shoulder.

"Hey, Druss," said Sieben. "You think there might be water in those rocks?"

"We don't need it," said the axman. "According to Nuang, the shrine should be no more than around ten miles from here."

"That may be true, old horse, but the child's blanket is beginning to stink. And I would appreciate the opportunity to wash some of my clothes before we make our grand entrance."

Druss chuckled. "Aye, poet, it would not be seemly for you to arrive looking any less than your glorious best." Tugging the reins to the left, Druss angled toward the dark volcanic rocks.

Sieben rode alongside him. "How will you find those healing jewels?" he asked.

The axman pondered the question. "I expect they are in the coffin," he said. "That would be usual, would it not?"

"It is an old shrine. I would think it would have been pillaged by now."

Druss was silent for a moment, then he shrugged. "Well, the old shaman said they were there. I'll ask him about it when I see him."

Sieben gave a wry grin. "I wish I had your faith in human nature, Druss, my friend."

The mare's head came up, nostrils quivering, and she quickened her pace. "There is water, right enough," said Sieben. "The horses can smell it."

They climbed the narrow, twisting trail, and as they reached the crest, two ancient Nadir warriors stepped out ahead of them. Both were carrying swords. A small priest in robes of faded blue appeared, and he spoke to the old men, who grudgingly backed away. Druss rode on, dismounting by the spring and casting a wary eye over the group of Nadir sitting close by.

The priest approached him. "You are welcome at our camp, axman," he said. The man's eyes were blind, their pupils of smoky opal. Laying Snaga against a rock, Druss took the baby from Sieben and waited as the poet swung down.

"This child needs milk," said Druss. The priest called out a name, and a young woman came forward, moving hesitantly. Taking the child from Druss, she walked back to the group.

"They are survivors from a Gothir raid," said the priest. "I am Enshima, a priest of the Source."

"Druss," said the axman. "And this is Sieben. We are traveling—"

"To the Shrine of Oshikai," said Enshima. "I know. Come, sit with me for a while." He walked away to a cluster of rocks by the spring. Druss followed him, while Sieben watered the horses and refilled their canteens.

"A great battle will be fought at the shrine," said Enshima. "You know this."

Druss sat down beside him. "I know. It does not interest me."

"Ah, but it does, for your own quest is linked to it. You will not find the jewels before the battle begins, Druss."

The axman knelt by the spring and drank. The water was cool and refreshing, but it left a bitter aftertaste on his tongue. Looking up at the blind man, he said, "You are a seer?"

"For what it is worth," agreed Enshima.

"Then can you tell me what this damned war is about? I see no sense in it."

Enshima gave a rueful smile. "That question presupposes that there is sense to any war."

"I am not a philosopher, priest, so spare me your ruminations."

"No, Druss, you are not a philosopher," said Enshima amiably, "but you are an idealist. What is this war about? As with all wars, it is about greed and fear: greed in that the Gothir are rich and desire to stay that way and fear in that they see the

Nadir as a future threat to their wealth and position. When has a war been fought over anything else?"

"These jewels exist, then," said Druss, changing the subject.

"Oh, they exist. The Eyes of Alchazzar were crafted several hundred years ago. They are like amethysts, each as big as an egg and each imbued with the awesome power of this savage land."

"Why will I not find them before the battle?" asked Druss as Sieben came up and sat alongside him.

"Such is not your destiny."

"I have a friend in need of them," said Druss. "I would appreciate your help in this matter."

Enshima smiled. "It gives me no pleasure to withhold help from you, axman. But what you would ask of me I shall not give you. Tomorrow I will lead these people deep into the mountains in the hope—vain though it may be—that I can keep them alive. You will journey to the shrine, and there you will fight. For that is what you do best."

"You have any bright words of comfort for me, old man?" asked Sieben.

The old man smiled and, reaching out, patted Sieben's arm. "I was set a problem, and you helped solve it, for which I give you my thanks. What you did back in the death chamber was a pure and good act for which I hope the Source blesses you. Show me the *lon-tsia*." Sieben fished into his pocket and produced the heavy silver medallion. The old man held it up before his face and closed his wood-smoke eyes. "The male head is that of Oshikai Demon-bane, the female that of his wife, Shul-sen. The script is Chiatze. A literal translation would be 'Oshka–Shul-sen—together.' But it really means 'spirit-entwined.' Their love was very great."

"Why would anyone want to torture her so?" asked Sieben.

"I cannot answer that, young man. The ways of evil men are lost to me; I have no understanding of such barbarity. Great magic was used to cage Shul-sen's spirit."

"Did I free her?"

"I do not know. A Nadir warrior told me that the spirit of Oshikai has been searching for her through the endless dark valleys of the Void. Perhaps now he has found her. I hope so. But as I said, the spells were very great."

Enshima returned the *lon-tsia* to Sieben. "This, too, has had a spell cast on it," he said.

"Not a curse, I hope," said the poet, holding the medallion gingerly.

"No, not a curse. I think it was a hide-spell. It would have masked it from the eyes of men. It is quite safe to carry, Sieben."

"Good. Tell me—you said the man was Oshikai, yet the name upon it is Oshka. Is that a short form?"

"There is no 'i' in the Chiatze alphabet. It is written as a small curved stroke above the preceding letter."

Sieben pocketed the medallion, and Enshima rose. "May the Source guard you both," he said.

Druss started toward his mare. "We leave you the two ponies," he said.

"That is most kind."

Sieben paused beside the old man. "How many defenders at the shrine?"

"I expect there will be fewer than two hundred when the Gothir arrive."

"And the jewels are there?"

"Indeed they are."

Sieben swore, then smiled sheepishly. "I was rather hoping they weren't. I am not at my best in battles."

"No civilized man is," said the priest.

"So why are the jewels hidden there?" asked Sieben.

Enshima shrugged. "They were crafted several hundred years ago and set in the head of a stone wolf. A shaman stole them. Obviously he wanted the power for himself. He was hunted and hid the jewels, then he tried to escape over the mountains. But he was caught, tortured, and killed near where you found the bones of Shul-sen. He did not reveal the hiding place of the eyes."

"The story makes no sense," said Sieben. "If the jewels were imbued with great power, why did he leave them behind? Surely he could have used their power against his pursuers?"

"Do the deeds of men always, as you say, make sense?" countered the priest.

"After a fashion," argued Sieben. "What kind of power did the eyes possess?"

"That is difficult to say. Much would depend on the skill of the man using them. They could heal all wounds and breach any spell. They were said to have powers of regeneration and replication."

"Could their power have hidden him from his pursuers?"

"Yes."

"Then why did he not use it?"

"I am afraid, young man, that that will remain a mystery."

"I hate mysteries," said Sieben. "You said 'regeneration.' They could raise the dead?"

"I mean regeneration of tissue, as in deep wounds or diseases. It was said that an old warrior became young again after being healed by them. But I think that is a fanciful tale."

Druss pushed himself to his feet. "Time to move on, poet," he said.

A young Nadir woman approached them, carrying the baby. Silently she offered it to Sieben. The poet stepped back. "No, no, my dear," he said. "Fond as we are of the little tyke, I think he is better off here, with his own people."

Talisman walked along the narrow wooden ramparts of the north wall, testing the strength of the structure and examining the ancient beams that held them in place. They seemed solid. The parapets were crenellated, allowing archers to shoot through the gaps. But each Nadir warrior carried only about twenty arrows, and they would be exhausted by the end of the first charge. The enemy would be loosing shafts, and they could be gathered. Even so, it would not be a battle won by archery. Gazing around, he saw Kzun directing building operations below the broken wall. A solid fighting platform had been constructed there. The Lone Wolves leader was still sporting the white scarf Zhusai had given him. Kzun saw him watching but did not wave. Quing-chin was working with a team on the gates, smearing animal fat on the hinges, trying to free them. How long since they have been closed? Talisman wondered. Ten years? A hundred?

Bartsai and ten of his men were working on the parapet of the eastern wall, where a section of ramparts had given way. Floorboards had been ripped from nearby buildings to be used in the repairs.

Quing-chin climbed the ramparts and gave a Gothir salute. "Make that the last Gothir tribute to me," said Talisman coldly. "It does not amuse the tribesmen."

"My apologies, Brother."

Talisman smiled. "Do not apologize, my friend. I did not mean to scold. You did well last night. A shame they saved their water wagons."

"Not all of them, Talisman. They will be on short rations."

"How did they react when disaster struck?"

"With great efficiency. They are well led," said Quing-chin. "We almost killed Gargan. I was watching from a rise, and I saw him stumbling around in the flames. A young officer rode in and rescued him; it was the same man who saved the wagons."

Talisman leaned on the parapet, staring out over the valley. "Much as I hate Gargan, it must be said that he is a skilled general. He has his own chapter in Gothir history books. He was twenty-two when he led the charge that ended the civil war, the youngest general in Gothir history."

"He's not twenty-two now," said Quing-chin. "He is old and fat."

"Courage remains even when youth has faded," Talisman pointed out.

"There is great venom in the man," said Quing-chin, removing his fur-fringed helm and running his fingers through his sweat-streaked hair. "An abiding malice that burns him. I think it will rage like last night's blaze when he learns that you are the leader here."

"With luck you will be proved correct. An angry man rarely makes rational decisions."

Quing-chin moved to the ramparts and sat down. "Have you thought about who will lead the fighters at the water hole?"

"Yes. Kzun."

Quing-chin looked doubtful. "I thought you said the Curved Horn men were to guard it?"

"They will. Under Kzun."

"A Lone Wolf? Will they stand for it?"

"We will see," said Talisman. "Get your men to gather heavy rocks and stones and place them around the battlements. We should have some missiles to hurl down on the infantry as they try to scale the walls."

Without another word Talisman walked away, climbing down from the wall and approaching Bartsai, who had stopped repair work while his people rested and drank from the well. "You have chosen your fighters?" he asked.

"I have. Twenty, as you ordered. We could make it more now. Another thirty-two warriors have come in."

"If the well is as you described it, twenty should be enough. Have the men come to me here. I wish to speak with them."

Bartsai moved away, and Talisman walked to where Kzun and his men were putting the last touches on the fighting platform. The top had been covered with wooden planks from the old tower. Talisman climbed to it and gazed through the jagged crack. "It is good," he said as Kzun moved alongside him.

"It will do," said Kzun. "Is this where you wish my men and me to fight?"

"Your men, yes. But not you. Appoint a leader for them. I want you to take command of the Curved Horn men at the well."

"What?" Kzun reddened. "You want me to lead those frightened monkeys?"

"If the Gothir take the well, they will take the shrine," said Talisman, his voice low and even. "It is the very heart of our defense. Without water the enemy will be forced into an all-out attack; if we can hold them long enough, they will start to die. With water they have a dozen options; they could even starve us out."

"You don't have to convince me of the importance, Talisman," snapped Kzun. "But why should I lead Curved Horn? They are soft. My own men could hold the well. I can trust them to fight to the death."

"You will lead the Curved Horn," said Talisman. "You are a fighting man, and they will follow you."

Kzun blinked. "Just tell me why. Why me?"

"Because I order it," said Talisman.

"No, there is more. What is it you are hiding from me?"

"There is nothing," Talisman lied smoothly. "The well is vital, and it is my judgment that you are the best man to lead the defense. But the well is on Curved Horn lands, and they would feel insulted if I asked another tribe to defend it."

"You think they will not feel insulted when you name me as their leader?"

"That is a risk that must be taken. Come with me now, for they are waiting for us."

Bartsai was furious, but he bit back his anger as he watched Kzun lead the warriors out through the gates. The nagging chest pain was back, a dull, tight cage of iron around his upper ribs. He had looked forward eagerly to the fight at the well. There were many escape routes open. He and his men would have defended it well but also would have slipped away to safety if the need arose. Now he was trapped in this rotting would-be fortress. Talisman approached him. "Come, we must talk," he said. A fresh pain stabbed at him as he looked at the younger man.

"Talk? I have had enough of talk. If the situation were not desperate, I would challenge you, Talisman."

"I understand your anger, Bartsai," said Talisman. "Now hear me: Kzun would have been useless in the siege. I have watched him pacing this compound and seen his lantern flickering throughout the night. He sleeps in the open. Have you noticed that?"

"Aye, he's a strange one. But what makes you think he should lead *my* men?"

Talisman led Bartsai to the table in the shade. "I do not know what demons plague Kzun, but it is obvious that he fears confinement. He does not like the dark, and he avoids enclosed spaces. When the siege begins, we will all be confined here. I think that would have broken Kzun. But he is a fighter and will defend the well with his life."

"As would I," said Bartsai, not meeting Talisman's eyes. "As would any leader."

"We all carry our own fears, Bartsai," Talisman said softly.

"What does that mean?" snapped the Curved Horn leader, reddening. Anxiously he looked up into Talisman's dark, enigmatic eyes.

"It means that I also fear the coming days. As do Quing-chin, Lin-tse, and all the warriors. None of us wants to die. That is one reason why I value your presence here, Bartsai. You are older and more experienced than the other leaders. Your calm and your strength will be of great importance when the Gothir attack."

Bartsai sighed, and the pain subsided. "When I was your age, I would have ridden a hundred miles to be at this battle. Now I can feel the cold breath of death upon my neck. It turns my bowels to water, Talisman. I am too old, and it would be best if you did not rely on me too much."

"You are wrong, Bartsai. Only the stupid are fearless. I am

young, but I am a good judge of men. You will stand, and you will inspire the warriors around you. You are Nadir!"

"I don't need pretty speeches. I know my duty."

"It was not a speech, Bartsai. Twelve years ago, when Chopbacks raided your village, you led a force of twenty men into their camp. You scattered them and recovered all the lost ponies. Five years ago you were challenged by a young swordsman from the Lone Wolves. You were stabbed four times, but you killed him. Then, though wounded, you walked to your pony and rode away. You are a man, Bartsai."

"You know a great deal about me, Talisman."

"All leaders must know the men who serve them. But I know this of you only because your men brag of it."

Bartsai grinned. "I'll stand," he said. "And now I had better get back to the work on the ramparts. Otherwise I'll have nothing to stand on!"

Talisman smiled, and the older man walked away. Nosta Khan came out of the shrine building and walked across the compound. Talisman's good mood evaporated as the shaman approached.

"There is nothing there," said Nosta Khan. "I have cast search spells, but they fail. Perhaps Chorin-Tsu was wrong. Perhaps they are not there at all."

"The eyes are here," said Talisman, "but they are hidden from us. The spirit of Oshikai told me that a foreigner was destined to find them."

Nosta Khan spit on the dust. "There are two coming: Druss and the poet. Let us hope one of them will prove to be the man of destiny."

"Why is Druss coming here?" asked Talisman.

"I told him the eyes would heal a friend of his who was wounded in a fight."

"And will they?"

"Of course, though he'll never have them. You think I would allow the sacred future of the Nadir to rest in the hands of a *gajin*? No, Talisman. Druss is a great warrior. He will be of use to us in the coming battle; after that he must be killed."

Talisman looked closely at the little man but said nothing. The shaman sat down at the table and poured himself a cup of water. "You say there is a *lon-tsia* inside the coffin?"

"Yes. Silver."

"That is curious," said Nosta Khan. "The shrine was plundered centuries ago. Why would the thieves leave a silver ornament behind?"

"It would have been worn next to the skin," observed Talisman, "underneath his shirt. Perhaps they missed it. The shirt then rotted away, which is why I found it."

"Hmm," murmured Nosta Khan, unconvinced. "I think a spell was placed on it that has faded with time." His glittering dark eyes fixed on Talisman's face. "Now let us talk about the girl. You cannot have her, Talisman; she is pledged to the Uniter, and you are not he. From his line will come the great men of the future. Zhusai will be his first bride."

Talisman felt a tight knot in his belly, and his anger rose. "I do not want to hear any more prophecies, shaman. I love her as I love life. She is mine."

"No!" hissed Nosta Khan, leaning in close. "The welfare of the Nadir is your first concern—indeed, it is your *only* concern. You want to see the day of the Uniter? Then do not meddle with his destiny. Somewhere out there," said Nosta Khan, waving his thin arm in the air, "is the man we wait for. The strands of his destiny are interwoven with that of Zhusai. You understand me, Talisman? You cannot have her!"

The young Nadir looked into Nosta Khan's dark eyes and saw the malice lurking there. But more than that, he saw that the little man was genuinely frightened. His life, even more than Talisman's, was devoted to one end: the coming of the Uniter.

Talisman felt as if a stone had replaced his heart. "I understand," he said.

"Good." The little shaman relaxed and gazed around at the

warriors working on the walls. "It looks impressive," he said. "You have done well."

"Are you staying with us for the battle?" Talisman asked coldly.

"For a while. I shall use my powers against the Gothir. But I cannot die here, Talisman; my work is too important. If the defense fails, I shall leave. I shall take the girl with me."

Talisman's heart lifted. "You can save her?"

"Of course. Though let me speak plainly, Talisman. If you take away her virtue, I shall leave her behind."

"You have my word, Nosta Khan. Is it good enough for you?"

"Always, Talisman. Do not hate me, boy," he said sadly. "There are too many who do. Most of them have justification. It would hurt me for you to be among them. You will serve the Uniter well; I know this."

"You have seen my destiny?"

"Yes. But some things are not to be spoken of. I need rest now." The shaman walked away, but Talisman called him back.

"If you have any regard for me, Nosta Khan, you will tell me what you have seen."

"I have seen nothing," said Nosta Khan without turning around. The little man's shoulders sank. "Nothing. I do not see you riding with the Uniter. There is no future for you, Talisman. This is your moment. Relish it." Without looking back, he moved away.

Talisman stood for a moment, then turned toward the sleeping quarters and made his way up the stairs to Zhusai's room. She was waiting for him, her long black hair sleekly combed and shining with perfumed oil. As he entered, she ran across to him, throwing her arms around his neck and kissing his face. Gently he pulled away from her and told her the words of the shaman.

"I don't care what he says," she told him. "I will never feel for another man what I feel for you. Never!"

"Nor I for any woman. Let us sit together for a while, Zhusai. I need to feel the touch of your hand." He led her to the small bed. She took his hand and kissed it, and he felt the warmth of her tears falling to his skin. "When all else fails," he whispered, "Nosta Khan will take you from here to a place of safety. He has great magic, and he will lead you through the Gothir. You will live, Zhusai."

"I don't want to live without you. I will not leave."

Her words touched Talisman, but they also made him fearful. "Do not say that, my love. You have to understand that for me your safety would be like a victory. I could die happy."

"I don't want you to die!" she said, her voice breaking. "I want to be with you somewhere deep in the mountains. I want to bear your sons."

Talisman held her close, breathing in the perfume of her hair and skin, his fingers stroking her face and neck. He could find no words, and a terrible sadness smote him. He had thought that his dreams of Nadir unity were more important than life itself. Now he knew differently. This one slender woman had shown him a truth he had not known existed. For her he could almost betray his destiny. Almost. His mouth was dry, and with a great effort he released his hold on her and stood. "I must go now," he said.

She shook her head and rose alongside him. "No, not yet," she told him, her voice controlled. "I am Chiatze, Talisman. I am trained in many things. Remove your shirt."

"I cannot. I gave my word to Nosta Khan."

She smiled then. "Take off your shirt. You are tense and weary, your muscles knotted. I shall massage your shoulders and neck. Then you may sleep. Do this for me, Talisman."

Shrugging off his goatskin jerkin, he doffed his shirt, unbuckled his sword belt, and sat back on the bed. She knelt behind him, her thumbs working at the knots in his muscles. After a while she ordered him to lie down on his stomach. He did so, and she rubbed perfumed oil into his back. The scent was delicate, and Talisman felt the tension flowing from him.

When he awoke, she was lying beside him under a single

blanket. Her arm was resting on his chest, her face next to his on the pillow. The dawn sun was shining through the window. Lifting her arm, Talisman eased himself from the bed and stood. She awoke. "How are you feeling, my lord?" she asked him.

"I am well, Zhusai. You are very skilled."

"Love is magic," she said, sitting up. She was naked, the sunlight turning her skin to gold.

"Love is magic," he agreed, dragging his gaze from her breasts. "You did not dream of Shul-sen?"

"I dreamed only of you, Talisman."

Pulling on his shirt and jerkin, he looped his sword belt over his shoulder and left the room. Gorkai was waiting below.

"Two riders coming," he said. "Could be Gothir scouts. One carries a great ax. You want them dead or alive?"

"Let them come. I have been expecting them."

Druss reined in the mare before the western wall and stared hard at the jagged crack that ran down it. "I have seen better forts," he told Sieben.

"And friendlier welcomes," muttered Sieben, staring up at the bowmen who stood on the ramparts, aiming down at them. Druss grinned and tugged on the reins, and the mare walked on. The gates were old and half-rotted, but he could see that the hinges had been recently cleaned of rust. The ground was scored under both gates in deep semicircles, showing they had been closed recently.

Touching his heels to the mare, he rode into the compound and dismounted. He saw Talisman walking toward him. "We meet again, my friend," he said. "No robbers hunting you this time?"

"Two thousand of them," Talisman told him. "Lancers, infantry, and archers."

"You had better set some men to soak those gates," said Druss. "The wood is dry. They'll not bother to smash them. They'll set fire to them." The axman cast his experienced eye over the defenses, impressed with what he saw. The ramparts had been restored, and a fighting platform had been raised beneath the crack in the western wall. Rocks and boulders had been set on each rampart, ready to be hurled down on advancing infantry. "How many men do you have?"

"Two hundred."

"They'll need to be fighters."

"They are Nadir. And they are defending the bones of the greatest Nadir warrior of all time. They will fight. Will you?"

Druss chuckled. "I love a good fight, boy. But this one isn't mine. A Nadir shaman told me there were jewels here, healing jewels. I need them for a friend."

"So I understand. But we have not found them yet. Tell me, did this shaman promise you the jewels?"

"Not exactly," admitted Druss. "He just told me they were here. Do you mind if we search?"

"Not at all," said Talisman. "I owe you my life; it is the least I can do." He pointed to the main building. "That is the Shrine of Oshikai Demon-bane. If the jewels are anywhere, they are hidden there. Nosta Khan—the shaman you spoke of—has searched with spells, but he cannot find them. For myself I summoned the spirit of Oshikai, but he would not divulge their whereabouts. Good luck, axman!"

Hoisting his ax to his shoulder, Druss strode across the compound with Sieben beside him. The shrine was dimly lit, and the axman paused before the stone sarcophagus. The chamber was dust-covered and empty of adornment.

"It has been plundered," said Sieben. "Look at the pegs on the wall. Once they would have carried his armor and his battle flag."

"No way to treat a hero," said Druss. "Any idea where to look?"

"Inside the sarcophagus," said Sieben. "But you'll find no jewels there."

Druss laid his ax aside and moved to the coffin. Grasping the stone lid, he tensed his muscles and heaved. The stone groaned and grated as he slid it aside. Sieben looked in. "Well, well," he said.

"Are they there?"

"Of course they are not there," snapped Sieben. "But the corpse is wearing a *lon-tsia* exactly like the one we found on the woman."

"Nothing else?"

"No. He has no fingers, Druss. Someone must have hacked them away to get at his rings. Put the lid back."

Druss did so. "What now?" he asked.

"I will think on it," said the poet. "There is something here that is not right. It will come to me."

"Make it soon, poet. Otherwise you may find yourself at the center of a war."

"A charming thought."

The sound of horses' hooves came from the compound. Druss walked to the door and stepped into the sunlight. Sieben followed him in time to see Nuang Xuan leap from his pony, his people streaming in through the gates behind him.

"I thought you were heading away from here," called Druss.

The Nadir leader hawked and spit. "So did I, axman. But some fool set a fire in our path, and we had no choice but to flee from it. When we tried to cut across to the east, we saw a column of lancers. Truly the gods of stone and water hate me."

"You're still alive, old man."

"Pah, not for much longer. Thousands of them there are, all heading this way. I will let my people rest for tonight."

"You are a bad liar, Nuang Xuan," said Druss. "You have come here to fight, to defend the shrine. It is no way to change your luck."

"I ask myself, Is there no end to Gothir malice? How does it benefit them to destroy that which we hold dear?" He drew in a deep breath. "I shall stay," he said. "I will send the women and children away, but I and my warriors will stay. And as for luck, axman, to die defending a sacred place is a privilege. And I am not so old. I think I will kill a hundred by myself. You are staying, yes?"

"It is not my fight, Nuang."

"What they are planning to do is evil, Druss." He gave a sudden gap-toothed grin. "I think you will stay, too. I think the gods of stone and water brought you here so that you could watch me kill my hundred. Now I must find the leader here."

Sieben walked to where Niobe was standing in the shade. She was carrying a canvas pack, which she had dropped to the ground at her feet. Sieben smiled. "Missed me?" he asked.

"I am too tired for lovemaking," she said tonelessly.

"Ever the Nadir romantic," said Sieben. "Come, let me get you some water."

"I can fetch my own water."

"I am sure that you can, my lovely, but I would cherish your company." Taking her hand, he led her to the table in the shade. Stone jugs had been filled with water, and there were clay cups on the table. Sieben filled one and passed it to her.

"Do men serve women in your land?" she asked.

"One way or another," he agreed. Niobe drained the cup and held it out to him, and Sieben refilled it.

"You are strange," she said. "And you are no warrior. What will you do here when the blood spills?"

"With luck I won't be here when the fighting starts. But if I am . . ." He spread his hands. "I have some skill with wounds," he told her. "I will be the fort surgeon."

"I, too, can stitch wounds. We will need cloth for bandages and much thread. Also needles. I will gather these things. And there must be a place for the dead; otherwise they stink, bloat, split, and attract flies."

"How nicely phrased," he said. "Shall we talk about something else?"

"Why for?"

"Because this subject is . . . demoralizing."

"I do not know this word."

"No," he said. "I don't think you do. Tell me, are you frightened at all?"

"Of what?"

"Of the Gothir."

She shook her head. "They will come; we will kill them."

"Or be killed by them," he pointed out.

She shrugged. "Whatever," she said grimly.

"You, my dear, are a fatalist."

"You are wrong. I am of the Lone Wolves," she said. "We were to be Eagle Wing tribe under Nuang. Now there are not enough of us, so we will become Lone Wolves again."

"Niobe of the Lone Wolves, I adore you," he said with a smile. "You are a breath of fresh air in this jaded life of mine."

"I will only wed a warrior," she told him sternly. "But until a good one approaches me, I will sleep with you."

"What gentleman would spurn such a delicate advance?" he said.

"Strange," she muttered, then walked away from him.

Druss strolled across the compound. "Nuang says he's tired of running. He and his people will stay here and fight."

"Can they win, Druss?"

"They look like a tough bunch, and Talisman has done well with the defenses."

"That doesn't answer the question."

"There is no answer," Druss told him. "Only odds. I wouldn't bet half a copper on their holding for more than a day."

Sieben sighed. "Naturally this does not mean we'll do something sensible—like leave?"

"The Gothir have no right to despoil this shrine," said Druss, a cold look in his gray eyes. "It is wrong. This Oshikai was a hero to all the Nadir. His bones should be left in peace."

"Excuse me for stating the obvious, old horse, but his tomb has already been plundered and his bones hacked around. I think he's probably past caring by now."

"It is not about him; it's about them," said Druss, indicating the Nadir. "Despoiling the shrine robs them of their heritage. Such a deed has no merit. It is born of spite, and I can't abide such things."

"We're staying, then?"

Druss smiled. "You should leave," he said. "This is no place for a poet."

"That is a tempting thought, Druss, old horse. I may just do that—as soon as we sight their battle flags."

Nuang called out to Druss, and the axman strode away. As Sieben sat at the table, sipping water, Talisman walked across to him and sat down.

"Tell me of the friend who is dying," he said. Sieben explained all that he knew about the fight that had left Klay crippled, and Talisman listened gravely.

"It is right," he said, "that a man should risk all for friendship. It shows he has a good heart. He has fought in many battles?"

"Many," Sieben said bitterly. "You know how a tall tree attracts lightning during a storm? Well, Druss is like that. Wherever he is battles just seem to spring up around him. It really is galling."

"Yet he survives them."

"That is his talent. Wherever he walks, death is close behind."

"He will be most welcome here," said Talisman. "But what of you, Sieben? Niobe tells me you wish to be our surgeon. Why should you do this?"

"Stupidity runs in my family."

Lin-tse sat on his pony and scanned the pass. To his right rose the sheer red rock face of Temple Stone, a towering monument to the majesty of nature, its flanks scored by the winds of time, its shape carved by a long-forgotten sea that had once covered that vast land. To Lin-tse's left was a series of jagged slopes covered with boulders. The enemy would have to pass along the narrow trail that led down beside Temple

Stone. Dismounting, he ran up the first slope, pausing at several jutting rocks. With enough men and enough time, he could dislodge several of the larger boulders and send them hurtling down onto the trail. He thought about it for a while.

Running back to his pony, he vaulted to the saddle and led his small company deeper into the red rocks. Talisman needed a victory, something to lift the hearts of the defenders.

But how? Talisman had mentioned Fecrem and the Long Retreat; that had involved a series of lightning guerrilla raids on enemy supply lines. Fecrem had been Oshikai's nephew and a skilled raider. Red dust rose in puffs of clouds beneath the ponies' hooves, and Lin-tse's throat was dry as he leaned in to his mount, urging the stallion up the steep slope. At the crest he paused and dismounted once more. Here the trail widened. A long finger of rock jutted from the left, leaning toward a cluster of boulders on the right. The gap between them was about eighteen feet. Lin-tse pictured the advancing line of lancers. They would be traveling slowly, probably in a column of twos. If he could make them move faster at this point . . . Swinging in the saddle, he scanned the back trail. The slope behind him was steep, but a skilled horseman could ride down it at a run. And the lancers were skilled. "Wait here," he told his men, then dragged on the reins. The pony reared and twisted, but Lin-tse heeled him into a run and set off down the slope. At the bottom he drew up sharply. Dust had kicked up behind him like a red mist over the trail. Lin-tse angled to the right and moved on more cautiously. Away from the trail the ground was more broken, leading to a crevice and a sheer drop of some three hundred feet. Dismounting again, he moved to the lip of the chasm, then worked his way along it. At the widest point there was at least fifty feet between the two edges, but it narrowed to ten feet where he knelt. On the other side the ground was angled upward and littered with rocks. But this part led to a wider trail, and Lin-tse followed it with his eyes. It would take him down to the western side of Temple Stone.

He sat alone for a while, thinking the plan through. Then he rode back to his men.

Premian led his hundred lancers deep into the red rock country. He was tired, his eyes bloodshot and gritty. The men behind him rode silently in a column of twos; all of them were unshaven, their water rations down by a third. For the fourth time that morning, Premian held his arm in the air, and the troops reined in. The young officer Mikal rode alongside Premian. "What do you see, sir?" he asked.

"Nothing. Send a scout to that high ground to the northeast."

"There is no *army* facing us," complained Mikal. "Why all these precautions?"

"You have your orders. Obey them," said Premian. The young man reddened and wheeled his horse. Premian had not wanted Mikal on this mission. The boy was young and hotheaded. Worse, he held the Nadir in contempt even after the fire at the camp. But Gargan had overruled him; he liked Mikal and saw in him a younger version of himself. Premian knew that the men did not object to the slow advance into enemy territory. The Royal Lancers had all fought Nadir warriors in the past and in the main were canny men who would sooner suffer discomfort in the saddle than ride unaware into an ambush.

One fact was sure: the man who planned the raid on the camp would not have only one string to his bow. Premian had not ridden these lands before, but he had studied the exquisite maps in the Great Library at Gulgothir and knew that the area around Temple Stone was rich with hiding places from which archers could attack his troops or send boulders hurtling down on them. Under no circumstances would he lead his men headlong into the enemy's arms. Sitting on his mount, he watched as the scout rode to the high ground. The man reached the top and then waved his arm in a circular motion, indicating that the way was clear. Premian led his four companies forward once more.

His mouth was dry. Fishing in his saddlebag, he produced a

small silver coin, which he put into his mouth to encourage salivation. The men would be watching him, and if he drank, then so would they. According to the maps, there was no major water supply in this region, though there were several dry riverbeds. Often solid digging produced small seeps that would at least give the horses a drink. Or there might be hidden rock tanks of which the cartographers were unaware. Premian kept watch for bees, which never strayed far from water. So far he had seen nothing. Nor had the horses reacted to the shifting of the hot winds; they could scent water from great distances.

Premian summoned his master sergeant, Jomil. The man was close to fifty and a veteran of Nadir campaigns. Heeling his horse alongside Premian, he gave a crisp salute. His grizzled face looked even older, with its two-day growth of silver bristles. "What do you think?" he asked the man.

"They're close," answered Jomil. "I can almost smell them."

"Lord Larness requires prisoners," said Premian. "Relay that to the men."

"A reward would be pleasant," suggested Jomil.

"There will be one, but do not announce it. I want no recklessness."

"Ah, but you are a careful man, sir," Jomil said with a grin.

Premian smiled. "That is what I would like my grandchildren to say as I sit with them in the cool of an autumn garden: 'He was a careful man.' "

"I already have grandchildren," Jomil told him.

"Probably more than you know."

"No 'probably' about it, sir." Jomil returned to his men, passing the word concerning prisoners. Premian lifted the white horsehair-plumed helm from his head and ran his fingers through his sweat-streaked blond hair. Just for a moment the wind felt cool as the sweat evaporated, then the oppressive heat began again. Premian replaced the helm.

Ahead, the trail twisted and Temple Stone came into sight. Shaped like a giant bell, it reared up majestically toward the sky. Premian found it an impressive sight and wished he had the time to sketch it. The trail steepened toward a crest. Summoning Mikal, he told him to take his company of twenty-five to the crest and wait for the main body to follow. The young man saluted and led his men away to the east. Premian scowled. He was riding too fast. Did he not understand that the horses were tired and that water was scarce?

Mikal and his men reached the crest just in time to see a small group of four startled Nadir warriors running for their ponies. Lord Gargan had said he wanted prisoners, and Mikal could almost hear the words of praise the general would heap upon him. "A gold Raq for the man who captures one!" he shouted, and spurred his mount. The gelding leapt forward. The Nadir scrambled to their mounts and kicked them into a run, sending up clouds of red dust as they galloped down the slope. The ponies were no match for Gothir horses, and it would be only a matter of moments before Mikal and his men reached them. Drawing his saber, Mikal squinted against the dust and leaned in to the neck of his mount, urging it to greater speed. The Nadir rounded a bend in the trail. He could just make them out through the dust cloud. His horse was at a full gallop, his men bunched behind him as he rounded the bend. He saw the Nadir slightly to the left; their horses bunched and jumped, as if going over a small fence.

In that terrible moment Mikal saw the chasm yawning before him like the mouth of a giant beast. Throwing himself back in the saddle, he hauled savagely on the reins, but it was too late. The gelding, at a full gallop, leapt out over the awesome drop and then tipped headfirst, flinging Mikal from the saddle. He fell screaming toward the distant rocks.

Behind him the lancers had also dragged on their reins. Seven fell immediately after him, the others milling at the edge of the crevice. Fifteen Nadir warriors, shouting at the tops of their voices, rose from hiding places in the rocks and ran toward the riders. The startled horses bolted, sending ten more lancers plunging to their deaths. The remaining eight men jumped from their saddles and turned to fight. Outnumbered and demoralized, with the chasm behind them and nowhere to run, they were hacked down swiftly and mercilessly. Only one Nadir warrior was wounded, his face gashed, the skin of his cheek flapping against his chin. Gathering the Gothir horses and the helms of the fallen men, they rode swiftly back down the trail.

Premian and his three companies topped the crest moments later. Jomil rode down and found the bodies. Returning to his captain, he made his report. "All dead, sir. Most of them appear to have ridden over a cliff. Their bodies are scattered on the rocks below. Some good men lost, sir."

"Good men," agreed Premian, barely keeping the fury from his voice. "Led by an officer with the brains of a sick goat."

"I heard your order to him, sir. You told him to wait. You're not to blame, sir."

"We'll detour down to the bodies and bury them," he said. "How many do you think were in the attacking party?"

"From the tracks, no more than twenty, sir. Some of the Nadir were riding ahead of our boys. They jumped the gorge at a narrow point."

"So, twenty-six men dead for the loss of how many of the enemy?"

"Some were wounded. There was blood on the ground where they hid their ponies—maybe ten of them."

Premian gave him a hard look. "Well, maybe one or two," Jomil admitted.

It took more than three hours to detour to the foot of the chasm. By the time the Gothir troops reached the bodies, it was almost dusk.

The eighteen corpses had all been stripped of armor and weapons and beheaded.

# ◇ **10** ◇

SIEBEN STOOD AND gazed around at the old storehouse.
Niobe and the other Nadir women had cleaned it of dust,
dirt, and ancient cobwebs, and five lanterns had been set in
brackets on the walls. Only one was lit now, and he used its
flickering light to study the layout of this new hospital. Two
barrels full of water had been set at the northern end of the
large, square room, placed close to the two long tables the
Nadir had carried in earlier. Sieben examined the tools set
there: an old pair of pliers, three sharp knives, several curved
needles of horn, and one long straight needle of iron. He
found that his hands were trembling. Niobe moved silently
alongside him. "Is this all you need, po-et?" she asked, laying a small box filled with thread on the table.

"Blankets," he said. "We'll need blankets. And food
bowls."

"Why for food bowls?" she asked. "If a wounded man has
strength to eat, he has strength to fight."

"A wounded man loses blood and therefore strength. Food
and water will help rebuild him."

"Why do you tremble?"

"I have assisted surgeons three times in my life. Once I even
stitched a wound in a man's shoulder. But my knowledge of
anatomy . . . the human body . . . is severely limited. I do not,
for example, know what to do with a deep belly wound."

"Nothing," she said simply. "A deep belly wound is death."

249

"How comforting! I could do with honey. That is good for wounds, especially when mixed with wine; it prevents infection."

"No bees, po-et. No bees, no honey. But we have some dried *lorassium* leaves. Good for pain and for dreams. And some *hakka* roots to ward off the blue-skin demons."

"Blue-skin demons? What are they?"

"Truly you know little of wounds. They are the invisible devils who creep in through the open flesh and turn it blue so it stinks and men die."

"Gangrene. I see. And what does one do with these *hakka* roots?"

"We make poultice and lay it over the wound. It smells very bad. The demons avoid it."

"And what cures do you have, my lady, for trembling hands?" he asked her.

She laughed and slid her hand over his belly and down. "I have big cure," she said. Curling her left arm around his neck, she drew down his head and kissed him. He felt the warmth and sweetness of her tongue on his. Arousal swept through him.

She pulled away. "Now look at your hands," she said. They were no longer trembling. "Big cure, yes?"

"I can offer no argument there," he said. "Where can we go?"

"Nowhere. I have much to do. Shi-sai will be in labor soon, and I have promised to help when the waters break. But if you have trembling hands in the night, you may come to me by the north wall."

Kissing him once more, she spun away from his embrace and walked from the room. Sieben took a last look at the hospital, then blew out the lantern and made his way to the compound. Some work was still being done in the moonlight, repairing the ramparts beside the crack in the west-facing wall. Elsewhere Nadir warriors were sitting around campfires. Druss was talking to Talisman and Bartsai on the ramparts above the gates.

Sieben thought of joining them but realized he did not want to listen to more talk of battles and death. His mind flickered to

Niobe. She was unlike any woman he had ever known. When first he had seen her, he had thought her mildly attractive, certainly no more than that. Up close, her laughing eyes had made him reappraise her. Even so, she would pale against the beauties who had shared his bed. Yet each time he made love to her, it seemed her beauty grew. It was uncanny. All his previous lovers were drab by comparison. As he was thinking, two Nadir warriors approached him. One of them spoke to him in Nadir.

"Sorry, lads," he said with a nervous smile. "I don't understand the language." The taller of the two, a ferocious-looking man with narrow, malevolent eyes, pointed to his companion and said, "This one have big pain."

"Big pain," echoed Sieben.

"You doctor. Fix it."

Sieben glanced down at the second warrior. The man's face was gray, his eyes sunken, and his jaws clenched. "We go in," muttered the first man, leading his friend into the new hospital. With a sinking heart Sieben followed them and, relighting the lantern, led them to the table. The small warrior tried to tug off his faded crimson shirt but groaned as he did so. The taller man dragged the garment clear, and in the flickering light Sieben saw a growth on the man's spine the size of a small apple. The area all around it was red, swollen, and angry. "You cut," said the taller man.

Sieben indicated that the warrior should lie down on the table; then he reached out and with great care touched the swelling. The man stiffened but made no sound. The lump was rock-hard. "Fetch the lantern," Sieben ordered the taller man. The warrior did so, and Sieben peered more closely at the growth. Then, taking the sharpest of the knives, he drew in a deep breath. He had no idea what the growth was. It looked like a giant boil, but for all he knew it might be a cancer. What was certain was that he had no choice of action, burdened as he was by the expectations of both men. Touching the point of the knife to the lump, he pressed down hard. Thick yellow pus exploded from the cut, and the skin peeled away as if from a section of rotten fruit. The warrior cried out, the sound strangled and inhuman. Laying aside the knife, Sieben gripped the lump and squeezed it. More pus—this time mixed with blood—oozed from the cut, covering his fingers. The wounded man sighed and relaxed on the table. Sieben moved to a water barrel and filled a wooden bowl, cleaning his hands and wrists. Then he returned to the warrior. Fresh blood was oozing from the three-inch cut and flowing down to the wood of the table. With a wet cloth Sieben cleaned the wound, then ordered the man to sit up while he applied a wedge of cloth to it, strapping it in place with a bandage around the man's waist. The patient spoke in Nadir to his companion; then, without another word, both men walked from the building.

Sieben sat down. "Not at all, it was my pleasure," he said not loudly enough to be heard by the departing warriors.

Once more extinguishing the lantern, he left the building by a side door and found himself standing close to the main entrance to the shrine. With Niobe otherwise occupied and with nothing else to do, Sieben pushed open the door and stepped inside.

Something about the place had been nagging at him from his subconscious, but he could not bring it to the surface. His eyes were drawn to the blackened iron plate on the stone coffin. The symbols on it were Chiatze, part alphabet, part hieroglyph, and Talisman had told him what they said:

*Oshikai Demon-bane—Lord of War*

Kneeling before it, Sieben scanned the symbols. They were deeply engraved into the iron, and they told him nothing. Irritated that he could not solve the problem, he left the shrine and climbed to the ramparts of the north wall, where he sat on the parapet in the moonlight, gazing out over the distant mountains. His thoughts turned once more to Niobe and her beauty, and he listened awhile in vain for the birth sounds of the newborn. Be patient, he told himself. Fishing the *lon-tsia* from his pocket, he looked at the profile of the woman embossed there. She, too, was beautiful. Turning the coin over, he looked down at the image of Oshikai. "You're causing a lot of trouble for someone who's been dead for ten centuries," he said.

Then it hit him . . .

Rising, he climbed down the steps and returned to the shrine, squatting down before the iron plate. Checking Oshikai's name against the embossing of the *lon-tsia*, he saw that the name on the plate boasted two extra and identical symbols. Peering more closely, he saw that the engraving of each was deeper than that of the other symbols.

"What have you found?" asked Talisman from the doorway. The slender Nadir leader moved forward and knelt beside the poet.

"Is this the original plate?" Sieben asked. "Was it made by Oshikai's followers?"

"I would imagine so," said Talisman. "Why?"

"What are these symbols?"

"The Nadir letter 'i.' "

"But the Chiatze had no such letter," said Sieben. "Therefore, the nameplate is not original or has been altered."

"I don't understand your point," said Talisman.

Sieben sat back. "I don't like mysteries," he said. "If this is original, there would be no 'i's.' If it is not, why is it in the Chiatze tongue? Why not fully Nadir?"

Moving forward on his knees, Sieben laid his hands on the plate, pressing a finger into each of the engraved symbols. Something gave way under his pressure; there was a dull clunk from within, and the nameplate fell clear. Behind it was a shallow niche cut into the coffin, and within that lay a small pouch of hide. Talisman pushed Sieben aside and grabbed the pouch. As he pulled it open, the hide split and the contents fell to the dusty floor. There were two knucklebones stained with black symbols, a small coil of braided hair, and a piece of folded parchment.

Talisman looked disappointed. "I thought you had found the Eyes of Alchazzar," he said.

Sieben lifted the parchment and tried to open it, but it broke into pieces under his fingers. "What are these objects?" he asked.

"A shaman's medicine bag. The knucklebones are used in spells of prophecy; the hair is that of the shaman's greatest enemy. The parchment? I do not know."

"Why would it be placed here?"

"I don't know," snapped Talisman. Reaching down, Sieben picked up the knucklebones.

The world spun. He cried out but was dragged down into the dark . . . .

Shocked by his sudden collapse, Talisman knelt over the still figure of the blond Drenai and placed his index finger on the pulse point of the neck. The heart was beating, but incredibly slowly. Roughly he shook Sieben's shoulders, but there was no response. Rising, he ran from the shrine. Gorkai was sitting on the ground, sharpening his sword with a whetstone. "Fetch Nosta Khan and the Drenai axman," commanded Talisman, then returned to where Sieben lay.

Druss arrived first. "What happened?" he asked, kneeling beside his friend.

"We were talking, and he collapsed. Is he subject to fits?"

"No." Druss swore softly. "His heart is barely beating." Talisman glanced at the axman and noted the fear on his broad, bearded face. Nosta Khan arrived, and Talisman saw his gimlet eyes fasten to the sagging nameplate on the coffin.

"The eyes?" he asked.

"No," said Talisman, and told him what they had found.

"You fool!" hissed Nosta Khan. "I should have been summoned."

"It was just a medicine pouch. There were no jewels," Talisman responded, feeling his anger rise.

"It is the medicine pouch of a *shaman*," snapped Nosta Khan. "A spell has been placed on it."

"I touched it also, and nothing has happened to me," argued Talisman.

The little shaman knelt beside Sieben, prying open the fingers of his right hand. The knucklebones lay there, but now they were white and pure, the black symbols having been transferred to the skin of Sieben's palm. "But the bag split," said Nosta Khan, "and it was not you who lifted the seeing bones."

The axman rose, towering over Nosta Khan. "I do not care who is at fault," he said, his voice dangerously even, his pale eyes glittering. "What I want is for you to bring him back. *Now!*"

Sensing danger, Nosta Khan felt a moment of panic as he looked into the axman's cold eyes. Placing his hand over his heart, he whispered two words of power. Druss stiffened and groaned. The spell was an old one and shackled the victim in chains of fiery pain. Any attempt on Druss' part to move would bring colossal agony and a subsequent loss of consciousness. Now, thought Nosta Khan triumphantly, let this Drenai *gajin* feel the power of the Nadir! The shaman was about to speak when Druss gave a low, guttural growl. His eyes blazed, and his hand snaked out, huge fingers grabbing Nosta Khan by the throat and lifting him into the air. The little man kicked out helplessly. As if through a sea of pain, Druss spoke: "Lift the . . . spell, little man . . . or . . . I'll snap . . . your neck!" Talisman drew his knife and jumped to the shaman's defense. "One more move and he dies," warned the axman. Nosta Khan gave a strangled gasp and managed to speak three words in a tongue neither Druss nor Talisman recognized. Druss' pain vanished. Dropping the shaman, he stabbed a finger into the little man's chest. "You ever do anything like that again, you ugly dwarf, and I'll kill you!"

Talisman could see the shock and terror on Nosta Khan's face. "We are all friends here," he said softly, sheathing his knife and stepping between Nosta Khan and the menacing figure of Druss. "Let us think of what is to be done."

Nosta Khan rubbed his bruised throat. He was astonished and could barely gather his thoughts. The spell had worked; he *knew* this. It was not possible that a mortal man could overcome such agony. Aware that both men were waiting for him to speak, he forced himself to concentrate and lifted the white knucklebones, holding them tightly in his fist. "His soul has been drawn out," he said, his voice croaking. "The medicine pouch belonged to Shaoshad the renegade. He was the shaman who stole the eyes, may his soul be forever accursed and burn in ten thousand fires!"

"Why would he hide it here?" asked Talisman. "What purpose did it serve?"

"I do not know. But let us see if we can reverse his spell." Taking Sieben's limp hand in his own, he began to chant.

*Sieben fell for an eternity, spinning and turning, then awoke with a start. He was lying beside a fire set at the center of a circle of standing stones. An old man was sitting by the small blaze. Naked but with a bulging bag hanging from one thin shoulder, he had two long wispy beards growing from both sides of his chin and reaching his scrawny chest; his hair was shaved on the left side of his head and gathered into a tight braid on the right.*

*"Welcome," said the old man. Sieben sat up and was about to speak when he noticed with horror that the speaker had been mutilated. His hands had been cut off, and blood was seeping from the stumps.*

*"Sweet heavens, you must be in great pain," he said.*

*"Always," agreed the man with a smile. "But when something never passes, remaining constant, it becomes bearable." Shrugging his shoulders, he let the bag fall, then reached into it with his mangled, bleeding arms. From the bag he produced a hand, which he held carefully between the stumps. Gripping it*

with his knees, he held his mutilated right arm to the severed wrist. The limb jerked, and the hand attached itself to the wrist. The fingers flexed. "Ah, that is good," said the man, reaching into the bag and producing a left hand, which he held in place over his left wrist. This, too, joined, and he clapped the hands together. Then he removed his eyes and dropped them into the bag.

"Why are you doing this to yourself?" asked Sieben.

"It is a compulsion engendered by sorcery," said the stranger amiably. "They were not content merely to kill me. Oh, no! Now I can have my hands or my eyes but never both at the same time. If I try—and I have—then the pain becomes unbearable. I have great admiration for the way the spell was cast. I did not think it would last this long. I managed to counter the curse on my ears and tongue. I see you found my medicine pouch."

The fire flickered down, but the old man gestured with his hands, and the flames sprang to new life. Sieben found himself staring at the man's empty eye sockets. "Have you tried using just one hand and one eye?" he asked.

"Is there something about me that suggests I am an idiot? Of course I have. It works . . . but the pain is too awesome to describe."

"I have to tell you that this is the worst dream I've ever had," said Sieben.

"No dream. You are here." Sieben was about to question him when a low, inhuman growl came from beyond the stones. The old man's hand came up, and blue forked lightning flashed from it, exploding between the stones with a loud crack. Then there was silence. "I need my hands, you see, to survive here. But I cannot go anywhere without my eyes. It is a sweetly vile punishment. I wish I had thought of it myself."

"What was that . . . thing?" asked Sieben, craning around to peer between the stones. There was nothing to be seen. All was darkness, deep and final.

"*Difficult to know. But it did not mean us any good. I am Shaoshad.*"

"Sieben. Sieben the Poet."

"*A poet? It is long since I savored the delicious sounds of exquisite wordplay. But I fear you will not be with me long, so perhaps another time . . . Tell me how you found my pouch.*"

"The use of the Nadir letter 'i,' " Sieben told him.

"*Yes. It was a joke, you see. I knew no Nadir would see it. Not given to jokes, the Nadir. They were searching for the Eyes of Alchazzar. Eyes and 'i's.' Good, isn't it?*"

"Most amusing," agreed Sieben. "I take it you are not Nadir?"

"*In part. Part Chiatze, part Sechuin, part Nadir. I want you to do something for me. I cannot offer you anything, of course.*"

"What do you require?"

"*My medicine pouch. I want you to take the hair and burn it. The knucklebones must be dropped into water. The parchment is to be shredded and scattered to the air, the pouch itself buried in the earth. Can you remember that?*"

"Hair burned, knuckles drowned, paper scattered, pouch buried," said Sieben. "What will that do?"

"*I believe the release of my elemental power will end this cursed spell and give me back my hands and my eyes. Speaking of which . . .*" He lifted the eyes from the bag and slid them back in their sockets. Holding his arms over the bag, he released his hands, which fell from the wrists. Immediately blood began to flow. "*You are a handsome fellow, and you have an honest face. I think I can trust you.*"

"You are the man who stole the Eyes of Alchazzar," said Sieben.

"*Indeed I am. A rare mistake it was. Still, the man who never made a mistake never made anything, eh?*"

"Why did you do it?"

"*I had a vision—false as it has so far turned out. I thought I could bring the Uniter to my people five centuries early. Arro-*

*gance was always my downfall. I thought to use the eyes to raise Oshikai from the dead, to regenerate his body and summon his soul. Well, I did summon his soul."*

"What happened?"

*"You will scarcely credit it. I still have difficulty believing it myself."*

*"I think I know," said Sieben. "He wouldn't accept life without Shul-sen."*

*"Exactly. You are a bright fellow. Can you guess what happened next?"*

*"You set off to find her body; that's why you were caught so close to her resting place. What I don't understand is why you did not use the power of the jewels."*

*"Ah, but I did. That is why I was caught and killed."*

*"Tell me," whispered Sieben, fascinated . . .*

He groaned and opened his eyes. Nosta Khan was leaning over him, and Sieben swore. Druss grabbed his arm, hauling him to his feet. "By heavens, poet, you gave us a scare. How are you feeling?"

"Miffed!" said Sieben. "A moment longer and he would have told me where he hid the jewels."

"You spoke to Shaoshad?" said Nosta Khan.

"Yes. He told me why he took them."

"Describe him."

"A man with a curious beard who has detachable hands and eyes."

"Aha!" Nosta Khan shouted happily. "The spell holds, then. Does he suffer?"

"Yes, but he is taking it rather well. Can you send me back to him?"

"Only by cutting out your heart and casting seven spells on it," the shaman told him.

"I'll take that as a no," said Sieben.

From outside came the cries of a newborn infant, and Sieben

smiled. "I hope you'll all excuse me. This has been a wearying experience, and I need some rest." Stooping, he gathered the hair, knucklebones, pouch, and shreds of parchment.

"What are you doing with those?" asked Nosta Khan.

"Souvenirs of an interesting experience," he said. "I shall show them to my grandchildren and brag about my visit to the underworld."

Zhusai was afraid, though not with a simple fear like the thought of dying. It was worse than that, she realized. Death was but another doorway, but this was a kind of extinction. At first her dreams of Shul-sen had been merely that—curiously unpleasant visions she suffered when sleeping. But now she was hearing voices whispering in her subconscious, and her own memories were becoming vague and blurred. Not so the memories of another life—a life as consort to the renegade chieftain Oshikai Demon-bane. Those memories were becoming sharper, more distinct. She remembered the ride through the long hills, making love in the grass in the shadow of Jiang-shin, the Mother of Mountains, wearing her dress of white silk on the day of the wedding in the White Palace of Pechuin.

"Stop it!" she cried as the memories seemed to engulf her. "It is not me. Not my life. I was born in . . . in . . ." But the memories would not come. "My parents died. I was raised by my grandfather . . ." For a moment the name was lost to her. Then: "Chorin-Tsu!" she shouted triumphantly. Talisman entered the room, and she flew to him. "Help me!" she begged him.

"What is wrong, my love?"

"She is trying to kill me," sobbed Zhusai. "And I cannot fight her."

Her almond eyes were wide open, fear radiating from them. "Who is trying to kill you?" he asked her.

"Shul-sen. She wants my life . . . my body. I can feel her within me, her memories swamping me."

"Calm yourself," he said soothingly, taking her to the bed

and sitting her down. Moving to the window, Talisman called out to Gorkai, who came running up the stairs. Talisman told him of Zhusai's fears.

"I have heard of this," Gorkai said grimly. "Spirit possession."

"What can we do?" asked Talisman.

"Find out what she wants," Gorkai advised.

"Supposing she just wants me?" asked Zhusai. "My life?"

"Why have you not spoken to your own shaman?" asked Gorkai. "His knowledge is greater than mine in these matters."

"I won't have him near me," said Zhusai, her voice breaking. "Not ever. I don't trust him. He . . . would want her to kill me. She is Shul-sen, the mother of the Nadir people. A witch. She has power, and he would seek to use it. I have nothing."

"I have not the skill to deal with this, Talisman," said Gorkai. "I can cast no spells."

Talisman took hold of Zhusai's hand. "Then it must be Nosta Khan. Fetch him."

"No!" shouted Zhusai, struggling to rise.

Talisman held her tightly, pulling her in to his chest. "Trust me!" he urged her. "I would let no harm come to you. I will watch Nosta Khan carefully. If there is danger, I will kill him. Trust me!"

Her body jerked in a wild spasm, and her eyes closed momentarily. When they opened, all fear was gone. "Oh, I trust you, Talisman," she said softly. He felt her shoulder draw back, and some sixth sense made him pull away from her just in time to see the knife blade. Throwing up his right arm, he blocked the blow and slammed his left fist into her jaw. Her head snapped back, and she slumped to the bed. Retrieving his knife from her limp hand, he flung the weapon across the room.

Nosta Khan entered. "What happened here?" he asked.

"She took my knife and tried to kill me. But it was not Zhusai. She is possessed."

"Your servant told me. The spirit of Shul-sen seeks release.

You should have come to me before, Talisman. How many more secrets do you keep from me?"

Without waiting for an answer, he moved to the bed. "Tie her hands behind her back," he ordered Gorkai. The warrior glanced at Talisman, who gave a curt nod. Using a slender belt of cord, Gorkai lashed her wrists together, and then he and Nosta Khan lifted her, propping her back against the bed pillows. From an old pouch that hung at his belt, Nosta Khan drew a necklace of human teeth, which he tied around the unconscious woman's neck. "From this moment," he said, "no one is to speak." Placing his hands on her head, he began to chant.

It seemed to the two watching men that the temperature in the room was dropping, and a cold wind began to blow through the window.

The chant continued, the sound rising and falling. Talisman did not know the language used—if language it was—but the effect within the room was astonishing. Ice began to form on the window frame and walls, and Gorkai was shivering uncontrollably. Nosta Khan showed no sign of discomfort. He fell silent, then drew his hand back from Zhusai's brow. "Open your eyes," he commanded, "and tell me your name."

The dark eyes slid open. "I am . . ." A smile formed. "I am she who was blessed above all women."

"You are the spirit of Shul-sen, wife to Oshikai Demonbane?"

"I am she."

"You are dead, woman. There is no place for you here."

"I do not feel dead, shaman. I can feel my heart beating and the rope around my wrists."

"The form is one you have stolen. Your bones lie in a chamber of volcanic rock. Or do you not remember the night of your death?"

"Oh, I remember," she said, her lips thinning, her eyes glittering. "I remember Chakata and his spikes of gold. He was human then. I can still feel the pain as he slowly pushed them home, deep enough to blind but not to kill. I remember. Oh, yes, I remember it all. But now I am back. Release my hands, shaman."

"I shall not," said Nosta Khan. "You are dead, Shul-sen, as your husband is dead. Your time is gone."

She laughed then, the sound filling the room. Talisman felt the terrible cold bite into his bones. Beside him Gorkai could scarcely stand and was trembling and shaking. The laughter died away. "I am a witch with great powers. Oshikai knew that, and he used me well. I know from the memories of the girl that you are facing an army, shaman. I can help you. Release me!"

"How can you help?"

"Release me and you will know."

Talisman's hand crept to his knife scabbard, but it was empty. Reaching out, he pulled Gorkai's knife clear of its sheath. The woman turned her dark eyes on him. "He means to kill you," she told Nosta Khan.

"Do not speak, either of you!" warned the shaman. Turning to the woman, he began to chant. She winced, then her lips drew back in a bestial snarl. One word of power she spoke. Nosta Khan was hurled from the bed, striking the wall just below the window. He rolled to his knees, but her voice sounded once more, and, flung back, his head cracked against the windowsill and he sank to the floor, unconscious.

The woman looked at Gorkai. "Release me," she said. On stumbling legs Gorkai tottered forward.

"Stand where you are!" ordered Talisman. Gorkai gave a cry of pain but forced himself to halt. Sinking to his knees, he groaned and fell face forward to the floorboards.

"So," she said, looking at Talisman, "you are a man of power. Your servant obeys despite the pain he feels. Very well, you may release me."

"Did you not love Oshikai?" he asked suddenly.

"What? You question my devotion, you ignorant peasant?"

"It was an honest question."

"Then I shall answer it: Yes, I loved him. I loved his breath upon my skin, the sound of his laughter, the glory of his rages. Now release me!"

"He searches for you still," Talisman told her.

"He died a thousand years ago," she said. "His spirit is in paradise."

"Not so, lady. I spoke with him when first I came here. I summoned his spirit. The first question he asked was, 'Do you bring news of Shul-sen?' I told him that there were many legends but that I did not know what had happened to you. He said: 'I have searched the Vales of Spirit, the Valleys of the Damned, the Fields of Heroes, the Halls of the Mighty. I have crossed the Void for time without reckoning. I cannot find her.' And as for paradise, he said: 'What paradise could there be without Shul-sen? Death I could bear, but not this parting of souls. I will find her, though it take a dozen eternities.' "

She was silent for a moment, and the feral gleam faded from her eyes. "I know you speak the truth," she said, "for I can read the hearts of men. But Oshikai will never find me. Chakata drew my spirit to the dark place, where it is guarded by demons who once were men. Chakata is there, but no human would recognize him now; he taunts me and tortures me whenever he wills. Or at least he did before I made my escape. I cannot go to Oshikai, Talisman. If I died here, I would be drawn back to the dark place."

"Is that where you have sent Zhusai?" he asked her.

"It is. But what is her life compared with mine? I was a queen. I will be again."

"Then you will leave Oshikai searching for an eternity, risking his soul in the terrors of the Void?"

"I can do nothing there!" she shouted.

By the window Nosta Khan was stirring, but he remained silent. Gorkai, too, lay very still, scarcely breathing.

"Where is this dark place?" asked Talisman. "Why can Oshikai not find it?"

"It is not a part of the Void," she said tonelessly. "Do you understand the nature of the underworld? The Void is set between two levels. In the simplest terms, it sits between paradise and Giragast, heaven and hell. The Void is the place in between where souls wander in search of final rest. Chakata chose to trap me in the dark center of Giragast, the pit at the center of the lakes of fire. No human soul would travel there voluntarily, and Oshikai would know of no reason why I would be there. He trusted Chakata. He would never have guessed the depth of the man's lust or the heights of his treachery. But if he were to know, then he would die the second death, the lasting death. There is no way a single warrior—not even one as mighty as my lord—could pass the demon-haunted passageways or conquer the creature Chakata has become."

"I will go with him," promised Talisman.

"You? What are you? Just a child in a man's body. How old are you, child? Seventeen? Twenty?"

"I am nineteen. And I will walk with Oshikai across the Void to the gates of Giragast."

"No, it is not enough. I see that you are brave, Talisman. And you are quick and intelligent. But to pass those gates takes something more. You are asking me to risk my soul in everlasting darkness and torment and the soul of the man I love. The mystic number is three. Do you have a warrior here who could match Oshikai? Is there one who would walk the Void with you?"

"I will," said Gorkai, pushing himself to his feet.

Her eyes fixed him, holding to Gorkai's gaze. "Another brave one. But not skilled enough."

Talisman strode to the window and leaned out over the sill. Below, Druss, stripped of his jerkin, was washing himself at the well side. The Nadir leader called out to him, beckoning him. Throwing his jerkin over his shoulder, Druss strolled to the building and climbed the stairs. As he entered, his pale blue eyes scanned the room. Gorkai was still on his knees, and Nosta

Khan was sitting below the window with a trickle of blood running from broken skin over his temple. He saw that Zhusai was tied and said nothing.

"This man has walked the Void," said Talisman, "in search of his wife. He found her."

"I can read his thoughts, Talisman. He has no loyalty to the Nadir. He is here seeking . . ." She stared hard at Druss. ". . . healing stones for a dying friend. Why would he risk the terrors of the Giragast? He does not know me."

Talisman swung to Druss. "This is not Zhusai," he said. "Her body is possessed by the spirit of Shul-sen. To free her, I must send my spirit into the Void. Will you travel with me?"

"As she said, I came here to find the jewels the shaman spoke of," said Druss, "and he lied to me. Why should I do this?"

Talisman sighed. "There is no reason I can offer you save that the woman I love is now trapped in that dark and vile place. And Oshikai, our greatest hero, has been searching for a thousand years to find the spirit of his wife. He does not know where to look. I can tell him, but Shul-sen says the journey would see his soul extinguished. Two men cannot fight the demons there."

"And three can?" asked Druss.

"I cannot answer that," Talisman told him. "She will not release the spirit of Zhusai unless I can find a man to match Oshikai. You are the only one here who has built a legend. What more can I say?"

Druss eased past him and moved to the bound woman. "How did you die?" he asked.

"Chakata put golden spikes in . . ." She hesitated, and her eyes flared wide. "You! You and your friend released me. I see it now, back in the chamber. He came back and removed the spikes. He found my *lon-tsia*."

Druss stood and looked Talisman in the eyes. "If I go with you, laddie, I want your word on something."

"Name it!"

"You will let me use the jewels to save my friend."

"Is that not why you are here?" hedged Talisman.

"Not good enough," said Druss, making for the door.

"Very well. You have my word. When we find the jewels, I will hand them to you and you may take them to Gulgothir."

"No!" shouted Nosta Khan. "What are you saying?"

Talisman held up his hand. "But I want your pledge to return them as soon as your friend is healed."

"It will be done," said Druss.

"Come to me, blackbeard," said Shul-sen, and Druss returned to the bed and sat. She looked deep into his eyes. "Everything I am or could ever be is in your hands now. Are you a man I can trust?"

"I am," he said.

"I believe you." Turning her gaze to Talisman, she spoke again. "I shall return to the dark place and free the soul of Zhusai. Do not fail me."

Her eyes closed, then flickered. A long, broken sigh came from her throat. Talisman ran to the bedside, untying the cord that bound her wrists. Her eyes opened, and a scream formed. Talisman hugged her to him. "It is all right, Zhusai. You are back with us!"

Nosta Khan moved to the bedside and placed his hand on her head. After a moment he said: "She has returned. This is Zhusai. I shall now cast spells to prevent any reentry. You did well, Talisman, to deceive her."

"I did not deceive her," replied the Nadir coldly. "I shall fulfill my part of the bargain."

"Pah! That is insane. An army is marching on us, and the destiny of the Nadir rests in your hands. This is no time to play the man of honor."

Talisman walked to the far wall and picked up his dagger. Slowly he moved toward Nosta Khan. "Who is the leader here?" he asked softly, his voice cold.

"You are, but—"

"Yes, I am, you miserable worm. I am the leader. You are *my* shaman. I will tolerate no further disobedience. I do not *play* at honor. It is what I am. My word is iron. Now and evermore. We will go now to the shrine. You will summon Oshikai, then do what you must to send Druss and myself into the Void. Is that clear, shaman?"

"It is clear, Talisman."

"Not Talisman to you!" thundered the warrior. "Now is it clear?"

"It is clear . . . my lord."

"Why do you hold to my hand, po-et?" asked Niobe as she and Sieben walked the ramparts of the western wall. Sieben, his passion spent during the last two hours with her, gave a weary smile.

"It is a custom among my people," he said, lifting her fingers to his lips and kissing them. "Lovers often walk hand in hand. It is perhaps a spiritual joining or at least a touching that proclaims that a couple are lovers. It is also considered pleasurable. Do you not like it?"

"I like feeling you inside me," she said, withdrawing her hand and sitting back on the battlements. "I like the taste of your tongue on mine. I like the many delights your hands can conjure. But I like to feel free when I walk. Hand-holding is for mother and small child. I am not your child."

Sieben chuckled and sat back admiring the way the moonlight made her long hair shine. "You are a delight to me," he said. "A breath of fresh air after a lifetime in musty rooms."

"Your clothes are very pretty," she noted, reaching out and stroking the blue silk of his shirt. "The buttons contain many colors."

"Mother-of-pearl," he said. "Exquisite, aren't they?" On an impulse he pulled the shirt over his head and stood bare-chested on the wall. "Here. It is yours."

Niobe giggled, then removed her own shirt of faded green wool. Sieben stared at her full breasts and saw that the nipples were erect. Arousal flared afresh within him. Stepping forward, he reached out to caress her. Niobe jumped back, holding the blue silk shirt to her body. "No," she said. "First we talk."

"Talk? What do you want to talk about?"

"Why no wife for you? Your friend has wife. And you are old."

"Old? Thirty-four is not old. I am in the prime of my life."

"You have balding patch at the crown. I have seen it."

Sieben's hand swept up to his blond hair, pushing his fingers through to the scalp. "Balding patch? It can't be."

Her laughter pealed out. "You are peacock," she said. "Worse than woman."

"My grandfather had a full head of hair to his death at ninety. Baldness does not run in our family."

Niobe slipped into the blue shirt and then moved alongside Sieben, taking his arm and pulling his hand from his hair.

"So why no wife?"

"It was a joke about the hair, yes?"

"No. Why no wife?"

"That's a difficult question." He shrugged. "I have known many beautiful women but none I would wish to spend my life with. I mean, I like apples, but I wouldn't want to live on a permanent diet of them."

"What is apples?"

"Fruit. Er . . . like figs."

"Good for bowels," she said.

"Exactly. But let's move on from that, shall we? What I'm trying to say is that I like the company of many women. I am easily bored."

"You are not strong man," she said, sadness in her voice. "You are frightened man. Many women is easy. Make children is easy. Life with them, help to raise them, that is hard. Watch babies die . . . that is hard. I have had two husbands. Both die. Both good men. Strong. My third will be also strong. Many babies, so some will survive."

Sieben gave a wry smile. "I tend toward the belief that life holds more than making strong babies. I live for pleasure, for sudden bursts of joy. For surprises. There are enough people making babies and eking out their boring lives in the harshness of deserts or the green splendor of mountains. The world will not miss my children."

She considered his words thoughtfully. "My people came over the tall mountains with Oshikai. They made babies, who grew proud and strong. They gave their blood to the land, and the land nurtured their young. For a thousand years. Now there is me. I owe it to my ancestors to bring life to the land so that in a thousand years to come there will be those with the blood of Niobe and her ancestors. You are good lover, po-et. You bring many joy trembles in your lovemaking. But joy trembles are easy; I can do that for myself. I feel great love for you. But I will not wed frightened man. I have seen strong warrior of the Curved Horn. He has no wife. I think I will go to him."

Sieben felt her words hit him like a blow to the belly. But he forced a smile. "Of course, lovely one. You go and make babies."

"You want shirt back?"

"No. It suits you. You look . . . very fine."

Without a word she left him there. Sieben shivered as a cold breeze touched his bare skin. What am I doing here? he wondered. A Nadir warrior with short hair and a pronounced widow's peak climbed to the ramparts and, ignoring Sieben, stood staring out to the west.

"A pleasant night," remarked Sieben.

The man turned and stared at him. "It will be a long night," he said, his voice deep and cold.

Sieben saw a candle flame flickering through the window of the shrine. "Still searching," he said.

"Not searching," said the man. "My lord, Talisman, and your friend are journeying to Giragast."

"I fear something has been lost in the translation," said Sieben. "Giragast isn't a place; it is a myth."

"It is a place," the man said stubbornly. "Their bodies are lying on the cold floor; their souls have gone to Giragast."

Sieben's mouth was suddenly dry. "Are you saying they are dead?"

"No, but they are going to the place of the dead. I do not think they will come back."

Sieben left the man and ran to the shrine. As the Nadir had said, Druss and Talisman were lying side by side on the dusty floor. The shaman Nosta Khan was sitting beside them. On top of the stone coffin was a lighted candle marked with seven lines of black ink.

"What is happening?" he asked the shaman.

"They go with Oshikai to rescue the witch Shul-sen," whispered Nosta Khan.

"Into the Void?"

"Beyond the Void." Nosta Khan glanced up at him, his eyes dark and malevolent. "I saw you scatter the parchment to the winds. Did you also throw the knucklebones into the well?"

"Yes. And I burned the hair and buried the pouch."

"You *gajin* are soft and weak. Shaoshad deserved his punishment."

"He wanted to bring Oshikai and Shul-sen back to life, to unite the Nadir," said Sieben. "That does not seem so terrible a crime."

Nosta Khan shook his head. "He wanted power and fame. Oh, he could have raised the body and perhaps even infused it with the soul of Oshikai. But the body would have needed the magic of jewels constantly; he would have been a slave to Shaoshad. Now, thanks to his arrogance, we have no jewels and the power of the land is lost to us. And *gajin* like you treat us like vermin. His lust for power sentenced us to five hundred years of servitude. He should have been left to rot for eternity."

Sieben sat down alongside the shaman. "Not a forgiving people, are you?"

Nosta Khan gave a rare smile. "Our babies die in childbirth. Our men are hunted down like animals. Our villages are burned, our people slaughtered. Why for should we forgive?"

"So what is the answer, old man? For the Nadir to mass into a huge army and hunt down the *gajin* like animals, burning their villages and towns and slaughtering their women and children?"

"Yes! That is how it will begin. Until we have conquered the world and enslaved every race."

"Then you will be no different from the *gajin* you despise. Is that not so?"

"We do not seek to be different," replied Nosta Khan. "We seek to be triumphant."

"A charmingly honest point of view," said the poet. "Tell me, why are they traveling through the Void?"

"Honor," said Nosta Khan admiringly. "Talisman is a great man. Were he destined to live, he would make a fine general for the Uniter."

"He is going to die?"

"Yes," Nosta Khan said sadly. "I have walked the many futures, but he is in none of them. Now be silent, for I have much work to do."

From his pouch Nosta Khan removed two small, dry leaves, which he placed under his tongue. Raising his hands, bony fingers spread wide, he closed his eyes. The bodies of Druss and Talisman began to glow, radiating light of many colors: purple around the heart, bright white pulsing from their heads, red from the lower torso, white and yellow from the legs. It was an extraordinary sight. Sieben remained silent until Nosta Khan sighed and opened his eyes.

"What did you do to them?" whispered the poet.

"Nothing," answered Nosta Khan. "I have merely made their life force visible. He is a powerful man, this Druss. See how the energy of his *zhi* dwarfs that of Talisman? And Talisman is greater than most men." Sieben gazed at the glowing figures. It was true. The radiance around Druss extended almost three feet, while Talisman's flickered no more than a foot from his torso.

"What is this . . . *zhi*?" asked Sieben.

Nosta Khan was silent for a moment. "No man fully understands the mystery," he said. "The energy flows around the human body, bringing life and health. It flickers and changes when disease strikes. I have seen old men with the rheumatism in their arms where the *zhi* no longer flows. And I have seen mystic healers transfuse their own *zhi* into the sick, making them healthy again. It is connected in some way to the soul. After death, for example, the *zhi* flares to five times its size. This happens for three days. Then, in a heartbeat, it is gone."

"But why have you chosen to make it visible?"

"Their souls have gone to a place of untold dangers, where they will be fighting demons. Each cut they take, each wound they suffer, will affect the *zhi*. I will watch, and when they come close to death, I hope to be able to draw them back."

"You mean you are not certain of your ability to do this?"

"In Giragast there is no certainty," snapped Nosta Khan. "Imagine a fight here. A soldier is wounded in the arm; he suffers but lives. Another man is struck to the heart; he dies instantly. Such can happen in the Void. I can see the wounds they suffer there. But a death blow will extinguish the *zhi* in an instant."

"But you said the *zhi* flares for three days after death," Sieben pointed out.

"That is when the soul is within the body. Theirs are not."

The two men lapsed into silence. For several minutes nothing happened, then Talisman's body jerked. The bright colors around him flickered, and a green glow showed on his right leg. "It has begun," said Nosta Khan.

* * *

An hour passed, the candle flame burning down to the first of the black lines marked on its shaft. Sieben found the tension hard to bear. Rising, he went outside to the eastern wall, where he had left his saddlebags. Pulling out a fresh shirt of white linen embroidered with gold thread, he donned it. Talisman's servant, Gorkai, approached him. "Do they still live?" he asked.

"Yes," answered Sieben.

"I should have gone with them."

"Why don't you come in with me? Then you'll see them for yourself."

The man shook his head. "I will wait outside."

Sieben left him and returned to the shrine. The glow around Druss seemed just as strong, though Talisman's *zhi* was weaker. Sieben settled himself down against the wall. It was so like Druss to volunteer for a trip to hell. What is it about you, my friend? he thought. Why do you revel in such unnecessary risks? Is it that you think you are immortal? Or do you believe the Source has blessed you above other men? Sieben smiled. Maybe he has, he thought. Maybe there *is* something indestructible in your soul. Talisman's body spasmed, bright green flaring within his *zhi*. Druss, too, shuddered, his fists clenching.

"They are in a battle," whispered Nosta Khan, moving to his knees with his hands outstretched. Talisman's *zhi* flickered and faded, the glow dying away. Nosta Khan shouted three words, the sound harsh and discordant. Talisman's back arched, and he groaned. His eyes opened wide, and a strangled cry came from his lips. His arm swept out as if still holding a sword.

"Be calm!" cried Nosta Khan. "You are safe." Talisman rolled to his knees, his face drenched in sweat. He was breathing heavily.

"Send . . . send me back," he said.

"No. Your *zhi* is too weak. You will die."

"Send me back, damn you!" Talisman tried to rise but slumped to his face in the dust.

Sieben ran to him, helping him sit up. "Your shaman is right, Talisman. You were dying. What happened there?"

"Beasts the like of which I have never seen! Huge. Scaled. Eyes of fire. We saw nothing for the first days of travel. Then we were attacked by wolves. Great creatures, almost the size of ponies. We killed four. The rest fled. I thought they were bad enough, but by the gods of stone and water, they were puppies compared with what followed." He shivered suddenly. "How many days have I been gone?"

"Less than two hours," Sieben told him.

"That is not possible."

"Time has no meaning in the Void," said Nosta Khan. "How far did you get?"

"We made it to the gates of Giragast. There was a man there. Oshikai knew him, a small shaman with a twin-forked beard." Talisman turned to Sieben. "He said to thank you for the gift. He will remember it."

"Shaoshad the Cursed," hissed Nosta Khan.

"Cursed he may be, but we would never have mastered the demons at the gates without him. Druss and Oshikai are . . . colossal. Never have I seen such power, such controlled rage. When the scaled beasts came, I thought we were finished. Oshikai attacked them with Druss beside him. I was already wounded and scarcely able to move." His hand moved to his side, seeking a wound. He smiled. "I feel so weak."

"You need to rest," said Nosta Khan. "Your *zhi* is diminished. I will cast healing spells over you as you sleep."

"They cannot succeed. More demons everywhere."

"How were they when you left?" asked Sieben.

"Druss has a wound in his thigh and his left shoulder. Oshikai is bleeding from the chest and hip. I last saw them enter a black tunnel. The little man, Shaoshad, was leading them. He was holding a stick, which burst into flame like a torch. I tried to follow them . . . but then I was here. I should never have agreed to

Shul-sen's request. I have killed Druss and destroyed the soul of Oshikai."

"Druss is still strong," said Sieben, pointing to the glowing aura around the axman. "I've known him a long time, and I'd wager on him returning. Trust me."

Talisman shivered again. Nosta Khan covered his shoulders with a blanket. "Rest now, Talisman," he told the younger man. "Let sleep wash away the weakness within."

"I must wait," he said, his voice slurred with weariness.

"Whatever you wish, my lord," whispered Nosta Khan. As Talisman lay down, Nosta Khan began to chant in a low voice. Talisman's eyes closed. For long minutes the chant continued, then at last the shaman lapsed into silence. "He will sleep for many hours," said the old man. "*Aya!* But my heart is filled with pride for him. He is a warrior among warriors. Aye, and a man of honor!"

Sieben glanced at Druss' body. The glow was fading. "You had better fetch him back," he said.

"Not yet. All is well."

Druss eased his huge frame against the black rockface, then slumped to his knees. His strength was all but gone, and blood the color of milk was flowing from numerous wounds in his upper body. Oshikai laid his golden ax on a rock and sat down. He, too, was sorely wounded. The tiny shaman Shaoshad moved to Druss, laying his skinny hand on a deep cut on Druss' shoulder. The wound closed instantly.

"Almost there," said the little man. "One more bridge to cross."

"I don't believe I could move another step," said Druss. Shaoshad touched all his wounds, and the milky ichor ceased to flow.

"One more bridge, Drenai," repeated Shaoshad, moving to Oshikai and treating his wounds also.

"Did Talisman die?" Oshikai asked the shaman, his voice weak.

"I do not know. But he is here no longer. Either way he cannot help us. Can you go on?"

"I will find Shul-sen," said Oshikai stubbornly. "Nothing shall stop me."

Druss gazed around the awesome black cavern. Towering stalagmites rose toward the high, domed ceiling, met there by colossal stalactites, like two rows of fangs in a vast maw. One of the surviving bat creatures was still in view, crouching high on a ledge above them. Druss stared up into its baleful red eyes. The bodies of its comrades lay scattered on the cavern floor, their gray wings outstretched and broken. The survivor made no move to attack. The journey there had been long and terrifying, across a landscape unlike any to be found in the world of flesh. Druss had walked the Void once before, to bring Rowena back from the dead. But then he had walked the Road of Souls, a veritable garden of delights compared with this journey. The land obeyed no laws of nature that Druss understood. It shifted and changed endlessly under a slate-gray sky, cliffs suddenly rearing from a desolate plain, showering boulders the size of houses down from the sky. Chasms would appear, as if an invisible plow were tearing at the dead soil. Black and twisted trees would sprout into forests, their branches reaching out to claw like talons at the flesh of the travelers. Some time before— it could have been days or hours—they had descended into a gorge, the floor of which was festooned with what appeared to be discarded helms of rusted iron. Lightning lit the sky endlessly, casting hideous shadows around them. Talisman was in the lead when the helms began to shake. The earth parted, and long-buried warriors erupted from the black earth. The skin of their faces had rotted away, and maggots clung to the flesh beneath. Soundlessly they advanced. Talisman beheaded the first but took a deep wound from the second. Druss and Oshikai charged, their axes slicing into corrupt flesh.

The battle was long and hard. Shaoshad blasted globes of explosive fire into the awful ranks, and the air stank with the smoke of burning flesh. At the last Druss and Oshikai stood back to back gazing around at the mound of corpses. Of Talisman there was no sign.

On the far side of the gorge they had entered a tunnel, which led into the heart of the highest mountain Druss had ever seen. In a cavern at its center they had fought off a frenzied attack from the demonic bats. "Tell me," said Druss to Shaoshad, "that there are no more guardians. That would please me greatly."

"Plenty more, axman. But you know what they say," he added with a mischievous grin. "Nothing worthwhile ever comes easy, yes?"

"What can we expect?" asked Oshikai.

"The Great Bear guards the bridge. After that I know not. But there is one who will remain. That is Chakata. He it was who murdered Shul-sen in a manner most foul. He is here . . . in one form or another."

"Then he is mine," said Oshikai. "You hear me, Druss? He is mine!"

Druss looked across at the stocky figure in his shattered golden armor. "No argument from me, laddie."

Oshikai chuckled and moved across to sit beside Druss. "By the gods of stone and water, Druss, you are a man I would be proud to call brother. I wish I had known you in life. We could have downed a dozen flagons of wine and filled the night with boasting."

"The wine sounds good," said Druss, "but I never was much of a boaster."

"It is an acquired skill," agreed Oshikai. "I always found that a story sounds better if a multiple of ten is added to the enemy. Unless of course it was known that there were, say, only three. Then they become giants."

"I have a friend who understands that very well," said Druss.

"Is he a fine warrior?"

Druss looked into Oshikai's violet eyes. "No, a poet."

"Ah! I always took a poet with me to record my victories. I am no mean braggart myself, but when I listened to his songs of my deeds, I felt put to shame. Where I would speak of slaying giants, he would sing of subduing the gods themselves. Are you feeling rested?"

"Almost," lied Druss. "Tell me, little man," he said to Shaoshad, "what is this Great Bear you spoke of?"

"The guardian of the Bridge of Giragast. It is said to be eight feet tall; it has two heads, one of a bear with sharp fangs, the other of a snake. The snake spits venom that will burn through all armor. Its talons are as long as a short sword and sharper than spite. It has two hearts, one high in the chest, the other low in the belly."

"And how do you propose we pass this beast?"

"My magic is all but spent now, but I shall cast one more hide-spell to mask Oshikai. Then I shall rest here and await your return."

Oshikai rose and laid his hand on the little man's shoulder. "You have served me well, Shaoshad. I am a king no longer, but if there is justice in this vile realm, you will be rewarded. I am sorry that my refusal of your offer led to your death."

"All men die, Great King. And my own actions led to my death. I bear no ill will toward anyone. But if . . . when . . . you reach paradise, speak a word on my behalf to the gatekeeper there."

"I shall." Taking up his golden ax, Kolmisai, the warrior turned to Druss. "Are you ready now, my brother?"

"I was born ready," grunted Druss, forcing himself to his feet.

"You will see the bridge about a hundred paces that way," said Shaoshad. "It spans the abyss of fire. If you fall, it will be for an eternity, then the flames will devour you. The bridge is wide at the start, maybe fifty feet, but then it narrows. You must draw the bear to you onto the wide section to allow Oshikai to slip past."

"No," said Oshikai, "we will face it together."

"Trust me, Great King, and follow my bidding. When the bear dies, Chakata will know you are coming. Then he will slay Shul-sen. It is vital that you cross the bridge to the dark place before that."

"In the meantime I dance with the bear and try not to kill it?" queried Druss.

"Delay for as long as you can," advised Shaoshad, "and do not look into its eyes. You will see only death there." The shaman closed his eyes and raised his hands. The air around Oshikai cracked with bright, flickering lights. The great king's image faded, becoming translucent and then transparent. Then it was gone.

Shaoshad opened his eyes, then clapped his hands with glee. "Arrogant I may be," he chortled, "but skilled am I!" His smile faded, and he turned to Druss. "When you approach the bridge, Oshikai must be close behind you. Otherwise the bear will sense both spirits. Once the beast is engaged, Great King, you must slip by him and run. Make no sound. Do not call out for Shul-sen; you will sense her when she is close."

"I understand," came the voice of Oshikai. "You move on, Druss, and I will follow."

Taking up his ax, Druss led the way. His legs were heavy, his arms weary. Never in his life, not even in his years in the prison dungeon, had he felt such a sense of physical weakness. Fear rose strong within him. His foot struck a stone, and he stumbled.

The sound of wings beating came to him. Swiveling, he saw the last of the bat creatures swooping down toward him, its black wings wide, its gray-taloned hands outstretched. Snaga flashed up, smashing through the thin neck, but not before the talons had scored across his face, ripping open his cheek. The creature's body struck him, toppling him from his feet. He felt the hand of Oshikai grasp him by the wrist, hauling him upright.

"You are exhausted, my friend," said Oshikai. "Rest here. I will try to slip by the bear."

"No, I will see it through," grunted Druss. "Do not concern yourself with me."

He staggered on, rounding a bend in the black cavern. Ahead of them an awesome bridge arced across a chasm. Druss stepped onto it and glanced over the edge. It seemed to him that he was staring down into infinity. It made him dizzy, and he swiftly stepped back onto the black stone. Holding Snaga in both hands, he walked on. From there he could not see the far side of the bridge. "It must be miles across," he whispered, a sense of despair filling him.

"One step at a time, my friend," said Oshikai.

Druss stumbled on through a haze of bone-numbing exhaustion. A cold wind blew across the chasm, and Druss could smell acrid smoke on it. On he struggled, forcing his body through each weary step.

After what seemed like hours they reached the midpoint of the bridge. The far side could now be seen, a towering hill of black rock set against a slate-gray sky. A figure moved on the bridge, and Druss narrowed his eyes, straining to see it. It moved slowly on its hind legs, mighty arms stretched wide. As it neared, Druss saw that Shaoshad's description had been correct in every detail: two heads, one a bear and the other a serpent. What Shaoshad had not conveyed was the sense of evil that radiated from the demon. It struck Druss like the numbing claws of a winter blizzard, colossal in its power, dwarfing the strength of man.

The bridge had narrowed to less than ten feet wide. The creature coming slowly toward them seemed to fill the gap.

"May the gods of stone and water smile upon you, Druss!" whispered Oshikai.

Druss stepped forward. The beast gave a terrible roar, thunder deep and deafening. The wall of sound struck the axman like a blow, pushing him back.

The beast spoke: "We are the Great Bear, devourers of souls. Your death will be agonizing, mortal!"

"In your dreams, you whoreson!" said Druss.

"Bring him back!" shouted Sieben. "You can see he is dying!"

"In a good cause," said Nosta Khan. Sieben looked at the little man and saw the malevolence in his eyes.

"You treacherous cur!" he hissed, scrambling to his feet and launching himself at the man. Nosta Khan threw up his right hand, and needles of fire sliced into Sieben's head. He screamed and fell back, yet even through the pain he scrabbled for the knife at his hip. Nosta Khan spoke a single word, and Sieben's arm froze.

"Don't do this to him," begged Sieben. "He deserves better."

"Deserving has nothing to do with it, you fool. He chose to walk in hell; I did not force him. But he has not yet accomplished what he set out to do. If he dies, so be it. Now be silent!" Sieben tried to speak, but his tongue stuck to the roof of his mouth. The pain subsided, but he was unable to move.

The beast spoke, the voice issuing from both heads: "Come to me and know death, Druss!"

Druss hefted his ax and moved forward. With astonishing speed the Great Bear dropped to all fours and charged. Snaga flashed up and then down with sickening force, plunging between the two heads, smashing through bone and sinew. The beast's body struck the axman hard, hurling him from his feet. Losing his grip on his ax, Druss skidded across the bridge on his back, his legs slipping over the chasm. Rolling to his belly, he scrabbled at the black stone, halting his slide, then hauled himself back onto the bridge. The Great Bear had reared up, black blood gouting from between its heads. Druss surged upright, charging the beast. A taloned arm swept down, ripping through his jerkin and scoring his flesh with the pain of fire. Reaching up, he grabbed Snaga's haft and wrenched the weapon clear.

Blood spurted over his face, burning like acid. The snake mouth opened, spewing a stream of venom that covered his jerkin, bursting into flame. Ignoring the pain, Druss hammered Snaga into the snake neck, severing it. The head fell clear, bouncing on the black stone as smoke spewed from the mutilated neck. The Great Bear lashed out once more. Druss was thrown clear and landed heavily but rolled to his feet with ax in hand. The beast tottered forward. The venom on Druss' jerkin burned through to the flesh beneath, and with a cry of rage and pain he threw himself at the mortally wounded guardian. The talons swept down, but the speed of Druss' charge carried him under the blow, and his shoulder hit the beast in the chest. The Great Bear staggered back, then fell from the bridge. Druss crawled to the edge, watching the body spiral down and down.

Sinking to the black stone, Druss rolled to his back. Exhaustion overtook him, and he longed for the bliss of sleep. "Do not close your eyes," came the voice of Shaoshad. Druss blinked and saw the little man kneeling beside him. Shaoshad touched his slender hands to Druss' wounds, and the pain subsided. "Sleep here is death," said the shaman.

Oshikai ran on, crossing the bridge at speed and reaching the other side just as the Great Bear fell into the chasm. Ahead of him the black hill beckoned. Swiftly he scaled the flanks of the hill, his thoughts reaching out to Shul-sen. At first there was nothing, but then, ahead, he saw a rectangular black stone doorway set into the hillside. And he felt the presence of Shul-sen's spirit beyond it. Oshikai pushed hard, but the door did not give. Stepping back, he struck the stone with his golden ax. Sparks flew from the stone, and a gaping crack appeared. Twice more Oshikai thundered Kolmisai against the stone. On the third stroke the door fell into four pieces.

Beyond it was a dark tunnel. As Oshikai stepped forward, a black lion with eyes of bright fire came hurtling out of the darkness. Kolmisai leapt to meet it, the ax blade ripping into the creature's chest, and with a terrible cry it fell to Oshikai's left. The king swung and slashed the ax through its thick neck, beheading it. Lifting the head by the mane, Oshikai strode forward. The eyes of bright fire were fading, but still they cast a dim light on the walls of the tunnel.

Oshikai moved on. A whisper of movement came from his left. Spinning toward the sound, the king threw the demon head. Huge serpentine jaws snapped down on it, the bones of the skull splitting, brains oozing out through the rows of crocodile teeth in the long snout. The lizard beast opened its jaws and shook its head, spitting out the broken skull. In that moment Oshikai leapt forward to smash Kolmisai into the thick, scaled head, the golden blade shearing through the bone. The beast slumped to the ground, gave one low groan, and died.

In darkness now, Oshikai moved forward with one hand on the wall. "Shul-sen!" he called. "Can you hear me?"

"I am here," came her voice. "Oh, my lord, is it you?" The sound came from ahead and to the left. Oshikai crossed the tunnel floor and found a sleek doorway. Blindly he struck at it; the door splintered and gave way. All was pitch darkness as he stepped into the room beyond.

A slender hand touched his face. "Is it truly you?" she whispered.

"Truly," he answered, his voice thick with emotion. His left arm drew her to him, and dropping his head, he held her close, his limbs shaking. "My love, the soul of my heart," he whispered. Their lips touched, and he felt Shul-sen's tears mingle with his own. For a moment only he forgot the perils and the dangers still to come.

Then, from the tunnel, came sounds of stealthy movement. Taking her hand, Oshikai backed out through the doorway. The sounds were coming from his right. Oshikai turned left and, still holding to Shul-sen, moved deeper into the tunnel. After a while the floor began to rise. Higher and higher they climbed. A faint light could be seen above them now, seeping through a crack in the rocks of the hillside.

Oshikai paused in his flight and waited.

A lion beast with eyes of flame padded into sight, and with a great roar it charged. Oshikai leapt to meet it, Kolmisai sweeping down and cleaving its skull. The beast sagged to the ground.

Oshikai climbed to the crack in the rocks and struck it with his ax. The crack opened to two feet wide, stones falling from it and showering the king. A boulder was lodged in the crack, and stretching up, he pushed at it. The boulder rolled clear. Climbing through the gap, he turned and reached down for Shul-sen. The mossy ground beneath him shivered. Oshikai was thrown to his left and almost lost hold of his ax. What he had taken to be moss below his feet quivered and lifted from the earth, and he was thrown into the air. The whole of the hillside seemed to shudder as two immense wings unfolded. The brow of the hill rose up, becoming the head of a giant bat. Oshikai clung to the wing as the colossal creature rose into the air. Higher and higher it flew out over the bridge and the bottomless pit. Oshikai sank his fingers deep into the fur and hung on. The head of the bat twisted around, and its huge mouth opened. Within the darkness of its maw there shone a face that he recognized.

"How do you like my new form, Great King?" sneered Chakata. "Is it not magnificent?"

Oshikai did not answer but began to crawl toward the creature's neck. "Shall I tell you how many times I have enjoyed Shul-sen? Shall I describe the pleasures I have forced her to undergo?" The king moved closer. The face of Chakata smiled. The bat banked suddenly, and Oshikai began to fall, then lashed out with his ax, burying it deep into the black wing. Slowly he hauled himself closer to the neck, dragging the ax clear and hammering it again through the fur, inching his way toward his enemy.

"Don't be a fool, Oshikai!" shouted Chakata. "If you kill me, you will fall with me. You will never see Shul-sen again!"

Slowly, inexorably the king moved onward. The bat flipped over into a backward dive, then rolled and beat its wings, trying to dislodge the tiny figure. But Oshikai clung on. Closer and closer he came to the head. The bat's jaws snapped at him, but he rolled wide of them. Dragging clear his ax, he dealt a mighty blow to the creature's neck. Black blood gouted from the wound. Twice more he struck. Suddenly the bat's wings folded, and the body began to plummet toward the bridge far below. Oshikai continued to hammer his blade into the half-severed neck, cleaving bone and sinew. The head fell clear, the dead beast spiraling down toward the pit.

Determined not to die alongside such vermin, Oshikai threw himself from the corpse.

Far below the naked Shul-sen had clambered free of the tunnel, and she stood now watching the epic battle in the gray skies above. Now free of the spells Chakata had woven, she felt her power returning. Instantly she clothed herself in a shirt and leggings of silver silk and a cloud-white cloak. Pulling her cloak from her shoulders, she spoke the five words of the eleventh spell. Then she hurled the cloak high into the air. It flew on, spinning wildly, a wheel of white cloth glistening against the smoke-gray sky.

Shul-sen stood with hand outstretched, directing the cloak with all the power she could muster. The dead creature that had once been Chakata plunged down into the abyss. Oshikai continued to fall, but the cloak soared up toward him, enveloping his body. For a moment only, the fall was halted, but then he plunged on with the cloak around him. Shul-sen cried out, the cloak flared open, and Oshikai's rapid descent slowed. The cloak floated down to the bridge, and Oshikai jumped clear. Shul-sen ran down the hillside toward him, arms outstretched. Dropping his ax, he went to meet her, drawing her into a tight embrace. For a long moment he held her thus, then drew back, and she saw tears on his cheeks.

"I have searched for so long," he said. "I had begun to believe I would never find you."

"But you did, my lord," she whispered, kissing his lips and tear-stained cheeks.

For a long time they stood, holding each other close. Then he took her hand and led her to where Druss lay on the bridge. Oshikai knelt beside him. "By all that is sacred, I never met a man like you, Druss. I pray that we meet again."

"Not here, though, eh?" grunted Druss. "Perhaps you could choose somewhere more . . . hospitable."

Two glowing figures appeared on the bridge, with light blazing around them. Druss squinted and shaded his eyes as the figures came closer. There was no threat from them, and Oshikai rose to meet them.

"It is time," came a gentle voice.

"You can take us both," said Oshikai.

"No. Only you."

"Then I will not come."

The first of the glowing figures swung toward the woman. "You are not ready, Shul-sen. You carry too much that is dark within you. All that was good came from your union with this man; the only selfless acts you committed were for him. Twice now he has refused paradise. This third refusal will be final . . . we will come for him no more."

"Give me a moment with him," she said. "Alone."

The glowing figures floated away some fifty paces. Shul-sen approached Oshikai. "I will not leave you," he said. "Not again."

Reaching up, she cupped her hand around his neck, drawing his head down into a long, lingering kiss. When at last they separated, she stroked his handsome face and gave a wistful smile. "Would you deny me paradise, my love?" she asked him.

"What do you mean?"

"If you refuse them now, you will never see the land of

heavenly dreams. And if you do not, then how can I? By refusing them, you sentence us to walk the Void forever."

Drawing her hand to his lips, he kissed her fingers tenderly. "But I have waited so long for you. I could not bear another parting."

"And yet you must," she said, forcing a smile. "We are united, Oshikai. We will be again. But when next I see you, it will be under blue skies, beside whispering streams. Go now and wait for me."

"I love you," he said. "You are the stars and moon to me."

Pulling away from him, she turned to the glowing figures. "Take him," she said. "Let him know joy." As they drew closer, she looked hard into the shining face of the first of the men. "Tell me, can I earn a place beside him?"

"What you have done here is a step toward it, Shul-sen. You know where we are. The journey will be long, and there will be many calls upon you. Travel with Shaoshad. He, too, has much to learn."

The second of the men floated alongside Druss, laying a golden hand on his body. All his wounds closed, and Druss felt new strength coursing through him.

Then, in an instant, they were gone, and Oshikai with them. As Shul-sen fell to her knees, her long, dark hair falling over her face, Shaoshad moved to her side. "We will find him, my lady. Together. And great will be the joy when we do."

Shul-sen gave a deep, shuddering sigh. "Then let us be away," she said, rising to her feet. Druss rose also.

"I wish I could help you," he said.

Taking his hand, she kissed it. "I knew you were the one," she told him. "You are like him in so many ways. Go back now to the world you know."

Her hand touched his head, and darkness swallowed him.

# ◊ 11 ◊

**D**RUSS AWOKE TO see the dawn sunlight shining through the window of the tomb. Never had he been happier to witness the birth of a new day. Sieben moved alongside him, and Nosta Khan edged forward, blocking the sunlight.

"Speak!" said the shaman. "Did you succeed?"

"Aye," muttered Druss, sitting up. "They were united."

"Did you ask about the Eyes of Alchazzar?"

"No."

"What?" stormed the shaman. "Then what was the purpose of this insane journey?"

Ignoring him, Druss stood and walked to where Talisman lay sleeping. Laying a huge hand on the young man's shoulder, Druss called to him.

Talisman's dark eyes opened. "Did we win?" he asked.

"We won, laddie, after a fashion." Quietly Druss told him about the appearance of the angels and the second separation.

Talisman pushed himself to his feet. "I hope she finds him," he said, and walked from the building, followed by Nosta Khan.

"Their gratitude brings a tear to my old eyes," said Sieben sourly.

Druss shrugged. "It is done. That is what counts."

"So, tell me all."

"I don't think so, poet. I want no songs about this."

"No songs; you have my word of honor," lied the poet.

Druss chuckled. "Maybe later. For now I need some food and a long, slow drink of cool water."

"Was she beautiful?"

"Exceptionally. But she had a hard face," said Druss, striding away. Sieben followed him out into the sunlight as Druss stood, gazing up at the rich blue of the sky. "The Void is an ugly place, devoid of color save for the red of flame and the gray of stone and ash and sky. It is a chilling thought that we must all walk it one day."

"Chilling. Absolutely," agreed Sieben. "Now the story, Druss. Tell me the story."

Above them on the ramparts, with Gorkai and Nosta Khan beside him, Talisman gazed down at Druss and the poet. "He should have died there," said Nosta Khan. "His life force was almost gone. But it surged back."

Talisman nodded. "I have never seen the like," he admitted. "Watching Druss and Oshikai together, battling demons and monsters . . . it was awesome. From the moment they met, they were like sword brothers, and when they fought side by side, it seemed they had known each other for an eternity. I could not compete, shaman. I was like a child among men. And yet I felt no bitterness. I felt . . . privileged."

"Aye," whispered Gorkai, "to have fought beside Oshikai Demon-bane is a privilege indeed."

"Yet we are no closer to the eyes," snapped Nosta Khan. "A great warrior he may be, but he is a fool. Shaoshad would have told him had he but asked!"

"We will find them or we won't! I'll lose no more sleep over it," said Talisman. Leaving the shaman, he moved down the rampart steps and crossed the open ground to the lodging house.

Zhusai was asleep in the bed, and Talisman sat beside her, stroking her hair. Her dark eyes opened, and she gave a sleepy smile. "I waited until Gorkai told me you were safe; then I slept."

"We are all safe," he told her, "and Shul-sen will haunt you no more." He fell silent.

Sitting up, she took his hand and saw the sorrow in his eyes. "What is it, Talisman? Why so sad?"

"Their love lasted an eternity," he said, his voice low. "Yet for us there will be no joining. All my life I have longed to help the Uniter band our people together. I thought there was no greater cause. You fill my mind, Zhusai. I know now that when the Uniter takes you, I will not be able to follow him. I could not."

"Then let us defy the prediction," she said, taking him in her arms. "Let us be together."

Gently but firmly he took hold of her arms, drawing away from her. "I cannot do that, either. My duty forbids it. I shall tell Nosta Khan to take you away from here. Tomorrow."

"No! I will not go."

"If you truly love me, you will, Zhusai. I need to clear my mind for the battle ahead." Rising, he left her and returned to the compound. For the next hour he toured the fortifications, checking the repairs to the ramparts. Then he sent Quing-chin and three riders to scout for the enemy.

"Do not engage them, my friend," he told Quing-chin. "I'll need you here when the battle begins."

"I will be here," the warrior promised. And he rode from the fort.

Gorkai approached Talisman. "You should take the woman," he said softly.

Talisman turned on him angrily. "You were listening?"

"Yes. Every word," Gorkai agreed amiably. "You should take her."

"And what of duty? What of the fate of the Nadir?"

Gorkai smiled. "You are a great man, Talisman, but you are not thinking this through. We won't survive here; we are all going to die. So if you wed her, she will be a widow in a few days, anyway. Nosta Khan says he can spirit her away. Good.

Then the Uniter will wed your widow. So how will destiny be changed?"

"What if we win?"

"You mean what if the puppy dog devours the lion?" Gorkai shrugged. "My view on that is simple, Talisman. I follow you. If the Uniter wants my loyalty, then let him be here fighting with us! Last night you united Oshikai and Shul-sen. Look around you. There are men here of five tribes. You have united them; that's enough of a Uniter for me."

"I am not the man prophesied."

"I do not care. You are the man who's *here*. I am older than you, boy, and I have made many mistakes. You are making one now regarding Zhusai. True love is rare. Take it where you find it. That is all I have to say."

Druss sat quietly on the ramparts, gazing around at the defenders as they continued their work on the walls, carrying rocks to hurl down on advancing infantrymen. There were now just under two hundred fighting men, the bulk of them refugees from the Curved Horn. Nuang Xuan had sent his people to the east, but several women remained behind, Niobe among them. The old man waved at Druss, then climbed the broken steps to the ramparts. He was breathing heavily when he reached the top. "A fine day, axman," he said, drawing in a deep breath.

"Aye," agreed Druss.

"It is a good fort now, yes?"

"A good fort with old gates," said Druss. "That's the weak spot."

"That is my position," said Nuang, his face devoid of expression. "Talisman has told me to stand among the defenders at that point. If the gate is breached, we are to fill it with bodies." He forced a smile. "A long time since I have known such fear, but it is a good feeling."

Druss nodded. "If the gate is breached, old man, you will find me beside you."

"Ha! Then there will be plenty of killing." Nuang's expression softened. "You will be fighting your own people again. How does this sit with you?"

Druss shrugged. "They are not my people, and I do not go hunting them. They are coming for me. Their deaths are on their own heads."

"You are a hard man, Druss. Nadir blood, maybe."

"Maybe." Nuang saw his nephew Meng below and called out to him. Without a word of farewell the old man strolled back down the steps.

Druss transferred his gaze to the west and the line of hills. The enemy would be there soon. He thought of Rowena, back at the farm, and the days of work among the herds, the quiet of the nights in their spacious cabin. Why is it, he wondered, that when I am away from her I long for her company, and when I am with her I yearn for the call to arms? His thoughts ranged back to his childhood, traveling with his father, trying to escape the infamy of Bardan the Slayer. Druss glanced down at Snaga, resting against the battlement wall. The dread ax had belonged to his grandfather, Bardan. It had been demon-possessed then and had turned Bardan into a raging killer, a butcher. Druss, too, had been touched by it. Is that why I am what I am? he thought. Even though the demon had long since been exorcised, still its malice had worked on him through the long years when he had searched for Rowena.

Not normally introspective, Druss found his mood darkening. He had not come to the lands of the Gothir for war but to take part in the games. Now, through no fault of his own, he was waiting for a powerful army and was desperate to find two healing jewels that would bring Klay back to health.

"You look angry, old horse," said Sieben, moving alongside him. Druss looked at his friend. The poet was wearing a pale blue shirt with buttons of polished bone. His baldric was freshly polished, the knife handles gleaming in their sheaths. His blond hair was newly combed and held in place by a headband at the center of which an opal was set.

"How do you do it?" asked Druss. "Here we are in a dust-blown wilderness, and you look as if you've just stepped from a bathhouse."

"Standards must always be maintained," Sieben said, with a broad grin. "These savages need to see how civilized men behave."

Druss chuckled. "You lift my spirits, poet. You always have."

"Why so gloomy? War and death are but a few days away. I would have thought you would have been dancing for joy."

"I was thinking of Klay. The jewels aren't here, and I can't keep my promise to him."

"Oh, don't be too sure of that, old horse. I have a theory, but we'll say no more of it until the time is right."

"You think you can find them?"

"As I said, I have a theory. But now is not the time. Nosta Khan wanted you to die, you know, and you almost did. We cannot trust him, Druss. Or Talisman. The jewels are too important to them."

"You are right there," grunted Druss. "The shaman is a loath-some wretch."

"What's that?" exclaimed Sieben, pointing to the line of hills. "Oh, sweet heaven, they are here!"

Druss narrowed his eyes. A line of lancers in bright armor was riding single file down the hillside. A cry went up on the walls, and warriors ran from the compound to take their places, bows in hand.

"They are riding ponies," muttered Druss. "What in hell's name . . . ?"

Talisman and Nosta Khan came alongside Druss. The riders beyond broke into a gallop and thundered across the plain with their lances held high. On each lance was a spitted head.

"It is Lin-tse!" shouted Talisman. The Nadir defenders

began to cheer and shout as the thirty riders slowed to a canter and rode along the line of the wall, lifting their lances and showing their grisly trophies. One by one they thrust the lances into the ground, then rode through the newly opened gates. Lin-tse jumped from his pony and removed the Gothir helm. Warriors streamed from the walls to surround him and his Sky Riders.

Lin-tse began to chant in the Nadir tongue. He leapt and danced to wild cheering from the warriors. On the battlements above Sieben watched in fascination but could understand none of the words. He turned to Nosta Khan. "What is he saying?"

"He is telling of the slaughter of the enemy and how his men rode the sky to defeat them."

"Rode the sky? What does that mean?"

"It means the first victory is ours," snapped the shaman. "Now be silent so I can listen."

"Irritating man," muttered Sieben, sitting back alongside Druss.

Lin-tse's story took almost a quarter of an hour to complete, and at the close the warriors swept in around him, lifting him shoulder-high. Talisman sat quietly until the noise died down. When Lin-tse was lowered to the ground, he walked to Talisman and gave a short bow. "Your orders were obeyed," he said. "Many lancers are dead, and I have their armor."

"You did well, my brother."

Talisman strode to the rampart steps and climbed them, swinging back to stare down at the gathered men. "They can be beaten," he said, still speaking Nadir. "They are not invincible. We have tasted their blood, and we will taste more. When they come to despoil the shrine, we will stop them. For we are Nadir, and our day is dawning. This is but the beginning. What we do here will become part of our legends. The story of your heroism will spread on the wings of fire to every Nadir tribe, every camp and village. It will bring the Day of the Uniter closer. And one day we will stand before the walls of Gulgothir, and the city itself will tremble before us." Slowly he raised his right arm, with his fist clenched. "Nadir we!" he shouted. The warriors followed him, and the chant was taken up:

> *"Nadir we,*
> *youth born,*
> *bloodletters,*
> *ax wielders,*
> *victors still."*

"Chills the blood, rather," observed Sieben.

Druss nodded. "He's a clever man. He knows there are disasters to come, and he's filling them with pride at the outset. They'll fight like devils for him now."

"I didn't know you could understand Nadir."

"I can't . . . but you don't need to be a linguist to understand what's happening here. He sent out Lin-tse to bloody the enemy, to give them a victory, to bond them together. He's probably just told them that they are all heroes and that together they can withstand any force. Something like that."

"And can they?"

"No way to judge, poet. Not until the first deaths. A fighting force is like a sword blade. You can't test it until it has passed through fire."

"Yes, yes, yes," said Sieben irritably, "but apart from the warlike analogies, what is your feeling? You know men. I trust your judgment."

"I don't know *these* men. Oh, they are ferocious, right enough. But they are not disciplined, and they are superstitious. They have no history of success to fall back on, to lift them in the dark hours. They have never defeated the Gothir. Everything depends on the first day of battle. Ask me again if we survive that."

"Damn, but you are gloomy today, my friend," said Sieben. "What is it?"

"This is not my war, poet. I have no *feeling* for it, you know?

I fought alongside Oshikai. I *know* that it doesn't matter a damn to him what happens to his bones. This is a battle over nothing, and nothing will be achieved by it, win or lose."

"I think you may be wrong there, old horse. All this talk of a Uniter is important to these people. You say they have no history of success to fall back on; well, perhaps this will be the first for them." Sieben hoisted himself to the wall and sat looking at his friend. "But you know all this. There's something more, isn't there, Druss? Something deeper."

Druss gave a wry smile, then rubbed his huge hand over his black beard. "Aye, there is. I don't like them, poet. It is that simple. I have no affinity with these tribesmen. I don't know how they think or what they feel. One thing is for damned sure: they don't think like us."

"You like Nuang and Talisman. They are both Nadir," Sieben pointed out.

"Yes, I know. I can't make sense of it."

Sieben chuckled. "It's not hard, Druss. You are Drenai, born and raised—the greatest race on earth. That's what they told us. Civilized men in a world of savages. You had no trouble fighting alongside the Ventrians, but then, they are like us, round-eyed and tall. We share a common mythology. But the Nadir are descended from the Chiatze, and with them we share nothing that is obvious. Dogs and cats, Druss. Or wolves and lions, if you prefer. But I think you are wrong to believe they don't think like us or feel like us. They just show things differently, that's all. A different culture base."

"I am not a bigot," Druss said defensively.

Sieben laughed. "Of course you are; it is bred into you. But you are a good man, Druss, and it won't make a damn bit of difference to the way you behave. Drenai teachings may have lodged in your head, but you have a fine heart. And that will always carry you through."

Druss relaxed and felt the tension flow from him. "I hope you are right," he said. "My grandfather was a butchering killer; his atrocities haunt me still. I never want to be guilty of that kind of evil. I never want to be fighting on the wrong side. The Ventrian War was just; I believed that, and it meant something. The people now have Gorben as a leader, and he is as great a man as I ever met."

"Perhaps," Sieben said doubtfully. "History will judge him better than you or I. But if you are concerned about this current . . . vileness, put your mind at rest. This is a shrine, and here lie the bones of the greatest hero the Nadir have ever known. This place means something to all their people. The men who are coming serve a mad emperor, and they seek to despoil this place for no other purpose than their desire to humiliate the tribes, to keep them in their place. The Source knows how I hate violence, but we are not on the wrong side in this, Druss. By heaven, we're not!"

Druss clapped him on the shoulder. "You're beginning to sound like a warrior," he said with a wide grin.

"Well, that's because the enemy hasn't arrived yet. When they do, you'll find me hiding in an empty flour barrel."

"I don't believe that for a moment," Druss told him.

In a small room alongside the makeshift hospital Zhusai sat quietly as Talisman and Lin-tse discussed the raid. The two men were physically very different; Lin-tse was tall, his solemn face showing his mixed-blood ancestry, the eyes only barely slanted, the cheeks and jawbones heavy. His hair was not the jet-black of the Nadir but was tinged with auburn streaks. Talisman, his hair drawn back into a tight ponytail, looked every inch the Nadir warrior, his skin pale gold, his face flat, the dark eyes expressionless. And yet, thought Zhusai, there was a similarity that was not born of the physical, an aura almost that spoke of brotherhood. Was it, she wondered, the shared experience in the Bodacas Academy or the desire to see the Nadir free and proud once more? Perhaps both, she thought.

"They will be here tomorrow afternoon. No later," said Lin-tse.

"There is nothing more we can do. The warriors are as ready now as they will ever be."

"But will they hold, Talisman? I have never heard much that is good of the Curved Horn. And as for the Lone Wolves ... well, they seem nervous without their leader. And I see the groups do not mix at all."

"They will hold," Talisman told him. "And as for what you have heard of the Curved Horn, I wonder what they have heard of the Sky Riders. It is not our custom to think well of tribal enemies. Though I note you have not mentioned the Fleet Ponies. Could that be because our friend Quing-chin leads them?"

Lin-tse gave a tight smile. "I take your point. The axman looks like a fighting man."

"He is. I have walked the Void with him, my friend, and believe me, he is awesome to behold."

"Even so I feel uncomfortable with a *gajin* within the walls. Is he a friend?"

"To the Nadir? No. To me? Perhaps. I am glad that he is here. He has an indomitable feel about him." Talisman stood. "You should go and rest, Lin-tse. You have earned it. I wish I could have seen you and your men leap the chasm. Truly you were Sky Riders in that moment. Men will sing of it in the years to come."

"Only if we survive, General."

"Then we must, for I would like to hear that song myself."

Lin-tse rose, and the two men gripped hands. Then Lin-tse bowed to Zhusai and left the room. Talisman slumped back into his seat.

"You are more tired than he," Zhusai admonished him. "It is you who need to rest."

Talisman gave a weary smile. "I am young and full of strength."

Zhusai crossed the room and knelt beside him, her arms resting on his thighs. "I will not go with Nosta Khan," she said. "I have thought long on this. I know it is the custom for a Nadir father to choose the husband for his daughter, but my father was not Nadir, and my grandfather had no right to pledge me. I tell you this, Talisman: if you make me leave, then I shall wait for news of you. If you die—"

"Do not say it! I forbid it!"

"You can forbid me nothing," she told him quietly. "You are not my husband; you are my guardian. No more. Very well, I shall not say it. But you know what I will do."

Angrily he grabbed her shoulders, lifting her. "Why are you torturing me in this way?" he shouted. "Can you not see that your safety would give me strength, give me hope?"

Relaxing in his arms, she sat down on his lap. "Hope? What hope for Zhusai with you dead, my love? What would the future hold? Marriage to an unnamed man with violet eyes? No, not for me. It will be you or no one."

Leaning forward, she kissed him, and he felt the soft warmth of her tongue on his lips. His mind screamed at him to pull away from her, but arousal swept over him and he drew her close, returning the kiss with an ardor he had not known he possessed. His hand slid over her shoulder, feeling the softness of her white silk shirt and the flesh beneath. His palm followed the contours of her body, moving down over her left breast, the hardness of the nipple causing him to slow and stroke it between thumb and forefinger.

He did not hear the door open but felt the warm flow of air from outside. Drawing back, he swung his head to see Nuang Xuan. "This a bad time, hey?" said the old warrior with a wink.

"No," answered Talisman, his voice thick. "Come in." Zhusai rose, then leaned forward and kissed his cheek. He watched her walk from the room, following the sway of her slender hips.

Nuang Xuan sat down awkwardly on the wooden chair. "Better to sit Nadir fashion on the floor," he said, "but I don't want to be looking up at you."

"What do you require of me, old one?"

"You wish me to guard the gate, but I desire to stand alongside Druss on the wall."

"Why?"

Nuang sighed. "I think I will die here, Talisman. I do not object to this, for I have lived a long time. And I have killed many men. You doubt me?"

"Why would I doubt you?"

"Because it's not true," Nuang said with a wicked grin. "I have killed five men in my life: three in duels when I was young and two lancers when they attacked us. I told the axman I would kill a hundred on the walls. He said he would keep count for me."

"Only a hundred?" queried Talisman.

Nuang smiled. "I have not been feeling well."

"Tell me the real reason you wish to stand beside him," said Talisman.

Nuang's old eyes narrowed, and he took a deep breath. "I have seen him fight, and he is deadly. Many *gajin* will die around him. If I am there, men will see me fight. I cannot reach a hundred, but it will seem like it to those watching. Then, when they sing the songs of this defense, my name will live on. You understand?"

"Nuang and the Deathwalker," said Talisman softly. "Yes, I understand."

"Why do you call him that?"

"He and I walked the Void. It is a good name for him."

"It is very fine. Nuang and the Deathwalker. I like this. Can it be so?"

"It can. I shall also watch you, old man, and keep count."

"Ha! I am happy now, Talisman." Nuang stood and rubbed his buttocks. "I don't like these chairs."

"The next time we talk, we will sit on the floor," promised Talisman.

Nuang shook his head. "Not much talking left. The *gajin* will be here tomorrow. Is your woman staying here?"

"Yes."

"As it should be," said Nuang. "She is very beautiful, and sex with her will aid you in the times ahead. Bear in mind, however, that her hips are very small. The first birth for such women is always hard."

"I will bear that in mind, old one."

Nuang strode to the door. He stopped there for a moment, then looked back at Talisman. "You are very young. But if you live, you will be a great man. I know these things."

Then he was gone.

Talisman moved to a second door at the back of the room and emerged into the hospital. Sieben was spreading blankets on the floor, and a young Nadir woman was sweeping the dust from the room.

"All ready here, General," said Sieben brightly. "Plenty of thread and sharp needles. And bandages and the most disgusting-smelling herbs I've ever come across. I would think the threat of them alone will have wounded men rushing back to the walls."

"Dried tree fungus," said Talisman. "It prevents infection. Do you have any alcohol?"

"I do not have the skill to operate. There will be no need to get men drunk."

"Use it for cleaning wounds and implements. This also helps prevent infection."

"Maybe you should be the surgeon," said Sieben. "You seem to know a lot more than I do."

"We had lessons on military surgery at Bodacas. There were many books."

As Talisman walked away, the Nadir woman approached him. Not conventionally pretty, she was devastatingly attractive. She moved in close. "You are young for a general," she said, her breasts touching his chest. "Is it true what they say about you and the Chiatze woman?"

"What do they say?"

"They say that she is pledged to the Uniter and that you cannot have her."

"Do they? And if it is true, how does that concern you?"

"I am not pledged to the Uniter. And no general should have to worry about both heads, above and below. It is said there is not enough blood in any man to fill both heads at the same time. Perhaps you should empty one so that the other may function."

Talisman laughed aloud. "You are one of Nuang's women . . . Niobe?"

"Yes. Niobe," she said, pleased that he remembered her name.

"Well, Niobe, I thank you for your offer. It is a great compliment, and it has lifted my spirits."

"Is that a no or a yes?" she asked, bemused.

Talisman smiled, then swung away and walked out into the sunlight. As Niobe turned back to Sieben, the poet chuckled.

"By heavens, but you are a brazen hussy. What happened to the warrior you had your pretty eye on?"

"He has two wives and one pony," she said. "And bad teeth."

"Well, don't despair. There are almost two hundred others to choose from."

She looked at him, then cocked her head. "There is no one here. Come, lie with me."

"There are men, my darling, who would feel hurt and humiliated to be second choice to a man with one pony and bad teeth. I, on the other hand, have no qualms about accepting such a graceless offer. But then, the men of my family have always had a weakness for attractive women."

"Do all the men in your family talk so much?" she asked, untying the cord belt and letting fall her skirt.

"Talking is the second best talent we have."

"What is the first?" she asked him.

"Sarcasm as well as beauty, sweet one? Ah, but you are an enchanting creature." Stripping off his clothes, Sieben spread a blanket on the floor and drew her down upon it.

"You will have to be quick," she said.

"Speed in matters of the loins is a talent that seems to have escaped me. Thankfully," he added.

\* \* \*

Kzun felt a roaring sense of exultation as he watched the two wagons burning. Leaping over the boulders, he ran down to where a Gothir wagon driver, shot through the neck, was trying to crawl away. Plunging his dagger between the man's shoulders, Kzun twisted it savagely; the man cried out, then began to choke on his own blood. When Kzun rose up and let out a bloodcurdling cry, the Curved Horn warriors rose from their hiding places and ran down to join him. The wind shifted, acrid smoke burning Kzun's eyes. Swiftly he loped around the blazing wagons and surveyed the scene. There had been seven wagons in all and a troop of fifteen lancers. Twelve of the lancers were dead: eight peppered with arrows, four slain in fierce hand-to-hand fighting. Kzun himself had killed two of them. Then the Gothir had turned the remaining wagons and fled. Kzun had longed to ride after them, but his orders were to remain at the pool, denying it to the enemy.

The Curved Horn men had fought well. Only one had a serious wound. "Gather their weapons and armor!" shouted Kzun, "then move back into the rocks."

A young man sporting a lancer's white-plumed helm approached him. "Now we go, hey?" he said.

"Go where?" countered Kzun.

"Where?" responded the man, mystified. "Away before they come back."

Kzun walked away from him, back up the boulder-strewn slope to the pool. Kneeling there, he washed the blood from his naked upper body. Then, removing the white scarf from his head, he dipped it into the water before retying it over his bald dome. The warriors gathered behind him.

Kzun stood and turned to face them. Scanning their faces, he saw the fear there. They had killed Gothir soldiers. Now more would come—many more. "You want to run?" he asked them.

A slender warrior with graying hair stepped forward. "We cannot fight an army, Kzun. We burned their wagons, hey?

They will come back. Maybe a hundred. Maybe two. We cannot fight them."

"Then run," said Kzun contemptuously. "I would expect no more from Curved Horn cowards. But I am of the Lone Wolves, and we do not run. I was told to hold this pool, to defend it with my life. This I shall do. While I live, not one *gajin* will taste of the water."

"We are not cowards!" shouted the man, reddening. An angry murmur rose up among the warriors around him. "But what is the point of dying here?"

"What is the point of dying anywhere?" countered Kzun. "Two hundred men wait at the Shrine of Oshikai, ready to defend his bones. Your own brothers are among them. You think they will run?"

"What would you have us do?" asked another warrior.

"I don't care what you do!" stormed Kzun. "All I know is that I will stand and fight."

The gray-haired warrior called his comrades to him, and they walked away to the far side of the pool, squatting in a rough circle to discuss their options. Kzun ignored them. A low groan came from his left, and he saw the wounded Curved Horn warrior sitting with his back against the red rock, his blood-covered hands clenched over a deep belly wound. Kzun lifted a lancer helmet and dipped it into the pool, then carried it to the dying man. Squatting down, he held the helmet to the warrior's lips. He drank two swallows, then coughed and cried out in pain. Kzun sat down beside him. "You fought well," he said. The young man had hurled himself upon a lancer, dragging the soldier from his horse. In the fight that had followed the lancer had drawn a dagger and rammed it in the Nadir's belly. Kzun had rushed to his aid and slain the lancer.

The sun rose above the red cliffs, shining down on the young man's face, and Kzun saw then that he was no more than fifteen years old.

"I dropped my sword," said the warrior. "Now I am going to die."

"You died defending your land. The gods of stone and water will welcome you."

"We are not cowards," said the dying boy. "But we . . . spend so much of our lives . . . running from the *gajin*."

"I know."

"I am frightened of the Void. If . . . I wait . . . will you walk with me into the dark?"

Kzun shivered. "I have been in the dark, boy. I know what fear is. Yes, you wait for me. I shall walk with you." The youngster gave a tired smile, then his head fell back. Kzun closed the boy's eyes and stood. Spinning on his heel, he walked across to the far side, where the warriors were still arguing. They looked up as he approached. Pushing through the circle, he stood at its center. "There is a time to fight," he said, "and a time to run. Think back over your lives. Have you not run enough? And where will you go? How far must you run to avoid the lancers? The fighters at the shrine will become immortal. How far must you run to escape the haunting words of their song?

"The enemy can fight only so long as they have water. This is the only deep pool. Every day we deny them water gives our brothers a further chance of victory, and in this we become part of the great song. I am a man with no friends, no sword brothers. My youth was stolen from me in the Gothir mines, working in the dark, my body covered in sores. I have no wife, no sons. Kzun can make no gifts to the future. When I am dead, who will mourn for me? No one. The blood of Kzun runs in no living creature. The Gothir put my spirit in chains, and when I slew the guards and freed my body, my spirit remained, trapped in the dark. I think it is there still, living in the black filth, hiding in the dark tunnels. I could not—cannot—ever feel the sense of belonging that is at the heart of all we are. All that is left to me is a desire to see the Nadir—my people—walk straight and free. I should not have called you cowards, for you are all brave men. But your spirits, too, have been chained by the *gajin*. We are born to fear them, to run from them, to bow our heads. They are the masters of the world. We are vermin on the steppes. Well, Kzun believes this no longer. Kzun is a lost and bitter man," he said, his voice breaking. "Kzun has nothing to lose. Your comrade back there is dead. He asked me if I would walk into the dark with him; he said his spirit would wait for me. I knew then that I would die here. I am ready for that. Perhaps I will be reunited with my spirit. But I will meet him on the dark road. And we will walk together into the Void. Any man among you who is not ready to do the same should leave now. I will not send him on his way with curses. Here is where Kzun stands. Here is where he will fall. That is all I have to say."

Kzun walked back through the circle and up into the rocks overlooking the steppes. The wagons were no longer burning, but smoke was still rising from the charred wood. Vultures had begun to tear at the corpses. Kzun squatted down in the shadows; his hands were trembling, and fear rose in him, bringing bile to his throat.

An eternity in the dark beckoned, and Kzun could imagine no greater terror. He glanced up at the clear blue sky. What he had told them was true: when he died, not one living creature on the surface of the steppes would mourn for him. He had nothing but a scarred, hairless body and rotting teeth to show for his life. In the mines there were no luxuries like friendship. Each man struggled alone. When he was free, the legacy of the years in the dark haunted him still. He could no longer abide sleeping in tents with others but needed the clean open air and the wondrous taste of solitude. There had been one woman he had yearned for, but he had never spoken of it. By then Kzun was a warrior with many ponies and could have bid for her. He had not and had watched in sick despair as she wed another.

He felt a hand on his shoulder. The warrior with the graying hair squatted down beside him. "You say you have no sword brothers. Now you have. We will stand with you, Kzun of the Lone Wolves. And we will walk the dark road with you!"

For the first time since he had been dragged to the mines Kzun felt the rush of hot tears to his cheeks. He bowed his head and wept unashamedly.

Gargan, Lord of Larness, reined in his massive gray stallion and leaned forward on the high pommel of his saddle. Ahead lay the buildings housing the Shrine of Oshikai Demon-bane. Behind him his troops waited: the 800 infantrymen standing in patient lines of four, and the 200 archers flanking the foot soldiers, with the Royal Lancers, in four columns of 250, fanned out on both sides. Gargan stared hard at the white walls, noting the V-shaped crack in the first. Shading his eyes, the warrior scanned the defenders, seeking the vile face of Okai. But at that distance they were all a blur.

Gargan's hands opened and closed, gripping the pommel so tightly that his knuckles shone white against the tan of his skin. "I will take you, Okai," he whispered. "I will put you through ten thousand torments before you die."

Raising his arm, Gargan called out for the herald. The young man rode alongside him. "You know what to say. Do it! And try to stay out of bowshot. These savages have no understanding of honor."

The soldier saluted and then rode his black gelding at a run toward the walls, drawing up in a cloud of red dust. The gelding reared, and the herald's voice rang out. "Know this, that Lord Gargan, with the full authority of the God-King, has come to visit the Shrine of Oshikai Demon-bane. The gate will be opened within the hour, and the traitor Okai, known now as Talisman, will be brought before Lord Gargan. If this is done, no harm will be offered to those within the shrine." He paused, allowing his words to sink in, then called out again. "If this is not done, Lord Gargan will have to consider all men inside the compound traitors. The army will surround them and take them captive. Every man will have his hands cut off, his eyes put out, before being hanged. You will all walk the Void blind and maimed. These are the words of Lord Gargan. You have one hour."

Swinging his horse, the young lancer rode back to the column.

Premian rode alongside Gargan. "They'll not surrender, sir," he said.

"I know," replied Gargan.

Premian looked up into the general's hard face, seeing the glint of triumph there. "We have only thirty ladders left, sir. An assault on the walls will be costly."

"That's what soldiers are paid for. Prepare the camp and send out fifty lancers to patrol the surrounding country. We'll launch the first attack at dusk. Concentrate on the broken wall and then torch the gates."

Gargan turned his horse and rode back through the men, while Premian ordered the troops to stand down and prepare camp. Gargan's tent had been destroyed in the fire, but a new one had been constructed from canvas sacking and cloth that had survived the blaze. The general sat his stallion as soldiers erected the tent; then he dismounted and strode inside. His chairs had been destroyed, but the pallet bed had survived. Gargan sat down, glad to be out of the blazing sun. Removing his plumed helm and unbuckling his breastplate, he stretched out on the bed.

A rider from the city had arrived the previous afternoon. There was great unrest in Gulgothir, according to the message from Garen-Tsen, but the secret police had arrested scores of nobles, and the situation was under control at the moment. The God-King was in hiding, guarded by Garen-Tsen's minions. Gargan was urged to complete his mission with all speed and return as soon as possible.

Well, he thought, we should take the shrine by dawn. With luck he could be back in Gulgothir in ten days.

A servant entered the tent, bringing a goblet of water. When

Gargan sipped it, the water was hot and brackish. "Send Premian and Marlham to me," he told the man.

"Yes, sir."

The officers arrived, saluted, then removed their helms, holding them under their arms. Marlham looked terribly tired, the iron-gray stubble on his cheeks adding ten years to him. Premian, though much younger, also looked weary, with dark rings under his pale blue eyes.

"How is morale?" Gargan asked the older man.

"Better now that we are here," he said. "The Nadir are not known for their defensive abilities. Most of the men believe that once we have reached the ramparts, they will run."

"Probably true," said Gargan. "I want lancers ringing the walls. They must not be allowed to escape, not one of them. You understand me?"

"I understand, sir."

"I do not believe they will run," put in Premian. "They will fight to the death. This shrine is their one great holy place."

"That is not the Nadir way," sneered Gargan. "You don't understand these vermin. Cowardice is built into them! You think they will care about Oshikai's bones once the arrows fly and cold steel scores their flesh? They won't."

Premian drew in a deep breath. "Okai will. He is no coward. He is a trained tactician, the best we ever saw at Bodacas."

Gargan surged to his feet. "Do not praise him!" he roared. "The man murdered my son!"

"I grieved for your loss, General; Argo was a friend of mine. But that evil deed does not change Okai's talents. He will have banded those men together, and he understands discipline and morale. They won't run."

"Then let them stand and die," shouted Gargan. "I never yet met any ten Nadir who could outfight a single Gothir swordsman. How many men do they have? Two hundred. By dusk we'll have twice that many infantrymen storming the walls. Whether they stand or run is immaterial."

"They also have the man Druss," said Premian.

"What are you saying? Is Druss a demigod? Will he cast mountains down upon us?"

"No, sir," Premian said evenly, "but he is a legend among his own people. And we know, to our cost, that he can fight. He slew seven of our lancers when they attacked the renegade camp. He is a fearsome warrior, and the men are already talking about him. No one relishes going up against that ax."

Gargan looked hard at the young man. "What are you suggesting, Premian? That we go home?"

"No, sir. We have our orders, and they must be carried out. All I am saying is that we should treat them with a little more respect. In an hour our infantry will assault the walls. If they believe—wrongly—that the defense will be no more than token, they will be in for a terrible surprise. We could lose a hundred men before dusk. They are already tired and thirsty; it would mean a bitter blow to morale."

"I disagree, sir," said Marlham. "If we tell them that the assault will be murderous, we risk instilling a fear of defeat in them. Such fears can prove self-fulfilling prophecies."

"That's not what I am saying," insisted Premian. "Tell them that the defenders are ready to lay down their lives and that the battle will not be easy. *Then* impress upon them that they are Gothir soldiers and that no one can stand against them."

Gargan returned to the bed, where he sat in silence for several minutes. At last he looked up. "I still think they will run. However, it would be a foolhardy general who did not allow for a margin of error. Do it, Premian. Warn them and lift them."

"Yes, sir. Thank you, sir."

"When the hour is up, release the prisoner. Send him toward their walls. When he is close enough for the defenders to see him, have three mounted archers cut him down."

Premian saluted and replaced his helm.

"No words of condemnation, Premian?" asked Gargan.

"No, sir. I have no taste for such things, but the sight of him will unnerve the defenders. Of that there is no doubt."

"Good. You are learning."

Sieben gazed out at the Gothir army and felt the cold touch of panic in his belly. "I think I'll wait in the hospital, old horse," he told Druss.

The axman nodded. "Probably best," he said grimly. "You'll soon have plenty to do there."

On unsteady legs, Sieben walked from the ramparts. Nuang Xuan approached Druss. "I stand with you," he said, his face pale, his eyes blinking rapidly.

Around twenty Nadir were standing silently close by. "What tribe are you?" Druss asked the nearest, a young man with nervous eyes.

"Lone Wolves," he answered, licking his lips.

"Well," said Druss good-naturedly, his voice carrying to the other men on the western wall. "This old man with me has pledged to kill a hundred Gothir soldiers. I am to keep count. I don't want any of you Lone Wolves to get in his way. Killing a hundred takes great concentration!"

The young man swung to look at Nuang. Then he grinned. "I kill more than him," he said.

"That sounds like a wager in the offing," said Druss. "What is your name?"

"I am Chisk."

"Well, Chisk, I have a silver piece that says when dusk falls old Nuang will have outscored you."

The man looked downcast. "I have no silver with which to gamble."

"What have you got?" the axman asked.

The Nadir warrior fished deep into the pocket of his filthy goatskin jacket, coming up with a small round charm inset with lapis lazuli. "This wards off evil spirits," he said. "It is worth many pieces of silver."

"I expect it is," agreed Druss. "You want to pledge it?"

The man nodded. "I bet I kill more than you, too," said the Nadir.

Druss laughed and patted the man's shoulder. "One bet per man is enough, lad. Any of you other Lone Wolves want to wager?"

Warriors pushed forward, offering ornate belts, curved daggers, and buttons of carved horn. Druss accepted all offers.

A burly warrior with deep-set eyes tapped him on the arm. "Who counts?" he asked. "No one can watch us all."

Druss smiled. "You are all heroes," he said, "and men to trust. Count for yourselves. Tonight, when the enemy has skulked back to his camp, we'll get together and see who has won. Now get back to your positions. The hour is almost up."

Nuang stepped in close. "I think you lose a lot of silver, axman," he whispered.

"It's only money," said Druss.

Talisman joined Druss. "What is the commotion here?" he asked. Several of the warriors gathered around him, speaking in Nadir. Talisman nodded and gave a weary smile. "They think you are a great fool," he told Druss.

"It's been said before," the axman admitted.

Three riders came from the enemy camp, one of them dragging a prisoner. As they came closer, they swerved their horses; the prisoner fell heavily and struggled to rise.

"It is Quing-chin," said Talisman, his voice flat and his expression unreadable.

The prisoner's hands had been cut off, the stumps dipped in black pitch. The rider leading him cut free the rope; Quing-chin stumbled on, turning in a half circle.

"He has been blinded also," whispered Nuang.

Several of the Nadir on the walls cried out to the maimed man. His head came up, and he staggered toward the sound. The three riders let him approach, then notched arrows to their bows and galloped toward him. One arrow struck him low in the back, but he did not cry out. A second arrow plunged between his shoulder blades. Quing-chin fell then and began to crawl. A horseman drew rein alongside him, sending a third shaft deep into his back.

An arrow flew from the ramparts, falling well short of the riders.

"No one shoot!" bellowed Talisman.

"A hard way to die," whispered Nuang Xuan. "That is what the enemy promises for all of us."

"This was their moment," said Druss, his voice cold and bitter. "Let them enjoy it. In a little while we will have *our* moment. They will not enjoy that!"

A drum sounded in the enemy camp, and hundreds of infantrymen began to move toward the western wall, the sun bright on their silver breastplates and helms. Behind them came two hundred archers, arrows notched to the strings.

Druss swung to Talisman, who had drawn his saber. "No place here for you, General," he said softly.

"I need to fight," hissed Talisman.

"Just what they'd want. You are the leader. You cannot die in the first attack; the blow to morale would be savage. Trust me. Leave the wall. I won't let it fall."

Talisman stood for a moment, then rammed his saber back in its scabbard and turned on his heel.

"Right, lads," shouted Druss. "Keep your heads down, for they'll pepper us with arrows at first. Spread yourselves and put away your swords. When the ladder men reach the walls, we'll pelt the whoresons with rocks. Then use daggers; they're better for the close work. Save the long blades for when they've reached the ramparts."

The lines of infantry slowed just out of bowshot range. Druss knelt and watched the archers run through their ranks. Hundreds of shafts slashed through the air. "Get down!" he yelled, and all along the wall the Nadir defenders ducked behind the crenellated battlements. Druss glanced back to the compound.

Talisman and the reserve force of twenty men, led by Lin-tse, were out in the open as the shafts soared over the wall. One man was struck in the leg; the rest ran back to the cover of the lodging building. Out on the plain the infantrymen began to move, slowly at first and then, as they closed on the wall, raising their round shields before them and breaking into a charge. Nadir arrows slashed at them, and several men fell. The Gothir archers sent volley after volley over the heads of the infantry. Two Nadir bowmen were cut down.

The ladder bearers reached the western wall. Druss knelt, wrapped his arms around a boulder as large as a bull's head, and with a grunt heaved it to the battlements. A ladder thudded against the wall. Gripping the boulder between his hands, Druss hoisted it above his head and sent it sailing out over the wall. Seven men were on the ladder as the boulder struck the first, smashing his skull to shards. The huge rock hit the shoulder of the third man, snapping his collarbone; he fell, dislodging three others. Rocks and stones rained down on the attackers, but they pushed on.

The first man reached the ramparts, his shield held above his head. Chisk ran forward, ramming his dagger through the man's eye, and with a choking cry the attacker fell.

"One for Chisk!" shouted the Nadir. Two more men reached the ramparts. Druss leapt to his right, sending Snaga crashing through a wooden helm and braining the second man with a reverse sweep. Nuang jumped forward, thrusting his dagger at the head of a climbing soldier. The blade gashed the man's forehead, but he stabbed out with his short sword, catching Nuang on the left wrist and scoring the flesh. Snaga crashed down on the man's shoulder, splitting his breastplate. Blood gushed from the wound, and the climber fell away.

To Druss' left four Gothir soldiers had forced their way to the ramparts, forming a fighting wedge that allowed more men to reach the walls unopposed. Druss charged the group, Snaga sweeping down in a murderous arc. One man was cut down instantly; Druss shoulder-charged a second, spinning him from the ramparts to fall headfirst to the compound below; a third went down to a terrible blow that caved in his ribs. The fourth thrust his sword at Druss' belly. Nuang's blade hacked down, parrying the thrust, then swept up to slash through the soldier's neck. Dropping his sword, the Gothir soldier staggered back with blood pumping from his severed jugular.

Dropping his ax, Druss grabbed the dying man by the throat and groin and heaved him high into the air. Spinning, he hurled the body at two more soldiers as they cleared the ramparts; both were thrown back from the walls. Nuang ran forward to plunge his sword into the open mouth of a bearded soldier who had just reached the top of the ladder. The blade smashed through the man's palate, emerging from the back of his neck. The sword was torn from Nuang's grasp as the man plummeted to the ground.

Druss swept up a short sword lying on the ramparts and tossed it to the old man. Nuang caught it expertly.

All along the western wall the Nadir struggled to block wave after wave of attackers.

Below, Talisman stood with Lin-tse and twenty warriors, trying to judge the best moment to send fresh troops into the fray. Beside him Lin-tse waited with sword drawn. The defense was briefly breached, five soldiers hacking and cleaving a path to the steps. Lin-tse started forward, but Talisman called him back. Druss had attacked the men, cutting three down in as many heartbeats.

"He is terrifying," said Lin-tse. "Never have I seen the like."

Talisman did not reply. The Lone Wolves were fighting like demons, inspired by the ferocious skills of the black-garbed axman. On the other walls Nadir warriors watched with awed admiration.

"They are coming for the gates!" shouted Gorkai. "They have fire buckets and axes."

Talisman lifted his arm to show that he had heard but made

no move. More than a dozen of the defenders on the western wall were wounded. Five fought on, with several others struggling down the steps and making their way to the hospital.

"Now!" he told Lin-tse.

The tall Sky Rider leapt forward, sprinting up the steps.

Axes thudded into the gate, and Talisman saw Gorkai and the men of the Fleet Ponies hurling rocks over the battlements. Smoke seeped through the ancient wood. But as Druss had suggested, they had soaked the gates every day, and the fires quickly died away.

Talisman signaled to Gorkai to send back ten men to stand with him.

The battle raged on. Druss, covered in blood, stormed along the ramparts, leaping down to the fighting platform and scattering the Gothir warriors who had forced their way over the battlements. Talisman committed his ten men to help, then drew his sword and followed them in. He knew Druss was right about the crushing blow there would be to morale if he died, but his men had to see him fight.

Climbing to the platform, he swept his saber through the throat of a charging Gothir soldier. Two more ran at him. Druss smashed his ax through the shoulder of the first; then the old man Nuang Xuan gutted the second.

The Gothir fell back, taking their ladders with them.

A great cry went up from the Nadir. They jeered and waved their swords over their heads.

Talisman called Lin-tse to him. "Get a count of the injured and have the more seriously wounded men carried to the hospital."

The Lone Wolves gathered around Druss, clapping him on the back and complimenting him. In their excitement they were speaking Nadir, and Druss understood not a word of it. He turned to the stocky Chisk. "Well, laddie," he said. "How many did you kill?"

"I don't know. But it was many."

"Did you beat this old man, do you think?" asked Druss, throwing his arm around Nuang's shoulder.

"I don't care," shouted Chisk happily. "I kiss his cheek!" Dropping his sword, he took the surprised Nuang by the shoulders and hugged him. "We showed them how Nadir fight, eh? We whipped the *gajin* dogs."

Nuang grinned, took a step, then fell to the ground with a surprised look on his face. Chisk knelt down beside him, dragging open the old man's jerkin. Three wounds had pierced Nuang's flesh, and blood was flowing freely.

"Hold fast, Brother," said Chisk. "The wounds are not bad. We get you to the surgeon, though, hey?" Two Lone Wolves helped Chisk carry Nuang across to the hospital.

Druss strode from the wall to the well, drawing up a bucket of clear, cool water. Pulling an old cloth from his belt, he sponged the blood from his face and jerkin, then emptied the bucket over his head.

From the battlements came the sound of laughter. "You could do with a bath, too, you whoresons!" he shouted. Dropping the bucket back into the well, he drew it forth again, then drank deeply. Talisman joined him. "We killed or wounded seventy," said the Nadir leader. "For the loss of nine dead and fifteen wounded. What next, do you think?"

"The same again, but with fresh troops," said Druss. "And before dark, too. My guess is there will be at least two more attacks today."

"I agree with you. And we will hold; I know that now."

Druss chuckled. "They're a fine bunch of fighters. Tomorrow it will be the gates—a concerted attack."

"Why not tonight?"

"They haven't learned their lesson yet," said Druss.

Talisman smiled. "You are a good teacher, axman. I am sure they will learn before the day is over."

Druss took another long drink, then pointed to a group of men working at the base of the old tower. They were separating blocks of granite and hauling them clear of the rubble. "What is the purpose of that?" asked the axman.

"The gates will fall," said Talisman, "but we will have a surprise for the first troops to get through."

Nuang Xuan lay quietly on the floor with his head on a pillow stuffed with straw, a single blanket covering him. The stitches in his chest and shoulder were tight, his wounds painful, yet he felt at peace. He had stood beside the axman and had killed five of the enemy. Five! Across the room a man cried out. Nuang carefully rolled to his side, seeing that the surgeon was stitching wounds in a man's belly; the wounded warrior thrashed out, and Niobe grabbed his arms. Waste of time, thought Nuang, and within moments the injured man gave a gurgling cry and was still. The surgeon swore. Niobe dragged the corpse from the table, and two men carried a freshly wounded man to take his place.

Sieben pulled open the man's jerkin. He had been cut across the chest and deep into the side; the sword had broken off above the hip. "I need pliers for this," said Sieben, wiping a bloodied hand across his brow, leaving a smear of crimson. Niobe handed him a rusty pair, and Sieben dug his fingers into the wound, feeling for the broken blade. Once he had it, he pushed the pliers against the split flesh and with a great wrench dragged the iron clear. Elsewhere in the room two other Nadir women were applying stitches or bandages.

Nosta Khan entered, looked around, and then moved across the room, past Nuang, and into the small office beyond.

Nuang could just make out the conversation that followed. "I leave tonight," came the voice of the shaman. "You must prepare the woman."

"She stays," said Talisman.

"Did you not understand what I said about destiny?"

"It is you who are without understanding," roared Talisman. "You do not know the future, shaman. You have had glimpses, tantalizing and incomplete. Despite your powers, you cannot locate Ulric. How hard should it be to find a violet-eyed leader? You cannot find the Eyes of Alchazzar. And you did not warn me they would take Quing-chin. Go from here if you must. But you travel alone."

"You fool!" shouted Nosta Khan. "This is no time for betrayal. Everything you live for hangs in the balance. If I take her, she lives. Can you understand that?"

"Wrong again, shaman. If you take her, she will kill herself. She has told me this, and I believe her. Go. Seek out the man with violet eyes. Let him build on what we accomplish here."

"You will die here, Talisman," said Nosta Khan. "It is written in the stars. Druss will escape, for I have seen him in the many futures. For you there is no place."

"Here is my place," responded Talisman. "Here I stand."

The shaman said more, but Nuang did not hear it, for the voices within were suddenly lowered.

Niobe knelt beside Nuang, handing him a clay cup full of *lyrrd*. "Drink, old father," she said. "It will put strength back into your ancient bones."

"Ancient they may be, but my blood runs true, Niobe. Five I killed. I feel so strong, I could even survive a night with you."

"You were never that strong," she said, patting his cheek. "Anyway, Chisk told us you killed at least a dozen."

"Ha! Good men, these Lone Wolves."

Rising, she moved back to the table. Taking a fresh cloth, she wiped the blood and sweat from Sieben's brow. "You are working good," she said. "No mistakes."

From outside came the screams of wounded men and the clash of swords. "It is vile," he said. "All vile."

"They say your friend is a god of battle. They call him the Deathwalker."

"The name suits him."

The doors opened, and two men were carried inside. "More bandages and thread," he told Niobe.

Outside on the walls Druss relaxed; the enemy had pulled back for the second time. Chisk came alongside him. "You hurt, Deathwalker?"

"The blood is not mine," Druss told him.

"You are wrong; your shoulder bleeds."

Druss glanced down to the gash in his jerkin. Blood was leaking from it. Doffing the jerkin, he examined the cut beneath, which was no more than two inches long, but deep. He swore. "You hold this damned wall till I get back," he said.

"Till the mountains crumble to dust," promised Chisk. As Druss walked away, he added, "But you don't take too long, hey?"

Inside the hospital Druss called out to Niobe, and she ran across to him. "Don't bother Sieben with it," he said. "It's no deeper than a dog bite. Get a needle and thread for me; I'll do it myself."

She returned with the implements and a long stretch of bandage. The wound was just below the collarbone, and Druss fumbled his way through the stitching, drawing the lips of the gash together.

"You have many scars," said Niobe, staring at his upper body.

"All men get careless," he told her. The wound was beginning to throb. Pushing himself to his feet, he strode from the room and out into the fading sunlight. Behind the gates some thirty warriors were manhandling blocks to form a semicircular wall. The work was backbreaking and slow, yet no word of complaint came from them. They had erected a rough hoist and pulley on the ramparts, and the blocks of granite were being hauled into place, blocking the gates. Suddenly the pulley gave way, and a huge block fell, hurling two men to the ground. Druss ran over to where they lay. The first was dead, his skull crushed, but the other man was merely winded. Pulling the corpse aside, the other warriors continued with their work, their faces grim. The blocks were being laid four deep, forming a curved wall eight feet wide.

"They'll get a nasty shock as they come through," said Lintse, striding down the rampart steps to join Druss.

"How tall can you get it?"

"We think twelve feet at the front, ten at the back. But we need a stronger hoist bar and supports."

"Tear up the floorboards in the upper lodging rooms," Druss advised. "Use the cross-joists."

Returning to the wall, Druss put on his jerkin and silver-skinned gauntlets. Talisman's man, Gorkai, joined him. "The Curved Horn will stand with you for the next attack," he said. "This is Bartsai, their leader."

Druss nodded, then reached out and shook hands with the stocky Nadir. "Well, lads," he said, with a wide smile, "do you fight as well as the Lone Wolves?"

"Better," grunted a young warrior.

"Would you care to make a wager on that, laddie?"

# ◇ 12 ◇

**T**HE MOON WAS bright as Talisman and Lin-tse watched the Gothir carrying away their dead and wounded. The stretcher bearers worked with great efficiency and no little courage, coming close to the walls to pick up the wounded. The Nadir did not loose shafts at them. Talisman had forbidden it—not for any reason of mercy but simply because every wounded Gothir soldier needed to be tended and fed, and that would help exhaust the enemy's supplies. The Nadir dead had been wrapped in blankets and placed in the coolness of the shrine.

"They lost sixty-four, with another eighty-one wounded," said Lin-tse gleefully. "Our losses are less than a third of that."

"Twenty-three dead," said Talisman, "and nine wounded who will not fight again."

"That is good, eh?"

"They outnumber us ten to one. Five to one for casualties is not good enough," Talisman told him. "However, as Fanlon used to say, the worst always die first: those with the least skill or the least luck. We did well today."

"The lancers are not riding out," observed Lin-tse.

"Their mounts are thirsty and tired," said Talisman, "as indeed are the men. Their wagons went out again this morning. They have not returned; Kzun is still holding them away from the pool."

Lin-tse moved to the edge of the battlements. "I wish we

could bring in Quing-chin's body," he said. "It saddens me to think of his spirit wandering blind and maimed."

Talisman did not reply. Two years before, the three Nadir warriors had sought revenge for the death of their comrade. They had found satisfaction in kidnapping and killing the son of Gargan; he, too, had been blinded and maimed. Now the circle of violence had swung once more, and Quing-chin's body lay as cold testimony to the cruel reality of revenge. Talisman rubbed at his eyes.

The smell of scorched wood drifted to him. The gates had come under two attacks, the Gothir using oil in an attempt to burn their way through. That had failed, and some twenty Gothir soldiers had paid with their lives. Talisman shivered.

"What is wrong, Brother?" asked Lin-tse.

"I do not hate them any longer," Talisman told him.

"Hate them? The Gothir? Why?"

"Do not misunderstand me, Lin-tse. I will fight them, and if the gods of stone and water permit, I will see their towers crumble and their cities fall. But I cannot hold to hate any longer. When they killed Zhen-shi, we lusted for blood. Do you remember the terror in Argo's eyes as we gagged him and carried him out?"

"Of course."

"Now his father nurses the hatred, and it hangs like a bat at his throat, ready to be passed on."

"But his father began it with his hatred of all Nadir," argued Lin-tse.

"Precisely. And what caused it? Some Nadir atrocity back in his own youth? My dream is to see the Nadir united, every man standing tall and proud. But I will never again hate an enemy."

"You are tired, Okai. You should rest. They will not come again tonight."

Talisman walked away along the ramparts. Nosta Khan had gone, and no man had seen him drop from the walls. He had tried to reach Zhusai but had found Gorkai standing guard at her door.

Even as he thought of her, Talisman saw her walking across the compound. She was wearing a white blouse of shining silk and silver-gray leggings. She waved and moved to him, throwing her arms around his neck.

"We are together, now and always," she said.

"Now and always," he agreed.

"Come. I have perfumed oil in my room, and I will ease away your fatigue." Taking him by the hand, she led him back to her room.

Druss and Sieben watched them from the ramparts of the western wall. "Love in the midst of death," said Druss. "It is good."

"Nothing is good here," snapped Sieben. "The whole business stinks like a ten-week fish. I wish I had never come."

"They say you are a great surgeon," said Druss.

"A fine seamstress, more like. Eleven men died under my hands, Druss, coughing up their blood. I cannot tell you how sick I am of it. I hate war, and I hate warriors. Scum of the earth!"

"It won't stop you from singing about it if we survive," Druss pointed out.

"What is that supposed to mean?"

"Who is it who tells of the glory, the honor, and the chivalry of war?" Druss asked softly. "Rarely the soldier who has seen the bulging entrails and the crows feasting on dead men's eyes. No, it is the saga poet. It is he who feeds young men with stories of heroism. How many young Drenai men have listened to your poems and songs and lusted for battle?"

"Well, that is a neat twist," said Sieben. "Poets are to blame now, are they?"

"Not just poets. Hell's teeth, man, we are a violent race. What I am saying is that soldiers are not the scum of the earth. Every man here is fighting for what he believes in. You knew that before the killing started. You'll know it again when it has stopped."

"It will never stop, Druss," said Sieben sadly. "Not as long as there are men with axes and swords. I think I had better get back to the hospital. How is your shoulder?"

"Stings like the devil."

"Good," Sieben said, with a tired smile.

"How is Nuang?"

"Resting. The wounds were not mortal, but he won't fight again."

As Sieben walked away, Druss stretched himself out on the ramparts. All along the wall exhausted Nadir warriors were sleeping. For many it would be the last sleep they ever enjoyed.

Maybe for me, thought Druss. Perhaps I will die tomorrow.

Perhaps not, he decided, and drifted into a dreamless sleep . . .

Gargan walked among the wounded, talking to the survivors and offering praise for their heroism. Returning to his tent, he summoned Premian. "I understand the Nadir are still denying us water," he said. "How many defend the pool?"

"That is hard to say, sir. The trail up to the pool is narrow, and our men are coming under attack from warriors hidden in the rocks. No more than thirty, I would say. They are led by a madman who wears a white scarf on his head; he leapt twenty feet from a tall rock and landed on the officer's mount, breaking its back. Then he killed the rider, wounded another, and sprinted back into the rocks."

"Who was the officer?"

"Mersham, sir. Newly promoted."

"I know his family. Good stock." Gargan sat down on his pallet bed; his face was drawn and strained, his lips dry. "Take a hundred men and wipe them out. The water here is all but gone, and without more we are finished. Go now, tonight."

"Yes, sir. I have had men digging at the bend of the dry

stream to the east, and we have uncovered a seep. It is not large, but it will fill several barrels."

"Good," said Gargan wearily. The general stretched himself out on the bed and closed his eyes. As Premian was about to leave, he spoke again. "They killed my son," he said. "They cut out his eyes."

"I know, sir."

"We will not attack before midmorning. I need you back with water by then."

"Yes, sir."

Sieben crossed the compound and quietly woke Druss. "Follow me," he whispered. Druss rose, and the two men moved down the rampart steps and across the open ground to the shrine. It was dark within, and they stood for a moment, allowing their eyes to adjust to the faint moonlight coming through the single window. The Nadir dead had been placed against the north wall, and already the smell of death clung to the air.

"What are we doing here?" whispered Druss.

"I want the healing stones," said Sieben. "No more dead men under my hands."

"We've already searched this place."

"Yes, and I think we have already seen them. Lift the lid." Moving to the stone coffin, Druss pushed at the lid, slowly easing it to one side to make enough room for Sieben to push his arm inside. His fingers touched dry bones and the dust of decayed garments. Swiftly he moved his hand upward until he reached the skull. Closing his eyes and concentrating, he searched below the fractured jaw until his fingers touched the cold metal of Oshikai's *lon-tsia*. Pulling it free, he brought it out into the pale moonlight.

"Now you have a pair," said Druss. "So what?"

"Shaoshad came here to ask Oshikai to agree to be regenerated. Oshikai refused unless Shul-sen could be with him. How, then, did he set about finding her?"

"I don't know," said Druss, holding back his impatience. "I do not understand magic."

"Bear with me, my friend, and look at the evidence. Both Oshikai and Shul-sen wore *lon-tsia*. Oshikai's tomb has already been plundered, but no one found the medallion. Why? The blind priest told me a hide-spell had been placed on the *lon-tsia* worn by Shul-sen. It is reasonable to suppose that a similar spell was cast upon that worn by Oshikai. Now, I believe Shaoshad lifted the spell on this one," he said, holding up the *lon-tsia*. "Why? In order to help him locate Shul-sen. Talisman's man, Gorkai, told me the *lon-tsia* of the rich were blessed with many spells. I think that in some way Shaoshad used this medallion to find the other. You follow me?"

"No, but I am hanging in," Druss said wearily.

"Why did he not have the stones when he was caught?"

"Will you stop asking me questions for which there are no answers?" Druss snapped.

"It was rhetorical, Druss. Now, don't interrupt anymore. According to Gorkai, a search spell is like a tracker dog. I think Shaoshad imbued Oshikai's medallion with the power of one of the stones and sent the other in search of Shul-sen's *lon-tsia*. Then he tried to follow the spirit trail. That is why he was caught between here and where we found Shul-sen's remains."

"And where does this leave us?" asked Druss.

Sieben fished in his pocket, producing the second *lon-tsia*, which he held close to the first. "It leaves us with this," he said triumphantly, clapping his hands and pushing the two medallions together.

Nothing happened.

"It leaves us with what?" asked Druss.

Sieben opened his hands. The two *lon-tsia* glittered in the moonlight, and he swore. "I was sure I was right," he said. "I thought if they were brought together, the stones would appear."

"I am going back to sleep," said Druss, spinning on his heel and striding from the room.

Sieben pocketed the medallions and was about to follow when he realized that the coffin was still open. He swore again and grasped the lid, straining to drag it back into place.

"So close, my friend," came a whispered voice, and Sieben swung to see the tiny, glowing figure of Shaoshad sitting cross-legged on the floor. "But I did not hide the eyes within the *lon-tsia*."

"Where, then?" asked the poet. "And why did you hide them at all?"

"They should never have been made," said Shaoshad, his voice edged with sorrow. "The magic was in the land, but now it is barren. It was an act of colossal arrogance. As to why I hid them, well, I knew I risked capture. There was no way I would allow the eyes to be retaken. Even now it saddens me to know they must surface once more."

"Where are they?"

"They are here. You were mostly right: I did use the power to locate Shul-sen's tomb, and I did indeed imbue her *lon-tsia* with enough power to regenerate her. Watch—and be suitably impressed!"

The two *lon-tsia* medallions rose up from Sieben's palm and floated across to the stone coffin, hovering just in front of the inscribed nameplate. "Can you guess?" asked the spirit of the shaman.

"Yes!" said Sieben, moving forward and retrieving the floating medallions. Holding them up before the engraved word "Oshikai," he pressed them into the two "i" indentations. Both *lon-tsia* disappeared. A violet glow radiated from within the coffin. Sieben rose and peered inside. Two jewels now rested in the eye sockets of the skull of Oshikai Demon-bane. Reaching inside, he drew them out; each was the size of a sparrow's egg.

"Tell no one you have them," warned Shaoshad, "not even Druss. He is a great man, but he has no guile. If the Nadir find out, they will kill you for them; therefore, do not use their powers too obviously. When treating the wounded, stitch them and bandage them as before, then concentrate on the healing. You will not need to produce the jewels. If you keep them hidden on your person, the power will still flow through you."

"How will I know how to heal?"

Shaoshad smiled. "You do not need to know; that is the beauty of magic, poet. Simply place your hands over the wound and *think* it healed. Once you have done this, you will understand more."

"I thank you, Shaoshad."

"No, poet, it is I who thank you. Use them wisely. Now replace the lid of the coffin."

Sieben took hold of the stone and, as he did so, glanced down. Just for a moment he saw the *lon-tsia* of Oshikai gleaming among the bones, then it faded. Dragging the lid back into place, he turned to Shaoshad. "He wears it once more," said the poet.

"Aye, as it should be, hidden again by a hide-spell. No one will plunder it. The other has returned to the resting place of Shul-sen."

"Can we win here?" Sieben asked, as the shaman's image began to fade.

"Winning and losing are entirely dependent on what you are fighting for," answered Shaoshad. "All men here could die, yet you could still win. Or all men could live and you could lose. Fare you well, poet."

The spirit vanished. Sieben shivered, then thrust his hands in his pocket, curling his fingers around the stones.

Returning to the hospital, he walked silently among the ranks of wounded men. In the far corner a man groaned, and Sieben moved to his side, kneeling beside the blanket on which he lay. A lantern flickered brightly on the wall, and by its light Sieben looked at the man's gaunt face. He had been stabbed in the belly, and though Sieben had stitched the outer flap of the wound, the bleeding was deep and internal. The man's eyes were fever-bright. Sieben gently laid a hand on the bandages and closed his eyes, trying to concentrate. For a moment nothing happened; then bright colors filled his mind, and he saw the torn muscles, the split entrails, the pooling blood within the wound. In that instant he knew every muscle and fiber, the attachments, the blood routes, the sources of pain and discomfort. It was as if he were floating inside the wound. Blood flowed from the gaping gash in a twisting purple cylinder, but as Sieben gazed at it, the gash closed and healed. Moving on, he sealed other cuts, his mind flowing back from the depths of the wound, healing as he went. At last he reached the outer stitches, and there he stopped. It would be wise to let the man feel the pull of the stitches when he woke, he thought. If any wound was utterly healed, the secret of the stones would be out.

The warrior blinked. "It is taking me a long time to die," he said.

"You are not going to die," Sieben promised him. "Your wound is healing, and you are a strong man."

"They pierced my guts."

"Sleep now. In the morning you will feel stronger."

"You speak the truth?"

"I do. The wound was not as deep as you believe. You are healing well. Sleep." Sieben touched the man's brow; instantly his eyes closed, and his head lolled to one side.

Sieben made his way to every wounded man, one by one. Most were sleeping. Those who were awake he spoke softly to and healed. At last he came to Nuang. As he floated within the old man's injuries, he found himself drawn to the heart, and there he found a section so thin that it was almost transparent. Nuang could have died at any time, he realized, for his heart, under strain, could have torn itself apart like wet paper. Sieben concentrated on the area, watching it thicken. The arteries were hard, the inner walls choked and narrow; those he opened and made supple.

Withdrawing at last, he sat back. There was no feeling of weariness in him but instead a sense of exultation and rare delight.

Niobe was asleep in another corner of the room. Placing the jewels in a pouch, he hid them behind a water cask, moved to Niobe, and lay down beside her, feeling her warmth against him. Drawing a blanket over them both, he leaned over and kissed her cheek. She moaned and rolled in to him, whispering a name that was not his. Sieben smiled.

She awoke then and raised herself up on one elbow. "Why you smile, po-et?" she asked him.

"Why not? It is a fine night."

"You wish to make love?"

"No, but I would appreciate a hug. Come close."

"You are very warm," she said, snuggling alongside him and resting her arm on his chest.

"What do you want from life?" he whispered.

"Want? What is there to want? Apart from a good man and strong babies?"

"And that is all?"

"Rugs," she said after thinking for a few moments. "Good rugs. And a fire bucket of iron. My uncle had a fire bucket of iron; it heated the tent on the cold nights."

"What about rings and bracelets, items of gold and silver?"

"Yes, those, too," she agreed. "You will give them to me?"

"I think so." Turning his head, he kissed her cheek. "Amazing as it might seem, I have fallen in love with you. I want you with me. I will take you to my own land and buy you an iron fire bucket and a mountain of rugs."

"And the babies?"

"Twenty if you want them."

"Seven. I want seven."

"Then seven it will be."

"If you are mocking me, po-et, I will cut out your heart."

Sieben chuckled. "No mockery, Niobe. You are the greatest treasure I ever found."

Sitting up, she looked around the large hospital. "Everyone is sleeping," she said suddenly.

"Yes."

"I think some must have died."

"I don't believe so," he told her. "In fact I am sure that is not the case, just as I am sure none will wake for several hours. So let us return to your earlier offer."

"Now you want lovemaking?"

"Indeed I do. Maybe for the first time in my life."

Master Sergeant Jomil pressed his thick fingers to the cut on his face, trying to stem the flow of blood. Sweat trickled into the shallow wound, the salt stinging him, and he cursed. "You are slowing down, Jomil," said Premian.

"Little bastard almost took my eye out . . . sir," he said.

The bodies of the Nadir defenders were dragged from the rocks and laid in a line away from the pool. The fourteen Gothir dead had been wrapped in their cloaks, the bodies of the six slain lancers tied across the saddles of their mounts, the infantrymen buried where they had fallen.

"By the blood of Missael, they put up a fight, didn't they, sir?" said Jomil.

Premian nodded. "They were fighting for pride and love of land. There is no greater motivation." Premian himself had led the charge up the slope while the infantry had stormed the rocks. Weight of numbers had carried the day, but the Nadir had fought well. "You'll need stitches in that face wound. I'll attend to it presently."

"Thank you, sir," Jomil replied without enthusiasm.

Premian grinned at him. "How is it that a man can face swords, axes, arrows, and spears without flinching yet be terrified of a small needle and a length of thread?"

"I get to whack the buggers with the swords and axes," said Jomil.

Premian laughed aloud, then moved to the poolside. The water was deep, clear, and cool. Kneeling, he cupped his hands and drank deeply; then, rising, he walked to the line of Nadir dead. Eighteen men, some of them little more than boys. Anger churned inside him: what a wasted exercise this was. What a futile little war! Two thousand highly trained Gothir soldiers marching through a wasteland to sack a shrine.

Yet something was wrong. Premian could feel it. An invisible worry nagged at his subconscious. An infantry soldier approached him and saluted. The man had a bloody bandage around his scalp.

"Can we start cook fires, sir?" he asked.

"Yes, but move farther into the rocks. I don't want the smoke to spook the wagon horses when they arrive. It'll be hard enough getting them up the slope."

"Yes, sir."

Premian walked to his horse and took a needle and thread from his saddlebag. Jomil saw him and cursed under his breath. It was only two hours past dawn, and already the heat was formidable, radiating from the red rocks. Premian knelt by Jomil's side and eased the flap of skin into place over his right cheekbone. Expertly he stitched the wound. "There," he said at last. "Now you'll have a fine scar to bewitch the ladies."

"I already have more than enough scars to brag of," grumbled Jomil. Then he grinned. "You remember that battle outside Lincairn Pass, sir?"

"Yes. You received an unfortunate wound, I recall."

"I don't know about unfortunate. The ladies love the story about that one. Not sure why."

"Buttock wounds are always a source of great merriment," said Premian. "As I recall, you were awarded forty gold crowns for bravery. Did you save any of it?"

"Not a copper of it. I spent most of it on strong drink, fat women, and gambling. The rest I wasted." Premian glanced back at the Nadir dead. "Something bothering you, sir?" asked Jomil.

"Yes, but I don't know what."

"You expected there to be more of them, sir?"

"Perhaps a few." Premian strolled to the line of dead warriors, then called out to a young Gothir lancer. The man ran to his side. "You were involved in the first attack. Which of these is the leader?"

The lancer gazed down at all the faces. "It is hard to say, sir. They all look alike to me, vomit-colored and slant-eyed."

"Yes, yes," Premian said irritably. "But what do you remember of the man?"

"He had a white scarf over his head. Oh . . . and rotting teeth. I remember that. They were yellow and black. Vile."

"Check the teeth of the dead," ordered Premian. "Find him for me."

"Yes, sir," the man replied, without enthusiasm.

Moving back to Jomil, he reached out, taking the man's extended hand and hauling him to his feet. "Time to work, Sergeant," he said. "Get the infantry out on the slope. I want all the boulders pushed from the trail. We've fourteen wagons on the way, and it will be bad enough trying to get them up the slope without needing to negotiate them through a maze of scattered rocks."

"Yes, sir."

The lancer returned from his examination of the corpses. "He's not there, sir; he must have run off."

"Run off? A man who would leap from a rock twenty feet high and launch himself into a group of lancers? A man who could inspire his warriors to die for him? Run off? That is most unlikely. If he is not here, then . . . sweet Karna!" Premian swung on Jomil. "The wagons; he has gone after the wagons!"

"He can't have more than a handful of men," argued Jomil. "There are fourteen drivers, tough and armed."

Premian ran to his horse and stepped into the saddle. Calling out to two of his officers, he ordered them to gather their companies and follow him. Kicking the horse into a run, he left the pool and galloped out onto the slope. As he breasted the rise, he saw the smoke more than a mile to the south. At full gallop he pushed the gelding hard. Behind him came fifty lancers.

It was a matter of minutes before they rounded a bend in the trail and saw the burning wagons. The horses had been cut free, and the bodies of several of the drivers could be seen with arrows jutting from their chests. Premian dragged his exhausted mount to a halt and swiftly surveyed the scene. Smoke was billowing around the area, stinging his eyes. Five wagons were burning.

Suddenly he saw a man with a blazing torch run through the smoke. He was wearing a white head scarf. "Take him!" bellowed Premian, kicking his horse forward. The lancers swept out around him, riding through the oily smoke.

A small group of Nadir warriors were desperately trying to fire the remaining wagons. As the thunder of hoofbeats reached them over the roaring of the flames, they dropped their torches and ran for their ponies.

The lancers tore into them, cutting them down.

Premian swung his horse just as something dark came at him from a blazing wagon. He instinctively ducked as a white-scarfed Nadir warrior cannoned into him, sending him hurtling from the saddle. They hit hard, and Premian rolled, scrabbling for his sword. But the man ignored him and, taking hold of the saddle pommel, vaulted to the gelding's back. Drawing his saber, the Nadir charged the lancers, hacking and cutting. One man fell from his mount with his throat slashed open; a second pitched to his left as the flickering blade pierced his face. A lance ripped into the Nadir's back, half lifting him from the saddle. Twisting savagely, he tried to reach the lancer. Another soldier heeled his horse forward, driving his longsword into the man's shoulder. The Nadir, dying now, sent one last lunge at the sword wielder, the blade piercing his arm. Then he sagged to his right. The gelding reared, throwing him to the ground with the lance still embedded deep in his back. He struggled to rise and groped for his fallen saber; blood was bubbling from his mouth, and his legs were unsteady. A rider closed in on him, but he lashed out, his sword cutting the horse's flanks. "Get back from him!" shouted Premian. "He's dying."

The Nadir staggered and turned toward Premian. "Nadir we!" he shouted.

A lancer spurred his horse forward and slashed his sword down at the man. The Nadir ducked under the blow and leapt forward to grab the lancer's cloak, dragging him down into the path of his saber, which sliced up into the man's belly. The lancer screamed and pitched from the saddle. Both men fell to the ground. Soldiers leapt from their mounts and surrounded the fallen Nadir, hacking and cleaving his body.

Premian ran forward. "Get back, you fools!" he yelled. "Save the wagons!"

Using their cloaks, the lancers beat at the flames, but it was useless. The dry timbers had caught now, and the fires raged on, unstoppable. Premian ordered the five remaining wagons pulled clear, then sent out riders to gather the wagon horses, which, having picked up the scent of water, were walking slowly toward the pool. Ten of the drivers were also found, hiding in a gully, and were brought before Premian. "You ran," he said, "from seven Nadir warriors. Now half our wagons are gone. You have put the entire army in peril by your cowardice."

"They came screaming out of the steppes in a cloud of dust," argued one man. "We thought there was an army of them."

"You will take your places on the remaining wagons and see them loaded and the water delivered back to the camp. Once there, you will face Lord Gargan. I don't doubt your backs will feel the weight of the lash. Now get out of my sight!"

Swinging away from them, Premian thought through the mathematics of the situation. Five wagons with eight barrels each. Some fifteen gallons could be stored in each barrel. In those conditions a fighting man needed, minimally, around two pints of water per day. By that rough estimate he calculated that one barrel could supply sixty men with water. Forty barrels would be barely enough for the men, let alone the horses. And the horses for only one day . . . From now on there would have to be a constant shuttle between the camp and the pool.

Still, he reasoned, it could have been worse. If he had not reacted when he had, all the wagons would have been lost. But the thought did not cheer him. If he had left a guard force with them in the first place, the Nadir attack would have failed.

His thinking was interrupted by the sound of savage laughter and the hacking of sword blades. The white-scarfed Nadir leader had been beheaded and dismembered. Furious, Premian ran into the jeering group. "Stand to attention!" he bellowed, and the men shuffled nervously into a line. "How dare you?" stormed Premian. "How dare you behave like savages? Do you have any idea what you look like at this moment? Would any of you wish to be seen by your loved ones, prancing about and waving the limbs of a dead warrior above your heads? You are Gothir! We leave this . . . barbarity to lesser races."

"Permission to speak, sir?" asked a lean soldier.

"Spit it out."

"Well, Lord Gargan said all Nadir were to have their hands cut off, didn't he, sir?"

"That was a threat made to frighten the Nadir, who believe that if they lose a limb, they will be devoid of that limb throughout eternity. It was not a threat, I believe, that Lord Gargan intends to carry out in reality. I may be wrong in this. But here and now I am in command. You will dig a grave for that man and place his limbs alongside him. He was my enemy, but he was brave and gave his life for a cause he believed in. He will be buried whole. Am I understood?"

The men nodded. "Then get to it."

Jomil approached Premian, and the two walked away from the surly group. "That wasn't wise, sir," said Jomil, keeping his voice low. "You'll get the name of a Nadir lover. Word'll spread that you're soft on the enemy."

"It doesn't matter a damn, my friend. I shall be resigning my commission the moment this battle is over."

"That's as may be, sir, but if you'll pardon my bluntness, I don't think Lord Gargan was making an idle threat. And I don't want to see him putting you on trial for disobedience."

Premian smiled and looked into the old soldier's grizzled face. "You are a fine friend, Jomil. I value you highly. But my father told me never to be a part of anything that lacked honor. He once said to me that there was no greater satisfaction for a man than to be able to look in the mirror while shaving and be proud of what he saw. At this moment I am not proud."

"I think you ought to be," Jomil said softly.

It was three hours after noon, and still the enemy had not attacked. The foot soldiers were sitting in the camp, many of them using their cloaks and swords to form screens against the harsh heat of the blazing sun. The horses of the lancers were picketed to the west. Most stood forlornly with their heads down; others had sunk to the ground for want of water.

Shading his eyes, Druss saw the five water wagons returning and gave a low curse under his breath. Gothir soldiers ran to the wagons, surrounding them.

Talisman climbed to the ramparts and stood beside Druss. "I should have sent more men with Kzun," he said.

Druss shrugged. "As I recall, they set out last night with fourteen wagons. Your man did well. There'll be scarcely enough water in those wagons, and they'll not last a day. The horses alone need more than those wagons will supply."

"You've been in sieges before?" asked Talisman.

"Aye, laddie. Too many."

"Then what is your appraisal?"

"I think they'll throw everything at us. They can't play a waiting game. They have no engineers to mine the walls; they have no battering ram to smash the gates. I think they'll send in every man they have, lancers and foot. They'll storm this wall by sheer weight of numbers."

"I think not," said Talisman. "It is my belief that they will try a three-pronged attack. This western wall will take the brunt, but I think they will also try to breach the gates and one other wall. They will try to stretch us. Only if that fails will they risk the final assault."

"We'll know soon enough," said Druss. "If they do what you surmise, how will you combat it?"

Talisman smiled wearily. "Our options are limited, Druss. We just hold as best we can."

Druss shook his head. "You've got to assume that some of their soldiers will get through to the ramparts and perhaps down into the compound itself. Our reaction to that will be crucial. Gut instinct tells a man to tackle the nearest enemy, but in that situation such instincts are liable to prove fatal. If a wall is breached, the first option must be to seal the breach. The men already inside are a secondary consideration."

"What do you suggest?"

"You already have a small reserve force ready to fill in the gaps. Draw more men to it and split them into two groups. If the enemy takes a section of wall, one group must join the defenders to win it back. The second group can attack those who have penetrated inside. We have only one outer perimeter. There is nowhere to fall back to, so these ramparts must be held. No defender must leave his post on them no matter what he sees in the compound below. The walls, Talisman! Nothing else matters."

The young Nadir nodded. "I take your point, axman. It will be relayed to the men. Did you know that the tribes have been drawing lots to see which group should have the privilege of standing beside you today?"

Druss chuckled. "So that's what they were doing. Who did I get?"

"The Sky Riders. They are greatly pleased. It is rare for a *gajin* to be so popular."

"You think so?" Druss hefted his ax. "I'm usually popular at times like this. Could be the song of the soldier, could it not? When war and the fear of war come upon people, they revere the warrior. Once the war has passed, he is forgotten or reviled. It never changes."

"You don't sound bitter about it," Talisman pointed out.

"I don't get bitter at the falling of the sun or the cold north wind. They are facts of life. I once took part in a raid that rescued a score of rich farmers from Sathuli tribesmen. Oh, they waxed eloquent about how heroic we were, how they would honor us always. There was a young soldier with us who lost an arm that day. He was from their town. Within six months he and his family had almost starved to death. Facts of life."

"And did they die?"

"No. I went back to the Sentran Plain and spoke to the leader of the farmers, reminded him of his obligations."

"I am not surprised that he listened," said Talisman, looking into Druss' cold blue eyes. "But you will not find that with us. Nadir memories are long. You are the Deathwalker; your legend will live on with us."

"Legends. Pah! I have had enough of legends. If I had half the courage of a farmer, I would be at home with my wife, looking after my lands."

"You have no sons?"

"None. Nor will have," said Druss coldly. "No. All I will leave behind are those damned legends."

"Some men would die for your fame."

"A lot of men have," observed Druss.

The two warriors stood in silence for a while, watching the Gothir surrounding the water wagons. "You regret being here?" Talisman asked.

"I try not to regret anything," replied Druss. "There's no point in it." Twenty Sky Rider tribesmen trooped up to the ramparts, standing by quietly as the two men spoke. Druss glanced at the first, a hawk-faced young man with brown eyes. "Were you one of those who leapt the chasm?" he asked him.

The man gave a wide grin and nodded.

"I would like to hear about that," said Druss. "Later, when we've seen off the Gothir, you can tell me of it."

"I shall, Deathwalker."

"Good. Now gather around, my boys, and I'll give you a few tips about siege warfare."

Talisman left the ramparts. As he reached the compound below, he could hear laughter coming from the men around Druss.

Lin-tse joined him. "I should be there, Talisman. With my men on the wall."

"No." Talisman told him to pick forty warriors from among the other tribes. "You will lead the first group, Gorkai the second." Then he outlined Druss' battle plan for a wall breach defense.

A young warrior moved past them, heading for the north wall. Talisman called him back. "What is your name?" he asked.

"Shi-da, General."

"You were a friend of Quing-chin's?"

"I was."

"I saw you wounded yesterday—in the belly and chest."

"It was not as deep as I feared, General. The surgeon has healed me. I can fight."

"There is no pain?"

"Aye, there is pain. The stitches are tight. But I will stand with the Fleet Ponies, General."

"Let me see the wound," said Talisman, leading the man to the shade and sitting him on the table that had been set there. Shi-da doffed his goatskin jerkin. There was blood on the bandage wrapped around his waist. The young warrior started to unravel it, but Talisman stopped him.

"The wound is bound well. Do not disturb it. Fight well today, Shi-da."

The young man nodded, his face grim, then walked away.

"What was that about?" asked Lin-tse.

"Every one of the wounded is back on the walls today," said Talisman. "Truly the poet is a fine surgeon. I saw Shi-da struck. I would have sworn the blade passed almost all the way through him."

"You think he has found the Eyes of Alchazzar?" whispered Lin-tse.

"If he has, then I will take them."

"I thought you said that Druss needed them."

"Druss is a fighting man I admire above all others. But the eyes belong to the Nadir. They are part of our destiny, and I cannot allow them to be taken by *gajin*."

Lin-tse laid his hand on Talisman's arm. "If we survive here, my brother, and if Sieben has the jewels, you know what will happen if you try to take them. Druss will fight for them. He is not a man to be frightened by weight of numbers. We will have to kill him."

"Then we will kill him," said Talisman, "though it would break my heart to do so."

Talisman poured water from a stone jug, drained the clay cup, and walked away with Lin-tse to the newly built wall around the gates. Niobe stepped from the shadows behind them and made her way to the hospital.

Sieben was sitting with Zhusai. They were laughing together, and Niobe was surprised to find a ripple of anger within herself at the sight of them. The Chiatze woman was slim and beautiful, her clothes of white silk adorned with mother-of-pearl. Niobe was still wearing Sieben's blue silk shirt, but it was stained with the blood of the wounded and with sweat from her tired body. Sieben saw her, and a broad smile showed on his handsome face.

He walked across the deserted room and hugged her. "You are a vision," he said, kissing her.

"Why is she here?" asked Niobe.

"She has offered to help with the wounded. Come, say hello."

Taking Niobe by the hand, he led her to Zhusai. The Chiatze woman looked nervous under Niobe's piercing gaze as Sieben introduced them.

"I should have offered help before," Zhusai said to Niobe. "Please forgive me."

Niobe shrugged. "We need no help. The po-et is very skilled."

"I am sure that he is. But I know much of the tending of wounds."

"She will be valuable," put in Sieben.

"I do not want her here," said Niobe.

Sieben was surprised, but he masked it and turned to Zhusai. "Perhaps, my lady, you should change your clothes. Blood will ruin that fine silk. You can return to us when the battle has started."

Zhusai gave a short bow of her head and walked from the room.

"What is the matter with you?" Sieben asked Niobe. "Are you jealous, my dove?"

"I am not a dove. And there is no jealousy. Do you not know why she is here?"

"To help. That is what she said."

"You are in much danger, po-et."

"From her? I do not think so."

"Not just from her, fool. Every Nadir knows the story of the Eyes of Alchazzar, the purple jewels of power. Talisman thinks you have found them, and so do I. There were men dying here yesterday who are now standing on the walls."

"Nonsense. They were—"

"You don't lie to me!" she snapped. "I hear Talisman. He says that if you have the jewels, he will take them; he says that they will kill Druss if he interferes. You give jewels to Talisman—then you are safe."

Sieben sat down on the newly scrubbed table. "I can't do that, my love. Druss made a promise to a dying man, and Druss is a man who lives by his word. You understand? But I won't keep them; I promise you that. If we survive here, which is doubtful at best, I will take them to Gulgothir and heal Druss' friend. Then I will return them to Talisman."

"He will not allow it. That is why he sent the woman; she will watch you like a snake. You heal no more dying men, po-et."

"I have to. That is what the power is for."

"This is no time to be weak. Men die in battle. They go to the earth; they feed the land. You understand?" She looked deep into his blue eyes and knew she was not convincing him. "Fool! Fool!" she said. "Very well. Keep them alive. But do not heal them so much that they walk from here. You hear what I say?"

"I do, Niobe. And you are right. I can't risk Druss being killed for them." He smiled and, reaching out, pushed his fingers through her dark hair. "I love you. You are the light in my life."

"And you are a trouble to me," she said. "You are no warrior, and you are soft like a puppy. I should have no feelings for a man like you."

"But you do, don't you?" he said, drawing her into an embrace. "Tell me!"

"No."

"You are still angry with me?"

"Yes."

"Then kiss me and feel it fade."

"I don't want it to fade," she said, pulling away.

Outside a battle horn sounded. "It begins again," sighed Sieben.

The Gothir infantry formed into three groups of about two hundred men. Druss watched them carefully. Only two of the groups contained ladder bearers. "The third group is going for the gates," he said to no one in particular.

Behind the infantry more than five hundred lancers waited on foot in two lines, their lances discarded and their sabers in their hands. A slow drumbeat sounded, and the army moved forward slowly. Druss could feel the fear in the men around him.

"Don't think of numbers," said Druss. "All that counts is the number of ladders, and they have fewer than thirty. Only thirty men can reach the wall at any time; the rest will be milling around below, useless. Never be cowed by numbers alone."

"Do you not know fear, axman?" asked Nuang Xuan.

Druss turned and grinned. "What are you doing here, old man? You are wounded."

"I am as tough as a wolf, as strong as a bear. How close am I to my hundred?"

"By my reckoning you need more than ninety more."

"Pah, you obviously miscounted."

"Stay close to me, Nuang," said Druss softly. "But not too close."

"I will be here at day's end, and the Gothir dead will be a mountain," promised Nuang.

Archers ran through the enemy lines, sending scores of shafts at the defenders, who ducked below the battlements. No one was struck. The drumbeat quickened, and Druss could hear the sound of running men drowning out the drums. Ladders clattered against the wall, and a man to Druss' left started to rise, but Druss dragged him down. "Not yet, laddie. The archers are waiting."

The warrior blinked nervously. Druss knelt for ten more heartbeats, then launched himself upright, the great ax shining in the sunlight. As he reared up, a Gothir warrior reached the top of the ladder and Snaga thundered down to smash the man's skull.

"Climb and die!" roared Druss, sending a reverse cut into the bearded face of a second warrior.

All around him the Nadir were hacking and slashing at the attackers. Two Gothir soldiers reached the ramparts but were cut down instantly. A Nadir warrior fell with an arrow jutting from his temple.

On the wall above the gate Talisman watched as Druss and the Sky Riders fought to contain the western ramparts. The second Gothir force had swung to the north wall, where Bartsai and his Curved Hornmen were battling to hold them.

Axes smashed into the gates, splintering the ancient wood. Nadir defenders threw rocks down on the enemy soldiers milling below, but the sounds of tearing wood continued.

"Be ready!" Talisman warned the men of the Fleet Ponies. Notching arrows to their bows, they knelt on the ramparts and the newly built curved wall inside the gates. In that moment Talisman felt a fierce pride surge through him. These men were Nadir, his people! And they were fighting together against the common enemy. This is how it should be, thought the young man. No more slavelike obedience to the cursed *gajin*. No more running from the threat of their lancers, their punitive raids, their slaughter.

Suddenly the gates were breached, and scores of men pushed through, only to be confronted by an eight-foot wall.

"Now! Now! Now!" yelled Talisman. Arrows lanced into the crowded mass below. So closely packed were they, with others pushing from behind, that few Gothir could raise their shields. Shafts tore into them, and rocks pelted them. As Talisman strained to lift a jagged boulder, two men helped him, and they pitched the stone over the ramparts and down into the death pit. Panicked now, the Gothir fought to retreat, trampling their own wounded.

Talisman gazed down with grim satisfaction at the thirty or more bodies. An arrow flashed past his face, and he ducked. Enemy archers were crowding around the breached gates, shooting up at the defenders. Two Nadir warriors fell, their chests pierced.

"Stay down!" shouted Talisman. As ladders suddenly clattered against the wall behind him, he swore. With archers shooting at them from the rear and an assault from the front, the section would be hard to hold.

Throwing himself flat, Talisman squirmed to the edge of the ramparts, calling down to the bowmen on the curved wall. "Ten of you pin down the archers," he commanded. "The rest to me!"

Ignoring the threat of arrows, Talisman surged upright and drew his saber. Three men appeared at the ramparts. Leaping forward, he plunged his saber into the leading man's face, spearing his open mouth.

In the compound below, Gorkai waited with twenty men. Sweat dripped from his face as he watched Talisman and the Fleet Ponies men battling against the warriors swarming over the ramparts. "I should go to him," he told Lin-tse.

"Not yet, Brother. Stand firm."

On the north wall Bartsai and his men fell back as the lancers gained the ramparts. With an awful suddenness the defending line broke, and a dozen enemy soldiers broke clear, swarming down the rampart steps and into the compound.

Lin-tse and his men charged to meet them. Gorkai transferred his saber to his left hand and wiped his sweating right hand on his leggings. The men of the Curved Horn tribe were on the verge of breaking, and Gorkai prepared himself to rush to their aid.

At that moment, seeing the danger, Druss ran along the ramparts of the western wall and leapt the yawning gap to the northern ramparts, his huge form crashing into the attackers and scattering them. The silver blades of his ax cut into the enemy ranks. His sudden appearance galvanized the Curved Horn men into renewed ferocity, and the Gothir were forced back.

Lin-tse had lost eight men, but the twelve Gothir lancers were reduced to four, fighting in two pairs, back to back. Two more Nadir fell before Lin-tse and his men cut the lancers down.

Gorkai swung to watch Talisman. The line was holding, but

more than ten Nadir were dead and the attack was no more than minutes old. Some wounded men were making their way to the hospital; others lay where they had fallen, trying to stop the flow of blood with their hands.

Lin-tse and the remainder of his men moved back to stand alongside Gorkai's group. The tall Nadir chief glanced at Gorkai. Blood was flowing from a wound in his face. "You can tackle the next breach," he said, forcing a smile.

Gorkai did not have long to wait. Talisman's men were swept aside as a section of the battlements gave way, and Talisman himself took a spear thrust into the chest. Gorkai screamed a battle cry and led his men forward, hurtling up the rampart steps two at a time. Talisman gutted the spearman, dragged the broken spear from his chest, and then fell. Gorkai leapt across his body as more Gothir soldiers made it to the ramparts.

Talisman's vision was blurring, and he felt a great dizziness sweep over him. I cannot die, he thought. Not now! Struggling to his knees, he scrabbled for his saber. Darkness loomed, but he fought against it.

Gorkai and his men retook the battlements, forcing the Gothir back. Blood was bubbling from Talisman's chest, and he knew that a lung had been punctured. Two men took him by the arms, hauling him to his feet. "Get him to the surgeon!" ordered Gorkai.

Talisman was half helped, half carried to the hospital building. He heard Zhusai cry out as he was brought in. Desperately trying to focus, he saw the face of Sieben above him . . . then he passed out.

The Gothir had given up their assault on the northern wall, and Druss, his helm struck from his head, jumped the gap in the ramparts and rejoined the Fleet Ponies. Nuang Xuan, wounded again in the chest and arms, was sitting slumped by the wall.

The Gothir fell back.

Druss knelt down by the old Nadir leader. "How goes it?" he asked.

"More than a hundred," said Nuang. "I think I have killed all the Gothir there are, and what you see outside are merely ghosts."

Druss rose and scanned the defenses. The north wall had only eighteen defenders still standing. Around him on the western ramparts there were some twenty-five Sky Riders. Above the gates he counted thirty, including Talisman's man, Gorkai. In the compound below Lin-tse had fewer than a dozen men. Druss tried to add the numbers together but lost them in a sea of weariness. Taking a deep breath, he recounted.

Fewer than a hundred defenders were visible to him, but the bodies of Nadir dead lay everywhere. He saw the Curved Horn leader Bartsai lying on the ground below the ramparts, three dead Gothir around his corpse.

"You are bleeding, Deathwalker," said a Sky Rider.

"It is nothing," replied Druss, recognizing the hawk-faced young man he had spoken to earlier.

"Take off your jerkin," said the youngster.

Druss groaned as he eased the ripped and nearly ruined leather from his huge frame. He had been cut four times around the shoulders and upper arms, but there was a deeper wound under his right shoulder blade. Blood had pooled around his belt.

"You need stitches, hey," the Nadir told him. "Or you bleed to death."

Druss leaned on the ramparts and stared down at the Gothir forces, which had moved back out of bowshot.

"Take the old man with you," said the Nadir, grinning. "He fights so well, he shames us all."

Druss forced a grin and hauled Nuang Xuan to his feet. "Walk with me a while, old man." Turning to the Nadir warrior, he said, "I'll be back before you know it."

Talisman felt the pain of his wounds recede and found himself lying on a bare hillside under a gray sky. His heart hammered in panic as he recognized the landscape of the Void. "You are not dead," came a calm voice from close by. Talisman sat up and saw the little sorcerer Shaoshad sitting beside a flickering blaze. The tall figure of Shul-sen stood beside him, her silver cloak gleaming in the firelight.

"Then why am I here?" he asked.

"To learn," said Shul-sen. "When Oshikai and I came to the land of the steppes, we were touched by its beauty, but more than this, we were called by its magic. Every stone carried it, every plant grew with it. Elemental power radiated from the mountains and flowed in the streams. The gods of stone and water, we called them. You know what gives birth to this magic, Talisman?"

"No."

"Life and death. The life forces of millions of men and animals, insects and plants. Each life comes from the land, then returns to the land. It is a circle of harmony."

"What has this to do with me?"

"Not so much with you, my boy, as with me," put in Shaoshad. "I was one of the three who robbed the land of its magic. We drew it forth and invested it in the Eyes of Alchazzar; we made the land barren; we sought to redirect the random magnificence of the energy, to focus it on behalf of the Nadir. In doing so we destroyed the link between the Nadir and the gods of stone and water. Our people became increasingly nomadic, feeling no love for the earth beneath their feet or the mountains that towered above them. They became split and divided, isolated from one another."

"Why are you telling me this?" asked Talisman.

"Why do you think?" responded Shul-sen.

"I do not have the eyes. I thought the poet might, but I think now he is merely a skilled surgeon."

"If you had them, Talisman, would you do what is right for the land?" asked Shaoshad.

"And what is that?"

"Return to it what was stolen."

"Give up the power of the eyes? With them I could bring all the tribes together into one unstoppable army."

"Perhaps," admitted Shul-sen, "but without love of land, what would they fight for? Plunder and rape, revenge and murder? And this army you speak of—it would be filled with men whose lives are but a fraction of a beat in the heart of eternity. The land is immortal. Give it back its magic, and it will repay you a thousandfold. It will give you the Uniter you dream of; it will give you Ulric."

"And how do I do this?" he whispered.

"It is not as deep as you thought," said Sieben as Druss lay on the table, feeling the poet's fingers probing at the wound in his back. Indeed, there was little pain now except from the ragged stitches.

"You are a revelation to me," said Druss, grunting as he sat up, the stitches pulling tight. "Who would have thought it?"

"Who indeed? How is it going out there?"

"The big attack is to come . . . soon," answered Druss. "If we hold that off . . ." His voice tailed away.

"We are going to lose, aren't we?" asked Sieben.

"I think so, poet, though it hurts me to say it. Is Talisman dead?"

"No, he is sleeping. His wounds were not as bad as we feared."

"I'd better get back to the wall." Druss stretched his back. "Amazing," he said. "I feel as if I've slept for eight hours. I can feel the strength flowing through me. Those poultices you use have great power. I'd be interested to know what's in them."

"Me, too. Niobe prepares them."

Druss shrugged on his jerkin and buckled his belt. "I am sorry I brought you to this," he said.

"I'm a free man who makes his own decisions," Sieben told him, "and I am not sorry at all. I met Niobe. Sweet heaven, Druss, but I love that woman!"

"You love all women," said Druss.

"No. Truly, this is different. And what is more incredible is that given the choice, I would not change a single thing. To die not having known true love must be terrible."

Nuang approached them. "Are you ready, axman?"

"You are a tough old goat," Druss told him, and together they returned to the battlements. Sieben watched them for a moment, then moved back among the wounded men. He caught Niobe's eye and smiled as she pointed to where Zhusai was sitting beside Talisman, holding the sleeping man's hand. The Chiatze girl was weeping. Sieben crossed the room, settling down beside her.

"He will live," he told her softly.

She nodded dumbly.

"I promise you," he said, gently laying his hand on Talisman's chest.

The Nadir warrior stirred and opened his eyes. "Zhusai . . . ?" he whispered.

"Yes, my love."

He groaned and struggled to rise. Sieben helped him to his feet. "What is happening?" he asked.

"The enemy troops are gathering for another charge," said Sieben.

"I must be there."

"No, you must rest!" insisted Zhusai.

Talisman's dark eyes turned to Sieben. "Give me more strength," he said.

The poet shrugged. "I cannot. You have lost a lot of blood, and you are weak."

"You have the Eyes of Alchazzar."

"I wish I did, old horse. I'd heal everybody here. By heaven, I'd even raise the dead."

Talisman looked closely at him, but Sieben met his stare with blank equanimity. Placing his arm over Zhusai's shoulder,

Talisman kissed her cheek. "Help me to the wall, my wife," he said. "We will stand upon it together."

As they moved off, Sieben heard a small voice whisper in his ear: *"Go with them."* He swung around, but there was no one close. The poet shuddered and stood where he was. *"Trust me, my boy,"* came the voice of Shaoshad.

Sieben walked out into the sunlight, then ran to catch Talisman and the woman. Taking the warrior's other arm, he helped him up the rampart steps to the western wall.

"Well, they're gathering again," muttered Druss.

On the plain beyond, the Gothir were once more in fighting ranks, waiting for the drumbeat signal. All along the wall weary Nadir defenders also waited, swords ready.

"Must be more than a thousand of them," said Sieben, feeling the onset of terror.

The drumbeat sounded, and the Gothir army began to move.

Zhusai stiffened and drew in a sharp breath. *"Put your hand on her shoulder,"* ordered Shaoshad. When Sieben reached out and gently touched Zhusai, he felt the power of the stones flow from him like a dam bursting. She released her hold on Talisman and moved to the ramparts.

"What are you doing, Zhusai?" hissed Talisman.

She turned to him and gave a dazzling smile. "She will return," said the voice of Shul-sen.

The woman climbed to the top of the ramparts and raised her arms. Overhead the sun—brilliant in a clear blue sky—shone down on the woman in bloodstained clothes. The wind picked up, stirring her raven-dark hair. Clouds began to form with astonishing speed, small white puffballs that swelled and grew, darkening down and obscuring the sun. The wind roared, buffeting the defenders. Blacker and blacker grew the sky, then a clap of thunder burst above the shrine. Lightning forked down, exploding in the midst of the Gothir army. Several men were hurled from their feet. Jagged spears of dazzling light flashed into the enemy force, while thunder rolled across the heavens.

The Gothir broke and ran, but still the lightning tore into them, catapulting men into the air. The fierce wind brought the smell of burning flesh to the stunned defenders. The Gothir horses uprooted their picket ropes and galloped away. On the plain, men were tearing off their armor and hurling aside their weapons—to no avail, it seemed. Sieben saw a man struck, his breastplate exploding. Those close to him were punched to the ground, where their bodies went into spasm.

Then the sun broke through the clouds, and the woman in white turned and stepped back to the ramparts. "My lord is in paradise," she told Talisman. "This is a debt repaid." She sagged against Talisman, who held her close.

On the plain more than half the Gothir force was dead, with many others suffering terrible burns.

"They'll not fight again," Gorkai said, as the clouds dispersed.

"No, but *they* will," muttered Druss, pointing to a line of cavalry breasting the hills and riding down toward the shattered Gothir camp.

Sieben's heart sank as more than a thousand men came into sight, riding in columns of twos.

"Who would have my luck?" said Nuang bitterly.

# ◇ 13 ◇

**P**REMIAN ROLLED TO his belly and pushed his blistered hands into the cold mud. Lightning had struck three men close to him. They were unrecognizable now. He staggered to his feet, his legs unsteady and dizziness swamping him. The dead and dying were everywhere, and the living staggered around as if drunk.

Some way to his left Premian saw Lord Gargan sitting beside his dead horse. The man looked old now and sat with his head in his hands. Premian had been wearing no armor—Gargan had stripped him of his rank and sentenced him to thirty lashes for disobedience—but the lack of metal on his frame had saved him during the lightning storm.

Slowly he made his way to the general. Half of Gargan's face was blistered and black. He looked up as Premian approached, and the younger man had to mask his horror at the sight. Gargan's left eye was gone, and blood flowed from the empty socket.

"All finished," mumbled the general. "The savages have won." Premian knelt by him and took his hand, unable to think of anything to say. "They murdered my mother," said Gargan. "I was five years old. She hid me under some sacking. They raped and murdered her. And I watched. I . . . wanted to help her. Couldn't. Just lay there and wet myself with fear. Then my son . . ." Gargan drew a long, shuddering breath. "Fetch me a sword."

"You don't need a sword, my lord. It is over."

"Over? You think it is over? It will never be over. Them or us, Premian. Now and forever." Gargan sagged to his right. Premian caught him and lowered him to the ground. "I can hear horses," whispered the general. And he died.

Premian glanced up to see the line of cavalry moving toward him, and he stood as they approached. A cavalry general rode up and glanced down at the dead Lord of Larness.

"I had orders for his arrest and immediate execution," he said. "It is just as well he is gone. I had great respect for him."

"Arrest? On what charge?" Premian asked.

"Who are you?" responded the general.

"Premian, sir."

"Ah, good. I am also carrying orders for you. You are to take command of the lancers and return to Gulgothir." Swinging in his saddle, he surveyed the chaos. "Your force will not be a large one, I fear. What happened here?"

Swiftly Premian told him. Then he asked, "Does the attack continue, sir?"

"The sacking of a shrine? Great heavens, no! What an utter waste of good men. I can't think what possessed Gargan to lead such a lunatic venture."

"I believe he was under orders, sir."

"All orders are changed now, Premian. We have a new emperor. The madman is dead, killed by his own guards. There is sanity once more in Gulgothir."

"Praise the Source for that," Premian said, with feeling.

On the walls of the shrine, Druss, Talisman, and the defenders watched a rider move slowly from the devastated camp. He was wearing no armor, and his silver hair shone in the sunlight.

"Shemak's balls, it's Majon!" said Sieben. "He rides that horse with all the grace of a carrot sack."

"Who is Majon?" asked Talisman, his face gray with the pain of his wounds.

"The Drenai ambassador. Best advise your men not to shoot

at him." Talisman relayed the order as Majon rode closer; his long face was pinched and tight, and Druss could see the fear in the man.

"Ho, Druss!" called Majon. "I am unarmed. I come as a herald."

"No one is going to hurt you, Ambassador. We'll lower a rope for you."

"I am quite comfortable here, thank you," he replied, his voice shaking.

"Nonsense," Druss called out. "Our hospitality is well known, and my friends here would think themselves insulted if you didn't join us."

A rope was lowered, and the ambassador dismounted. Removing his sky-blue cape, which he draped over his saddle, he took hold of the rope and was hauled to the ramparts. Once he got there, Druss introduced him to Talisman. "He's one of the kings among the Nadir," said Druss. "An important man."

"Delighted to meet you, sir," said Majon.

"What words do you bring from the enemy?" countered Talisman.

"There are no enemies here, sir," Majon told him. "The . . . battle is over. The cavalry force you see before the walls was sent to arrest the renegade Gargan. The general Cuskar has asked me to assure you that all hostilities are now at an end and that the shrine will not be despoiled by any Gothir soldier. Equally, you and all your men are free to go. Your actions against the renegade Gargan will not be seen as crimes against the new emperor."

"New emperor?" put in Druss.

"Yes, indeed. The madman is dead, killed by two of his guards. There is a new order now in Gulgothir. The scenes in the city were wonderful to behold, Druss. Dancing and singing in the streets, no less. The new emperor's government is being led by a minister of rare culture and breeding: his name is Garen-Tsen, and it seems he has been working behind the scenes for some time to overthrow the God-King. A charming man with a great understanding of diplomacy. Already we have signed three trade agreements."

"You mean we won?" said Sieben. "And we are all going to live?"

"I believe that puts the facts succinctly," said Majon. "One small matter, Druss, my friend," added the ambassador, drawing the axman away from the others. "Garen-Tsen asked me to mention the matter of some jewels said to be hidden here."

"There were no jewels," said Druss bitterly. "Just old bones and new deaths."

"You . . . er . . . searched the coffin, did you?"

"Yes. Nothing. It's all a myth."

"Ah, well. It matters not, I am sure." Returning to Talisman, the ambassador bowed again. "The general Cuskar has brought three surgeons with him. He has asked me to offer you their services for your wounded."

"We have a fine surgeon, but thank the general for his kindness," said Talisman. "In return for such goodwill, do tell the general that if he brings his water wagons to the walls, I will see that the barrels are filled."

Druss and Gorkai lowered Majon to the ground. The ambassador mounted his horse, waved once, then cantered back to the Gothir camp.

Talisman sank back to the ramparts. "We won," he said.

"That we did, laddie. But only just."

Talisman held out his hand. "You are a man among men, Deathwalker," he said. "On behalf of my people, I thank you."

"You should get back to the hospital," said Druss, "and let our 'fine' surgeon tend to you."

Talisman smiled and with the support of Zhusai and Gorkai made his way down the rampart steps. In the compound below, the Nadir had formed into loose groups, talking excitedly about the battle. Lin-tse watched them dispassionately, but in his eyes there was sadness.

"What is wrong?" asked Sieben.

"Nothing a *gajin* could see," said the warrior, walking away.

"What was he talking about, Druss?"

"They are all with their own tribesmen. The mixing has ended. They came together for this one battle, and now they are drawing apart again—the way of the Nadir, perhaps." Druss sighed. "Ah, but I am weary, poet. I need to see Rowena again, to breathe the air of the mountains. By heavens, it would be nice to smell the sweet breeze coming over the long grass and the pine meadows."

"It would indeed, Druss, old horse."

"First we must return to Gulgothir. I want to see Klay. We'll rest for a couple of hours, then ride out."

Sieben nodded. "Niobe is coming with us. I'm going to marry her, Druss, give her babies and an iron fire bucket!"

Druss chuckled. "I expect it will be in that order."

Sieben returned to the hospital, where Talisman was sleeping soundly. In the small office he found a strip of parchment, a quill pen, and an inkwell that was almost dry. Adding a little water to the ink, he penned a short message on the parchment. When the ink was dry, he folded the parchment into four and walked back into the larger room. Kneeling by Talisman, he slid the message under a fold of the bandage around his chest and used the power of the Eyes of Alchazzar to heal the Nadir leader.

One by one he visited all the wounded, leaving them all asleep, their wounds vanished.

At the last, he stood in the doorway and looked back, satisfied. Many men had died defending this shrine, but there were others, Talisman among them, who would have died if it had not been for him. The thought pleased the poet.

He glanced up at the battlements, where Druss was stretched out asleep. Sieben climbed the rampart steps and healed him also.

Lin-tse and his Sky Riders were dismantling the wall around the gates. Sieben sat on the walls watching them. The sky was a glorious blue, and even the hot breeze tasted good on the tongue.

I am alive, he thought. Alive and in love. If there is a better feeling in all the world, I have yet to taste of it, he decided.

# ◇ 14 ◇

O KAR, THE FAT gatekeeper at the hospice, cursed as the pounding on the front door continued. Rolling from his pallet bed, he pulled on his leggings, stumbled along the corridor, and dragged back the bolts. "Be quiet!" he ordered as he dragged open the thick door. "There are sick people here trying to sleep."

A huge man with a thick black beard stepped into the doorway, seized him by the arms, and hoisted him into the air. "They won't be sick for much longer," he said with a wide grin. Okar was not a small man, but the giant lifted him and moved him aside as if he were a child.

"You must forgive my friend," said a slim, handsome man, "but he is very excitable."

A young woman followed the two men inside. She was Nadir and strikingly attractive.

"Where do you think you are going?" asked Okar as the group made its way up the stairs. They did not reply, and he hurried after them. The abbot was waiting at the top of the stairs; still in his night robe, a candleholder in his hand, he blocked their way.

"What is the meaning of this intrusion?" asked the abbot sternly.

"We've come to heal our friend, Father Abbot," said the giant. "I kept my promise."

Okar waited for the harsh words he was sure would follow.

But the abbot stood in silence for a moment, his expression unreadable in the flickering candlelight. "Follow me," he said softly, "and please be silent."

The abbot led the way through the first ward and on to a small office in the western part of the building. Lighting two lanterns, he sat down at a desk littered with papers. "Now explain," he said.

The giant spoke first. "We found the healing stones, Father. And they work! By all that's holy, they work! Now take us to Klay."

"That is not possible," the abbot told him, and sighed. "Klay passed from this life three days after you left. He is buried in a simple grave behind the gardens. A stone has been fashioned for him. I am truly sorry."

"He promised me," said Druss. "He promised me he would live until my return."

"It was a promise he could not keep," said the abbot. "The bolt that struck him was tainted with some vile substance, and gangrene set in almost immediately. No man could have withstood the deadly effect."

"I can't believe it," whispered Druss. "I have the stones!"

"Why is it so hard for you warriors to believe?" snapped the abbot. "You think the world revolves around your desires. Do you honestly believe that nature and the laws of the universe can be changed by your will? I have heard of you, Druss. You crossed the world to find your lady. You have fought in many battles; you are indomitable. But you are a man of flesh and blood. You will live, and you will die—just like any other man. Klay was a great man, a man of kindness and understanding. His death is a tragedy beyond my ability to describe. Yet it is part of the cycle of life, and I do not doubt that the Source received him with joy. I was with him at the end. He wanted to leave you a message, and we sent for pen and ink, but he died very suddenly. I think I know what he wanted to ask you."

"What?" Druss asked numbly.

"He told me of the boy Kells and how he had believed that Klay was a god who could lay his hands on his mother and heal her. The boy is still here. He sat with Klay, holding to his hand, and he wept bitter tears when the fighter died. His mother still lives. If the stones have the power you say, then I think Klay would want you to use their power on her."

Druss said nothing, but sat slumped in his chair, staring down at his hands. Sieben stepped forward. "I think we can do a little better than that, Father. Take me to the boy."

Leaving Druss alone in the office, Sieben, Niobe, and the abbot walked silently through the hospice, coming at last to a long, narrow room in which twenty beds were set against the walls, ten on each side. Kells lay curled up and asleep on the floor by the first bed; a tall thin woman was sleeping in a chair beside him. In the bed, her face pale in the moonlight from the high window, lay a wasted, dying figure, the skin of her face drawn tightly around her skull, no flesh visible, black rings beneath her eyes.

Sieben knelt by the boy, lightly touching his shoulder. Kells came awake instantly, his eyes flaring wide in fear. "It is all right, boy. I come with a gift from Lord Klay."

"He is dead," said the child.

"But I bring his gift anyway. Stand up." Kells did so. The movement and the voices awoke the thin woman in the chair.

"What is happening?" she asked. "Is she gone?"

"Not gone," said Sieben. "She is coming home." To the boy he said, "Take your mother's hand," and Kells did so. Sieben leaned forward and laid his palm on the dying woman's fevered brow. The skin was hot and dry. The poet closed his eyes and felt the power of the stones flowing through him. The woman in the bed gave a weak groan, and the abbot moved in closer, looking down in wonder as her color deepened and the dark rings beneath her eyes slowly faded. The bones of her face receded as the wasted muscles of her cheeks and jaw swelled into health.

Her hair, which had been dry and lifeless, shone upon the pillow. Sieben took a deep breath and stepped back.

"Are you an angel of the Source?" asked the thin woman.

"No, just a man," said Sieben. Kneeling down by the boy, he saw the tears in his eyes. "She is healed, Kells. She sleeps now. Would you like to help me heal all these others?"

"Yes. Yes, I would. Lord Klay sent you?"

"In a manner of speaking."

"And my mother is going to live?"

"Aye. She is going to live."

Together Sieben and the boy moved from bed to bed, and when the dawn sun rose over Gulgothir, the sounds of laughter and unfettered joy came from within the walls of the hospice.

It was all lost on Druss, who sat alone in the drab office, his feelings numbed. He could help hold a fortress against all odds but could not prevent the death of a friend. He could cross the ocean and fight in a hundred battles. He could stand against any man alive, yet Klay was still dead.

Rising from his chair, he moved to the window. The dawn sun had filled the gardens beyond with color: crimson roses growing around the white marble fountain, purple foxglove amid carpets of yellow flowers beside the curving paths. "It is not fair," Druss said aloud.

"I cannot recall anyone saying that it would be," came the voice of the abbot.

"That bolt was meant for me, Father. Klay took it for me. Why should I live and he die?"

"There are never answers to such questions, Druss. He will be remembered with great fondness by a great many people. There will even be those who will revere his memory enough to try to emulate him. We are none of us here for very long. Would you like to see his stone?"

"Aye. I would."

Together the two men left the office and walked down the rear stairwell to the gardens. The air was sweet with perfume, the sun bright in the morning sky. Klay's grave was beside a drystone wall, beneath an ancient willow. A long, rectangular slab of white marble had been set into the earth, and on it were carved the words

*Any good that I may do, let me do it now,*
*for I may not pass this way again.*

"It is a quote from an ancient writing," said the abbot. "He did not ask for it, but I thought it was fitting."

"Aye, it is fitting," agreed Druss. "Tell me, who is the woman Klay wanted saved?"

"She is a prostitute; she works the southern quarter, I understand."

Druss shook his head and said nothing.

"You think a whore is not worth saving?" the abbot asked.

"I would never say that," Druss told him, "nor would I think it. But I have just come from a battle, Father, where hundreds of men lost their lives. I have returned here to find a great man dead. And at the end of it I have ensured that one more whore will work the southern quarter. I'm going home," Druss said sadly. "I wish I had never come to Gulgothir."

"If you hadn't, then you would not have known him. And that would have been your loss. My advice is to hold to the memory of what he was and think about him as you live your own life. There may come a time when you will draw on those memories in order to achieve some good for others, just as he would have done."

Druss took in a deep breath, glanced down once more at the simple grave, then turned away. "Where is my friend? We should be leaving soon."

"He and his wife are gone, Druss. He said to tell you he will meet you on the road. He is returning the stones to a man named Talisman."

\*   \*   \*

Talisman, Gorkai, and Zhusai rode up the dusty rise, cresting the slope and pulling back on the reins of their weary ponies. Below them, spreading right across the valley, were the tents of the Northern Wolfshead.

"We are home," said Talisman.

"Now perhaps, my general," said Gorkai, "you can tell me why we have ridden so hard."

"This is the Day of the Stone Wolf. All the captains of every Wolfshead tribe are gathered here. At noon there is a ceremony in the High Cave."

"And you must be there?"

"Today I will stand before my people and take my Nadir name. That right was denied me when I returned home from the academy; some of the Elders believed I had been tainted by Gothir education. Nosta Khan named me Talisman and said that I would keep that name until I found the Eyes of Alchazzar."

"What name will you now choose, my love?" asked Zhusai.

"I have not yet decided. Come, let us ride." And Talisman led the trio down into the valley.

High on the hillside, from the mouth of a huge cave, Nosta Khan watched them. His emotions were mixed. He could sense the presence of the eyes and knew that Talisman had fulfilled his quest. That alone was cause for rejoicing, for with the power restored to the Stone Wolf, the Day of the Uniter was infinitely closer. Yet there was anger, too, for Talisman had disobeyed him and had despoiled the woman. Even now she was pregnant and almost lost to the cause. There was only one answer, and it saddened Nosta Khan. Talisman, for all his strength and skill, had to die. After that there were herbs and potions to rob Zhusai of the babe. Perhaps then all could proceed as it should.

Rising, he turned from the sunlight and entered the cave. It was huge and spherical, great stalactites hanging like spears from the domed ceiling. The Stone Wolf had been carved from the rock of the rear wall centuries before, and it sat now, its great jaws open, its sightless eyes waiting for a return to the light.

This day, at noon, the eyes would shine again, albeit briefly. They were too powerful to be left in the stone sockets, prey to whatever thief had the wit or courage to steal them. No. From now on the Eyes of Alchazzar would be carried on the person of Nosta Khan, shaman to the Wolfshead.

Three acolytes entered the cave, bearing bundles of oil-soaked torches, which they placed in rusting brackets on the walls around the Stone Wolf.

Nosta Khan strolled back into the sunlight and watched the steady stream of men moving purposefully up the hillside. "Light the torches," he commanded the acolytes.

Returning to the Stone Wolf, he squatted down before it and closed his eyes, focusing his powers. More than forty leaders would be there that day; not one of them had violet eyes, but after the ceremony he would question all of them. The Uniter was out there somewhere on the steppes. With the power of the eyes, Nosta Khan would find him.

The leaders trooped into the cave and sat in a wide semicircle some twenty feet back from the Stone Wolf. Each leader had his own champions with him, chosen warriors. They stood behind their warlords with their hands on their sword hilts, ready for any treachery. Truly, thought Nosta Khan, we are a divided people.

When all the leaders were present, Nosta Khan rose. "This is a great day," he told the assembly. "What was lost has been returned to us. This is the first day of the Uniter. The Eyes of Alchazzar have been found!"

A gasp went up from the crowd, followed by a stunned silence. "Step forth, Talisman," commanded the shaman.

Talisman rose from the center of the group and made his way through the ranks to stand beside the shaman. "This is the man who led the defenders at the Shrine of Oshikai Demon-bane. This is the man who inflicted defeat on the *gajin*. Today, with pride, he will take his Nadir name and be remembered for all time as a great Wolfshead hero." Turning to Talisman, he said, "Give me the eyes, my boy."

"In a moment," said Talisman. The young warrior turned to the assembly. "The Shrine of Oshikai stands," he said, his voice ringing out. "It stands because Nadir warriors aimed straight and stood tall. Here in this place I praise Bartsai, leader of the Curved Horn, who died defending the bones of Oshikai. Here in this place I praise Kzun of the Lone Wolves, who was slain leading Curved Horn warriors in defense of our holiest shrine. Here in this place I praise Quing-chin of the Fleet Ponies, who was maimed and butchered by the *gajin*. Here in this place I praise Lin-tse of the Sky Riders. And I bring a new warrior to the ranks of the Wolves. Come forward, Gorkai."

Gorkai rose and marched to the front. Across his shoulder he carried a long hammer with a head of heavy iron. "This is Gorkai, who was Notas and is now Wolfshead.

"Nosta Khan has told you that the Day of the Uniter is close, and he is right. It is time to put aside the stupidity of the past. Look at you all! You are Wolfshead, and yet you sit here with your champions behind you, fearing the brothers who sit beside you. Rightly fearing them! For given the chance, there is not one of you who would not slay the other in order to rule. Each man here is an enemy. It is folly of the worst kind. While the Gothir wax rich, we starve. While the Gothir raid our villages, we plan wars among ourselves. Why is this? Were we born stupid?

"Centuries ago, wise men of the Nadir committed an act of appalling stupidity. They drew the magic from the land and set it in these," he said, drawing the Eyes of Alchazzar from the pocket of his goatskin jerkin. The jewels shone in the torchlight as he raised them up.

"The power of the steppes and the mountains," he said. "The magic of the gods of stone and water. Trapped here . . . with these purple jewels any man here could be khan. He could be immortal. I saw their power. I was struck down at the shrine, pierced through the body, yet I have no scar."

All eyes were on the jewels now, and he felt the lust in every gaze.

"The Eyes of Alchazzar!" he shouted, his voice echoing around the cavern. "But does any man here believe that Bartsai or Kzun or Quing-chin died so that one petty Wolfshead leader could command the magic of the gods of stone and water? Is any one of you worthy to wield this power? If he is here, let him stand now and tell us why he deserves this honor!"

The leaders glanced one to another, but no one moved.

Talisman spun on his heel and walked to the Stone Wolf. Reaching up, he pressed the stones back into the eye sockets. Then, turning once more, he gestured to Gorkai, who threw the long hammer through the air. Talisman caught it.

"No!" screamed Nosta Khan.

Talisman took one step back, then swung the hammer in a mighty blow, the iron connecting with the stone brow and shattering the wolf's head. In that moment the jewels flared in a blinding blaze of purple light, engulfing Talisman and filling the cavern. Lightning crackled between the stalactites, and a great rumble like distant thunder caused the cavern floor to tremble and groan.

Dust fell from the ceiling, the purple light shining on the motes like a thousand jewels hanging in the air. As the dust settled and the light faded, Talisman dropped the hammer and stood staring at the ruins of the Stone Wolf. Of the Eyes of Alchazzar there was no sign.

"What have you done?" screamed Nosta Khan, rushing at him and grabbing his arm. Talisman turned, and the shaman gasped and fell back, his jaw slack, his eyes blinking rapidly.

Gorkai moved forward . . . and stopped. Talisman's eyes had changed, as if the blazing purple light of the jewels had lodged there, glittering in the torchlight. No longer dark, they shone with violet light.

"Your eyes . . ." whispered Gorkai.

"I know," said Talisman.

Moving past the stunned shaman, Talisman stood before the awed leaders.

"Today I take my Nadir name," he said. "Today Talisman is no more. He died as the magic returned to the land. From this day, I am Ulric of the Wolfshead."

# ◇ Dros Delnoch ◇

### Thirty years later

**D**RUSS THE LEGEND sat beside the young soldier Pellin and chuckled as he concluded his tale. "So, in the end," he said, "we did it all for a young whore! Sieben didn't seem to mind; he had Niobe, and he took her home and bought her a fabulously ornate fire bucket. She was a good woman, outlived him by ten years. He wasn't faithful to her. I don't think Sieben knew what faithful meant. He was loyal, though, and I guess that counts for something."

The surgeon, Calvar Syn, moved alongside the axman. "The boy is dead, Druss," he said.

"I know he's dead, damn you! Everyone dies on me." Tenderly he patted Pellin's still-warm hand, then rose from the bedside. "He fought well, you know. He was frightened, but he didn't run. He stood his ground like a man should. You think he heard any of my story?"

"It is hard to say. Perhaps. Now you should get some rest. You're no youngster."

"Aye, that is the advice from Rek and Hogun and all the others. I'll rest soon enough. We all will. They've all gone, you know—all my friends. I killed Bodasen myself, and Sieben fell at Skeln."

"What about Talisman? Did you ever see him again?"

"No. I expect he died in one of Ulric's battles." Druss forced a laugh and ran his gnarled hand over his silver beard. "He would have been proud to see the tribes now, though, eh? Battling before the walls of Dros Delnoch? All the tribes united?"

"Get some rest, old man," ordered Calvar Syn. "Otherwise tomorrow you may be in one of these beds and not sitting alongside it."

"I hear you, surgeon."

Taking up his ax, Druss strolled out into the moonlight and made his way to the ramparts, staring out over the awesome camp of the Nadir, which filled the pass for as far as the eye could see.

Three of the six great walls had fallen, and Druss stood by the gate towers of Wall Four. "What are you thinking, old horse?" asked Bowman, moving out of the shadows.

"Ulric said his shaman warned that I would die here, by this gate. It seems as good a place as any."

"You won't die, Druss. You're immortal. All men know this."

"What I am is old and tired," said Druss. "And I knew before I came here that this would be my last resting place." He grinned. "I made a pact with death, boy."

Bowman shivered and changed the subject. "You liked him, didn't you? Ulric, I mean. What else did he say to you?"

Druss did not answer. Something about the meeting with Ulric had been bothering him, but he had not yet figured it out.

He never would . . .

Several days later, alone in his tent, Ulric was also thinking about the axman, remembering their last meeting on the killing ground between Walls One and Two. The sun was bright in the sky, and the enemy had fallen back from Eldibar, Wall One.

Ulric had walked out onto the killing ground and spread a purple rug on the ground. A jug of wine, a plate of dates, and some cheese had been brought forward by one of his men, and the great khan had sat waiting.

He had watched as Druss was lowered from the ramparts of

Wall Two. He looked old, his beard shining silver in the sunlight. Will you remember me, Druss? he thought. No, how could you? The fresh-faced, dark-eyed young man you knew thirty years ago is now a violet-eyed, battle-scarred warrior. As the axman approached, Ulric found his heart hammering. In Druss' hand was the terrible weapon Snaga, which had wreaked such a heavy toll at the Shrine of Oshikai. Will you use it on me? wondered Ulric. No, he realized. As always, Druss would be the man of honor.

"I am a stranger in your camp," said the old man.

"Welcome, stranger, and eat," said Ulric, and Druss sat cross-legged opposite him. Slowly Ulric unbuckled his lacquered black breastplate and removed it, laying it carefully at his side. Then he removed his black greaves and forearm straps. "I am Ulric of the Wolfshead."

"I am Druss of the Ax." The axman's pale blue eyes narrowed as he stared at the great khan. Was recognition flickering? Ulric wondered. Tell him! Speak to him now. Voice your gratitude.

"Well met! Eat," bade Ulric.

Druss took a handful of dates from the silver platter before him and ate slowly. He followed with goat's milk cheese and washed it down with a mouthful of red wine. His eyebrows rose, and he grinned.

"Lentrian red," said Ulric. "Without poison."

Druss grinned. "I'm a hard man to kill. It's a talent."

"You did well, and I am glad for you."

"I was grieved to hear of the death of your son. I have no sons, but I know how hard it is for a man to lose a loved one."

"It was a cruel blow," said Ulric. "He was a good boy. But then, all life is cruel, is it not? A man must rise above his grief."

Druss was silent, helping himself to more dates.

"You are a great man, Druss. I am sorry you are to die here."

"Yes, it would be nice to live forever. On the other hand, I am beginning to slow down. Some of your men have been getting damn close to marking me. It's an embarrassment."

"There is a prize for the man who kills you: one hundred horses, picked from my own stable."

"How does the man prove to you that he slew me?"

"He brings me your head and two witnesses to the blow."

"Don't allow that information to reach my men. They will do it for fifty horses."

"I think not. You have done well. How is the new earl settling in?"

"He would have preferred a less noisy welcome, but I think he is enjoying himself. He fights well."

"As do you all. It will not be enough, however."

"We shall see," said Druss. "These dates are very good."

"Do you believe you can stop me? Tell me truly, Deathwalker."

"I would like to have served under you," said Druss. "I have admired you for years. I have served many kings. Some were weak, others willful. Many were fine men, but you . . . you have the mark of greatness. I think you will get what you want eventually . . . but not while I live."

"You will not live long, Druss," said Ulric gently. "We have a shaman who knows these things. He told me that he saw you standing at the gates of Wall Four—Sumitos, I believe it is called—and the grinning skull of death floated above your shoulders."

Druss laughed aloud. "Death always floats where I stand, Ulric! I am he who walks with death. Does your shaman not know your own legends? I may choose to die at Sumitos. I may choose to die at Musif. But wherever I choose to die, know this: as I walk into the Valley of Shadows, I will take with me more than a few Nadir for company on the road."

"They will be proud to walk with you. Go in peace."

A movement came at the tent flap, jerking Ulric's mind back to the present. His lieutenant, Ogasi, son of the long-dead

Gorkai, stepped inside. Fist to chest, he saluted his khan. "The cairn is ready, lord," said the warrior.

Ulric took a deep breath and then walked out into the night.

The body of Druss the Legend lay on the cairn, his arms folded across his chest, his great ax held in his dead hands. Ulric felt the jolt of inner pain as he gazed on the cairn, and the sick empty suffering of bereavement followed. Druss had killed the Nadir champion Nogusha in single combat. Nogusha, however, had smeared poison on his sword blade. When the next attack came, the old warrior was already dying in agony, yet still he fought, his great ax dealing death until at last, ringed by Nadir warriors, he was cut down.

"Why are we doing this honor for him, lord?" asked Ogasi. "He was *gajin* and our enemy."

Ulric sighed. "He fought beside your father and me at the Shrine of Oshikai. He helped bring the magic back to the land. Without him there would have been no Nadir army. Perhaps no future for our people."

"The more fool him, then," observed Ogasi.

Ulric quelled the rush of anger he felt. Ogasi was brave and loyal, but he would never understand the greatness of men like Druss the Legend.

"It was my honor and my privilege to stand beside him," said Ulric. "He was a man who always fought for what he believed in, no matter what the odds. I know you hate the *gajin*, Ogasi. But Druss was special; he transcended race. A long time ago he and I walked the Void to save the soul of Shul-sen and re-unite her with the spirit of Oshikai. Yes, he fought us. But there was no malice in him. He was a great man and—for a time— my friend. Do him honor for my sake."

"I will, lord," said Ogasi. The warrior was silent for a moment, then he smiled. "By the gods of stone and water, but he could fight, hey?"

"Yes," said Ulric softly. "He could fight."